Acclaim for Francesca Marciano's

CASA ROSSA

"A family epic [that] revolves around three generations of extraordinary women. . . . Fans of Marciano's first novel will once again embrace her sensual descriptions of exotic lands."
—*San Francisco Chronicle*

"Lyrical. . . . Romantic. . . . The story of a family whose secrets collide with history." —*Deseret News*

"A passionate tale. . . . [Marciano] imperturbably weaves . . . together . . . a glamorous, romantic whole."
—*Publishers Weekly*

"Marciano . . . casts a sharp eye on the society that surrounds the family of the Casa Rossa. Her Italy is full of lies. . . . But the search for truth takes courage, and the lesson learned in her novel is that the violence of the *anni di piombo* achieved nothing." —*The Economist*

"Lyrical. . . . Spiced with those special Italian flavors: beauty, melodrama, and—of course—murder. . . . Thank heaven for life's little pleasures." —*Daily Candy NYC*

"Marciano effectively intermingles family secrets, Italian history, and the loves and lives of her characters. A good read."
—*Library Journal*

FRANCESCA MARCIANO

CASA ROSSA

Francesca Marciano is also the author of *Rules of the Wild*. She lives in Rome.

ALSO BY FRANCESCA MARCIANO

Rules of the Wild

CASA ROSSA

CASA ROSSA

A Novel

FRANCESCA MARCIANO

Vintage Contemporaries
Vintage Books
A Division of Random House, Inc.
New York

FIRST VINTAGE CONTEMPORARIES EDITION, OCTOBER 2003

Copyright © 2002 by Audenspice Ltd.

All rights reserved under International and Pan-American Copyright
Conventions. Published in the United States by Vintage Books, a
division of Random House, Inc., New York, and simultaneously in
Canada by Random House of Canada Limited, Toronto. Originally
published in hardcover in the United States by Pantheon Books,
a division of Random House, New York, and in Great Britain
by Jonathan Cape, Ltd., London, in 2002.

Vintage is a registered trademark and Vintage Contemporaries
and colophon are trademarks of Random House, Inc.

A Cataloging-in-Publication record has been established for the
Pantheon edition of *Casa Rossa* by the Library of Congress.

Vintage ISBN: 0-375-72637-3

Book design by M. Kristen Bearse

w w w . v i n t a g e b o o k s . c o m

Printed in the United States of America
10   9   8   7   6   5   4   3   2   1

FOR DONATA

CASA ROSSA

When we were small, my sister Isabella and I used to wonder whether Alba had murdered our father.

Murdered him, and then made up the suicide story.

We'd be in the kitchen, hunting for food, two skinny girls, ten and twelve. Murdered. We'd let that possibility hang in the air, to see if anything crashed or shattered, but nothing ever moved. The house remained perfectly still.

"Who knows, anyway," we'd say, to finish it off. We didn't really want to know. If she had done it, eventually they would come and lock her up.

It was bad enough, what had happened already. Dad vanishing, like a card in a trick.

We'd hear the keys in the door. She'd come in smiling, wearing her green dress and sandals, her arms full of groceries.

There she was: Alba. Our mother. The Murderer.

"Want a prosciutto sandwich, darlings?"

When we were that small, things shifted proportions all the time: the really dangerous stuff shrunk, curled up in a ball so that we could juggle it, study it closely, let it drop from our hands the minute it began to bother us.

It was a silent agreement between my sister and me. To move on, to survive.

To eat that sandwich.

CHAPTER ONE

⬦

Careful now. Watch what you do.

You keep staring at the living room, you don't think you can follow this task. It feels like sacrilege to alter its order, like rummaging a temple.

How long has this dark red armchair been sitting across from the threadbare sofa, right next to the painted lampshade? How many years has the faded rug sat on these stone tiles? Renée's portrait hung on the wall? The opaline vase stood on the mantelpiece?

My grandfather bought this house in the late twenties. It was a crumbling farmhouse then, nobody wanted it. My mother grew up here. My sister and I did, too.

Casa Rossa has been my family house for over seventy years.

I know its smell like I know the smell of cut grass. Its map is imprinted in me, I can walk it blindfolded.

Why did I think these objects would stay like this forever and that I could always come back, find the chair and the sofa and the rug and the painting in their place? That way I assumed I could always reenact all the different moments that shaped our story. Like the day when Renée was sitting for my grandfather on the wicker chair and, as he was painting another one of her portraits, she told him about Muriel. The summer day Oliviero came for lunch and sat outside on the patio under the trellis and fell in love with my mother. The times my sister lay awake at night, wrapped in her hatred, fearing every noise. Or the night I took Daniel Moore in here for the first time. I opened the door and showed him this room. This rug, this faded sofa, that yellowing lampshade. The room smelled of firewood. "This is it," I said.

I hoped it would stay like this forever, so that, by coming back and finding everything still arranged exactly as I had left it, I would believe I had secured my history in a safe place. Inside a shrine, where nothing would get lost. Just as prayers are never lost in a church. One can always go back and light another candle.

As I walk across the ground floor of Casa Rossa, as I move from the large kitchen into the living room, then through the big wooden door into my grandfather's studio, I look around, I count my steps, I mark my territory as if it's the last time I will ever do this. And, guess what. It is.

I talk out loud to myself—like I always do when I'm scared. Careful now, watch what you do. Everything, from now on, will be final and surprisingly quick.

The movers will arrive and wait for me to give them a sign. Then they will heft the table, then the sofa, they will roll up the rug and take down the painting. They will wrap the furniture in blankets and tie it with rope. They will blindfold and choke the familiar shapes and will pile them up one on top of the other in the truck. An armrest will show from under the blanket. The stain on its faded fabric will look pathetic. The scratches on the table legs, the pale circle a cup had once left on its top: all these familiar marks will look spooky now, like scars. One didn't notice them so much before. But it will be impossible to look at them now without shame. You will have to admit that these things have turned into what they have always been but which you always refused to see: a pile of sad, old junk.

Once every single piece of furniture and every single box are loaded onto the truck, this house, stripped bare in a single morning, will go back to being mute. A white canvas, where someone else will write their story.

That's how fast our memories disintegrate.

I've been procrastinating about calling the movers, of course. Who wouldn't? It's like phoning in your own death sentence and prodding the executioner.

Instead I've been wandering around the rooms in a daze, touching surfaces, sizing things up. Every time I open a drawer or look in the back of an armoire, some new discovery stuns me. I keep turning between my fingers what I have just found, as if expecting it to talk to me. An old dusty ribbon (a hat? gift wrapping?), a newspaper clipping from the fifties, the obituary page (whose death are we looking at here?), a single light-blue silk shoe, custom-made in Paris (Renée's?), a tiny photograph in black-and-white, of a group of young people huddled together on a beach in thirties-style bathing suits (which one is my grandfather?), a single page from a letter (no date, no signature, written in French).

It's like trying to trace the history of an Egyptian mummy from her ring, a few glass beads, bits of broken pottery, a faded inscription. Yes, she was a merchant's wife—no, a pharaoh's sister, or maybe a high priestess. History demands a plot with a proper beginning and a proper end.

This is not a story about what we know, nor about what we have.

This story is about what gets lost on the way.

My mother, Alba, rings me twice a day from her house in Rome. She wants to know how I'm proceeding with the move.

"Oh," I say gingerly, "I'm not quite ready yet. I still have to go through all the drawers upstairs in the bedrooms. There are all these papers, photographs, you have no idea how—"

"Just chuck everything in the boxes," she interrupts. "You'll never get out alive if you start looking at everything. Those people said they want to move in next week."

"It's all right. They have the house for life now. They can wait another day or two. By the way, I found your wedding dress."

"Oh my *God*."

"It doesn't even look like a wedding dress. I only recognized it from of the photos."

"You found those as well?" she asks.

"Yes. Everything was kind of stuffed inside a box on top of the armoire in your room. There were hats, printed wedding invitations, an envelope full of pictures. Papà looks like this smart kid with glasses. Like a math genius or something. Why didn't you wear a long white dress?"

"Oh, I don't know. It was a country wedding. . . . I kept it simple," she sighs, impatient with me already. "I remember it was a pretty dress."

"Knee-length, full skirt. Tiny poppies embroidered here and there. Fifties-style, you know. I'm wearing it right now."

"You are?"

"It barely fits me, but it makes this whole process a bit more fun. You know, wearing something so nice."

"Alina," she sighs . . . . "are you okay doing this on your own? Do you want me to come down? I could get on the train tomorrow if you need me."

She asks this question twice a day, her voice full of dread that I'll say yes.

"No, I'm fine. You would only get in the way."

"Are you sure? I'll come if—"

"No, really. I'm actually enjoying it. It's kind of . . . therapeutic."

I don't hear anything coming from her end, so I add:

"It's like, you don't even begin to realize someone you love is really dead until you see their body go underground. It's part of the process."

"Jesus, you are morbid," she says, but I can feel her relief: she can stay in Rome.

I always knew she wouldn't have anything to do with sorting out old, forgotten boxes. Alba has never been big on remembering.

Puglia is the heel of Italy, the thinnest strip of land between two seas. Lorenzo, my grandfather, said it was exactly this—the refraction of the sun hitting the water on both sides—that made the light of Puglia so rich and warm. He had chosen to buy a house there because of it. He needed to paint in that light, he said.

Way before it was called Casa Rossa, the house had been a crumbling farmhouse—a *masseria*—built in the eighteen-hundreds, surrounded by a wall in the midst of an olive grove among the open fields in the countryside south of Lecce.

One could see it from miles around: tall, squared, simple and yet majestic. A large building that closed itself in a U-shaped courtyard. It had a barn, a granary, a cowshed, a crumbling chapel. It had belonged to rich landowners whose last generation had emigrated to America. Lorenzo had bought it for a few thousand liras with the money he'd made in Paris selling his paintings to a banker. He was proud of it, it was the first thing he owned that he didn't owe to his family.

They had plenty of money: his family had been dealing in marble for centuries. They owned quarries in Carrara, in the mountains that separate Tuscany from Liguria. This was considered the purest marble in the world, a material that, like diamonds or gold, seemed to exude its own magic. When it was cut, sometimes its surface split with a soft undulation that resembled waves and showed its original nature. A calcified ocean, trapped inside the mountain.

Everyone wanted it, as if a divine quality were trapped in its candor, something unique other granites didn't have. The white marble was shipped all over the world, wherever someone needed to build something that might consign them to posterity.

Of five brothers Lorenzo was the youngest, and by the time he was born, in 1900, his parents were ready for something else for him than the family business. They had named him Lorenzo after the sculptor Bernini in the hope that he would contribute to the immortality of their name. By then they were selling marble for more prosaic purposes: rich people wanted to line their bathroom walls in it, and its fine powder was used to make toothpaste. It was losing its nobility. So Lorenzo was sent to art school in Milano and then on to Paris to be an artist. He was the family's luxury item. Their single extravagance.

Paris in the twenties was a city in love with painters. Lorenzo joined in, found his niche. He paid for lots of the drinks and the restaurant bills his friends couldn't afford. He worked a lot, he sold enough, he had a few shows, a few dealers, and lots of women. My guess is that Paris was the happiest season of his life—I have a storybook image of him living his twenties in a kind of inebriated obliviousness.

Paris had an insane but heartless vitality in those years. I doubt it had any time for people with little talent, and I suspect Lorenzo was considered mediocre by his painter friends. He had a good technique but his work was derivative.

I wonder if he knew it, and how much it bothered him.

In fact, my grandfather's name did not go down in history. It barely managed to gain an entry in the encyclopedia, and he was given a proper exhibition only for his centennial. But even that, the retrospective at the Galleria d'Arte Moderna in Rome, occurred at a particular moment when the museum curators had simply run out of ideas. They had already done "I Futuristi," "I Macchiaioli," "I Surrealisti," and suddenly my grandfather's birth date was the perfect excuse to resurrect another minor Italian artist.

Renée, my grandmother, was an incredible beauty.

I know everybody tends to idealize the physical attributes and the eccentricities of their grandparents: it provides necessary interesting background, and there are hardly ever any witnesses to contradict you and spoil your story. But in this case I'm not exaggerating.

Anyway, you can see for yourself in the photos.

There is one where she leans with her back against a railing over the sea—it must be somewhere in the South of France. She's wearing loose white sailor's pants, a tight striped top that bares her arms and has a graceful low-cut neckline. Her skin is very tanned, her lips perfectly painted a dark red. Her hand, resting on the rail, holds a cigarette between two fingers. In another one—it's my favorite—she's riding in an open car, the wind is messing up her cropped curly hair, and she's laughing, throwing her head back a little. She wears small, round, dark glasses that give her an allure of mystery and intrigue. Lorenzo must have been the one behind the camera. Only a man in love would have had the doggedness to record every possible pose and shift of mood of his subject.

The Côte d'Azur in the twenties had a unique elegance. A particularly bright reflection—that Mediterranean glare—bounced on the white buildings lining the Promenade des Anglais. Nobody could look bad in that summer light.

Lorenzo saw the two girls sitting at the bar of the Grand Hotel Negresco one evening.

He watched them from his table—he was waiting for a friend who was invariably late—and he noticed the way the girls whispered, smoked, and laughed, one very close to the other, their heads almost touching.

These two girls aren't waiting for anybody, he thought, they are just waiting to see what happens.

The one with the short hair had a long neck like a gazelle, and a husky voice he liked. He noticed the way her dress fell gracefully around her lean body and over her dark legs. It was a heavy crêpe de chine in a subtle paisley design.

He did what arrogant men do in these instances: he sent over a waiter with a chilled bottle of champagne and responded to their surprise with that lame gesture, that imperceptible sign of recognition, lifting his chin up a bit and barely waving a finger. As if to say, "Yes, it's me who just bought your attention for the price of a bottle." But he was good looking and well dressed enough to get away with it.

When they finally came to join him, he felt pleased with himself. They were indeed striking and different.

"Lulu," said the smaller one, pouting her red lips.

"Renée," said the gazelle. Her bony hand felt fresh and strong.

They were too young, too giggly and nervous, to be what they were pretending to be: sirens on holiday in an expensive hotel. But it was part of the game everyone played, taking on roles they couldn't afford to match.

"Do you live here in the hotel?" Renée asked, feigning indifference.

"No, I'm staying with some friends in a villa just outside of town, up on the hill. I'm here till mid-September."

"So are we," said Lulu. "We're here for the whole season."

"Good, I should introduce you to my friends. They have a boat. Do you enjoy sailing?"

They shrugged and looked at each other, not knowing what to say.

There was something about them he couldn't place. Something untamed beneath the makeup, the perfectly manicured hands, the orderly curls. Then he heard them exchange a quick comment. It was more like a hissing sound, a secret code.

"What was that?" he asked.

"Arabic," said Renée, smiling. "We're from Sidi Bou-Sahid, a village near Tunis. We grew up together, Lulu and I."

Of course, he thought. They aren't just tanned.

He told them he was a painter, that he lived in Paris, where he had a big studio in Montmartre. It was the thing to say, in a bar like that, to girls like that.

Renée sat up on her chair and stretched her long neck, proudly.

"I sit for painters. I'm a model."

Lulu looked at her in disbelief.

"Are you really?" Lorenzo asked.

"Yes. When you go back to Paris I could come and sit for you if you like." She puffed on her thin cigarette and turned her head to the side, blowing the smoke. "I've been doing it for a long time."

She made it up just this minute, Lorenzo thought and raised his flute.

"Let's drink to that, then," he said. "To this perfect coincidence."

I don't even have Renée's family name. Not a single record from her childhood in Tunisia. No pictures of veiled great-grandmothers in the village of Sidi Bou-Sahid, wearing slippers, palm trees in the courtyard. All I'm left with is a single blue silk shoe, a few photos, and a page ripped from a letter—no date, no signature—written in French. I'm pretty sure she wrote it because of the spelling mistakes. And I'm left with the portraits, of course. There were so many of them, they filled a whole room at the Galleria d'Arte Moderna when they had my grandfather's retrospective. What's left of them—the museum now owns quite a few, and there are some private collectors, of course—has been split in three equal parts between Alba, Isabella, and me. I was the one to decide which canvas was going to whom, and I have prepared three big crates, each bearing a different name.

Renée has no clothes on in any of his paintings. Her small breasts are like a little girl's. Narrow hips, long torso, and thin legs, like an Ethiopian runner. She doesn't seem to worry about her nakedness— she lies on the sofa, she sits in the wicker chair, she's cross-legged on the floor, she lies across the unmade bed, she hugs her knees on a stool. The backgrounds are rich oranges, reds, and thick pistachio greens. In them you can smell Matisse, Mediterranean light, Picasso, Kandinsky.

But above all else, you smell his obsession for Renée. As if it wasn't enough to have her in flesh.

She wasn't a model, my grandfather said once. Let's get this straight. She was a whore. I painted a whore, and I married a whore.

Whore. I was too small to know what that word actually meant, but I could tell it wasn't good. It sounded mysteriously interesting to me, though.

And even then I knew he was only talking like that because she must have hurt him. Children are pretty good at recognizing that kind of anger.

It's almost six, and it's getting cold inside the house. These walls are thick, and by the end of summer the sun isn't strong enough to keep them warm. I'm shivering, so I put on a cardigan over this wedding dress, which smells of mildew and dust, as I climb the narrow staircase that leads to the roof. Outside I immediately feel the warmth of the sandstone under my bare feet. These southern farmhouses have vaulted ceilings in each room, so the roofs look like a series of giant half-egg shapes covered in black tar. I sit on top of the highest egg, crossed-legged, and as the stone begins to release the heat it has collected all day, I look out on a view that hasn't changed in hundreds of years; it's still just a sea of olive trees, their tiny silver leaves crackling and shimmering like sparks of light bouncing on water. I love how red the earth looks against the blue sky at this time of day. The air feels crisp on my legs. I watch the sun go down, as the olive leaves turn from silver to blue, and then I go inside and light a fire.

I have a little mission to accomplish this evening before I go to sleep. I need to go over that handwritten page, it's just one sheet with no date, no signature. I found it neatly folded inside a leather folder, eaten by moths and stuffed full of papers in my grandfather's studio. I looked quickly at the old bills, the receipts, and some old telegrams from the forties. Then I saw this crackling piece of paper, thinned by age, with a slanting handwriting—big and bold—in a faded blue ink. It must've been part of a longer letter Renée wrote, perhaps to Lorenzo, a few years after she left him. My French is faltering, and I need to check a few words in the dictionary, but I have a feeling that this single page— torn, hidden, and then forgotten for so many years—may open a door into a room kept dark for too long.

There is something that has been handed down from woman to woman in my family. I don't know how to call it. A secret, an unspoken legacy—it needs to remain concealed, it's something to be ashamed of. Its burden has shaped each one of us, has twisted us into what we are today, as vines are slowly forced by wire.

Renée was the first to bestow that inheritance. But to this day, I still don't know exactly what it was she left behind for Alba to take on. All I know is the outcome: the way that nameless something crippled Alba, and then, in turn, crippled Isabella and me.

That's why, before I close this door for good behind me, I must look at every little scrap of paper, every hidden meaning. Everything counts, especially if those words come from her.

Renée had moved in with Lorenzo right after they went back to Paris from the Côte d'Azur.

I'd like to think that their life, at least in the beginning, was light and carefree. But if one looks carefully, Renée seems more and more melancholic in every succeeding picture that first summer. Something about her has shrunk. She looks smaller, she doesn't smile into the camera, she doesn't stand up straight, arms outstretched, chest open, cigarette between her fingers, proud and bold. She has retreated.

In a photo dated 1933 she's out on the porch of Casa Rossa, the house still a ruin, before Lorenzo restored it. She's sitting on a chipped stone step, barefoot, looking away from the camera toward the olive grove, her arms hugging her knees tightly. She's not even aware someone is taking her picture. She's not really there. She was already gone by then, although she may not have known it yet.

Lorenzo and Renée still lived in Paris then, but they came to Italy every summer to spend the holidays. Lorenzo had fallen in love with Puglia and decided he had to have a place there that he could come back to for the rest of his life. "A place our children will be able to call home," he had said to Renée, and it had sounded more like a threat than the plan of a man in love.

He had bought Casa Rossa around the year that picture was taken. In those days to buy a crumbling ruin like that, in such a remote place, was unheard of. People from the north of Italy like my grandfather never considered going that far south to live. It was too backwards, too poor—foreign.

A young man from the village—stocky and strong like a bull, with gentle deep blue eyes—had been the one to show my grandfather the ruin buried in thorny bushes. His name was Stellario. His middle name was Immacolato Concetto, which made him a Starry and Immaculate Concept, and Lorenzo thought nobody with a name like that could ever lead him wrong.

As they opened the squeaking wooden door, a couple of doves fluttered out of a crack in the roof. Lorenzo stepped onto a soft layer of hay. Then, as he walked into what used to be the kitchen, he noticed a young olive tree sprouting in the middle of the room, its roots splitting the terra-cotta tiles.

"You can fall in love with a place just like with a person, and suffer from the same obsessions," he explained to me once. "You believe you are the one and only capable of understanding its beauty. It was destiny, you say. We were meant for each other. That's exactly what happened the minute I walked into this place."

Possessive as he was, I'm not surprised he couldn't bear the thought someone else might own it, live in it, love it. So he bought it right away.

Stellario knew wood, stone, sand, beams, bricks. He and my grandfather rebuilt the house with their own hands, in the course of two years. Every bit of building material had to come all the way from Lecce. In those days it had to be carried all the way on a donkey's back, because there was no road to the house. After the house was finished Lorenzo hired Stellario to look after the olive trees on the land. He planted the almond trees around the house, the lemons and the oranges in the orchard, the sweet grapes on the trellis, the *zagara* that climbed the wall and diffused its scent at night. He worked as my grandfather's *fattore* for the rest of his life. The house became as much his as ours. But that's another story.

After the house had been entirely rebuilt, Lorenzo and Renée came to Puglia every year and spent the summer months there. He shut himself in the barn, which he had converted into his studio, and painted all day, hardly taking a break to eat.

To the villagers, this young couple who came all the way from Paris looked so foreign that, as far as they were concerned, they could have come from the moon. They had never seen a woman with cropped hair wearing trousers, nor a man who spent the whole day inside painting and letting the garden become overgrown. But once Alba was born, in 1935, Lorenzo and Renée began to look more like a family, and the locals got more used to them. Women brought dried figs and sweets to Renée, they sent fresh baked bread and ricotta with their younger daughters. They insisted she was too thin to breast-feed her baby properly.

I know what Lorenzo would say if he saw me now, methodically wiping out all our memories, making room for strangers who might cut his trees, bring their own furniture and disfigure the order of his rooms forever.

A place you love that much should cease to exist without you, or better still, it should turn to rubble.

But the thing is, I'm trying to have a different outlook on life from his.

I doubt very much Renée ever cared for Casa Rossa.

Had she been still in love with Lorenzo, maybe she would have tried to see it through his eyes. Then she would have seen the same things he loved and would have been moved by them.

During the long winters in Paris she, too, would have been longing for the smell of green figs in the early morning air, the coolness of the stone floors under her bare feet, the fat lizards crossing her path, the mulberry juice dripping like blood on her fingers. Had she still been in love with him, all that would have meant something to her. But she probably had had enough of poverty, illiteracy, and hunger in Tunisia to fall in love with a place like that. Her idea of a good life was more like nice clothes, cocktail parties, and glamorous friends. I'm sure she didn't see the point of hauling water out of a well and having to light kerosene lamps at night. That was precisely what she had run away from when she had left her village.

I can just see her, sitting on that stone step on the porch, staring into the distance, like a prisoner counting the days. Her little baby girl, Alba, is being lulled to sleep by Celeste, Stellario's young wife, somewhere inside the house. She can't find the energy or the desire within her to be a good mother.

They say women can suffer from depression after delivery, that it's perfectly normal to feel shattered for no apparent reason. But this sadness feels to her like it's been sitting inside her, quiet and still, for a very long time, way before the baby was born.

Lorenzo is painting inside the barn, wrapped in his gloom. There's no joy, no kindness left in him. There's no trace of the gallant dandy she had met at the bar of the Hotel Negresco a few years earlier.

He needs to own her. He doesn't let her out of his sight. But there's no love, no warmth in that need. There's only greed and fear.

Their marriage has turned into a cold and silent place.

The light blue shoe I found is pointed and has a sequined strap that goes around the ankle. It was inside a felt box in the bottom of a closet.

This is no ordinary shoe. This is the silk shoe one wears at a ball.

It was custom made in Paris, and I suspect there must be a light blue dress made of the same silk somewhere that went with it.

I think it was worn by my grandmother at a big reception given by some American heiress, patron of the arts, who had come to live in Paris and wanted to make an impression. I like to think of Renée entering the room, wearing this light blue dress and these custom-made shoes, cigarette holder between her fingers, silver bangles on her thin wrist, her eyes darting right and left. After the months she has spent in Puglia over the summer, she probably has been looking forward to this: the thrill of flirting again, the tinkling of crystal, the swish of shiny fabrics. Lorenzo, however, is in a bad mood, hates the idea of having to go to this party, feels uncomfortable in his dinner jacket. He finds the whole atmosphere pretentious and ridiculous.

"I want to leave early," he says as they check their coats, "so don't start drinking."

"You don't need to warn me," Renée snaps without even looking at him. "I didn't expect you'd let me have a bit of fun for once."

He doesn't even answer. They are used to being curt and nasty to each other by now. The bitterness they are capable of has ceased to surprise them.

Renée moves swiftly across the crowded room, trying to lose contact with him, even if only for a few minutes. Just so that she can savor what it would be like to be on her own again, like she had been when she and Lulu first came to France. To move through a crowd, collecting glances, responding to smiles. As she feels the animal heat in the room rising around her, she realizes it's been too long since she has felt the attention of a man. The last time had been at a dinner party at the French Embassy in Rome, where they had stopped on their way south to Puglia. An antiques dealer was he? Or maybe an archaeologist. He was sitting across the table from her and had kept his foot pressed on hers throughout the entire dinner. An attractive Englishman in love with Roman ruins. Lorenzo had raised hell afterwards. God only knows how, but he always felt it, whenever someone had been sniffing around her.

She picks a glass of champagne from a tray balanced on a waiter's gloved hand.

Her eyes meet the eyes of a stranger in the crowd. They find themselves very close to one another. The woman is tall, blond, has porcelain skin. She raises her glass, as if proposing a toast to her, and Renée raises hers in turn. As their two flutes touch and the crystal tinkles, they burst out laughing.

"To what?" asks Renée.

"To us, here, tonight," says the blonde promptly, in a foreign accent.

"All right—to us, here, tonight," Renée repeats, slowly, giving strength to every syllable.

"Oh my God!" The woman laughs and closes her eyes, as if Renée is too much to look at. "Do you mind if I tell you this? You are so beautiful!"

She must be drunk, Renée thinks. But she's flattered.

Later that evening Lorenzo crosses the room, then the room after that, and the room after that. He looks around, not too quickly and not too anxiously. He doesn't want to give the impression he's angry or disturbed. More and more often, whenever they are with other people, she gets out of hand. She does it on purpose, to spite him. Her reminder that he can't lock her up, that there is—and there always will be—a way to escape him.

He can't find her.

The orchestra is playing a tango, the dance floor is crowded. He keeps moving on, slowly scanning the room.

Renée is in the arms of a tall blond woman dressed in white. They are staring into each other's eyes as they dance, smiling. They know the steps, as if they have been dancing for a while, and as Renée arches all the way back, the woman's lips move very close to hers. It's not clear whether she's kissing her or is just whispering something to her. But when Renée comes back up, proud and tall like a tango dancer should be, she's laughing a throaty, drunken laugh.

Her name is Muriel, she's German. She's twenty-eight years old, the heiress to a fortune built on steel. Her father is an industrialist, her older brother is some high-ranking officer in the Reich. She's extravagant, spoiled, too confident in her own power. Renée receives six phone calls and a few letters from her the week following the ball. The effect is dazzling, pitched with drunken excitement, slightly melodramatic.

"I must see you again before I leave Paris at the end of the month. I haven't stopped thinking of you since I met you. I beg you to give me a chance to see you once more so that you can at least get to know me a little bit."

Renée hasn't made up her mind about this yet. She doesn't really know what to think—she has never been pursued by a woman—but she finally agrees to meet her for tea in Montparnasse in the middle of the day.

As she enters the café she sees Muriel sitting at a small round table in the back of the room. She's wearing a red beret over her blond hair, which makes her look more girlish than the tall imposing woman she remembered from the ball. Muriel waves her hand like a child. Renée sits down without smiling, unwraps the scarf from her neck, and unbuttons her coat.

"I thought you might not come," Muriel says, her cheeks flushing.

"Why? You're not going to eat me up, are you?"

They stare at each other for a few seconds, not knowing how to proceed. Muriel looks almost frightened, as if all her confidence has disintegrated. Suddenly what had seemed so natural to say on paper is impossible to pronounce. Renée has silenced her. Her physical presence, her scent, the way she carries herself, her long fingers, the orange gloves on the table, the color of her nail polish, everything dumbfounds Muriel.

"It's a bit more difficult to be with you without being drunk," she admits in her heavily accented French.

"But it's more real," says Renée. Then she smiles, as if the situation is beginning to amuse her. "This is actually who I am: I have a husband, a little two-year-old girl, and you are—"

Muriel puts a finger on her lips to prevent her from saying any more.

"I just wish it would be possible to get close to you, but I mean *really* close, and skip all this"—she waves a hand in the air as if searching for a good enough word—"all this *history* that needs to be said beforehand."

"I don't see how you can ignore it, this *history*," says Renée and nonchalantly turns to the waitress, who's been standing beside her with a pen in her hand. "Yes, a tea with milk please. Muriel, what would you like?"

"Tea is fine," says Muriel, looking into the ashtray, discouraged. She's not used to this, someone else dealing briskly with the waitress. She's usually the one in charge.

Then she lifts her eyes again.

"I feel pathetic. I should have known this was hopeless."

"Maybe you feel like that because you're used to always getting what you want at the snap of a finger."

"Is that what you think?"

Renée shrugs and fiddles with her handbag, in search of her cigarettes.

"It's possible."

She lights a cigarette and inhales deeply, closing her eyes

"I know because I've been bought by someone who is used to getting anything he likes, just like this"—and she snaps her long fingers as she blows out the smoke.

"And now I'm angry," Renée continues. "I get very angry at people who do that."

Muriel stares at her, surprised.

"You sound so bitter. I didn't mean to stir that in you."

"You didn't stir anything. It's not your fault. And I don't even know you, so don't pay any attention to what I say."

The waitress comes back with the tea and they both fiddle for a few seconds with the pot, the milk, the sugar. There's only the tinkling sound of spoons swirling in the china. Muriel sips her tea slowly. This is not going in the direction she has hoped. She has lost control over the situation and is not capable of steering it back into place. It's better to retreat now, before it's too late, before any damage is inflicted. She knows how to do it graciously, she's had to do it before.

"I'm sorry I insisted and made you come. I don't know what I was thinking. I'm going back to Berlin soon and I probably won't ever see you again."

Renée doesn't say anything. She just stares at her, so serious.

"You are so *charmante* . . . . I mean . . . not just the way you look." Muriel hesitates. "Inside as well. I felt it right away when I saw you among all those people at the ball. I . . . I guess I wanted to see you because I needed to tell you how beautiful I think you are . . . that's all."

Renée doesn't say anything. She sips her tea and keeps her dark eyes fixed on Muriel's.

"And maybe I should leave it at that instead of going on making a fool of myself."

She grabs her coat on the back of her chair and starts to get up.

"Wait."

Renée gently presses her arm till she has to sit down again. They look at each other, holding their breath. Renée comes forward, stretches lightly across the marble-top table and touches Muriel's pale hair with her fingertips, then smooths a strand behind her ear, as a mother would for a child.

"Don't go. I'm just scared."

"Scared of what?"

"Of what might happen between us."

"So am I."

They both smile at each other now and begin to feel this warmth—it's rising, from lungs to chest, all the way to their cheeks. Their breathing is heavier. Muriel feels her tension release, and begins to laugh. They are shaking with laughter, holding hands across the table.

Later, years later, they will remember that particular moment and go over it, hoping to discover something they might have forgotten.

"When did it happen, for you?"

"When you touched my hair."

"For me, too. I needed to touch you. I couldn't resist."

In the catalogue of the show for my grandfather's centennial there was a black-and-white photograph of the inner patio of Casa Rossa, dated 1940. It shows an enormous portrait of Renée reclining on her side, naked. It spanned the lime-washed wall. Her legs stretched beneath the windows, her arms curved under the vine. Like a giantess, her body in the fresco loomed across the courtyard, her bare breasts, her thighs, the darkness between her legs stark against the whiteness of the wall.

Renée's portrait on the patio appeared practically overnight one summer.

The afternoon of the next day the whole village was talking about it. Women weren't allowed to look at this giant naked body. They stopped coming to the house. Their husbands, their fathers, and their brothers forbade it. So no one showed up to cook a meal, light the fire, wash the floor. No one came to bring figs and ricotta. No one changed the sheets or opened the shutters. The village staged a silent mutiny against the *forestieri,* whose behavior they couldn't comprehend.

Renée had left a few days earlier. The villagers had seen her get into a hired car with a lot of luggage. The driver said she had been crying the whole way to the train station in town.

And then, out of the blue, Lorenzo painted that indecency on the wall of the house. There were rumors, all sort of conjectures, but nobody dared to come too close. They could smell his madness even at a distance.

Someone said he wasn't getting out of bed at all. Others said they heard him throwing things around, breaking glass, cursing. He made the perfect subject for village gossip.

But as days passed, they began to feel sorry for the little girl. Someone should go and make sure Alba was all right. She was only five, was she getting her meals? So they sent Stellario to have a look. Stellario came back and reported dutifully to the others in the café on the piazza. The doctor was sent for, phone calls were made, a doctor from town was duly consulted. Telegrams were sent to the rest of his family. His sister came all the way from Carrara with their family doctor. They took him and the girl, packed all their things, and put them on the train.

Lorenzo didn't come back the following summer. Nobody in the village knew exactly where he'd been taken. The rumor at the café in the piazza was that he'd had a breakdown and had been sent to Switzerland for shock treatments. Alba had to stay with her aunt and uncles in Carrara. Renée was never mentioned, as if she had never existed or was never to reappear in their lives.

While my grandfather was away, the house stayed closed, the furniture covered in white sheets, spiderwebs dangling in the dark. Someone had taken that photo—I like to think it was Stellario, with my grandfather's camera—before shrouding her body in a white sheet: he buried Renée's fresco under a coat of white paint. Yet a dim trace of her emerged through the lime wash.

When Lorenzo finally came back to Puglia the next summer, he looked thinner. But he was smiling when he got off the train in Lecce; he was holding Alba's hand and there was another woman with them. This one looked very different from Renée. This one was plump, had bleached blond hair, thick wrists, and thin lips.

"This is Signora Jeanne," Lorenzo said when Stellario and his wife, Celeste, came to greet him. Then he pointed at the big trunks that sat on the floor. "I've decided to move here and stay. For good. I'm never going back to Paris."

"I'm happy to hear that, Don Lorenzo," said Stellario. "This is your real home. You don't need to go live in France and speak a different language. If you stay, then we can really do something with the property. We can make oil and sell it. Have a business."

For Stellario the concept of the world outside his village was vague. He couldn't even begin to picture it. Anything outside his domain, his trees and goats, felt like a vast, useless space, where people wasted their time doing things that didn't matter.

"Yes, this is my country," Lorenzo sighed. "For better or worse."

Over that summer, Lorenzo settled back into the house. He pretended not to notice that the fresco was still there, sprawled across the patio, seeping through the white paint. He simply ignored it.

Every day he and Stellario would make a list of things which needed to be done to improve the house now that he was going to spend the winters there: the leaky roof needed to be repaired, they had to build another fireplace upstairs, and dig a second well under the almond tree. The shutters had to be repainted, the doors fixed. But he never mentioned a second coat of white paint to cover the ghost of Renée.

One day, shortly after their arrival, Jeanne showed up in the *drogheria,* the grocery store across from the church, wearing a large straw hat that made her look like a mushroom.

The store was dark, and it had a strong smell of garlic and rotting tomatoes. There were dusty sacks of hemp on the floor stuffed with dry lentils and beans; bars of soap, candles, jars of capers in salt sat on the dark wooden shelves. Jeanne wandered around, sighing, picking up this and that, putting things back in place with an expression of distaste. She kept shaking her head, as if nothing seemed fresh or clean enough for her to buy. Domenico and his wife, Addolorata, kept still behind the marble counter, watching her slow procession through the aisles. They listened to her sniffing and sighing.

"Like a dog in a heap of trash," they muttered to each other without offering to help her, just whisking flies away.

"Must be the nanny," Domenico said to his wife after she left, "come to take care of Alba."

"Why did he bring her here?" Addolorata said, irritated. "Celeste could have taken care of the child, he didn't need to have this woman come and live in the house with him."

Jeanne came back to the *drogheria* once or twice a week. She never smiled or said anything friendly to Domenico and Addolorata. Not even a comment on the weather. She treated them as if they were invisible. She kept her money in a tiny pouch, wrote down every single lira she spent in a notebook in her neat handwriting with the zeal of an accountant.

Once Domenico, as he was counting the change to give her back, couldn't restrain his curiosity. Addressing her in his most formal Italian, he asked, "Where are you from, Signora Jeanne? Excuse me for asking, but you have an unusual way of talking. Sometimes I don't understand you very well."

"I come from Switzerland."

"Is that where you met Don Lorenzo?" Addolorata asked.

Jeanne imperceptibly stepped back, as to protect herself from the intrusion. She wasn't used to strangers asking such personal questions.

"Yes, I was a nurse at the hospital," she offerred.

"The hospital for his nerves?"

Jeanne hesitated, then nodded quickly. They had definitely crossed the line, those two. She thrust her arm forward for her change. They smelled of sweat and onions. Nobody smelled like that in Geneva.

Domenico and Addolorata watched her go out in the fierce summer light, stumble across the square under the wide-brimmed hat, carrying her groceries. They didn't think she would last long. She didn't seem fit for that kind of heat—no constitution for the flies, the spicy food, the thorny cacti.

But she would have to be. Lorenzo married Jeanne a year later, in the Church of San Matteo in Lecce. It was a hot day. The light was glaring on the white steps of the church. Jeanne's makeup was running with her sweat, and her wedding dress looked too tight across her hips.

"All my life I'd wanted a muse, but as it turned out all I really needed was a nurse," he said to Alba years later, speaking of his marriage to Jeanne. "Just think, what a waste of time and energy."

Actually, Domenico wasn't so very wrong when he mistook her for the nanny: Jeanne had the nature of a caretaker, never expecting to be thanked for the care she took. And in fact, nobody did. Everyone in my family, Lorenzo, Alba, even my sister and I, expected Jeanne to see us through rages, despairs, fevers, depressions, hatreds, jealousies, financial ruins without blinking an eye. She kept the accounts, made sure the balance would be even. She always put back the same amount she had been given.

She believed she had been chosen to save the life of a genius, or at least that's the way she decided to perceive her fate when Lorenzo materialized at the hospital in Geneva.

From the moment she agreed to follow him back to Italy after he was discharged, and said she'd be happy to go and live in with him and his little daughter, she could no longer think of herself as separate from him. What could she do—already forty years old—who could she be, in a foreign place where she knew no one else, a place not of her choosing? She had the faith of the survivor. And the discipline.

Plump, short, bleached. Thick wrists and thin lips. There isn't a single canvas of Jeanne, he wasn't interested in using her as a model, of course. But there she is, in almost every single family photo since 1940. She was always at the edge of the photo, never in the center, never looking comfortable in a chair, always in the wrong clothes. You, too, would think she was the governess, or his secretary. You could tell she didn't belong there. You could tell our blood hadn't mixed with hers.

One day Jeanne went to the *drogheria* and instead of buying her groceries she asked Domenico if he would order red pigments for her from the town's hardware store, to mix with lime wash.

"What for, Signora Jeanne?"

"I would like to repaint the exterior of the house."

Domenico burst out laughing.

"You can't paint it red, *Signora*. That house has always been white, for hundreds of years."

"I don't care."

"It has to be a light color—yellow maybe, or cream. But red . . ." He shook his head. "It's impossible."

"Just order it, please, Domenico," she said in her usual flat tone. Not kind, not rude. Domenico stopped laughing and scribbled down a note.

People in the village watched the sacks of pigment being delivered to the house on the back of a donkey. They waited to see what would happen, if Lorenzo would let her go ahead with this. They watched as the house was painted a rich deep red by a few men she had hired from the next town.

Casa Rossa.

People started to call it that, because every other house in the village was white or the creamy yellow of eggnog. One could see it for miles away, sunk among the olive trees, the extravagant color of a Pompeiian villa.

It's a good name for a house, said Jeanne.

Lorenzo still said nothing. He pretended not to hear her. She didn't care, this was not a matter of approval. She was marking her territory.

"That was Jeanne drowning Renée in a bloodbath," said my grandfather many years later. And he laughed.

I wake up before seven to the sound of rain and thunder. I jump out of bed and run outside. The sky is leaden, a nasty wind is shaking the olive branches.

I'm always for a storm. When we were small, Isabella and I loved to wait for the first downpour in Casa Rossa at the end of the summer. It meant the end of the sultry heat, of the relentless cicada song, and it meant we could ride our bicycles wearing the cheap blue sweaters we loved so much.

Sometimes Alba, bored by the rain, would call for us. She would be standing by the open door of her red Fiat 500, wearing a black turtleneck and cotton trousers, her hair tied up in a bun.

"Shall we go for a little ride? Today is market day in Martano. I was thinking we could get some baskets . . ."

I knew she felt restless as well. By the end of September we were all ready to leave Lorenzo and Jeanne behind and go back to Rome, to city life and school.

So this morning this sudden rain fills me with unexpected euphoria. I don't even know why I'm happy. This is the end of all summers for me here, after all.

But today is Wednesday, market day in Maglie. As when I was small, the market still moves every day from village to village in Puglia. Except that now, along with the handmade pottery, the fresh goat cheeses, and the sturdy hand-embroidered sheets, you'll find endless rows of fake Fendi bags, Dolce e Gabbana underwear, and fluorescent track suits.

I wonder if Andrea, the old man, is still alive and still does the market rounds.

"You'll never find anything like this, remember," Alba would warn us, holding one of his tight-woven baskets up in the air, turning it

27

around, checking every detail, sniffing it. "This is wild reeds, the kind that grows by the sea. See how fine this is? Nobody uses it anymore, I'm telling you."

What I most remember about the old man Andrea was his scary raspy voice. He always wore the same threadbare suit and black beret. We always found his stall in the crowded open market: it was impossible to miss, with that colorful pile of straw mats and baskets. He always sat back quietly as he watched Alba inspect his baskets, his coarse hands resting in his lap. Then he would pick one from the pile and stroke it, pat it, show her how flexible it was, how finely woven. In his hands it would almost come alive. The two of them went on and on, while Isabella and I sat on a pile of smelly mats, wishing we had stayed home to ride our bicycles in the dusty tracks around the house.

In the car, on the way back home, she kept pushing the basket under our noses.

"Smell this. It reminds me so much of my childhood." She would press it till the rough weeds scratched my nostrils. "God, how I love this smell! Wild reeds. You can tell it comes from the sea."

She would sniff it again with her eyes closed. It made us nervous, that she would close her eyes while driving.

"That man is a master, nobody in the world makes baskets like him. When that man dies, you won't be able to get anything like this anymore, I'm telling you. These baskets are going to be worth a fortune."

They really were beautiful, so thin, so soft. And they did smell good, especially in the rain. If I close my eyes I can still recall that fragrance: like the sea at the end of the summer. Salty and cool.

On June 10, 1940, a young boy pushed his bicycle up the road to Casa Rossa, raising a cloud of white dust. He knocked lightly on the kitchen door and walked in clutching a beret in his hands. Lorenzo and Jeanne were eating their midday meal in silence.

"What is it?" asked Lorenzo.

"Stellario sent me," said the boy, blushing. "He says you must come to listen to the speech at three."

"What speech?"

"Il Duce is going to give a speech. Everybody is going to the square at three o'clock sharp to listen. They've hung a speaker up on a pole, so everybody can hear.

Lorenzo put down his napkin, turned to Jeanne.

"It's the war," he said.

Everyone knew it was coming, that it was only a matter of months till Italy plunged into war alongside Hitler, but till the very last moment everyone hoped some miracle might happen.

At three the whole village gathered in silence under the white-hot sun across from Domenico's store, where a loudspeaker was lashed to a lamppost. They wiped their foreheads with their handkerchiefs and stared up toward the loudspeaker, waiting for their fate to be spelled out. First thing they heard coming from its dark mouth was a raucous sound, like a lion's roar: it was the clamor of the crowd greeting Mussolini as he stepped onto the balcony of Piazza Venezia in Rome. But nobody was cheering in the small piazza of the village. Now all heads drooped, as Mussolini pronouced his triumphant declaration.

Down in Salento, in southern Puglia, life went on as usual in the following years, save for the evening radio bulletins. The food was there, all you needed to do was go out and pick it: figs, oil, wheat, *cicoria*—the bitter herb peasants cooked with their homemade pasta—sun-dried tomatoes, and beans. Every household baked fragrant maize bread and *friselle*—the dry-roasted buns that could last for months—and made fresh ricotta with the sheep's milk. The black market thrived, and farmers went up north to sell their produce in the cities where food was rationed and people were starving. Oil had become more precious than gold.

Stellario and Lorenzo found themselves with a pretty good business.

Throughout the following years Puglia was virtually spared the conflict. There were no soldiers, no tanks, no bombing. Especially in the interior, people hardly knew there was a war going on.

In the elementary school of the village there were only five children in the class, and often the school was shut because nobody could afford to send their kids to school full-time. Families, especially in those days, could always do with an extra hand in the fields.

By the time Alba was ten, she had become some strange hybrid. She had hardly a notion of geography or history, and she spoke the tight, guttural dialect the villagers taught her. Yet at home she still conversed in French with Jeanne, and Lorenzo would read to her from Homer. She was different from every other child she knew. She grew up awkward and moody.

Whenever he found her lolling about aimlessly, Stellario took her along with him on his cart to the tiny farm where he had his olive trees and his orchard. He would sit under a tree in the middle of the day, after he had tended the trees and the plants since early morning, and share with Alba his favorite meal.

"A slice of fresh bread, anchovies, and ricotta. This is the peasant's lunch. Nothing at the rich man's table tastes so good." He would laugh as he unwrapped the handkerchief slowly, took out the round bread, and sliced it carefully with a big wood-handled knife. She watched his rough hand place a thick anchovy on each slice, then spread some of the soft cheese with great care. He served Alba her slice on a fig leaf, and they would chew and nod at each other with pleasure at every bite. It was almost religious, the way Stellario prepared that slice of bread. She loved to eat like that: sitting under the shade of an olive tree, on its twisted root with Stellario. Everything tasted strong and delicious.

If he went back to work in the fields, sometimes she helped him spray the plants, or she would run around barefoot, catching lizards or picking blackberries while he worked.

"Beware of the tarantulas," Stellario warned her. "If they bite you, you will get so sick, like something has cut you in two. Like you have swallowed a stone."

"Will I die?" Alba asked, wide-eyed.

"No, but you'll have to dance for a whole month to get rid of the poison."

"Why?"

"Because only the music can cure the bite. It'll shake the poison out of your blood. And then, on the twenty-ninth of June you'll have to go to Galatina, to the Church of San Paolo, and he'll grant you the grace and you'll be rid of the tarantula forever. Otherwise, every summer it'll come back in your blood and shake it, and you'll have to dance again."

"For how long?"

"Every summer, for a month. Till San Paolo in Galatina cures you for good, I told you."

She had heard many stories about the tarantulas. Every summer one could hear music coming from a house far away, and whenever the frenzied rhythm was heard, she'd see women crossing themselves several times and praying. Grown-ups whispered; something bad had happened. It was the tarantula, which had stung yet another woman working in the tobacco fields. When Alba went home and asked Jeanne about it, Jeanne would shake her head again.

"These peasants, they believe anything. It's because they haven't had an education. You shouldn't listen to them."

It was always like this: whatever she learned from Stellario she had to dismiss immediately once back in the house. There were always two ways of looking at things.

In summer afternoons, when the heat became unbearable, Stellario would lie down for a quick nap in the *furneddhu,* the oval-shaped stone hut that peasants have built all over the countryside for centuries. These were small cairns where they could rest, keep their tools, spend the night if the orchard or the olive trees were too distant from their house. They were made of rough stones piled up, one on top of the other, nothing holding them together but their weight. It smelled good inside: stone, hay, and heat. In the winter, when it was damp and windy, the stones seemed to be able to absorb even the faintest ray of light. Sometimes Alba would squeeze in with Stellario and lie down on the mattress of olive leaves Stellario had prepared for them. She'd close her eyes, falling asleep for only a few minutes, lulled by his snoring. The olive leaves rustled under her back; they felt soft and dry.

This was what my mother remembered most, whenever she thought of her childhood. The contrast between the harsh light and the dark, that sudden change that blinded her everytime she entered the *furneddhu.* The crackling of the tiny olive leaves under her back. The slice of bread with the anchovy and the ricotta.

The smell of wild reeds.

The square of our village is tiny, but like every other village here in Puglia, it still has the three essential elements which make a piazza a *piazza*. The church, the palazzo of the most important family (usually a baron's), and the main café. Our baroque church is small and austere, built in sandstone with a carved door; the palazzo from the 1700s is unpretentious and stark (the Sanguedolces are very minor barons); but the Caffè Sport has been recently redone and looks pretty snazzy. It's all steel and fake wood and bright lights. An old man in a beret and overalls sitting in the corner lifts his head from the paper and nods as I come in. A local rock station is blasting from the speakers.

"Hi, Enzo. Cappuccino, please."

Enzo smiles and starts steaming the milk behind the espresso machine. His narrow hips bounce slightly to the music as he does that. He must love the way he looks, I can tell by the confidence he shows moving his body around behind the counter, as if he were on a dance floor. He looks like every other twenty-five-year-old around the globe obsessed by fashion labels: dark hair slicked back, biceps bulging through the black Versace T-shirt, tight jeans, a kneeling samurai tattooed on his forearm. He sets the foamy cappuccino in front of me. He always swirls a little heart shape with the foam right at the center.

"Thanks."

"Where are you going in this weather?" He points with his chin to the rain outside. Then he smiles. "That's some outfit."

"It's an old dress. My mother's."

"You're so crazy," he chuckles. "It's only eight in the morning and she looks like she's ready to rock and roll."

"I am ready, in fact. But where's the party? I'd go in a second."

He rolls his eyes to the ceiling.

"Don't even talk about it. I got home four hours ago. Danced all night at Guendalina's."

"How can you do it?"

"You should come with me sometime," he says, then leans over the counter and whispers, "I'd show you how to have a really good time."

"I don't think I have the stamina to dance till dawn."

He winks at me mischievously and moves closer. I can smell his expensive cologne.

"There are ways to stay up, if you're interested."

"I bet there are."

The old man reading the paper behind me coughs, and we instinctively straighten up, as if warned by a cop.

"Are you coming to the opening of the Gulliver Supermarket tomorrow?" he asks.

"Where?"

"You know—the big one on the highway. There's an opening party tomorrow evening. Everyone is going."

"I don't think so. You know, I hate to think they're opening that monstrosity. I'd rather shop just at Domenico's."

Domenico of course is dead, but everyone still calls the store by his name. His son has taken over with his wife. It's still dark and smelly, but the hemp bags are gone, and so are the dark wooden shelves, replaced by refrigerators and shiny aluminum racks.

"Domenico's got only a few things." Enzo shrugs. "This supermarket will have everything. All the things they advertise on TV. Like in America."

His lack of loyalty irritates me. How can he not see it, this ugliness that is taking over all the places we loved and cherished, that keeps swallowing the landscape slowly, with its bright signs and parking lots?

"I'm off to the market in Maglie," I say as I lick the foam off my upper lip. "I want to buy a basket from that old man . . . Andrea, I think he's called."

He arches one eyebrow quizzically. The old man sitting in the corner reading La Gazzetta senses the gap in our dialogue and promptly fills it.

"Andrea Sartano, the man from Parabita," he says with his thick southern accent. He shakes his head. "He's too old to do the market now. Sometimes he sends his son, but he hardly weaves anymore. You can try."

Enzo asks him something using the dialect they still speak in the area, which I hardly understand. Suddenly his voice turns a shade harder, more masculine. Even his body language shifts as he speaks to the old man. It's tougher.

"I know who you mean," he says and turns back to me. "He's the old man who used to have the movie house Cleopatra. It's closed now, but that's where he keeps all his old baskets, if you want to have a look. Go to Parabita and ask for the old cinema house."

The old man intervenes again and gives me detailed instructions: get on the highway, exit at Parabita, turn right at the second light, then left again after the cemetery, then go behind the church across from the railway, make a left, you'll find it right in front of you. I nod and I pretend I follow exactly what he's saying.

I always do that. For some reason, I prefer to get lost than ask things twice.

During and after the war, when Alba was growing up here, few people around her knew how to read or write, or speak proper Italian—just the local dialect. Women dressed strictly in black, they kept their gaze down, and worked out in the fields bent in two, picking tobacco leaves till sunset. Girls from good families, who didn't need to work, stayed secluded in the house, and if they went for a stroll in the evening, they would always be escorted by family members. The only form of entertainment were the tales the family elders told. The stories were always the same, but nobody seemed to mind hearing them over and over again. Everyone believed in the same myths, in magic, in the power of invisible things. Tradition still stood in the place of education, and strongly held its ground.

Stellario had lots of children. One of his oldest daughters, Rosa, was around Alba's age. She had green eyes and black curly hair, the scrawny body of a monkey, her forearms and legs covered in a light fuzz. What Alba particularly envied her were the small golden hoops dangling from her ears. Sometimes Stellario would bring Rosa to Casa Rossa on his cart so that she and Alba could play together in the garden. But Rosa was too shy to be fun as a playmate. She would stare at Alba's clean clothes and shoes, her eyes wide open, dumbfounded. Like a little animal who has finally been let out of its cage and can't take a single step forward.

As they began to grow up, they saw each other less and less. Celeste didn't like the idea of her daughter picking up the habits of the *signori,* by hanging around a house that had so many luxuries, plenty of food, and sofas covered in flowered fabrics. She sent Rosa to pick tobacco leaves with other girls her age instead.

One day, when Alba was about ten, Stellario came early in the morning to Casa Rossa to speak to Jeanne. Alba watched him from a distance, his hat clutched in his hands, his head slightly bowed.

"We have called the musicians"—she overheard him say. "They will play till she shakes the poison off."

"Rubbish," said Jeanne, "I can't believe you and Celeste believe this stuff."

"It's the tarantula, *Signora.* It cannot be anything else. The doctors don't know what's wrong with her. We even took her to Lecce, to the big hospital. She doesn't eat, she has pains here," he said, touching his stomach. "She turns and turns in bed all day, covered in sweat. She was stung picking the leaves, she told me."

Jeanne shrugged, impatiently, in her usual brusque manner.

"If you say so. So what is it you want?"

"The musicians are coming today. I have to go home and look after everything."

"All right . Do what you need to do. Stay home today and tomorrow, but be back on Monday."

Alba grabbed Stellario's arm before he hopped on his cart to leave.

"Is it Rosa?" she whispered.

Stellario nodded.

"Take me to your house," she said. "I want to see her."

Stellario and his family lived in a small, square, stone house on the side of the road. She had seen it many times but had never gone in. A scruffy yellow dog always barked wildly and scared her. But today there were many people outside the house: all the women were dressed in black, many were praying. And the dog was quiet.

Inside it was close, dark and stuffy. A pungent whiff, like fermented fruit. The insistent buzzing of flies. Garlic and red peppers hanging from the ceiling. Sweat.

Rosa was lying on a bed, quite still but breathing heavily, in the biggest room of the house, dressed in an immaculate white dress, like a bride. She looked much older than her age. Alba was almost frightened to see how full her breasts were, and the way her expression had changed since she had seen her last. She looked like a sad, skinny woman. Celeste and her two other daughters, all dressed in white, entered the room and spread a white sheet on the floor beneath the bed, in the center of the room. A rope tied on a ring hung from the ceiling. People started streaming in quietly, till the room was full. Everybody was careful not to step on the sheet.

Alba felt scared, but it was too late. Too many people were pressing her on every side, she was trapped in the heat and the darkness.

Then the musicians began. A violin, a tambourine, and a mandolin.

Rosa started rocking her head, then spread her legs and arms and began to move them slowly, as if her body were being driven by waves. Then she slid down from the bed and grabbed the rope.

She held on to it and started swinging slowly, with her head bowed. In her white dress, in her pallor, she looked like she had been hanged. Suddenly she woke up from this trance-like movement, raised her head, clutched the rope tight, and started to climb the rope, keeping it between her feet. Her slender body curled nimbly as she went up.

"You see, she's turned into a spider," whispered a woman next to Alba. "You know, when I was your age, I saw a woman who had been stung, she climbed the walls, all the way up to the ceiling, and fell down without even getting hurt. They become like spiders. They can crawl anywhere they like."

The rhythm accelerated as one of the old men started singing. The sound was strident, somehow unpleasant. But Alba knew this music: she'd heard it many times, always in the summer, the season of the tarantulas.

Rosa jumped down from the rope, she landed with a thud and now was dancing on the sheet. She was wriggling and stomping, then whirling on all fours. She did look like a spider, crawling on the floor, moving faster and faster.

The music got louder, speeding up its tempo.

An old woman dressed in white came forward, holding different colored ribbons in her hand. She waved them in front of Rosa, like a bullfighter incites a bull with his red cloth.

"The *nzaccareddhe*," someone whispered.

The girl started thrashing around, writhing to a fevered pitch. Sweat poured copiously from her forehead, her hair was drenched, her breathing heavier.

"Why is she doing that?" Alba tapped the arm of the woman next to her. She was very frightened now.

"She has to pick from the *nzaccareddhe* the color of the tarantula that has stung her," the woman said. "Tarantulas come in different colors. You have to know if it's a red one, a black one, a yellow one. You have to rip the ribbon of that same color if you want to kill the tarantula inside you."

Rosa threw herself onto the woman and grabbed at the ribbons. She started tearing one with her teeth. Her eyes had turned white. She was foaming at the mouth.

She looked like the devil herself.

Everything turned black as Alba gently slid to the floor.

When she opened her eyes again, she was outside, in the blaring light. The first thing she saw was the whitewashed wall of the house against the deep blue sky. She could still hear the music coming from inside the house. But she was breathing again now, and could even smell the sweet lattice of figs in the heat.

Voices around her were whispering.

"She'll be fine. Give her some water."

"Take her back to Casa Rossa. Don Lorenzo doesn't even know she's here."

"Holy Mary! Ntoni, you take her home in the cart."

She felt a hand sliding behind her head, holding it gently, and the coolness of the deep well water on her lips.

As far as Lorenzo was concerned, his daughter's upbringing never seemed to require a particular strategy. But Jeanne, by the time Alba turned thirteen, became concerned, and issued her pronouncement:

"She can't grow up like a peasant. She needs to see people of her own social background."

To begin with, Jeanne couldn't tolerate hearing Alba speak with that thick accent. Therefore Alba was sent to a private school in Lecce so that she might become acquainted with the offspring of the southern aristocracy. But she was too different, an oddity that the rigid code of a provincial town could not allow for. She wasn't much of a success with her schoolmates.

It's no surprise Beniamino Sanguedolce was the only real friend she ever made. Two stray dogs that didn't fit anywhere, they were a perfect match.

He was the youngest son of the baroness Alearda Sanguedolce. The baroness had given her husband four daughters already, and she kept praying to Santa Caterina, the patron of the village, to grace her with a son. When the the fifth daughter was born, the baron suggested that she stop asking, that they should resign to God's will, but Alearda wouldn't hear of it. She prayed one last time and promised to donate a golden crown to be put on the Saint's statue whenever it was taken out of the church for the yearly procession.

That did it.

Alearda was awarded a son at last, the lovely Beniamino. That year the statue of Caterina came out of the church crowned in twenty-two-karat gold, with a dazzling smile on her face.

Alba went to school with the Sanguedolce sisters, and Jeanne often sent her to their palazzo to do their homework together. Alba didn't like the palazzo, she found it spooky and freezing cold.

But then she discovered Beniamino, the brother nobody liked to talk about. They were the same age, about twelve years old. He was a very different boy from the boisterous ones Alba had met so far. He looked like a chubby girl who just wore the wrong sort of clothes. He was soft, squeamish, hilarious.

They locked themselves in his room as he played with her hair, dressed her up in his mother's clothes like a doll. He sometimes wore Alearda's gowns as well. He adored Alba because she didn't mind one bit whenever he did that. Unlike his dull sisters, she didn't think there was anything wrong in dressing up.

"You should've been a girl," she once said to him as he walked past her in high heels and a silk kimono, his face made up like a clown.

"You think so?"

He felt relieved to hear her verbalize his problem for him: he had long felt trapped in the wrong body and didn't know how to be released from it.

All because of that golden crown. And of the greediness of Santa Caterina.

"Maybe I'll be a woman when I'm older. I can always wear a wig, nobody will know the difference," he said, looking at his made-up face in the mirror. That seemed like a good solution, for the time being.

Beniamino had two souls: one was the frivolous girl who kicked to be freed at last, who longed to grow long curls and wear makeup. But there was another side to him, which Alba particularly admired. He could be serious and authoritative. He was a passionate reader. She would often find him lying on his bed, buried in a book he had found in the library of the house. He looked so intent, this funny boy with black-rimmed glasses, his shorts too tight around his round bottom and fat thighs. She preferred him when he was quiet like this.

One day they were in his room, and he had been reading aloud a gruesome passage from a book he particularly liked on the French Revolution. He loved to impersonate Charlotte Corday when she stabs Marat in his bath. He had closed the book and remained silent for a few seconds.

"I have to ask you something. I hope you don't mind. It's about your mother," he said.

"What is it?" Alba stiffened.

"My mother said this is something I shouldn't talk about, but I don't think you'll mind if I ask you."

Alba's heart started beating faster, as it did every other time someone mentioned Renée's name.

" I don't mind," she said and shrugged, taking the book from his hands and pretending to look at the illustrations.

"You can answer yes or no."

"Okay."

"Is it true your mother was a spy for the Germans?"

Alba remained silent. She raised her eyes from the book and stared at Beniamino. There was no malice in his question, just curiosity.

"I don't know," she admitted. This was so unexpected, it almost choked her.

"My mother says she was working for the Nazis during the war, and that's why she had to go live in Germany and can never come back."

"Why can't she come back?"

"Because the Germans have become our enemies, *scema*. Because now if your mother comes back to Italy, they will kill her. Or shave her head."

"Why? Why will they shave her head?" she whispered.

"That's what they do to women traitors. They shave their heads so that when they walk down the street everybody knows they helped the Nazis and so everyone can spit at them."

Beniamino stared at her, studying the effect of this information. He saw her eyes fill with tears. That worried him.

"Maybe it's not true," he said quickly. "My mother says a lot of things."

"It's not true," Alba said, turning her head to the side to hide her shiny eyes from him. "My mother went to Germany because . . . she had a very good friend there."

"The rich woman?" Beniamino asked. "I know, my mother said—"

"No," Alba interrupted him with sudden energy, "not her. Someone else you don't know."

There was a pause. She kept looking at the book, as if her interest in the conversation had ceased. Beniamino felt bad; he hadn't meant to upset her. He knew what it was like to feel different.

"I hate my parents," he said at last, hoping this might cheer her up. "I envy you. At least you only have one. Jeanne doesn't count."

"No, she doesn't count," Alba agreed.

They smiled at each other.

"I hate them so much," he stressed, wanting her to forget the subject of Renée. "I can't wait to leave and never come back."

"You can't." Alba looked frightened by his energy. "You have to fin-ish school."

"I don't care about school."

"Your father will kill you."

Beniamino shrugged. "I'm never coming back here. You know, I could go to Rome, change my name, and nobody would ever find me."

"No, you can't leave," Alba said again, feebly.

But she knew he would.

Silence had become one of Alba's best skills. She knew not to ask her father about Renée. On the one hand, she hated his lies and spiteful fabrications, and on the other, she feared hearing the truth, which might be even worse. She simply avoided the whole subject, hoping that one day it would slide past her for good. Maybe she would stop wondering about her mother and the reasons she'd vanished.

But that day, after the conversation with Beniamino, she felt unusually brave and resolute. Jeanne was in the kitchen, preparing dinner, when she got home.

"Come and look, Alba," she said and opened the lid of a big pot where a stew was cooking. "We are going to say this is rabbit, *d'accord*? Your father hates lamb, but he will eat it if we don't tell him what it is. I always do it, because *j'adore l'agneau*," she said with a satisfied laugh.

That was typical Jeanne. She always preferred to have accomplices to share her little secrets. Even Jeanne, the impassive caretaker, when it came to Lorenzo, had her tricks and childish revenges.

"Yes, we won't tell him," said Alba, wanting to ingratiate herself. Then, instead of running upstairs to her room, she sat on a chair, her eyes fixed on Jeanne, who had forgotten all about her.

"Jeanne."

"Yes, *chérie.*"

"Is it true that if my mother comes back to Italy, they will kill her or shave her head?"

Jeanne froze, her ladle in midair, but said nothing.

"Did my mother work for the Germans? Is that why she can't come back?"

"Who told you this story?"

"Someone at school."

Jeanne pulled up a chair and sat across from her at the table, squinting.

"Well, I don't know that she actually worked for—." She stopped and looked around the room, to make sure nobody else was listening, then lowered her voice. "You know, your mother, she . . . she was .. how can I say . . ."

"What?"

41

"A bit of a mystery."

"What do you mean?" Alba was alarmed again.

"Well, you see, nobody really knew the story of your mother, where she came from, what her real name was." Jeanne paused, then went on. "She always claimed she had lost her documents."

She looked at a stain on her apron and absentmindedly tried to scrape it off.

"It wasn't clear whose money she had been living on before she met your father. It was all very, very . . . dodgy."

Alba nodded, pretending to understand.

"And then, when she suddenly left your father and went to Germany with this woman . . ." Jeanne sighed and shook her head. "You can imagine the rumors, right?"

Alba nodded again.

"Well, it affected your father terribly. And it ruined his reputation, as you can well imagine. He was shattered. He ended up in the hospital because of it."

"Mmmmm . . ." Alba lowered her eyes.

"She did not have a lot of scruples, your mother."

Jeanne went back to the stove and checked the stew in the pot. She muttered something to herself concerning the state of the lamb and turned off the stove with a sigh of satisfaction. Alba would have liked to ask again, perhaps be more specific with her question this time. She wanted to have a yes or no, something definite that she could report back to Beniamino. But Jeanne turned to Alba, pointing a finger sharply at her.

"But you should never mention any of this to your father. It's still very very sensitive for him. Don't ever tell him that you heard about this at school, *d'accord*?"

"*D'accord.*"

"Otherwise he'll remove you from that school and you'll have to study at home. He'd be furious if he knew people were still gossiping about this."

Jeanne shivered and wrapped her pink, hand-knitted cardigan tightly around her shoulders. She looked at her tiny wristwatch and reached for the door.

"I'm going upstairs now to take a nap. Make sure you keep quiet down here. Your father is probably asleep on the sofa in the living room."

She was gone. The kitchen was suddenly very quiet, except for the intermittent drip of the tap in the sink and the ticking of the wall clock.

Alba felt nauseous. She wasn't going to mention this again. It made her feel too sick in the stomach, it wasn't worth it. She was going to forget this conversation, pretend it never happened. Jeanne didn't count, as Beniamino had put it. Alba didn't trust anything she said.

After all, she had been the one to drown Renée in red paint.

And to turn a lamb into a rabbit.

Of course it wasn't just my family who covered the past with paint: it was the whole of Italy.

Italians had turned away from Germany from one day to the next, and by the time our generation was born, that swift movement—that sudden pirouette—was conveniently forgotten, as if it had never happened. As if we had always been on the right side.

That's how we inherited a different story.

According to all our families, we'd all been fervent antifascists. They had all hated the Germans. They had all known all along that Hitler was a dangerous psychopath and Mussolini a violent fanatic. They had all been waiting anxiously to be "liberated" by the Allies. Each one of our families made sure to forget anything that might embarrass them in the future. They got rid of all the junk of the past and hid it in the attic, as if it had never been part of their lives. The bronze bust of the uncle who had been a *prefetto,* the letters from the Ministry of Interior that addressed the father as *Camerata,* the photos of the children at school wearing the *camicia nera,* arms stretched in the Roman salute.

That stiff salute. Nobody wanted to remember it, or be reminded of it. Nobody had liked it.

Overnight it had turned into the simple V for victory.

CHAPTER TWO

———◆———

I like to imagine the particular moment when Alba's and Oliviero's trajectories crossed, and the story took an unexpected turn.

Summer, 1958. The train is heading south.

Every small-town train station south of Rome looks the same: dusty oleanders, gravel, cracked orange walls, peeling green shutters. It's unbearably hot in the dusty compartments, the passengers keep fanning themselves with newspapers as sweat dribbles down their backs. Exhausted from the heat, they keep dozing off, chins dangling, snoring lightly, and wake up with a grunt at every jolt of the train.

Oliviero Strada is in his early thirties. You couldn't call him handsome, he's the studious type, thin and wiry, messy hair and thick glasses. He wears a shapeless corduroy jacket and worn-out English shoes. He's a romantic, an ardent Anglophile. Unlike his companion, Giorgio Morelli, he can't concentrate on his book. He keeps looking at the girl sitting across from them in the compartment. The three of them boarded the train together in Rome, early in the morning. Many passengers have gotten off in Naples, others in Benevento. New ones have boarded and are gone by now. It's late afternoon but the sun is still fierce. As the train continues farther south, toward Puglia, fewer passengers board, most of them are peasants who travel third class, loaded with cardboard boxes and baskets.

Oliviero, Giorgio, and the girl have been alone for quite some time in the second-class compartment. This has created an air of unspoken intimacy, as if the compartment belonged to them by right. They feel at ease with each other by now, they have become somewhat familiar: the occasional cigarette, a few polite words, a quick nap. She's been leafing through cheap magazines and has dozed off a couple of times.

Which has given Oliviero a chance to study her with a clinical eye.

She must be in her early twenties, olive skin, slim, yet strong. Her dark hair is a mess: tangled, precariously pinned up, sticky with sweat. She's wearing a sleeveless cotton dress, a thick cotton print of giant peonies that looks more like old-fashioned upholstery than dress material. It has been hand-stitched and the seams are giving out at the waist. Her cheap pink sandals are dirty, one of the broken straps is hanging loose. The nail polish on her toes is chipped, her feet are in rough shape, as if she's been walking barefoot. She wears no rings.

There's something unusual about this girl. Oliviero has been trying to tailor a story to fit her for some time now.

She's not a peasant, she's not a gypsy.

Her features are too refined. A long, rather prominent nose, thick, arched eyebrows, full lips. Dark circles under her almond-shaped eyes. She's not a mother, nor a secretary, nor a student.

She's something Oliviero can't quite grasp.

Making stories is Oliviero's job. That's how he makes a living in Rome; he and Giorgio Morelli have been writing films together for quite some time and have had a couple of successful hits. Since the war, it's as if the whole country were swept away by optimism and renewed energy. The theaters are full—everybody seems to have money for a movie. Italian cinema is booming; producers are constantly hunting for ideas. The two of them still cannot get used to it: every time they succeed in selling one of their stories they feel like they have just robbed a bank. They can hardly believe their luck.

"To be paid money . . . "

". . . to write stories . . . "

"While other people toil in a factory, or die of boredom behind a desk."

They usually hop in a taxi straight outside the producer's office and head straight for Caffè Rosati on Piazza del Popolo and then move onto

Via Veneto, to celebrate with their friends the checks they just put in their pockets. Everyone in the film business hangs out here. Oliviero and Giorgio drift from one table to the next, shaking hands, patting backs, kissing the pretty girls, ordering another round of drinks for everybody. Giorgio is the properly handsome one of the two—the paparazzi, who always hang out in the vicinities of Via Veneto, jokingly call him "Gary Cooper" because of his height and fine features, though some girls are undone by Oliviero's tortured look, his gaunt face and slim hands. They think him sensitive and uncannily gifted.

Via Veneto, the only proper boulevard in Rome that could claim to be Parisian, has obliterated its very recent past. Only a few years earlier, during the war, it had housed the headquarters of the Nazis. It had been lined with barbed wire to protect the Hotel Flora, the "German Special Courthouse," while Field Marshal Kesselring lived in the Excelsior, across the street. And the fascist police headquarters in Via Tasso, where suspects were held and tortured, was only around the corner.

But these days it's hard to remember Via Veneto was ever that gloomy: in less than ten years the memories of the Nazis and the barbed wire have faded, and Via Veneto has gotten so happy that it resembles a beach more than a boulevard. From a distance all one can see is a sea of umbrellas covering the tables of the outdoor cafés. Some have the bright red Campari sign written across, others are made of straw, with long fringes flowing in the breeze in a sort of Hawaiian fantasy. The girls—mostly aspiring actresses, aspiring poets, aspiring muses—look so cheerful in their low-cut summer dresses, strawberry-red earrings, and bright pistachio shoes, their silky legs already tanned. They sip brightly colored cocktails, a symphony of reds, oranges, and pinks dotted by the occasional cherry or Japanese umbrella. It's as if the whole Via Veneto crowd were made of ice cream: colorful, smooth, frothy.

Later in the evening, Oliviero and Giorgio move to Otello's, a trattoria in Via della Croce, right around the corner from the Spanish Steps. The food is good and cheap, and they always run into familiar faces. At Otello's they pay only periodically, only when they have received an advance; otherwise Otello doesn't mind putting it on their tab. Sometimes it's months before they can clear it.

Before the trattoria closes, around eleven-thirty, they collect other friends from the neighboring tables and stumble to someone's apartment, in Via Margutta or Via Borgognona, all the way to the top floor, up a narrow spiral staircase. Here they sit on the floor, play charades, silly games that involve embarassing questions and frank answers, read aloud from their favorite books, gossip about the latest literary prize, drink some more. It's the mating dance, the necessary prologue to picking who you'll spend the night with.

A last drink before Caffè Rosati. Sometimes Oliviero and Giorgio make it just on time—the two girls they have secured for the night tightly tucked under their arms—as the waiter is mopping the floor inside and all the chairs are tipped over the tables.

"The last one, Alberto!" they scream and roar with laughter.

"I can't. The cashier's closed."

"Oh, don't be like that, my friend. We need a last one for the road!"

They tip him and persuade him to hand over the half-empty bottle of scotch. They are good clients, and Alberto likes them.

It's late. Piazza del Popolo is deserted. The moonlight brushes the silvery pines of Villa Borghese, the thin Egyptian obelisk, and the marble sphinxes of the fountains, transforming the familiar square into a mysterious landscape, eerie and empty like a De Chirico painting. Oliviero and Giorgio sit with the girls on the steps of the Church of Santa Maria del Popolo, across from the fountains, and stare at the iridescent reflections of the water on the marble obelisk, sipping in turn from the bottle of scotch. They would like to sit and talk for a while longer, now that everything is quiet again. Their voices echo and bounce around the square; the water gurgling from the fountain is the only sound of the night. The girls are giggling and pressing their heads on their dates' shoulders, their warm bodies leaning on theirs, moving in short shivers. The two men are exhausted and aroused. It's time to go.

So they finally say goodbye and each one goes home with his nightly prey, the mysterious Silvana, or the beautiful Maria Grazia. Once they reach the bed they make love quickly and then collapse on top of the girl, their head still spinning from all the drinks.

For Oliviero sex is a sort of vertigo. He rarely remembers what it was like the next morning when he wakes up with a nasty hangover.

The next morning Silvana appears in the door frame of his bedroom, wearing one of his shirts, holding a coffee cup in her hand. She's dark, curvaceous, pretty. She looks good in a man's shirt. She curls up next to him, trying to look like the French actress with cropped hair they have recently seen in a movie. She hands him the cup.

"Coffee? It's almost eleven, my love."

It's an easy life. It's *la dolce vita*.

"What a Scarlett O'Hara," says Giorgio, finally waking up from his book as the girl leaves the compartment to go to the rest room.

"What? . . . You mean *her*?" Oliviero is surprised Giorgio has even noticed the girl, he seemed so engrossed in his Faulkner.

"Yes," says Giorgio. He smiles and shakes his head. "And I'll bet she's cut that dress out of the curtains.

Oliviero laughs.

"Curtains. I was thinking more like sofa cushions . . . Who do you think she is?"

"I'd guess she's from Sicily. Good family, I think. Sicilian aristocracy.

"Really? She doesn't look quite—"

"Check the nose. Aquiline, like one of those portraits."

"Yes, but the way she's dressed . . ."

"Couldn't they have lost all their money?"

"Right! The father is a gambler and he went bust—"

"Yes! Absolutely, And he's either committed suicide or gone to jail, and she had to get a job in Rome . . . as a . . ."

"Seamstress."

"Of course—for the Fontana sisters. She stitches haute couture and lives in a pensione around Via Belsiana."

They are good at this game. They play it all the time, almost automatically, hoping by chance they might stumble upon something worthwhile that they can sell to another producer.

The girl returns to the compartment. She sits up straight, across from them, and this time she stares at them. Both Oliviero and Giorgio feel that she's expecting them to maybe introduce themselves, or entertain her in some way. As if she's suddenly tired of daydreaming and flipping through magazines. There's something almost imperious in her stare.

"*Signorina,* where are you getting off?" Oliviero can think of nothing better to say."

"Lecce," she replies. She continues to stare at them, as if waiting for more. As if that's not enough.

Giorgio smiles at her, boyishly, almost blushing.

"We were wondering, my friend and I . . . we were playing a bit of a game, trying to guess what—"

Oliviero elbows him in the ribs. Giorgio stops in mid-sentence, words evaporating from his lips. But the girl doesn't stir. She's looking at them as if they were a rare species of animal, something she's never come across before. It's a purely scientific gaze.

"What do you do?" she inquires softly. She drags her vowels, with a southern inflection.

"We work for the cinema," says Oliviero, proud to be able to impress her right away. "We're screenwriters."

"We're supposed to write a film that takes place in Puglia, a story about tobacco pickers. We're also going to Lecce. To do some research," adds Giorgio.

"And talk to a few people."

The girl reflects for a second or two.

"Oh."

Oliviero is disappointed, he was hoping for a warmer reaction.

"We'd like to find out more about this business of the"—he hesitates—"the tarantula. These women who are stung in the fields and then are possessed. We might use it for the film."

"Have you heard anything about it?" Giorgio asks.

"Yes," she says. "They have to go to Galatina and ask San Paolo to grant them grace. Every twenty-ninth of June.

"So you know about this."

"Oh yes," she says, and then looks out of the window as if that's the end of the conversation.

The two men exchange a quick glance. They can't figure this girl out at all.

"Is it true they dance for days on end, like in a trance?" asks Giorgio.

"We heard that there are musicians who play a special music they have to dance to . . ."

The girl turns her head slowly from the window and looks at him. She seems bored already.

"The *pizzica*. They play the *pizzica*."

"Would you . . . would we be able to meet some of these women, to talk to them, do you think?" Giorgio asks.

The girl doesn't seem to understand what he means. She shrugs.

"Yes, why not. Of course you can talk to them."

Then she looks at Oliviero.

"I don't see a lot of films. There's nothing to do where I live. It's just farmland."

Oliviero and Giorgio don't know how to react. The girl, for some mysterious reason, has intimidated the both of them.

"You can come stay with us at the house if you like," she says. "We have lots of room at home."

"Well, actually we're . . . we have to . . . we have a hotel in Lecce," says Oliviero politely, yet stunned by her audacity.

"But it would be wonderful if we could come and see you," Giorgio adds eagerly. "In fact, it might be useful for our research."

"My father is a painter. He doesn't know much about tobacco. But maybe you could come and look at his paintings."

"A *painter?*" Oliviero asks as if the word is the key to the plot he had been looking for. "How interesting."

She doesn't say anything. She's neither flirtatious nor excited. It's almost as if she has asked them to visit merely for the sake of doing something different, not because she finds them attractive or fun to be with.

"We live near Tricase. It's not far from Lecce."

They diligently take down the name of the village, and she draws a map so they can find the house.

"It's called Casa Rossa. Anyone can tell you where it is."

A few days later, while they are in Lecce, Giorgio receives a phone call from Rome. It's Maria Grazia, with whom he has been sleeping lately. She's pregnant.

"My father is going to kill me," she is saying, between sobs.

Giorgio turns white, he knows right away this is not to be taken lightly. That night he keeps tossing and turning in bed, realizing how Maria Grazia's phone call will mark, on the map of his life, the point where he had to turn back. Just at a time when he was traveling so light.

Maria Grazia. A baby. He might have to marry her now. His Gary Cooper days are over. But deep down, something about this terrifying prospect thrills him. This is something he doesn't dare admit even to himself.

He gets up at dawn and wakes up Oliviero. They attack the subject from every possible angle, until it's decided that Giorgio should catch the first train back to Rome and deal with this issue personally and without any procrastination.

Oliviero is left alone amid the heat, the flies, and the smelly streets to interview a few more people, to check some books at the public library in Lecce. He even calls the university and gets hold of an anthropology professor. They meet for breakfast in a café in the old city; they sit at a marble-top table under the ceiling fan, surrounded by mirrors and brass lamps. The professor is a small chubby man in his forties who wears thick glasses. He orders *caffè al ghiaccio* with almond milk and has Oliviero try one as well.

"This is how we drink coffee here in the summer," he says, interrupting his own discussion of the myth behind the tarantula bite and its cure.

"It's an orgiastic dance. A venting of repressed sexual desire," the professor explains dismissively. "It only happens to women, in fact. You could say it still bears a trace of Dionysiac rituals. That archaic world, it's all here, you know. Just look around."

He does look around. The old city of Lecce is ferociously beautiful. The buildings are carved in a soft, creamy stone, porous and light. Angels, gargoyles, hydras, hippogriffs, dragons, Madonnas, mermaids, saints—they're staring down from windows and roofs at every corner of the shady streets. There are faces and wings, fishtails and sharp paws twirling in spirals around the columns of the many churches. Each door, window, balcony, every decoration, ends in a ripple or a swirl, as if they have been curled out of meringue. In the midst of this creamy yellow surface, smooth like a ripe peach, a green ficus patiently blasts a wall, pushing its roots through the bricks. A bougainvillea throws a violent purple stain against a gate. A wall has collapsed to reveal a thick dark jungle inside a courtyard.

Oliviero hadn't expected it to be so intense. There are moments when the sensuality of the city pains him.

During the day, he drives out into the countryside to do his research. Right outside Lecce the landscape opens up in a flat, endless line. Miles and miles of centenarian olive trees, twisted trunks on the red soil. Nothing else, but the essential silhouette of the white *masserie,* the fortified farmhouses scattered in the plain.

Sometimes he drives his battered rental car along the sea, all the way south of Otranto, where the medieval watch towers dot the coastline. You can see them from miles away, perched on the edge of the steep cliffs, half crumbled. Dark-blue fjords cut deep into the land. At times he stops the car and walks across the yellow plain that reaches the sea and stops abruptly in a stony precipice. He walks through the yellow grass bent by the wind and climbs up to the crumbling tower. He touches its stones, listens to the short gusts of wind, smells the thyme and wild sage. The sea is right below him, a sheet of emerald glass, at the bottom of the cliff.

All this makes him sad.

He comes back to Lecce in the evening and sits in the deserted square on the steps of the church, watching the glow of the orange light dim on the façade of the buildings. By that time everyone has gone home and he's completely alone, he and the pigeons, like on an empty stage. He has his meal always in the same small trattoria. The food is good, hearty, deliciously rough. He always brings a book with him, so that the other diners don't feel obliged to talk to him. In the south a person does not eat out alone, it's just not done, and they all wonder about this young man always by himself. Why does he not have a wife?

By now he has talked to enough people, seen enough churches and villages, scribbled enough notes. The prospect of writing a movie about an illiterate tobacco picker begins to bore him. There's so much more to this place. It's darker, stranger, more complex than he ever expected.

Sometimes he wakes up very early and goes walking around the narrow alleys, when the city is still asleep and all he can hear are his own footsteps. They resonate, stark and clear on the pebbled pavement.

There's often a fresh breeze at that hour, and the crispness in the air helps him think straight.

He looks at his own fleeting reflection in the windows: a man in his early thirties, hands clenched in the pockets of his crumpled jacket, shoulders slightly hunched, dark glasses. It's good to feel like a stranger, not to recognize anybody on the street, and to look so out of place. Oliviero does a lot of thinking as he walks, this is the way he works best, head down, gaze fixed on his shoes. He sorts out all the images that come to mind, lays them on an imaginary table, like cards. These images are all new, all surprising, seductive. But none of them has to do with the film he's supposed to be writing. Where do they come from, and why?

He lies on his bed in the small hotel room during the siesta hour, listening to the flies buzzing around the ceiling. What is it? It's a certain kind of sexual alertness that has seeped through from the blinds along with the afternoon sun. He can't sleep it off, he's too restless.

The next day he pulls out that piece of paper with the map and heads toward Tricase.

So this is how they met.

It could have been just a brief encounter on the train, had it not been for that piece of paper, which he had kept in his pocket. The map Alba had given him must have been the same she still draws today for any visitor who comes to Casa Rossa for the first time. I've seen her draw it quickly so many times, always in the same fashion. Two parallel lines for the bridge, a cross for the Madonna shrine under the tall tree, an arrow to the left, a dotted line to the wooden gate. I myself don't know how to draw it any other way.

The house looked the same as today, except the road wasn't paved then, one had to trudge along slowly in the dirt, raising a cloud of red dust behind. After turning left past the Madonna shrine, he must have recognized the house resting on top of the field. Its red walls emerging amongst the olives. He had no idea how familiar that sight would become to him.

How blithely did he drive into his destiny that first time.

He didn't fall in love with her immediately. He hadn't even ventured to Casa Rossa to see her especially. He was just bored eating always on his own and was curious about meeting a painter. At least that's what he was telling himself.

The father's paintings impressed him—he had expected to see bad, amateurish art. He didn't believe a real painter would live in such a remote place. In fact, Lorenzo by then had spent too much time alone, and now there was a rough edge to him that spoke more of the peasant than the sophisticate. The charm he had displayed so lavishly in his Parisian days had worn off. Obsession and resentment had gnawed at his spirit.

"Stay for lunch," Lorenzo commanded him. "We hardly ever have visitors I can discuss anything with."

When Oliviero saw the girl again he was slightly disappointed. Somehow she didn't look as attractive as she had on the train.

She didn't look or act anything like the girls he went out with in Rome. She wore strange clothes, things you wouldn't see in the shops or in the fashion magazines. She put together incongruous colors and went barefoot. Yet she had a kind of style—Oliviero had noticed it immediately on the train—that, like her father's, intimidated him. He wasn't sure what to make of them.

The girl seemed disappointed when she heard that Giorgio had left so unexpectedly.

"What kind of a problem?" she asked when Oliviero told her he had had to go back.

He was used to it, girls were always more attracted to Giorgio when they met the two of them together. He always had to work a bit harder to get their attention.

"I don't know exactly. I think his fiancée wasn't feeling well," he said, from a sudden urge to disappoint her.

She shrugged—apparently his answer had indeed annoyed her. She walked out onto the porch and began to set the table for lunch. He watched her organize the table under the jasmine trellis as she moved back and forth from the kitchen.

In the shady studio, under the high vaulted ceiling, Lorenzo kept talking to Oliviero about African art, the Dadaists, Giacometti, De Chirico. A world hard to believe he had ever been part of. The vehemence with which Lorenzo talked about those days in France made

Oliviero feel claustrophobic. He could smell Lorenzo's frustration right away. He felt trapped by his unhappiness.

From the corner of his eyes he saw the girl out on the porch set a vase of poppies and jasmine at the center of the lunch table.

She stepped back to look at it, tilted her head to one side as a painter would do. Then she picked a jasmine bud and stuck it behind her ear.

Oliviero couldn't help wonder whether she might have done this for his sake, but immediately felt ridiculous for even considering it. It was so obvious this girl wasn't interested in him in the least. She largely ignored him, just stared into the distance as her father got drunker and gloomier—merely passed the food around, then cleared the plates, without ever addressing him. She treated him as if he had been one of her father's aquaintances she needed to be polite to and was hoping would leave soon.

The stepmother, Jeanne, was dull and looked like an aging nurse. She had a slight accent and looked out of place.

What a weird bunch of people, living in a world of their own, Oliviero thought. After lunch he felt sleepy and melancholic and had a sudden urge to escape back to his hotel room. He scribbled his address down for Lorenzo.

"In case you ever happen to be in Rome . . ."

But he knew he never would.

One night, weeks later, Oliviero and Silvana stumbled up the stairs to his apartment in Rome.

"I can't stay," Silvana had whispered earlier, as he pulled her in the direction of his flat after they had left Caffè Rosati. "My mother is in town. I have to go back home."

"Just come up for a last drink," Oliviero had begged her. He was longing to undress her quickly and make love to her, yet he was relieved she had to go, so he didn't have to face her the next morning. Whenever he woke up with a hangover he preferred to be alone. Sometimes Silvana purred too much like a kitten. Her cuteness annoyed him. Lately he had begun to feel guilty for wanting her with such urgency and such lack of tenderness.

As they climbed the stairs he was thinking about making love to her against the wall, just pulling up her dress. That way they wouldn't even have to get into bed. The thought excited him.

Alba was sitting on the steps of the landing. She was curled up before his door, a small bag between her feet.

"Hi," she said quietly. "I came on the train tonight. I've been waiting for you here. I was hoping you'd let me sleep on your couch."

She was wearing a maroon linen dress; it was crumpled and a button was missing. She shivered and pulled the hem of the dress over her bare knees.

"I'm cold."

Oliviero suddenly felt something open up in his stomach. Something swelled. It all happened there, on the steps. It took only a couple of seconds.

"Yes," he said and smiled, "of course you can. Just let me take my friend here to a taxi."

Silvana didn't say a word as he led her down the stairs again. She had gone stiff, like a rod of iron. Oliviero walked her across Piazza del Popolo to the taxi station and put her in a car. He handed some banknotes to the driver.

"Who is she?" Silvana asked, her chin trembling.

"The daughter of a friend of mine. It's hard to explain—but it's not what you think."

He ran back home, flying up the steps. The dark contraction in his loins had dissolved, leaving in its place an exhilarating sensation of lightness.

How strange. This girl. Right there, on his doorstep, patiently waiting for him in the dark. Her bizarre behavior had suddenly eliminated all distance between them. Whatever that might mean for her, for him it was clear what he wanted. But without the urge, the cold desire he had felt for Silvana. He wanted to lift her from the marble steps and place her on his bed like a doll. Undress her slowly and kiss her lightly, taking all the time in the world.

This was an entirely different plan than the one he had devised only a few minutes earlier.

Alba didn't say much. She didn't explain why she had come to his home, of all places, nor what were her plans. She just followed him into the bedroom and looked out the window. The river was flowing below, Castel Sant'Angelo was shimmering in the water. The trumpeting angel on its top looked like a figurine on a wedding cake.

"So pretty here," she said and sunk into a small armchair. She brushed the armrest with her fingertips. "I would love to live in place like this."

She smiled at him, like a child opening a Christmas present.

"I want to come and live in Rome."

"Where exactly?" Oliviero asked, amused by her boldness.

"Here. On your couch, if you'll let me."

"I'd prefer if you slept in my bed."

Alba laughed and stretched both her hands toward him.

You live with someone for two, ten, twenty years. Are you surprised at how much you forget? Whole chunks of your life just disappear, your memories muddle. What were you doing all that time? How did you spend your days as a couple?

Scattered fragments may reemerge here and there, but you never forget that first moment. Those hands pulling you closer, closing your eyes as you taste the sweetness of this stranger's mouth. Glimpses of skin, eyes, hair getting in the way, shoulders. You have strung those images together in this glorious chain, and the chain has never broken, the beads have never fallen off the string. It'll stay with you forever. And you'll be surprised to realize how, often, it's all you have managed to keep of the other.

Sometimes I think Alba must have succeeded in erasing almost every single memory of Oliviero from her life. You can tell, just by looking at her today, that she no longer carries any trace of him. She walks around in this world as someone who hardly even knew him. Which was difficult for Isabella and me to come to terms with, because for us it felt like losing Oliviero twice. First when he died, and then when she failed to remind us of him.

But I like to think that she kept that single string of images, of the night they first made love. I like to think they had at least one memory in common, and that it should be that one.

The next morning, as he opened his eyes, Oliviero rolled over and gazed at Alba's back. Her skin was dark against the white sheets, her hair all tangled up in knots.

The girl on the train, he said to himself. That stranger.

There she was now, naked in his bed, breathing peacefully. Not only had he not woken up with a hangover, but he remembered perfectly well how they had made love the night before. How quiet she had been, as she had let him undress her. The surprise of her skin, dark and soft, her bushy armpits, the long thin scar on her thigh, the fine dark fuzz on her arms . Her smell, a mix of sweat and salt.

"Don't move, please," she had said to him in a whisper after he had come inside her. He felt the pressure of her hand behind his neck. She was holding on to him, she didn't want to let go. And then, in a few seconds, the hand loosened its grip. She had fallen asleep. Without another word, as if this was the bed she slept in every night and his was the body she always fell asleep next to. As if she had come home after a long trip.

Oliviero reached for his cigarettes on the night table, lit one and inhaled, looking at the ceiling. He caught himself grinning like an idiot.

Maybe I'll make some coffee and then wake her up, he thought. It's almost ten. Maybe I'll run her a bath first.

Maybe I'm in love.

I picture it a glorious morning. One of those September days when Rome is bathed in a warm light, and one can sense the first colder note in the air. I picture him walking to his appointment from his flat—along the river, only a few cars would drive by then—not even realizing he was late. Still wrapped in that unexpected warmth, grinning.

Peppino Esposito, the Neapolitan film producer, had his headquarters in the grandest suite of the Hotel Excelsior—probably, in fact, in the same suite once occupied by Field Marshal Kesselring. His office sat right above the swaying Hawaiian umbrellas of the cafés on Via Veneto. He liked to start his meetings very early; often he received writers, directors, agents while still in his pajamas and silk robe, as his barber,

Toto, whom he had brought to Rome with him from Naples, shaved him with religious zeal.

The American stars and Hollywood screenwriters who came to Rome to work on his films thought this charming and exquisitely Italian. They wrote colorful letters to their agents in Los Angeles describing Esposito making deals on the phone, screaming in his striped pajamas, as Toto—steady and imperturbable—kept shaving him. Everybody was in love with Italian histrionics.

Esposito was the quintessential self-made man. As a teenager, he made pizzas in Posillipo and had been a tour guide in Pompei. He then proceeded to make a fortune in ways directors and writers had always preferred not to investigate. He still lapsed into Neapolitan dialect whenever he lost his temper (which was often) and chain-smoked Nazionale nonfilter cigarettes. He wasn't handsome; he was short and hairy and wore thick black-rimmed glasses, but he exuded a peculiar charm. Women adored him: he had an extraordinary ability to always make them feel safe and loved. Men respected him because of the mercurial speed of his thought and his success. Esposito was ambitious; he wanted to become a *famoso produttore internazionale*. Although he spoke a very poor English, he was perfectly suited for Hollywood grandeur. Art and the avant garde didn't intimidate him; on the contrary, he had a sixth sense, a street sense, that enabled him to produce films he didn't even fully understand. He could recognize talent, the way a dog smells a truffle.

He liked Oliviero Strada and Giorgio Morelli as writers. They had no idea how good they were, which was for the better because it added to his control over them. Now there was this script about the illiterate tobacco picker in Puglia. He had insisted they weave a love story in. As long as there is a love story, the audience can identify with almost anything. That was his credo. Plus he had just met this formidable girl from Sicily whom, with the right script in his hands, he could turn into the next Sofia Loren. He had already picked the perfect screen name for her: Elsa Dern.

Puglia, he was thinking that morning as he was being lathered up by Toto. He had recommended that Oliviero and Giorgio write a love scene between the farmer and a pretty tobacco picker in the hay barn.

Would they have hay barns in Puglia? *Must check this with Strada.*

It was very important that the girl wear black stockings, he had stressed in their meeting a few days earlier, the same sort Silvana Mangano wore in *Riso Amaro,* where she had played a stunning rice picker.

The white of Elsa Dern's thighs against the black of the stockings—he savored the image as Toto delicately skimmed the lather off his chin. It felt like whipped cream. *Delicious contrast.*

Peppino believed that for a movie to be a commercial success, you needed a single indelible image. The rest is just support—background noise, he always used to say to his writers.

"Nobody ever remembers the plot of a film for long. It all evaporates. But if you can create one single scene that survives the destruction and will stay with the audience, well, that moment *becomes* the film for the rest of their lives. Then it means we've succeeded in making the film immortal. We've created a masterpiece."

"What time is it? Wasn't Strada supposed to be here at ten?" he asked Luisa, his plump, middle-aged secretary.

Checking her watch, Luisa nodded. Her brows furrowed.

"Yes, yes, he's late. Unfortunately he doesn't have a phone. Maybe I could send someone down to . . ."

Peppino nodded energetically. He liked the way Luisa always anticipated him. She was exceedingly efficient.

"Send a driver to get him. I don't have all day, you know."

That morning Oliviero felt particularly inspired. He had never been so charged, so ebullient. He hardly apologized for being late when, around eleven o'clock, he showed up at the suite at the Hotel Excelsior. He looked so radiant, so confident, that for once even Peppino Esposito was impressed and decided to forget his impatience.

Strada hadn't shaved and his shirt was crumpled. He was disheveled, but somehow looked more relaxed than usual.

Sex, thought Esposito.

He could smell sex on anyone's skin. He always smiled whenever he spotted it. After all, he considered himself an expert on the subject.

Good sex makes good movies. Don't ever hire writers, directors, or actors who aren't getting laid regularly. They're dry and mean. That was Esposito's favorite dictum on moviemaking.

Oliviero grabbed a ham sandwich from the tray Luisa was offering him. Only then did he realize how starved he was. He leaned back on the small chintzy armchair and began to chew the sandwich slowly, as if he had all the time in the world. Esposito was staring at him, waiting. Oliviero could feel his own eyes shine. He had never felt so sure of himself.

"Esposito, I'm late because I've been up all night. Thinking about this idea. I've been completely obsessed by it."

"Let's hear it, what is it? Is it the love scene with the black stockings?"

"The black . . .? Oh yes, right, the stockings. Well . . . actually no, this is an entirely different idea. In fact, it has nothing to do with the other script. This is a new idea, for a brand-new film."

"Strada, you can't show up like this with a new idea every day. I don't need another script from you. I want you to write me a good love scene in the hay barn for—"

"Yes, yes, I know, but listen to me, please. Giorgio and I are almost through with that script. I promise you, he's working—*as we speak*—on your love scene. Stockings, haybarn, the works. You'll see the final draft on Wednesday, and I have a feeling you'll love it . . ."

Oliviero couldn't believe his ears. He had never heard himself speak to Esposito like this before. He was usually sweating and hesitant, stumbling over words, like a poor gambler attempting a last, desperate bluff.

". . . but this is one of those ideas that comes like a shooting star—"

"A shooting star?" Esposito arched his bushy eyebrow and impatiently grabbed a Nazionale. "What's *that* supposed to mean, Strada?"

Oliviero smoothly lit his cigarette with a Zippo, then leaned back against the pillow of the armchair and crossed his legs, totally at ease.

"I'm talking about one of those rare ideas that appears with a perfectly clear trajectory in the middle of the dark. Something one would be a fool not to follow, if you know what I mean."

"Then you mean a comet," Esposito corrected him. Strada was beginning to amuse him in a very unexpected way.

"A comet, precisely. That's the image I was looking for."

"So what is this comet of yours?"

Oliviero forced himself to pause, to create suspense.

"A love story."

"Ha!"

Esposito began to tap his fingers rapidly on the table. This was the first signal he usually gave when his attention began to drift. This better be good.

"Go on, then."

"A man, a successful writer, young, good-looking but a little ragged, okay? A Mastroianni type, let's say. His fiancée has just told him she's pregnant and he has made up his mind to marry her. He feels the time has come for him to take some responsibilities, make certain decisions, etcetera. As the movie starts, he's on his way to meet her family somewhere near Milano. She comes from a solid background, her father is an industrialist, something like that. Anyway, he's on the train, and there's this girl sitting across from him, okay? She's asleep and he looks at her for a long time. His eyes scan her body, every inch of her. It's very sensual. Nothing happens, just the man staring at this sleeping girl. She has taken off her shoes, a pair of old sandals. When she wakes up, they stare at each other. As if she knows he's been looking at her all that time. There's a sort of unspoken intimacy between them, even though they don't exchange words. Then she picks up one of the sandals and slides her foot into it. To buckle the strap, she rests her foot on the man's knee. Just like that, without asking permission."

Esposito's eyes narrow as he exhales smoke.

"Just like that," he echoes.

"Yes. She ties one strap around her ankle and then puts her other foot on his knee and ties the other. Which is broken."

"The strap."

"Yes."

Luisa appears, carrying a small tray with two small cups of espresso. She quickly exchanges a glance with Oliviero. She signals him imperceptibly to go on, that he was doing just fine.

"So she leaves her foot on his knee. She has beautiful legs, but very strong, like a dancer, if you know what I mean. This girl is dark, has curly hair, she looks like a Carmen. A flamenco type."

Esposito nods. He is seeing the leg, the broken strap, the bare foot on the man's knee. He can't help visualizing Elsa Dern's round calves . . .

"Go on," he says, his lips curled in a smile. The indelible scene. Yes. He can smell it.

That night Oliviero took Alba out for dinner to celebrate the contract for the new script.

They drove to Otello's on the back of his Vespa. She held him tight as they whizzed through the narrow streets, and he felt her breasts pressing against his back, the warmth of her breath behind his neck. He held her hand whenever he didn't have to change gears.

This is crazy. I didn't even think she was that special.

Their bodies, pressed so close together, were exchanging precious information, about scent, temperature, texture. But otherwise they continued to be two strangers as far as their conversation went.

"Are you hungry?"

"Yes, a little bit."

"What do you feel like eating?"

"Anything, really."

"Fish? Would you like fish?"

"Yes. That would be nice."

Is this what he found so attractive about her? Her elusiveness, the way one always felt she was somewhere else, in a place where nobody was allowed? Maybe he imagined that one day she would allow someone to get close at last. Maybe that's what he found challenging about getting to know her.

People must have watched them that night. The new lovers, oblivious to the other tables, focused in their minute exchanges. A hand brushes a hand, a smile, a slight hesitation, another smile.

Giorgio walked in with Maria Grazia, waved to Oliviero, and went straight to the table. It took him a few seconds to realize how he knew Alba.

"Of course, from the train! Yes, how could I forget!" he said and she beamed. Then her smile wilted as he introduced Maria Grazia as his fiancée. She looked very Audrey Hepburn, Oliviero thought, in her little black dress, a string of pearls around her neck. Alba and Maria Grazia shook hands without smiling.

After dinner the four of them went for a drink on Via Veneto. They climbed the Spanish Steps, then walked along Via Gregoriana. The rich tourists waiting for a taxi in front of the Hotel Hassler watched them as they strolled by, laughing, the two young men holding the girls by the waist. A perfect quartet.

They took a table in the crowded café, the waiters welcomed them warmly and greeted Oliviero and Giorgio by name as they pulled out a chair for Alba. Oliviero was euphoric, he felt Rome had never been so intoxicating. He wanted Alba to like his friends, to be impressed by his wit.

Alba sat quietly, drinking her cherry-colored cocktail, listening carefully as more and more people pulled up a chair and joined their table. They were all discussing a film they had seen and loathed, directed by someone they all knew, and whom they considered pompous and reactionary. Maria Grazia was smoking one cigarette after another with a thin black cigarette holder and seemed to have an opinion about almost everything. She made cutting remarks that drew roars of laughter from everybody. Alba had never heard any of the names, read any of the articles, seen any of the films they were mentioning. It stunned her how little she knew about anything. The drink was going to her head. She felt Oliviero's hand sliding and pressing behind the small of her back. It was a delicious, proprietary gesture that made her feel safe in the midst of all that confusion.

I would like the same color lipstick as that girl in the red skirt.

She closed her eyes and tried to conjure up Lorenzo and Jeanne sitting alone in the big kitchen after dinner, the clock ticking, the slow buzz of crickets coming from outside. She could see the thin film of dust that had descended upon the furniture, the cracks of the pottery in the cupboard, the water stains on the ceiling, the peeling walls. All the scars they pretended not to see.

She thought of the stuffy smell in Stellario's house. Garlic and chili hanging from the ceiling. Rosa's pallor and sweat in the season of the tarantulas.

No way I'm going back there again.

She kept her eyes closed as Oliviero's hand slid slowly up her spine,

64

to the nape of her neck. She felt his fingers find their way into her hair, now damp with sweat. He pressed his fingertips lightly around the base of her head. It felt good.

She pictured the old barn at home, the rays of the afternoon sun seeping from the cracks in the roof, cutting the shadow in luminous strips. The insistent buzzing of flies, the smell of firewood and dust, the sweet aroma of dry tomatoes.

And then it hit her. Just like it had hit her mother, twenty years earlier, as she was sitting on that stone step of Casa Rossa, feeling trapped. What a long time she had spent by herself, barely ever talking to anybody.

I want a different life. I want to be like these people.

Then she heard someone yelling her name.

"Alba! Alba! I don't believe it!"

A tall, curvaceous girl, squeezed in a white dress, shaking her blond curls. Her lipstick too bright, her eyelashes too long, her heels too high.

The table froze. Maria Grazia stopped in mid-sentence and looked up in disbelief.

"Alba, my sweet, what are you doing here?"

A whiff of cheap perfume. A voice so familiar. The beautiful hooker was now leaning over her, embracing her, her skin lightly damp. Alba knew that smell.

"Beniamino!"

"Rita! It's Rita, my love," Beniamino whispered and then grabbed a chair and squeezed between her and Oliviero. He stood up straight, showing off his full bosom.

"Can you believe this?"

"Oh my God, you look so . . . amazing!"

"Do I? You, too, my love. You're gorgeous."

Alba, who had seemed so poised and enigmatic up until then, was suddenly shrieking with laughter, squeezing Rita's breasts, howling with a thick southern accent.

"Look at these! Holy Mary Jesus, how did you do it?"

"I'm going to Casablanca to do the whole thing. I'll be the first Italian ever to become legally a woman. They'll have to change my ID, everything," Beniamino said proudly. "I could even get married."

"You're so crazy, look at you, you look like a princess!"

"Did you know I had a small role in *La Dolce Vita*? Fellini's mad about me. He takes me out to lunch every now and then. He absolutely loves me."

Then he turned to the others, arching an eyebrow.

"So let's see, who are these friends of yours? I know the cute one in the blue shirt, he's a film director, right?"

Alba couldn't remember everybody's name, so she recomposed herself and introduced Rita to the rest of the table.

"This is *Baronessa* Rita Sanguedolce, my childhood friend."

Everyone cheered, glasses were raised, drunken toasts overlapped.

Oliviero smiled, proud of her like a father watching his little girl making her first entrance in the school play.

Alba and Oliviero got married a few months later, here in Casa Rossa.

I keep brushing the fabric of her wedding gown with the tip of my fingers. It must be organza, from the way it swishes as I move. I'm sure she only wore this dress that one day and then stuffed it in the box along with the rest of the mementos: photos, invitations, all the paraphernalia that goes along with a wedding ceremony. She didn't even hang it in a closet, I bet. She probably rolled it up in a tight ball and put it away, like she didn't care if it crumpled.

In one of the photos Oliviero holds her hand as she attempts to cut the cake. One of her feet is curled against the other, in the awkward pose of a self-conscious child. All around them people are cheering and clapping. I recognize Jeanne, in another one of her absurd, wide-rimmed hats, Lorenzo looking like a mad Prospero with his white hair flowing behind his ears, Giorgio and Maria Grazia, Peppino Esposito smoking a cigar.

I stare at all the pictures, hoping to find a new detail, searching for clues in her body language. I try to analyze her frozen smile, the way she clutches her hands around the bouquet, the stiffness in her shoulders.

What was she thinking? What did she want? Who did she want?

And, more than anything else—after all that has happened—one feels like asking this simple question: Why?

Sometimes I think she was like an illiterate person who pretends all along that she can read: after all, nobody had bothered to teach her anything, she wasn't the one to blame.

She probably thought, like so many girls her age then, that she could easily get away with it, that all it took was a white dress, a ceremony, the cutting of a cake, and then, somehow, things would slip right in place by themselves.

Nobody would notice, for years, that she hadn't a clue.

Andrea, the old man of the baskets, looks much smaller than I remembered. He must have shrunk with age. His voice, too, has withered, to an almost inaudible rasp. I can hardly catch his words.

It didn't take me long to find him; he lives on the edge of the village of Parabita. Everybody I asked on the way, from the gas station attendant to the guy selling vegetables from the back of his pickup truck, they all knew where he lived. But it took a long time to persuade him to open the warehouse for me. It was his old movie theater, which has been closed for years.

He keeps shaking his head, as if my request is utterly impossible.

"I don't work anymore. My eyes are bad. I have only a few things left."

But I persist, and finally he agrees to show me what he has. I follow him as he stumbles across the street, holding a heavy set of keys close to his chest. It's still pretty early in the morning, there's nobody around save for a couple of scrawny dogs barking in the rain. He stops in front of a rundown building and opens the thick padlock. Inside it's dark, but there's some light coming from above, through a skylight. The chairs of the cinema have been ripped out; there are only a few left in a corner, old wooden seats covered in cheap red velvet. But I instantly recognize the smell. Dry, dusty straw. Wild reeds.

" You see? That's all I have, just some old ones." He makes an indefinite gesture somewhere in the half-light. Now that my eyes have adjusted, I can make out some baskets and mats scattered all around.

"Do you sell them?" I ask cautiously.

He nods.

"Pick whatever you want," he says and motions toward a huge pile up on top of the loft.

"What did you call the theater?" I ask as I climb up the squeaking wooden ladder that gives onto the loft.

"Cleopatra. Cinema Cleopatra," he says.

"That's a great name. Why did you close it down?"

"I had to, in '78. People started watching television at home and didn't care for films anymore."

I crouch on the floor as I start sorting out the baskets. They are all rectangles of different sizes, one placed inside the other. They have a different geometrical pattern and a lid that latches with a button. Andrea coughs, coming up the ladder slowly. He sits, cross-legged, next to me, then picks one up and turns it around, slowly, like he's looking at it for the first time. And once again, as I see his hand stroke the reeds, his fingers rub the weave, the basket turns into a wonderful, unique object. I immediately want to touch the one he's handling.

"This one is good," he says in his rasp. "Look how tight the weave is on this one. Feel how soft."

"I would like to buy one for my mother. She loves your things, you probably remember her. She grew up around here, in Casa Rossa. Her name is Alba."

He stops stroking the basket and thinks for a moment.

"I know Alba. She always used to buy from me." He raises his head from the basket and stares at me. "I remember you, too. You and your sister. A blond one and a dark one. I haven't seen any of you in a long time."

"Yes, we've been away. My mother doesn't come much anymore. She lives in Rome now."

"Give her my regards." He checks underneath the pile and pulls out a small basket with a lavender motif.

"Take this one. She will like this one. I remember she liked them small. And your father, didn't he pass away?"

"Yes, many years ago. Do you remember him as well?"

"Yes. He made films. I showed one he had made, right here." He pats with his hand on the floor. "Even the mayor came that night."

"Really? Which film was that, do you remember?"

The old man pauses, looks away. His breathing is heavy, I can almost feel a hissing in his lungs.

"It was a good film, a love story. I remember people liked it, it made them cry." He turns to me, surprised that I shouldn't remember the title. "Your father made it."

"He wrote it. He was a writer, he didn't actually direct—" I stop myself in mid-sentence. I don't want to confuse him. "Was it called *The Summer of Alina*? That's his most famous film."

"Yes, maybe." He shakes his head and his gaze goes back to the basket. "He was a fine man. He came here that night and explained the film to the people. He said this place had inspired him to write it."

"It's true. He loved it here. You know, he called me Alina, after that film."

He doesn't say anything. We sit like this, in silence, for a few seconds, then he puts the small lavender basket in my lap.

"This is for Alba. You don't have to pay for this. Just tell her it's me sending it to her"—he makes a gesture with his hand, rubbing the palm quickly over his eyes—"and that she should come and see me before these get too weak. Tell her I told you this."

Every now and again, late at night, they still show *The Summer of Alina* on television. It's become a classic of sorts.

Black-and-white, shot in the summer of '60. Starring Elsa Dern and Vittorio de Luca. Directed by Renato Fegiz, screenplay by Oliviero Strada. Winner of two Nastro d'Argentos, one for best film script and one for best actress. Some of its sequences have become so famous that they have inspired other films, fashion spreads on glossy magazines, even TV commercials.

It's pure sixties iconography.

Maybe Esposito was right: all you need is a couple of great images to make a film immortal. For example:

Elsa Dern, who plays Alina, sitting sideways on the back of the Vespa behind the handsome Vittorio de Luca, a scarf tied under her chin, the legendary legs, her bare arms wrapped around his waist.

Elsa Dern swimming naked at night in the Blue Grotto in Capri, singing "Milord," completely drunk, mascara streaking her cheeks.

Elsa Dern barefoot, doing a mambo on top of an unmade bed, wearing only a man's shirt with a wilted flower stabbed in her hair bun.

And, of course, the opening shot—on the train, where Elsa Dern delicately places her bare foot on the man's knee.

Just like that. Without asking permission.

Alba is somewhere in there, a faint refraction, a shadow behind Elsa Dern's curves. Although she's not visible, I recognize her voice like a familiar song that comes and goes. It flutters across the dialogue like a breeze.

The character of Alina was clearly Oliviero's fantasy of Alba, what he had chosen to see in her, what he'd fallen in love with. By freezing her forever on celluloid, he had managed to turn her into an icon. But my mother always resented that film. She felt trapped by it. "*That* Alina," she huffed, referring to the character, as if to establish a distance between her and me.

There is no happy ending in *The Summer of Alina*. Which, in a sense, is only fair, considering the way things played out in real life.

The character played by Vittorio de Luca finally makes up his mind that he can't marry the industrialist's daughter. He realizes he cannot live without the sultry and whimsical Alina. He sees that it would be a mistake to lose her, so he turns back, determined to find her. Well, unfortunately he's driving too fast on the Amalfi drive in a desperate attempt to catch her before she takes the ferry across to Sicily, and makes a final exit from his life.

Bang. End of story.

Last shot: the car crash, the faint strains of a mambo rising over the credits, a reminder that life will go on. At least for Alina, who by now, we understand to be a survivor, despite the tears and the running mascara.

Maybe the plot was an omen. Or maybe it was just a coincidence, one that only later earned the status of prophecy.

In any case, Alba always seemed uneasy whenever someone mentioned the film to her. Invariably she'd shrug and try to steer the conversation elsewhere, almost as if she only vaguely remembered the plot. In fact, she hardly ever talked about Oliviero's work.

It's hard to figure out what she really felt at the time.

Maybe it annoyed her that her husband would jot down notes as she was talking, bits of dialogue that would come back to her as lines delivered by Elsa Dern on the screen. Maybe it disappointed her that he saw her as a character in a film and not as a real person. Maybe she felt manipulated. Or maybe *The Summer of Alina* was just another film he wrote, something she had absolutely nothing to do with it. It's hard now to put the pieces together and reassemble the picture now. They have been scattered all over, thrown up in the air, as if a bomb went off.

It's virtually impossible to know, now that Oliviero is dead. When people die, and especially when people die tragically, others can't help but get carried away. They come up with their implausible interpretations and usually resort to cheap psychology. A sense of fatalism is the only form of relief left.

Nobody could have done anything to prevent this from happening.

What could serve their separate destinies better than a film, really? All you need to do is lie back on the sofa and watch. The story will unravel by itself, no need for complicated interpretations. It's all there, crane shots and heartbreaking soundtrack included.

That's why my sister, Isa, and I felt increasingly paranoid about *The Summer of Alina* when we were growing up. By the time we were teenagers we were convinced that the film contained evidence of our mother's heartlessness and premeditation. Had it been admissible as evidence in court, for sure they would have put her away for life.

She never loved him. That's why, in the end, he dies.

"Alina . . . it's Alba here. Just checking how you were doing and if—"

I pick up the receiver and the answering machine gives out a distorted whistle.

"Mamma, hi, I've just come in this minute."

"Oh, were you out?"

"Yes."

There's a slight pause. Somehow it disappoints her, as if I'm taking time off from work.

"Every now and again I do enjoy a breath of fresh air," I say. "Even lifers get their half-hour a day."

"Don't be silly. I was just asking. How are you getting along?"

"I'm almost through. I think by the day after tomorrow I'll be finished and will call the movers. It'll take them only half a day to load everything on the truck. So, basically, yes, it's done. It looks pretty hellish in here, though. More like a warehouse than a house."

"Mmm . . . I'm sure. Well I guess that's the way it has to be." Her voice sounds gloomy.

"What's wrong?"

"Nothing . . . it's just . . . oh, I don't know, I have lots on my mind. I guess, maybe . . . I don't know . . . I suddenly realized I'll never see the house again. That these English people will live there till I die."

"They're Australian."

"What's the difference? They're from another place."

"We can always visit. They're really nice people. They said they'd be happy to have us come and stay if we want."

"We won't. You know that."

"Why? Not right now, but maybe one day we'll feel it's okay."

"No. It would drive me crazy to be a guest in my own house."

"At least they have good taste. They're going to keep the house just as it is, only they'll take better care of it than we did."

"I hope you're right," she sighs. "I just hope she won't build a swimming pool for the kids.

"She didn't say anything about that. But they do have three kids."

"There you go. They always build pools, these English people. Look what they did in Tuscany."

"Mamma," I can't help laughing, "what do you care? The whole point is to let go. *Let . . . go.*"

"It's not easy to give up something you've had all your life."

We both sigh and wait for the other to change the subject. It's a game we play all the time. I usually fold first.

"It's been raining here."

"Really?"

"Now the sun's just come out. Everything smells fresh."

"I bet the light is gorgeous."

She sighs again. Suddenly I feel another rising of an urge I've had for days, and I'm tired of fighting it.

"You should . . . you should come. Really. Before they move in."

She doesn't say anything, but I can see her, either biting her nails or scribbling her crazy patterns on a piece of paper by the phone.

"It would do you good. And it would be fun, just the two of us. Everyone here would be so happy to see you."

I hear her breathing in the receiver.

"I went to see Andrea today. You remember, the old man who made baskets."

"He's still alive?"

"He told me you should come and see him before he turns completely blind. He gave me a basket for you. It's really beautiful."

She starts laughing.

"He wouldn't let me pay for it. It's a present."

"I can't believe he even . . . he even remembered me."

"Of course he did. People remember stuff, Mamma. This is a small place. And one thing that hasn't changed around here is that. They remember everything."

CHAPTER THREE

My sister is almost exactly two years older than me. As children, we shared a room, wore identical clothes—only one size apart—and played with the same toys. In order to economize, we had been squeezed into being one child. We even shared our birthday cake, since we were born only a few weeks apart. We grew up believing we had exactly the same taste and the same desires, that our futures would unravel in one identical pattern.

Of the two of us, Isabella was the beautiful child.

People were amazed by the color of her eyes: one moment they were gray, then they would shift to green, at times they turned into an icy blue. They were transparent, one could almost see through them. She would stare at grown-ups with those big eyes wide open, her mass of blond hair crowning her perfectly round face like a halo, and managed to shut them up just by looking at them.

She bullied me, of course, being the older. But it wasn't just that. If I think about it now, I realize that there was always something I feared in Isabella. As if I always perceived her power, a strength I didn't have. She was fearless from a very early age.

"No," she would say and shake her head, whenever Alba told her to give someone a kiss. I admired her for being so firm. I, on the other hand, always sheepishly did whatever Alba asked of me. A sucker for approval.

We lived in a big apartment on Via del Babbuino, just off Piazza del Popolo, on the top floor of an old building. The apartment overlooked the gardens of the old Hôtel de Russie. The hotel was built at the turn of the century and had been popular with Russian émigrés. It had been closed for years and years, and the overgrown garden and the rusted-out greenhouses we saw from our windows looked like the setting for a mystery in a castle.

I remember our flat as untidy and old-fashioned. It had a very intricate web of piping and wiring that ran along the walls, old sofas covered in faded cottons, threadbare carpets, and chipped octagonal tiles on the floors. The walls were stained, the ceilings had spiderwebs, the lightbulbs were too dim.

Everything either squeaked, peeled, or cracked. I remember a broken bicycle parked for ages in the living room, the spring of the big cherry armchair popping out beneath the pillow, a perfectly dead record player that sat like a gray mausoleum without a purpose. Things didn't often get repaired. They seemed to have come to us with an unchangeable expiration date. When something died, it was left there, as if it were inconceivable to resurrect it.

I think maternal life and its daily chores bored Alba. She tried to reduce them to a minimum. I don't remember her ever baking a cake for our birthday, giving us a bath, or reading us bedtime stories. I don't think she ever helped us with our homework or took us shopping for clothes or toys. I have no idea what she was doing most of the time; although she didn't have a job then, she was out of the house a lot. So, Isabella and I, bored, spent way too many hours on our own in the big, silent apartment.

Isabella developed an amazing talent for creating exciting new games we could play to liven up our otherwise dull afternoons, fantastically complicated plots in which she played the part of a brilliant detective and I was her assistant.

The large Persian rug in the living room provided an intricate map for us to decode, a map that would eventually lead us to find a hidden treasure. We spent hours down on all fours, scribbling notes on our pads, translating the hieroglyphs we found in the rug's design. Every time I made believe I had found the way to the secret place, Isabella would shake her head, depressed by my lack of sophistication.

"No, that's not a door, you stupid. That's not it. This is a much more complicated map than you think."

Isabella didn't want the mystery to end. She never liked to find an easy way out of anything.

The rusty greenhouse of the Hôtel de Russie, which we could see from our bedroom window, had turned into the hiding place of an extremely dangerous thief. We spied on him for hours and hours on end. We'd take turns watching, in the event that he might slip up and let himself be seen.

"Then we can report him to the police," said Isabella. She had scribbled down the phone number of the nearest police station, just in case we had to make that call fast. But nothing ever moved, at least whenever it was my turn to watch. I would have to sit by the window and look down for very long stretches, sometimes I would even doze off for a few minutes. I hated to admit that being a detective's assistant wasn't as thrilling as I had expected. I didn't dare suggest to Isabella I'd rather we played a different game.

Right when I was about to fall asleep, she would barge into the room, looking intent and preoccupied, just as I imagined a very busy detective would.

"Anything happening down there?" she would bark.

"No . . . I don't think so."

"Okay, then move. It's my turn now."

I always felt relieved when she took over. I ran to the kitchen for milk and cookies or to watch TV.

"I saw him!" Isa would scream, running into the kitchen to find me, flushed with excitement. "I promise you, I saw him move. Come quick!"

Invariably, by the time I looked down into the abandoned greenhouse, nothing was ever moving. Still, I believed her. I believed the legendary thief would only allow her to see him. It made sense to me, that he, too, would recognize her authority.

It feels almost impossible now, to think how close Isabella and I were as children. It felt like we were part of the same breathing organism. At the time it seemed inconceivable that we could ever spend more than a few hours apart, that our lives would ever diverge the way they did.

That we would turn first into enemies and then into strangers.

Most of the time, Oliviero wrote at the production office, but whenever he worked at home, he typed away in a little room at the end of the corridor. What exactly he was doing was a mystery to me. I didn't really understand what a screenplay was, but Papà's little den felt like a good place to be. I remember the mess on his desk, the overflowing ashtrays, the piles of newspapers and magazines, sheets of paper flowing all around. I liked the manly smell of the room. I loved watching him when he worked. I would sit next to him and pretend I was doing my homework, but I kept staring at him, trying to imitate the way he wrote.

It's astonishing how quickly he flashed through my life.

Oliviero is a series of jagged pictures in the kaleidoscope of my childhood. I think part of me doesn't want to remember him, for fear of missing him too much. That's why the contours of my days with him have now become slack. But I have strung my own chain of memories. I like to go over them, savoring and separating each one, as one does with a string of prayer beads.

The smell of leather in his Giulietta Alfa Romeo. It made me slightly dizzy whenever I got inside it. The feeling was a mixture of nausea and delight.

Oliviero's clothes, the way he rolled up the sleeves of his crumpled shirts, the warm colors of his worn-out corduroy jackets.

His tiny handwriting crawling over the typed pages like a column of industrious ants. His hairline beginning to recede and show some gray at the temples, and my realizing he was getting old.

It's not very long, my string of beads.

But I remember having lemon sorbet at the Caffè Rosati with him on sticky summer evenings. Isabella and I were still so little. I can see our feet dangling from the aluminum chairs. He always acted very formal, as if we had been invited to celebrate something special. He ordered a bright-red Campari while we would have our sorbet. It seemed that the whole point of the mission for him was to talk to us as if we were not his children, but as two grown-up ladies he had asked out for an aperitif.

If someone he knew happened to walk by and come over to the table, he always introduced us.

"This is Alina, and this is Isabella. We are having a drink together before dinner," he would declare, as if reminding the person that he or she should adopt a proper demeanor. He wanted to make sure they knew this was a very specific occasion, not to be interrupted by just any acquaintance.

We shook the stranger's hand with poise and dangled our feet nervously from the chair. We knew he was treating us to a sneak preview of what grown-ups did.

I particularly remember one afternoon when Oliviero took Isabella and me to the Cinecittà studios, where they were shooting a film from one of his scripts.

There wasn't anything glamorous about the studio lot: it looked more like a modern university campus—just ugly boxes amidst pine trees. But its school-like architecture had a surreal quality, as if characters and places had slipped out of history texts and walked around the place like zombies. There were bits and pieces of Imperial Rome scattered here and there, broken columns of papier-mâché stucco fountains, chariots. Bored centurions sipped espresso at the cafeteria, smoking Marlboros with ladies-in-waiting from the court of Louis XIV. A cardinal snored on the lawn. Nobody seemed to mind being caught in such ridiculous attire. I felt embarrassed for all of them.

We walked into one of the square buildings with a big red "5" painted on the door. Inside, it felt like a beehive. There were lots of people running around, trampling on cables, switching on hot lights, hammering somewhere up a ladder. The director, a small man wearing a large floppy hat, was sitting on top of a crane over a plush bedroom set and screaming into a bullhorn. An actress was sitting on a chair with her hair in curlers and fluffy slippers on. She was wearing way too much makeup and her face looked like an ugly mask.

We were mesmerized by how complicated everything was: it seemed impossible to take it all in, to figure out how this or that worked, what the purpose of the crane was, of the tracks, the lights, the massive equipment, where everyone was running too. Oliviero moved swiftly amidst all this confusion of bodies, movement, and voices. We were surprised to see him so at ease in this incomprehensible world we knew nothing about. Men patted him on the shoulders, women holding notebooks and pens strung around their necks stopped to kiss him on the cheeks and exchanged rapid comments under their breath.

"Hi, darling."

"Good thing you came. I think he could use some help."

"Peppino wants to see you."

Peppino Esposito waved to Oliviero and signaled him to come over. He was wearing a white turtleneck under his jacket and gave off a strong whiff of French cologne. I found him a bit scary, with his bull terrier face and bushy eyebrows.

"Oliviero! Good, you're here! We've got a problem. We have to change some of Laura's lines in the bedroom scene." He raised his eyes to the ceiling and sighed. "You know what she's like."

"Fine, no problem," Oliviero said. "Everything else okay?"

Esposito glanced at the funny little man screaming on top of the crane.

"Sort of. Except I wish I had never hired him. Let's go talk to him. Come on."

Oliviero had us by each hand. He raised both his arms, lifting us up slightly to show us to him.

"These are my two little girls."

"Oh, how nice." Esposito seemed fretful and concerned about whatever he needed to discuss, but then I think he caught a glimpse of disappointment in Oliviero's eyes, so he took a second look at us. He smiled and placed his hand on my head.

"Lovely girls. So which one are you, Alina or Isabella?"

I blushed. I had no idea this stranger knew our names.

Oliviero put on a motherly smile.

"Alina. Let me find a seat for them and I'll be right with you."

He took us over to the costume designer, a chubby redheaded woman named Eleonora and asked her if she could look after us while he was going to deal with the "maestro" for five minutes. She giggled when he said "maestro," as if it was a joke.

Isa and I sat quietly in a corner next to Eleonora and watched the beehive buzz on. Oliviero, the funny man with the hat, and the actress in curlers were sitting together on folding chairs. Esposito hovered around them, pacing up and down and puffing from his cigarette. My father was scribbling. I felt proud of him. He looked important.

"God, these two girls are angels," Eleonora whispered to Oliviero when he came to get us, and he smiled at her with gratitude in his eyes. He clutched our hands and then we slipped through the busy crowd, across the dark studio. He pushed the heavy door and we were back out in the afternoon sun. Everything looked quiet and normal again.

"That was Papà's office, one could say," he said to us with childish ostentation as we drove out of the gates. "It looks more like a circus, doesn't it?"

I don't know why I remember this particular afternoon so well, or why I don't remember the details of him and Alba arguing, slamming doors. Sleeping in different rooms. I can't say why some memories float and others sink.

Obviously Isabella saved a lot of the memories I had sent to the guillotine. Every image survived in her, and by the time we were grownups, they were alive and well, and kicking to get out. Strange how she kept throwing them at me like arrows, at a time when I wished all that stuff was dead, buried, and forgotten.

Another faded photograph, this one in color.

On the back, written in my father's tiny handwriting: *1971, Delos, Aegean Sea, Greece.*

That was the last summer we were to spend together.

An early summer day: the ground is covered in poppies, a red fluttering wave curled by gusts of wind coming from the sea. The blue of the water is the deepest blue you will ever see. Nothing else on the island: not a house, not a single taverna. Only the blinding white marble of the temple ruins, the bloody stains of the poppies, and that ultramarine blue.

"This tiny island is said to have been Apollo's birthplace"—Alba had read to us from the guidebook—"and nobody is allowed to live here. Only the gods."

Alba, Isabella, and I walk under the midday sun between the nine lions flanking the Sacred Way that leads to the temple. The lions, smoothed by time and wind, crumbled in parts, are drowned in the swaying grass and the cruel red of the poppies.

Look at us.

Alba is wearing her hair tied back and hides behind dark glasses, Jackie Onassis style. A guidebook clutched in her hand—she loved to read aloud to us wherever we went, she loved the sense of authority the book gave her. The dark glasses give her a certain tragic flair.

My sister and I are twelve and ten. We wear short dresses in a small flower print and sport beads on our wrists, stringy hair to the middle of our backs. We still do not dare wear different clothes. Our skinny legs are brown, our bodies still an uncertain shape.

On our feet we wear the leather sandals we just bought in Athens from an old man in the Plaka district.

We had seen these sandals on the feet of a statue in the National Museum only a few days earlier. It was an Artemis resting after the hunt. Alba had quickly sketched the sandals on a pad and had this old shoemaker in the Plaka make them for us. We had to put our feet on a piece of paper so he could trace the shape with a pencil, and to our delight he made the sandals in less than twenty minutes, right in front of our eyes.

The "Artemis sandals" we called them ever after. If and when she was in the mood, Alba was good at things like that: turning something small like a shoe into magic, and giving it a name, bestowing special power on it.

But then, just as quickly, Alba had the power to turn our golden carriage into a pumpkin again. She could behave like she hated everything, like nothing could cheer her up. Whenever she got like that, she simply stopped talking and looked off into the distance. You could hear her thoughts rustle, dark and furious.

We never knew when it was coming, it just happened. But by then we had pretty much figured out it had to do with Oliviero.

"Angry again," Isabella would warn me, and make a face, rolling her eyes, like we had no chance.

Whenever we went on holiday it got worse between Alba and Oliviero, or maybe it just seemed that way because Isabella and I could hear them at night. We usually slept in a room right next to theirs in the little guesthouses where we stayed, and there was no way to avoid overhearing them. We didn't know what their fights were about, since during the day they said practically nothing to one another. But the minute they closed the door of their bedroom at night, it took only a few minutes before their hisses and grumbles would flare and erupt into screaming.

The day that picture was taken on the island of Delos must have come after a particularly bad night, judging from the tragic look Alba had put on, just as someone else would put on lipstick. The night before, we had heard her yell at him through the wall of our room in the pension in Mykonos, her voice so cold, so full of hatred.

"You're disgusting! You try and do that to me again and I'm going to kill you!"

Isabella and I lay frozen on our twin beds. I was pretending to be fast asleep, just to avoid having to say anything. But Isabella wouldn't let me be. She never wanted to be alone in this.

"I think he's crying," she declared. I kept still, my eyes closed, hoping she would leave me out of it. But I could hear Oliviero's muffled voice coming from the next room.

"You're a liar," he was saying, and he repeated that over and over again.

"Hey, Alina, listen," she continued as she got out of bed and pressed her ear to the wall. But I kept my eyes closed.

"Wake up, come on." Then she shook my shoulder and I had to open my eyes. She motioned me to listen, ignoring the fact that I was pretending to be asleep. I obeyed. We stared at each other, our ears glued to the wall.

"You're a liar, a fucking liar. You've always lied," Oliviero kept saying, his voice breaking.

"He's not crying," I whispered. "He's just upset."

Isabella shook her head.

"She makes him cry all the time. You don't know because you always fall asleep."

I hated the way she always wanted to make sure I knew all the stuff I was trying to avoid. She seemed to enjoy spoiling my peace of mind.

The next day we had a particularly silent breakfast.

Oliviero kept looking at Alba, and passing her coffee, bread, sugar.

"Do you want to order yogurt with honey? Or you can have some of mine if you'd like."

She wouldn't even look at him.

"I have a splitting headache," is all she said.

A small fisherman's boat was waiting for us on the dock to take us across to Delos.

"Shall we not go?" Oliviero asked her. I was always surprised at his meekness. It hurt me to see him like that.

"Would you rather stay and rest?"

"No. We've come this far," she said with her usual shrug. "And at least I'll have something beautiful to look at. Better than lying on my bed and thinking."

I remember the two women very well, almost as if there was no one else but us walking around the ruins on Delos that morning. They must have been in their mid-sixties. They were speaking German; one had a pair of binoculars dangling from her neck. They seemed engrossed in every small detail of the temple, I don't think they took any notice of us. There was something about them that said they had spent a long time in each other's company and had absorbed each other's style. The same short haircut, one dark-haired, one blond, the same kind of amber and coral jewelry, the same opaque deep tan that mercilessly showed all their wrinkles.

Suddenly Alba said she wasn't feeling well. Oliviero had to sit her down in the shade of a tree. She was faint.

"It's the heat," Oliviero said. "She'll be all right in just a minute."

We had to hurry to the harbor and hire another small fishing boat to get back to Mykonos. I kept my eyes on Alba, because something about her expression alarmed me: she was deadly pale, and whatever it was, she wasn't faking it.

Later that evening in Mykonos we saw the women again. They were drinking ouzo at a café along the harbor. They had changed for the evening and wore long flowing caftans. They didn't even notice us, they were so intent on writing a stack of postcards.

As we walked past their table I could smell the anise in their drink, and I still remember that strange feeling of suspension, as if we had all been holding our breath.

Nobody said anything. We sat in Vangelis's taverna like every other evening and ordered dinner. Loud Greek music was blaring from a speaker, a string of lightbulbs strung across the trees lit the tiny square.

Acrid smell of souvlaki and octopus smoking on the grill hung in the air. Isa and I ordered moussaka and fries, like every single night. We loved life on a Greek island.

The next morning, we had breakfast early, under the canopy of a large tree at Vassili's, our favorite taverna.

Papà finished his coffee in haste and went to check schedules at the boat ticket office on the waterfront. He came back holding a scrap of scribbled paper.

"There is a boat at nine tomorrow morning that goes to Patras." He looked exhausted, at the end of his rope.

"Perfect," she said, smiling now, as she did when she got things her way. "Girls, you'll have to be packed by tonight, okay?"

"Why? Are we leaving tomorrow?" Isabella asked, her eyes alarmed.

"Yes," said Oliviero. "Your mother isn't feeling well and I think it's better we go home."

"But"—Isabella kicked me under the table, soliciting my support— "I don't want to go back to Rome now. You said we were staying till the end of the month. It's not fair."

"Just do what I tell you, *bambine*." Oliviero lit a cigarette and puffed angrily. He had dark circles under his eyes.

Isa and I walked down to the beach by ourselves. We always knew when it was time to leave them alone. We swam and picked bits of colored glass, which we were religiously collecting. We had filled two jars already.

"I bet she wants to leave because of those two women," I said.

I wanted to blame this change of plan on someone. I couldn't bear to see it all go to pieces like that, for no apparent reason. And I wanted to impress Isabella with my detective skills for once.

We were lying in the sun on a flat rock. Isa didn't say anything for a while. I turned to look at her. She lay perfectly still, and droplets of seawater streamed down her golden skin, darkening the warm rock.

"The one with the binoculars, I think that one is Renée," I said with my eyes shut, feeling the sun burning on my face. I was hoping to shock her with this piece of unexpected news.

"Oh yeah? And how would you know?" Isa challenged me.

"I just know it." I propped myself up on my elbow and looked at her.

"Plus, Mamma looked like she had seen a ghost when she saw her. She nearly died."

It sounded like such a perfect little plot. I had always imagined Renée looking something like that: a dark, skinny older woman, a manic chain-smoker. And I wanted Alba's sudden change of mood to have a cause that we could sympathize with.

Isa kept perfectly still on the rock as if she had fallen asleep. Then she made a face.

"Nah. She just wants to go back to Rome fast," she sneered.

"But why?"

"She has a boyfriend. She can't wait to see him. That's all."

I waited for her to say something more, but she didn't. She just lay there, eyes shut, feeling the salt dry slowly on her body and prickle her skin. I hated the way she would unload these bits of classified information on me, like bombs dropped from high altitude. She didn't even have the grace to open her eyes and review the damage. And I didn't want to give her the satisfaction of letting her see how wounded I was.

"Oh," I said nonchalantly and lay down on the flat rock next to her again. "And how do you know *that*?"

Isa sighed, as if I were annoying her with so many stupid questions.

"You just have no idea what's going on. You're asleep all the time."

That shut me up. She was right: I'd rather stay asleep than have to learn all those frightening secrets.

"Shall we go for another swim?" I asked her timidly.

"No," she said.

We lay there, listening to each other breathe. Letting it all sink in, pretending it didn't make a difference.

Angelica was Alba's best friend. She was tall and skinny, always dressed in black. She had a long dark braid, pale skin, and wore bright-red lipstick. We were told she was a harpist with the Philharmonic. She looked frightening.

Morticia, Isabella used to call her with a snigger.

We desperately wanted to see her play the harp, but she never bothered to show it to us. It was too bulky to carry around, she said, but I think the truth was that she wasn't interested enough in winning our affection to make the effort. She didn't have children and clearly had no patience for them. We wondered if this famous harp even existed.

Every time she came to the house, she and Alba headed straight for the living room and carefully closed the door behind them. We could see them through the opalescent glass doors, curled up on the sofa, coiled like snails among the puffy pillows. We could hear the ice in their scotch glasses, clinking in counterpoint to their whispers. Anytime Isa or I found an excuse to stick our heads into the living room they would both freeze and look at us disapprovingly as if we had interrupted a delicate surgical operation. They would raise their eyebrows, outraged that we would dare disrupt their concentration.

"What is it?" Alba would ask, brisk, stretching her neck to see what I was holding in my hand.

"Can you . . . show me how to do this, please"—and I would offer her my math exercise book.

"Not now. Just go to your room. Come on, off you go." She would raise her chin, move it up and down a couple of times as if to push me away.

Then came the indelible day. The day when everything happened in slow motion. All sounds were muffled. There was no soundtrack.

It was the end of May. School was almost over and we could smell the summer in the air. All we could think about was that soon we'd be swimming again.

That day no one showed up to pick us up at school. We waited outside the building in the heat, hungry and tired. Everything had gone quiet, the street was empty. All the other children were gone. We were the only ones standing in front of the building. I was sweating and felt very hungry.

"Let's just walk," Isa said.

Then we saw Angelica running toward us from the other side of the street. She looked frightened, her face was white.

"Oh, thank God, there you are!" She took our hands and ordered, "Come, let's go have something to eat."

"Where's Mamma?" I asked.

"She couldn't come," she said stiffly. "She asked me to come and pick you up. I'm taking you out to lunch."

"I don't want to go out to lunch," Isabella said, hostile. "I want to go home."

"Me, too," I added.

"*Please,* girls," she begged us, "we'll go home later. Alba said you might like a pizza."

"Really?" I lightened up. "Did she say we can have pizza *for lunch*?"

"I don't want pizza." Isabella wasn't buying any of that. "Where is Papà?"

"Listen, girls, let's go and sit down first of all, it's so hot. Oh my, it's two o'clock, you must be starving."

Angelica parked us at a table in an empty pizzeria near Via Flaminia and kept going back and forth to the pay phone in the back of the restaurant. She whispered and sucked anxiously at her cigarette, giving us her back while we fiddled with stringy mozzarella on our pizza Margherita. She kept coming back with a frozen smile, trying to look reassuring.

"All right, who wants dessert now?"

We could smell a rat. This had never happened before. Never pizza in a restaurant right after school. Never lunch with Angelica on our own.

After Isabella finished her ice cream, she burst out crying.

"I want to go home now," she sobbed and started stomping her feet.

That really frightened me: Isabella never cried like that. And if she could break down like that in front of Angelica, this had to be serious.

The waiters looked over at our table. Maybe they thought Angelica had kidnapped us, I thought with a hint of satisfaction. Maybe they would come to our rescue.

Maybe.

Angelica gave up, she had no clue how to handle this and hated to be the center of attention in the empty restaurant.

"All right, then, what can I tell you? I was only trying to . . . Oh, forget it, let's just go."

She clutched her bag. I could tell she was about to start crying, too.

We rode home in an eerie silence. My head glued to the car window, I watched the familiar shape of the buildings go by slowly, the leafy branches of the plane trees sway in the breeze, and the pollen float. Somehow I knew none of it was ever going to be the same again.

There were various police cars parked outside our building when we finally got home. Men in blue uniforms were coming down the stairs. The apartment door was wide open. Inside there were lots of people moving around. It was a bit like the beehive activity we had seen on the movie set the day Oliviero took us; I think I even remember someone taking photographs with a flash.

I caught a glimpse of Alba among all those strangers. She looked like a child. Pale, her dark hair a mess. She saw us coming through the open door, but she didn't come close. She just turned to someone and said in a whisper:

"Please take them upstairs. I don't want them to see any of this."

You can smell death in your own house. Even the most familiar objects and faces shine with a very particular electricity. They take on a strange vibrancy. It's like a hallucination. People look and sound the same, but it's like seeing them from the bottom of a glass, slightly deformed.

By then I just knew Oliviero was dead. It couldn't have been otherwise.

I could feel his absence. I just knew he was no longer here.

We were taken upstairs to our neighbor Olga's, the old Russian lady. She gave us tea in glass cups and poppy-seed cake, put us on a couch with lots of beautiful books with color plates to flick through, and played soothing classical music. It was nice to borrow a slice of extra time. Whatever amount still separated us from what Alba didn't want us to see. Nobody was telling us anything yet, but the clock was ticking and we knew eventually we would have to be told.

I don't know what time it was when we were finally allowed downstairs again. By then we were tired, hungry, sleepy. Meanwhile, Jeanne and Lorenzo had arrived from Casa Rossa. They had taken a long train ride and looked gloomy and exhausted. Jeanne had made us hot soup. She made us take a bath and wear pajamas. Alba was in the study with someone who was asking her questions, Jeanne said. We should get into bed, and then, as soon as Alba was finished with this gentleman, she would come to give us a goodnight kiss.

Neither Isa nor I dared ask about Oliviero.

We went to bed and listened to the sounds of the house.

A stranger's voice, very formal and authoritative, seeped through the door. I knew it was the police.

Then I heard the door of the study open and Alba take the man down the corridor to the door. They exchanged formalities.

Thank you so much . . . your kindness . . . You have to excuse us but it's part of the procedure . . . Of course . . . don't worry . . . Whenever you are ready . . . I will call you tomorrow . . . yes, but of course . . . Just a formality . . . I totally understand . . .

Then the door of our room opened slowly and I saw her come in. She sat on the edge of my bed. As I pretended to be asleep, she stroked my hair and then kissed me on the forehead. Her cheeks were damp with tears.

"Mamma . . . ," Isabella whispered from her bed.

"Come here, come to Alina's bed, quick. I need to hug you both."

She held us tight and hid her face in the pillow. I could feel the tears running down her neck.

Then she sat up straight, and wiped off the tears like a child would.

"Listen to me now," she whispered, "something terrible has happened. But you don't have to be scared."

"I know. Papà's dead," said Isabella. "right?"

"Yes. He died."

We held the silence. I could hear the three of us breathing. Alba kept stroking our head.

"Why did he die?" I asked.

"Because he . . . because he was . . . There has been an accident."

Then she corrected herself

"A mistake. It was a mistake.

"He killed himself," said Isabella without inflection.

"Yes. But I will explain it to you," Alba sighed, "tomorrow."

Then she lay down again on her stomach, her arms stretched across our chests. The minute she closed her eyes her breathing suddenly changed. It got thicker, deeper. She was asleep. It was as if she had slipped into a black pit, and she was now irretrievable.

Isa and I wiggled out from underneath her body, as if crawling out of a car wreck. We climbed into the other twin bed.

We didn't say anything for a while.

"How did you know he killed himself?" I whispered to Isa. I was horrified to pronounce those words.

"I heard Olga say it on the phone. She said, 'He shot himself in the temple with a gun.' "

We lay very still in the dark, listening to Alba's regular breathing from the other bed, not really knowing what we were supposed to do. Should we be crying, howling, or simply going to sleep, like all the other grown-ups in the house seemed to have done? We had been left without instructions.

Then I heard Isabella's muffled sobs and something loosened up in my stomach. I quietly began to cry next to her, careful not to wake Alba up.

"She did it," Isabella whispered in a broken voice. I could feel her rage.

"What?" I panicked. "What did she do?"

"She killed him," Isa said. "I know she did." Her voice sounded flat, as if it had frozen.

"That's why that policeman was here. They also know she did it."

We kept perfectly still, our eyes glued open, listening to every squeak, as if we were waiting for someone to come and tell us that everything was going to be all right, that this was just a bad joke or a nightmare. But nothing moved.

I remember how we woke up the next day. Alba was still lying next to us, her arms and legs falling out of the bed, like Alice in Wonderland grown big again.

CHAPTER FOUR

What happens to the shoes, the socks, the underwear, the shaving cream, the notebook, the pen, the handkerchiefs of the dead? Whose hands choose whether to chuck them in the trash or slip them in a paper envelope and keep them inside a drawer? What kind of heart does one have to have in order to be able to get rid of these, without regret, as if they were empty beer cans?

I don't know who had been the undertaker for Oliviero's personal effects; whoever it was, he or she had done a pretty clean job. Already by the next day after his death his presence had been eradicated from the house. All that was left was his Giulietta Alfa Romeo parked downstairs on the corner. Isa and I kept glancing at it, expecting it to perform some miracle, like driving around the block or conjuring up our father at the steering wheel. But no, the Giulietta sat still, lifeless and dormant, just like a parked car.

Once the feverish days that surrounded Oliviero's death were over, once the visits, the confusion, and the voices subdued, once we came back from the funeral—red-eyed, exhausted from crying and kissing and being hugged by too many strangers—a different kind of silence welcomed us as we came through the door of our apartment.

Alba kicked her shoes off and went straight into her room. She re-emerged a few minutes later, barefoot, her hair undone, in a short green dress. It struck me that she had disposed so quickly of her mourning outfit. I had fantasized that from that day on she would be wearing black, like Sicilian widows did in movies.

"Do you want to eat something?" she asked, and stroked my hair.

Warm food seemed like a good idea. I realized we were to start a brand-new life, now, a life we knew nothing about.

"Set the table, will you, darlings?" I heard her say, as she started opening and shutting drawers in the kitchen.

I took out the place mats from the cupboard in the dining room. I automatically picked four. I felt Isabella's eyes on me and looked at her. We froze in midair for a split second, without saying anything, but I could see something between terror and admonishment in her eyes. She didn't want me to make that mistake, as if it would be too much to bear. I rushed back to the cupboard and put the fourth mat back in its place. I laid the plates at the three sides of the table. The empty side of the table suddenly seemed impossible for me to look at. I felt my lungs fill with air and I ran into my bedroom. I didn't want Alba to hear me cry.

That was it. Neither Isa nor I knew how we were supposed to react, what we were or were not allowed to feel. We knew nothing of loss. Nobody had taught us about pain. Until that moment, the word *death* had just amounted to a scary sound.

We looked for a place to grieve for him, but we couldn't find any within our house. We watched Alba in the weeks that followed, waiting for a sign that would dissipate our worse suspicions. But she kept listening to music, painting her toes red, going to the hairdresser on Thursdays. She never wore black. We never caught her crying or just sad and silent. She mentioned him rarely, and always as "your father." The only thing we were left with to remind us of his absence was that empty place at the head of the table.

Children know so little, they must learn quickly to imitate grown-ups whenever they feel unsure in a situation. So we mimicked her indifference, we emulated her cool lack of grief, till we slowly started to believe ourselves that death was perhaps not such a big deal after all. That it was no more than removing a place setting from the table or a tweed jacket from the closet.

Isabella and I didn't talk about this. We lay in our beds at night in silence, unable to share our feelings. I guess we were busy attempting to tame the pain we had pushed down, so that we could stop wrestling with it and finally be able to go to sleep.

One day I walked into our bedroom and found that Isabella had framed a photo of Oliviero and put it by her bedside table. It was a picture probably taken around the time he had met Alba. He was wearing a white shirt with the sleeves rolled up to the elbow, round horn-rimmed glasses, a cigarette between his fingers, a big smile for the camera. He looked tanned, happy. Young.

"Where did you find it?" I asked.

"In a drawer, with masses of others. She shoved them all in there," she said and gave me one of her looks, arching an eyebrow. "And I bet she'll never open it again."

"Did you get the frame yourself?"

"I bought it at the flea market in the piazza."

She took the photo in her hands and looked at it with pride. She brushed the dust off the glass with her index finger and put it back. Her personal shrine.

"You can get one, too. There are millions of photos in that drawer," she offered.

I wanted to, but I didn't. I felt that if Alba saw how the two of us had rescued Oliviero's pictures, she might interpret it as a tacit reproach. I didn't want to upset her. She was all I had left and I wanted to hold on to her.

Isabella, on the other hand, enjoyed showing her resentment to Alba. Her silences at mealtime took on a hostile quality. She spent more and more time in our room, the door closed. Her answers became curt, sarcastic, her manners ungraceful. She looked at me with contempt every time she caught me acting like a puppy around Alba, wagging my tail in search of her attention.

She was two years older, stronger than me. Or maybe it was just the way she was: more prepared to face the consequences of her anger. But to think of it now, that's when our paths started to diverge.

That summer, Alba got her driver's license. She bought driving gloves made of soft leather, the kind that leave your knuckles exposed. Every-time she put them on, she clutched and stretched her fingers out a couple of times.

"We're going back to Greece for the holidays," she announced.

"We'll catch the ferry and I'll drive you girls all the way up to Mount Olympus. I want you to see the place where the gods sat and decided things. It'll be great fun."

I guess she wanted to make us feel like nothing had changed. Like now that she was in charge, our lives were going to run just as smoothly. But it was a different world without Oliviero.

Greece didn't feel the same.

The colors on the islands were identical: whitewashed houses with bright-blue shutters and potted basil on the windowsills. The taste of salt on our skin, the way the sun streaked our hair, the way the fishermen beat the octopus on the rocks and mended their nets on the harbor. Isabella and I tried to order the same food at the outdoor restaurants, go swimming early in the morning when the water was the clearest, collect green glass pebbles on the beach like we always had. But it didn't feel right. The more we tried, the more melancholic we got.

We pretended to ignore Alba's moodiness, the way she lost her temper with the waiters at the local taverna if the service was too slow, or the way she sulked and wouldn't pay attention to us for hours on end. She had started to keep a journal and sometimes she wrote for what seemed an eternity on the terrace of our little guest house. We were not to interrupt her when she was writing, we had been warned. There were always these boundaries one wasn't allowed to cross, even when she made it sound like we were supposed to have fun together.

She did drive us to see some ruins up on a mountain somewhere in the North as she had promised. It was a hot afternoon, and the road was very steep and winding. Isa and I were excited, this was to be our great expedition. We kept reading aloud from the guidebook to Alba, hoping she'd get excited, too. But she kept checking the road map over and over again and looked pretty tense. She wasn't even listening to us, nor was she having any fun.

"It'll be hours before we get there," she said, frowning and looking over the top of the mountain.

"No, it won't," Isa said lightly, "it just *looks* far."

"Right. As if you've been there already!" Alba said.

It was beautiful. We had left the pavement and were climbing the side of the mountain on a dirt track. The Giulietta trudged along with some difficulties as the track got steeper and steeper; rocks kept slipping from underneath the tires and tumbling down the precipice on our right. The view was breathtaking. The afternoon sun had lit the plain below us and we could see for miles. Rocky terrain, scattered bushes here and there. One expected any minute to see a Greek warrior clad in his bronze armor. Yes, this was what we'd pictured ancient Greece to be like.

Alba pressed down on the brake, the car shuddered abruptly to a halt.

"I can't do this," she said, crossing her arms on the steering wheel, hiding her face in them.

We waited for her to say something else. We peeked out the window. It was very silent, except for an occasional gust of wind in the shrubs.

Then she hit the steering wheel with one of her fists, hard. We jolted.

"I hate heights. I'm not driving on this road anymore."

"Let's go back then," Isabella said abruptly, in a flat, expressionless tone, completely devoid of sympathy.

By then Isabella was no longer intimidated by Alba's moodiness or her inexplicable behavior the way I was. She felt insulted every time Alba failed to perform her maternal duties, like an angry customer who had paid an exorbitant price for damaged goods.

"And just how are we suposed to do that!" she snapped. "I can't turn the car around, as you can see. It's too narrow."

Isabella looked at me and made a face, tapping her finger at the temple, meaning "cuckoo." I shrugged. I wanted to stay out of it.

"And now what? Are we supposed to sit here all night?" Isa asked, her rage mounting.

Alba didn't move.

"I'm sorry but you can't just stop like this in the middle of the—"

"Oh shut up, you!" Alba yelled and glared at Isabella. She was flushed, her eyes looked wild. "Why don't *you* drive, then?"

"I wish I could. Then I wouldn't have to depend on a psychopath like you," Isa yelled back. I saw her face reddening and the vein in her forehead pulse.

I poked my elbow lightly into Isabella's side. I knew it was better to keep quiet when Alba got like that. But Isa pushed my arm away and threw the passenger door open.

"She's totally crazy. You can sit with her, I've had it," she hissed to me as she got out of the car. I watched her sit on a rock on the side of the road, her back to us.

I sat in the car, not saying a word, for what seemed a very long time. Alba kept perfectly still, her head hidden between her arms over the steering wheel, as if I weren't even there. The sun got lower and lower, till it disappeared behind the ridge. I kept looking out the window as if something might be happening out there, but it was only getting darker, colder, and spookier. Isabella was drawing circles in the dirt with a stick, her head between her knees.

"Look! There's a car coming down!" Isa called out, and she suddenly got up and pointed toward the mountain. I could see its faint headlights coming around, way up on the top. Alba raised her head slowly and looked. Her mascara had gotten all messed up and she looked like a crazy woman who had been in a fight.

It was an English couple with two teenage boys sitting in the back. They were obviously coming back from the same ruins we were supposed to have seen. Alba got out of the car and flagged them down. She spoke French to them through their window. They kept nodding sympathetically as she gesticulated, pointing repeatedly at us and the car. There were a lot of *bien sûr*'s and *pas de problem*'s. Then the wife, a skinny blonde with freckles, moved over to the driver's seat, while the husband got into our car. He smiled to us, said "Hallo there," started the engine, and switched on the lights. Alba sat next to him and didn't even turn to look at us for a second. As he drove our car downhill they chatted, Alba in her impeccable French (she liked to show it off). He said the ruins on top of the mountain were simply magnificent, that there was an extraordinary monastery, still in use, that he had never seen anything like it. She asked a lot of questions, as if the place was interesting to her, not like before, when Isabella was reading from the guidebook and she couldn't have cared less. Then she told him we came to Greece every summer, that we had seen a lot of the sights. Had they been to Delos yet? When he answered they hadn't, she shook her head, gravely, and said they simply couldn't leave Greece without going there.

Once back on the plain, back on the pavement road, the Englishman pulled the car over to the side of the road. His wife had pulled up behind us. We watched him exchange a few more pleasantries with Alba, shake her hand, and climb back into his car. I had this crazy feeling that Alba felt disappointed that the Englishman was so eager to be back with his own family. I remember thinking that because she went right back into a sulk the moment it was just the three of us again.

The English boys waved to us as they overtook our car and sped ahead. They probably thought we were pathetic. I pictured the four of them laughing at us as they drove on. This crazy Italian woman and her two girls stuck halfway up the mountain. She's so pretentious—and she can't even drive her own car, can you imagine?

When school started again, after that first summer without Oliviero, we hoped things would take a familiar shape again and that the winter would turn our apartment into the cozy place we used to know. But somehow it didn't work out that way.

In the evenings there was a lot of Angelica and Alba talking behind closed doors in the living room, ice tinkling in their scotch. Meals were erratic: often there was nothing to eat in the fridge and we had to run to the shops before they closed. The phone would ring at odd hours of the night. Doors would swiftly slam whenever it rang, and one could detect Alba's whispers, sometimes her muffled giggles, coming through the door.

It was a man's voice that always asked to speak to her. It startled me the first time I heard it. It was imperious, unfriendly.

"Is Alba there?"

There was no *hello,* no *please,* no *may I,* no *who am I speaking to,* no *my name is.*

Hers—whenever I was standing nearby and was able to catch a few syllables—were pretty much where-what-and-when conversations. Invariably, a few minutes after she hung up, she would peek into our room, one hand twisting her hair in a bun, the other on the zipper of the dress, a hairpin secured between her teeth.

"I'm off. I'll be back later, darlings. There's ham and cheese in the fridge if you get hungry."

One day the man called while she was out.

"Tell her Bruno rang," he said briskly, as if he were leaving a message with her secretary.

Bruno.

I played with the sound of it for a while. I didn't like it. Too menacing.

I just couldn't bring myself to say the name when Alba came back. It seemed as if by the mere action of pronouncing it I was going to finally make the man real. But I wanted to keep him a ghost, so I pretended that he never called, and that the phone never rang.

The next day, when she came home in the evening from one of her mysterious wanderings, Isabella and I were eating a ham sandwich in the kitchen. Alba didn't even take her coat off. She glared at me from the door, clutching the strap of her bag.

"Someone phoned for me yesterday and you didn't even bother to tell me."

"No, I—"

"Don't you ever do that again," she threatened, pointing at me, then she stormed out of the room.

Isabella made a face and waited for my reaction.

"Why are you staring at me like that?" I asked. I felt like bursting into tears.

We sat in silence around the kitchen table. We could hear Alba running a bath.

"Why didn't you tell her? See how *furious* she is now," Isa said with her usual hint of sarcasm.

"I forgot."

Then I tried to challenge her.

"I thought this guy could be someone from the police," I said, hoping she would support another impromptu theory of mine and dissipate my worse suspicions.

"No," she said, biting her sandwich. Then she added, almost savoring the words, "I think this one is the lover."

Once again, she broke the spell. Of course I knew he must have existed all along, since she had mentioned him that day in Mykonos. Why would anybody keep a journal so obsessively, share secrets with a girlfriend behind closed doors, or space out for hours, unless they were in love?

"This has been going on for some time, by the way. Time to wake up," Isabella said, snapping her fingers in my face, and walked out of the kitchen.

Then one night Bruno finally materialized. He came into the living room behind Alba. Isa and I looked at him in amazement. We couldn't believe he actually dared to show his face.

"*Bambine,* this is Bruno," Alba said, a new anxious pitch in her voice. Then she added, as if to justify his presence, "He's Angelica's brother."

It all fell into place. We had suspected all along the harpist was bad news.

Bruno was just like his name: dark, small, menacing. He had hair on his knuckles and on his chest up to his neck. He wore a sparkling white unbuttoned shirt and a dark-blue suit that was too tight on the shoulders. There was something of the bullfighter in him, small yet strong, a bundle of muscles and nerves. I guess one could say he was sexy, or that he was sexually charged. I could sense something alarming in the way he looked at my mother, although at the time I didn't yet know what lust was.

"These are my little girls, Alina and Isabella," she said hesitantly, then turned to us for reassurance. "Bruno has heard so much about you two, he's dying to meet you at last."

Bruno gave us a half-smile and shook our hands awkwardly. He, just like his sister, had obviously never been around kids much. We could tell by his stiff awkwardness.

"Hello," he said, which wasn't much for someone who had been so looking forward to meet us.

Alba fixed him a drink as he sat on the sofa tapping the armrest, looking uneasy. He looked out of place in our messy living room. She brought two glasses of scotch on a fancy tray. We'd never seen her serve drinks on a tray before.

"Bedtime. Come on, you two. Brush your teeth and off you go," Alba announced to us, gesturing with her chin, up and down, like she always did when she was on the sofa with Angelica. But this time she was curled on the sofa next to *him*. Her bare feet brushing *his* legs.

For once Isa didn't say anything as she slipped into her bed. I had been expecting her to produce the final, sarcastic comment on the situation, come up with the evening headline. Name our new enemy and make fun of him. Her silence worried me: what was taking place in the living room had crushed her to the point that there was no room left for mockery.

As it turned out, she had a very good reason to feel crushed.

They got married only a few months later. It was all done in a rush: Alba was pregnant.

"I don't want to get married when my belly shows," she told us one morning as she looked at herself sideways in the mirror in her bathroom.

Bruno had money. His family owned a chain of furniture stores. He was a very busy man, we learned, and he traveled abroad a lot. He drove a big car and started taking us for Sunday lunch at expensive restaurants. He invariably had little to say, but he wasn't unkind. We ignored him, we learned never to get in his way. Thus, it was easier than we thought, getting used to this stranger.

Their wedding was to be a very simple ceremony, there was going to be no party, no toasts. Isa and I were shipped to Casa Rossa for the week when the wedding took place. It was the first time we were allowed to ride a train by ourselves—we were told we were old enough to do that now. Alba and Bruno were going to Capri for a quick honeymoon and that was going to be it.

Stellario came to get us at the station. He drove us to Casa Rossa in his brand-new pickup truck. On the way, he talked about the weather, the preserves Celeste had made for the winter, how well his granddaughter Adele was doing in school. He didn't mention Alba. At home we found a strange, suspended atmosphere. Jeanne looked embarrassed.

"It's not even a year," we overheard her say to Celeste, Stellario's wife. They were whispering in the kitchen as they were preparing lunch. "I mean, couldn't she have been a little more careful?"

"There are ways to . . ."

"I know, that's what I'm saying. She's a woman, she should know."

"I feel sorry for the girls."

"They'll be all right," Jeanne said. "He's a nice man, I think. And he's got means."

The stepmother, siding with the newcomer. The wicked stepfather of this ugly fairy tale.

But Lorenzo was beside himself.

"Your mother is an imbecile," he said as soon as we sat at the table for lunch. "I want you to know that."

"Lorenzo, please don't start," Jeanne tried to prevent him. "They are only—"

"Shut up. They better find out right away who they are dealing with. A totally undiscerning, obtuse, sexually obsessed creature who can only follow what she calls 'her instinct.' Who now marries a gangster only because she got knocked up. As if one can't get an abortion these days. As if we couldn't help her financially. No, she needs to be his *wife*." He shook his head in disbelief. "So that we'll be appalled by him and his offspring for the rest of our lives. Jesus Holy Christ."

Our grandfather's rage felt reassuring. At last, someone was openly admitting there *was* something to be upset about. Really really upset, too.

As soon as we were sent back to Rome, we moved out of our apartment in Via del Babbuino. We left the spacious tall rooms, the old-fashioned piping and the cherry armchairs, the shady garden and rusty greenhouses of the Hôtel de Russie. We left Oliviero behind for good, in that little room at the end of the corridor, the scent of his cigarettes still hovering about.

We moved to a new part of town, to a neighborhood without shops or cafés, that had no charm. There were no arches, no vaults, no curls or swirls, everything was in the shape of a box. Our new apartment had squared balconies, bright-green tiles in the bathrooms, and shiny cold floors.

How can we live here? We silently asked ourselves the first time we walked through the empty rooms and sat on top of our carton boxes. It felt like such a dreary place, so inhospitable, so sterile, still smelling of paint. A place hard to imagine ever becoming a home.

"Bruno didn't want to live downtown, too much confusion," Alba said. "Here we have a garage, and a doorman."

The apartment slowly filled with new furniture. Modern design.

I loathed its lack of warmth, its lifelessness. There were no more soft cushions, or round armrests on the sofas. No more threadbare turkish carpets, or thick oil paintings by Lorenzo on the walls. It was the end of deep oranges and reds, thick greens and creamy yellows, the end of soft light seeping through old lampshades. This place was all beiges and grays, steel and glass, spikes and angles, low rectangular tables, hard couches, harsh light glaring from hideous plastic balls. It looked like the interior of a shop. The windows looked out on an ugly street lined by young trees where old ladies or their maids took out tiny dogs on a leash. The whole place felt silent and lifeless; one could spend the whole morning listening to flies buzzing and hitting against the glass of the kitchen window. The world outside seemed perfectly groomed and perfectly dead, as if everyone else were lying inside an identical box, arms crossed upon the chest, waiting for the organ to start the Requiem.

It was like having been kidnapped overnight and waking up in a foreign country where we didn't understand the language. Nothing matched, and our sense of orientation simply wasn't good enough.

To make things worse, Alba now seemed even more distant. Although she had nowhere to go now that she had married Bruno, no trysts to organize, we still felt like she wasn't around. What she did now was shut herself up in the bedroom all the time. She said she felt tired, that she needed to sleep. Something made her dizzy and listless; she said it was the pregnancy. Whenever Bruno came home, there were always lots of closed doors, conversations we were not supposed to hear, although we often heard her whimpering.

I think till then I had refused to admit she had been a stranger all along. Probably Oliviero's presence had made her distance more bearable, but now I couldn't stand the idea that she had drifted away for good when we needed her so badly.

I wanted desperately to sneak back into Oliviero's world, a place where there were still great bedtime stories, Campari-and-sodas at Caffè Rosati, offices that looked like circuses, intricate film plots, a world where one could enter into a small room and sit next to a man who was smoking, smiling and typing, who made room for your exercise book next to him and called you "monkey face." A world that had existed just across town, but it felt like light years away.

We were not to mention his name again. We had never been officially told, but it was implicit in the way Alba behaved. She stiffened anytime either Isa or I would mention the word *papà*.

"Yes, love?"

"What happened to Papà's typewriter?"

"Oh God." Her back would arch like a cat raising its fur, and she would look away. "I have no idea. I really don't know."

Then she would frown.

"What do you need it for, anyway?"

"I have to type a paper for school."

She would sigh and look at me blankly, as if I were trying to squeeze money from a beggar.

She wanted us to forget. This was a new life—there was a new house, a new baby. Why did we keep coming back asking for scraps of the past?

The incident, the accident, the mistake. Whatever she had called it, whatever had happened in that room that day, couldn't we be kind to her and just forget once and for all?

One day we came home from school and found the house empty, a note sitting on the dining room table: *We are at the doctor's. There's roast chicken in the fridge, you can heat it up.*

Later that evening, Isabella and I were playing a game of cards at the kitchen table, we heard the key in the door and their muffled voices. We waited a few seconds and then heard Alba's bedroom door open and close. Water running from the tap in her bathroom. Bruno walked into the kitchen and sat at the head of the table. He looked tired.

"Your mother's had a miscarriage," he said and looked at us awkwardly. I guess he didn't feel comfortable having to be the one to tell us. But she obviously had sent him.

I didn't feel sad, or shocked. For me—and I think for Isabella as well—this baby Alba was expecting had been just an abstraction, it meant nothing at all to us. It would have been *their* child, the evidence that they had become a couple like all the others. This baby would have turned them into parents at last and they no longer would be seen like Aegisthus and Clytemnestra. Something inside me rejoiced. I felt relieved that this little family situation wasn't going to happen for them after all.

"Is she in pain?" Isabella asked absentmindedly as she studied her cards and started pulling one out slowly.

"No, she's okay. Just a little tired, that's all." He stood up and leaned slightly over Isabella's shoulder, checking what she was holding. "The doctor said she needs a good night's sleep and she should be perfectly fine by tomorrow."

As Isabella was about to lay a card on the table, he tapped his index finger on a different one.

"Trust me," he said.

Isabella looked at him, then shook her head.

"No," she said, "I don't think so."

We watched him leave the room and wave goodnight at the door. We ignored him.

Isabella showed her card. It was the king of hearts. I had the ace, and she lost the hand.

There we were: two sulking adolescents who didn't like their new home, their new school, who were angry at their mother, hostile toward her new husband, and didn't care that they had lost a child.

It was strange, learning so fast how not to love. And surprising, how easy it proved to be.

Then came the terrible revolution, the overnight coup d'état that takes over the adolescent girl's body, turns everything upside down, and leaves her exhausted, unprepared and wary of the future under the new regime.

The way Isabella changed shocked me. It wasn't just that she had grown into a young woman. It was more like her body had completely changed its inner chemistry. It had hardened, she was all nerves and muscles braided in knots. Her skin had turned a translucent white: one could see the intricate web of blue veins crossing the whiteness of her forearms, ripping the pallor of her neck and forehead like a wound. There was heat, blood, streams of fluids flowing under that skin cool as snow. One always knew something was pulsating furiously right underneath.

Her eyes, that gray-blue, had become a color so light it seemed someone had dipped a brush in stained water. At times they could turn so cold, so blank, like the eyes of a white rabbit when it freezes with fear. It was as if her heart had slipped under, into the depths of a smoldering crater, while the outside had crystallized. Her body harbored a silent hatred.

She had been taking ballet classes at a small school near our old house in Via del Babuino. I envied her the bus ride downtown, the duffel bag slung across her shoulders, her lessons in the mirrored studio with the wooden floor, the other girls in leg warmers and black tights, the sound of the piano, the French words spoken by the teacher in a high voice while they stretched at the barre. I was jealous of those hours she carved out for herself, away from the silence of the apartment, the melancholy of our long, empty afternoons.

The physical strain had bent her, stretched her, flattened her. She had given herself in, like a soldier, to the idea of hard discipline. It hurt me to see her doing a split. The way her legs opened, her torso flattened on the floor, the way her body twisted and arched. Her new body seemed to me more the result of a self-inflicted torture than a beautiful gift. There was something painful in her suppleness, something I could hardly bring myself to look at. She was like a bonsai—perfectly shaped, yet warped.

My body, meanwhile, had gotten softer, rounder at the edges. The increasing flesh around my arms and thighs concealed the tension; you could detect no nerves, no tendons, no pulse in my wrists. My hair was curlier, my eyes darker, my skin thicker.

I had made myself easier, friendlier. People were eager to smile back at me—unlike Isabella, who made them nervous.

It happened so suddenly that it took us almost by surprise whenever we looked in the mirror to see how we differed. It was as if we had pushed our bodies in different ways, to match what we'd become.

I was fifteen.

Peppino Esposito had aged, but I recognized him right away through the glass door of the Caffè Greco, stirring his espresso at the counter. I walked in, and there he was, pinstriped suit and dark glasses Aristotle

Onassis–style, broadcasting the familiar scent of his English cologne all around.

I had read about him in the papers: he'd gone to Hollywood in the early seventies, moved to Beverly Hills. He had produced a couple of catastrophe movies—one, about a bunch of people stuck inside a tunnel in the Alps, had been a terrible fiasco and nearly bankrupted him; the other one, about a boat trapped in the ice, made a fortune and put him back on the map, stronger than ever—then decided to come back to Cinecittà, where everybody knew him and where he felt at home.

I noticed his stiff cuffs, his shirt collar, his manicured nails: everything about him was starched, trimmed, prim; it said "Everything's under control." I liked that.

I pushed through the people crowding the counter and introduced myself.

"Alina Strada. Incredible! I would have never recognized you." He patted me vigorously on the shoulder, exhilarated, smiling, warm.

He said he was on his way to buy a tie at Hermés, around the corner, would I walk him there. The salesmen in the store all knew him and called him *Dottore*. He knew exactly which tie he wanted—burgundy color, thin stripes—and the whole operation didn't take more than ten minutes. He paid from a wad of cash that he kept in a silver clip in his pocket. Then he grabbed my arm.

"Let's go for an aperitif at Mario's, right around the corner."

He behaved as if he had had his secretary call me a long time ago to fix this meeting. As if we had lots to talk about and we needed a quiet place to do it. He didn't even bother to ask me if I was on my way anywhere else. His confidence was soothing, just like his cologne. I followed him, hypnotized by his manners.

We entered the wood-paneled bar of the Hôtel d'Angleterre, where the graying barman greeted him graciously.

"Dottor Esposito, how nice to see you. It's been a while."

"Mario"—he was all excited, he still gripped me tightly by the arm—"guess who this beautiful young girl is? It's Oliviero Strada's daughter, can you believe it?"

Mario stared at me with a smile.

"Yes, she does look like Signor Strada. The eyes, the smile. Look at that." He took my hand and held it, incredulous.

Esposito proceeded to order two glasses of champagne and warm truffle canapés. Mario insisted it would have to be on the house.

"Your father was one of my favorite people," he explained as he poured the champagne slowly into the flutes. "Such a clever, distinguished man. He used to come here often. I can say that he became more of a friend than a customer. Sometimes he even discussed his ideas with me. He always appreciated a bit of feedback, other people's reactions always interested him."

"Your father was a very fine man," said Esposito, raising his glass. Truly a rare individual."

We sat at the empty bar with Mario, who poured himself a glass, and we toasted.

"To Oliviero."

It was dark, the canapés were delicious, the wooden bar smelled of wax and nicotine. I had never drunk champagne in the morning. Esposito wiped his dark glasses with the tip of his tie.

"I heard your mother has remarried, right? She is such a lovely young woman, of course she would"—he cleared his throat—"you know . . . marry again."

"Yes," I said, "although my sister and I don't really get along with her or our stepfather." The champagne had made me bold.

"Really? I'm sorry to hear that. Well, of course your father was quite an irreplaceable man. I still feel rather haunted by his . . . by the way he passed away."

Mario shook his head slowly, lowering his eyes. Esposito went on, holding the lenses in front of him, making sure he had cleaned them thoroughly.

"Totally unexpected. I mean, nobody would have ever thought someone like him would commit suicide. Inexplicable. I still wonder why he did it."

These two men, I could feel it, they still cared, they still wondered, they still searched for an answer. The Barman and the Producer. My father's loyal friends, shaking their heads, lighting a cigarette with a golden Cartier, glass in hand. It suddenly dawned on me they might have an answer and that this could be the day I discover why. I felt confident, sheltered by the darkness of the bar, still so quiet in the morning hours, like a church. The wood paneling, the silence, it was a perfect setting for a confession.

I began by testing how far I could go.

"I think he was very much in love with my mother, and maybe she—"

"Yes, true . . ." Esposito waved his hand in the air, cutting me short. "That could have been part of it."

I could tell he didn't want to get into that.

He dragged on his cigarette for a few seconds, staring into the bottles across from his stool.

"Now that I think of it, I still have a wonderful screenplay of Oliviero's. His best script, really." He lightly tipped his flute over to Mario, who filled it up slowly. "Absolutely brilliant. A story on the order of *The Conformist*. With the right cast it would have made a major hit in America."

"Why didn't you make it?" I asked.

"He didn't want me to. In fact, he bought the rights back from me."

"Why?"

"Because of your mother. When she read it, she told him she would leave him if the film ever got made. So he begged me to let him buy it back."

"You mean he gave you back the money?"

"Yes. And I was furious with him," he said, smiling. "It was such a brilliant script, I wasn't happy at all to have to give it back."

"I can imagine." I picked an olive from a dish and played with it for a few seconds. "And why do you think my mother got so upset?"

Esposito adjusted the knot of his tie and waved vaguely in the air.

"Well, it was the story of her family—you know, your grandparents, in Paris just before the war."

"Oh, *that* story. My grandmother running away with a woman. People said she was a Nazi."

"Right. But you see, I had no idea it was a true story. To me it was just a great film plot! But of course she didn't want to have her father exposed like that. And, for God's sake, I can totally see why."

Then he turned to Mario and began to gesticulate, as if he himself were the screenwriter pitching his story.

"You see, the main character is this Italian painter who goes to live in Paris in the late twenties to mingle with the avant garde—really just to be a bohemian and have a good time. The Ovra, the Fascist secret police, manage to get ahold of him and get some information from him about a group of Italian refugees—writers, intellectuals, very active antifascists—who are living in France. When these people eventually are arrested, the painter has to leave Paris to avoid retaliations from the antifascist community, who label him as a spy. And for his whole life he swears up and down that it wasn't him who gave those names to the police but his wife. He persuades everybody that he was always a staunch antifascist, but that his wife—a foreigner—was to blame. She becomes the scapegoat. It's a wonderful story of betrayal."

I nodded and gulped down the rest of my champagne.

"It's subtle. You see, the whole point is, he's not *really* a spy: when he spills this information about his friends, the painter has no idea how dangerous the Ovra is. At the time—this is the late twenties, early thirties—intellectuals still had mixed feelings about fascism. Lots of artists had joined the party, or were at least sympathetic. Don't forget, it had sprouted from socialism, so people were still ambivalent about it. So your grandfather—no, I mean the character in the film—when the Ovra agents come to Paris and press him, he doesn't fully realize how bad these guys are or what the consequences might be. And of course, there's no denying, he's a bit of an opportunist. You wanted to please the party, then, if you wanted to get ahead. Only later on does he realize he's responsible for these people's arrest, maybe their death."

Esposito paused, checked on his audience, and lit another Nazionale.

"So he leaves Paris and returns to Italy, and after the war he manages to save his reputation by blaming it all on the wife, who in fact has left him for a German woman. Then years go by, and the great twist in the plot is that you realize he has actually *convinced himself* that he's innocent, he totally believes that his wife has been working for the secret police all along. And that it was because of politics and power that his wife had an affair with the other woman, rather than because she simply fell in love with her. And not only does he rewrite history but everyone else around him agrees to believe his version of the story. In a way you could say it's a brilliant metaphor for Italy's dirty conscience. Something like that."

"A terrific story," said Mario, presenting us with a small tray of fresh canapés. "Herring fillet and hard-boiled egg?"

"Thank you." I picked one up with a toothpick and swallowed it in one go. "So, Signor Esposito"—I was trying to sound nonchalant—"you say you still have this script?"

"Yes. And call me Peppino."

"Okay." I smiled quickly, to show him gratitude for allowing me that intimacy.

I could feel my heart racing but I tried not to show it.

"I would love to read it."

Esposito stared at me. He probably realized only then that I knew nothing. That it had always escaped me, the wonderful story about betrayal in my family. And the twist in the plot.

I decided it was better to admit it.

"You know, there's so much stuff, so much that isn't clear to me, about what happened then. Everyone keeps their mouth shut. And now that Oliviero is gone, there's nobody left I can ask."

"In fact, you *should* read it," Esposito said. He always made up his mind fast. "It's all in the past now and I don't think you would find it so disturbing as your mother did. How old is your grandfather now?"

"Almost eighty. But still going strong. Why?"

"Nothing," he said. "Just checking. For the sake of the lawyers—ha!"

We walked out into the sunshine, both slightly tipsy. He said I could call his office and he would arrange for me to pick up the script. He signaled a taxi that was unloading an American tourist in front of the Hôtel d'Angleterre and got in.

"Remember," he said, his head sticking out of the taxi window, "technically speaking, you're free to sell those rights back to me. They belong to you now. Goodbye, my dear. Give me a call whenever you want. We'll have lunch."

Once I read the script, I immediately gave it to Isabella. She became obsessed with it. I think for her the story was a kind of retribution; she said it made everything fall into place. Our mother being so fucked up, and Lorenzo so bitter. She didn't have doubts about any of it being true; she always believed things were either black or white.

To me, that script was more like a fetish. I loved to touch it, feel the impression of the letters from my father's old-fashioned typewriter. The notes in his tiny handwriting scribbled on the margins. A dark circle on the first page—probably his coffee cup.

The first time I read it, I forced myself to take it just as another film plot. Who knows what was true and what Oliviero had made up in order to make the story work "on the screen." I didn't want to believe any of it was true, not only for the sake of Lorenzo—I needed to hold on to my grandfather, to think of him as a man of integrity, despite his resentment and his bitterness—but mostly because I couldn't bear the idea that my father had taken Alba's family secrets and sold them for money. That was not the way I liked to think of him. I couldn't believe Oliviero ever had a mercenary thought in his life, and I wasn't going to acknowledge it now. In my own story, Oliviero was the hero, and he'd have to play that role throughout.

I didn't call Esposito about selling him back the rights. I wasn't ready yet to strike a deal with that bit of past, not even twenty years later.

Jeanne died in 1976.

Her heart. It stopped beating, just like that, during the night. She had gone the same way she had come: quietly, careful to avoid all commotion.

Alba, Isabella, and I took the train down to Casa Rossa for the funeral. It was nice to be just us in the same place for so many hours. Alba looked sad for most of the trip. She was looking out of the window, and I could almost see her thoughts, wandering at random, crowding over her eyebrows. But once we were south of Bari, she lightened up and sat straight on her seat, suddenly elated as the landscape became more and more familiar. It had been a while since she had been back home. Only then did I realize that she might have felt lonely, too, just like us, in that big, cold apartment, a place so different from anywhere she had ever lived before.

It was November, and it was windy and cold. A gray sky threatening rain hovered over the fields.

"Look, look! The color of the clouds, the silver of the olives! Isn't this just . . . beautiful?" She couldn't stop pointing, as if she were showing us something for the first time. By the time we reached Casa Rossa she was smiling.

"Look how bright the red of the house is in this light! They must have repainted it recently."

The house was full of people. Celeste and her daughters were cooking a huge meal, homemade *orecchiette* were laid on the marble-top table, bread was baking in the oven, the fireplaces were lit in every room. Old women in black whispered their rosaries in the corners, young girls served soup and wine to the men.

Signora Jeanne. She had been less of a stranger to them than to us.

It was another death in the family, but a quiet one. At least for Isa and me. Jeanne had been a familiar presence, but we knew we were never going to miss her. In the same way we had gotten used to her presence, we knew we would get used to her absence. We watched Alba. She looked sad, but we never caught her crying.

Why should she? It wasn't her real mother, I kept thinking in order to justify her, yet surprised at my own lack of emotion.

But for Lorenzo it was different. He sat in the center of the kitchen, looking brittle, like he had been turned into stone. I tried to picture him in his Parisian days—his thick hair swept back in the bohemian fashion, greedy for life and success—talking to this Italian "official" who had invited him for a drink in a discreet café. I imagined him gesticulating, smoking, "just having a friendly conversation," trading his friends' names, their addresses, quoting their words, in exchange for the Fascists' benevolence. I kept my eyes on him, searching for a trace of the ruthless spy, the heartless traitor, or simply the cynical opportunist, but all I saw was my grandfather. Holding his plate and spoon, in the eerie stillness of his posture, looking like an old, hardened peasant.

It made me sad to observe his vitreous stare: he wasn't made to be left alone, without a woman. I couldn't imagine how Lorenzo would clear his table after dinner, make his coffee in the morning, sleep alone in his bed. I could tell he too was scared.

Alba slipped back into her young girl's body like into an old dress: I saw her help Celeste with the food, fan the coals in the fireplace, lay the table, and I knew she was savoring the familiarity of each gesture.

The wind was banging windows upstairs, we ran to shut them. It felt good—the house so warm, the rain outside, the smell of wax and incense in the church, the children singing, the big lunch in the house for all the people of the village, the kisses, the faces warm with tears, the blessings, the smell of flowers. It was like Christmas.

"Why don't we move here? We can't really leave grandfather alone, can we?" I said to Alba the day after the funeral.

She gave me a hard look. I knew I annoyed her when I said things like that; she didn't want to be reminded of how much I hated living with her and Bruno.

"Don't be ridiculous. He can always come and stay with us if he wants to."

It was impossible to picture Lorenzo trapped in that living room, among the low glass-top tables, the hideous lamp fixtures, the hard rectangular sofas. Walking on the sidewalk next to old ladies with their bluish hair and odious poodles. The image was preposterous.

We left a couple of days later. She said it was because we shouldn't miss too much school, but I knew she wanted to hurry back home to be with Bruno.

And I knew this had nothing to do with love: it had to do with fear. I smelled it in her. It was something sick, scary.

And I knew what her fear meant: she was either going to kill or be killed, there were no half measures. She either possessed men or was possessed by them.

This time it was Isabella and I who looked melancholic all the way back on the train. Neither of us wanted to leave Casa Rossa. We'd already learned to shed so much from our lives; somehow, to leave Puglia then made us feel as if we were left with nothing at all.

When we got home, late that night, Bruno wasn't there. She immediately got on the phone, without even taking off her coat. She slammed the door with a kick, and we could hear the desperate clicking of the rotary dial, her angry words, her pleading.

Bruno came back home in the middle of the night. She was screaming so loud, sleep was impossible. I think she must have been drinking, because she slurred her words with a nasty, snappy edge in her voice. I could hardly make out what she said, but I knew it was the desperate, stale sequence of accusations women throw at men, like sand in the face.

"You liar . . . I know you've been fucking her . . . you bastard . . . don't you ever come near me again . . . I can smell it on you . . ."

"You're not well," I heard him say. "You're too upset. You better take something to calm down."

His voice was flat. Cold. He didn't love her, anyone could see that.

"You, you are . . . I can't believe what you . . ." But now she was sobbing too hard—heaving, choking—to be understood.

"Get up," he said, without pity.

"How could you . . . how could you . . . ," she cried.

I think she had thrown herself on the floor. She was determined to get something out of him. But the more she went on with her pathetic performance the less one believed her.

"I've given you everything . . . everything."

He wouldn't help her up. I knew that. He must have been just standing there, perfectly still, staring at her. With contempt.

Something crashed. Glasses, bottles, a lamp. I shut my eyes tight.

"Shit!" I heard Isabella say in the dark. She was sitting upright in her bed. She opened the drawer from her night table and took out something, then struck a match. She lit a cigarette. I said nothing, although it was the very first time I had seen her do that. She inhaled deeply, I could see the tip of the cigarette burn redder in the dark.

"I hate her," she said. "She has no self-respect. She should just throw him out of the house."

I said nothing.

"I hate them both. I wish they would both die and leave us alone," she added, as if she were casting a spell. She waited for me to say something, she wanted to know whether I was with her or not on this.

But I couldn't bring myself to side with her. I still wanted to believe Alba and Bruno were a mistake that could be fixed. I didn't want anybody else to die in order to settle things.

The next morning, we went into the kitchen to make ourselves breakfast and found her there, in her silk kimono, making coffee.

"Good morning, girls." She smiled at us. "Did you sleep well?"

Bruno walked in, smelling of his pungent aftershave, ready to go to work. She brushed his sleeve with the tip of her fingers and then slid her hand under his jacket.

"Coffee, darling?"

"No, I've got to run."

She kissed him lightly on the lips.

"I'll call you later," he said, trying his best to look cheerful. "Goodbye girls. See you all tonight."

Isabella and I exchanged a glance.

It made us anxious to think that we were all walking on such thin ice. It could crack anytime, without warning.

Darkness, a bright cone of light on stage, and Isabella coming forward under it, barefoot, doing a little solo dance. The audience (it was a very small theater, downtown, a low-budget production) held their breath. She came forward under the lights, swaying lightly (by then she had abandoned ballet and joined a small contemporary dance company), as a tightrope walker would, in her light-blue dress. I remember the music: a high-pitched voice, female singer (from Mali?) on a single-string instrument. She looked small, strong, wild. A little Artemis holding her bow and arrow.

I knew right away what it was that she was doing: it was Alba, the essence of Alba.

That dance was Alba walking barefoot in the country as a girl, her strong calves showing under the dress. Quiet yet cruel. The victim and the killer.

She was so perfect, she made everybody understand what she meant, just by coming forward like that, in her little barefoot dance.

Then, once the lights came on and the audience broke into applause, she reappeared on stage, holding hands with the other dancers. Their hair was drenched in sweat, their clothes damp with exertion, their eyes blinded by the stage lights. They held hands and bowed, with this unrestrainable smile, this magnificent glow on their faces, a sense of release, of complete satisfaction. That expression in their eyes, of pure joy, when they looked out toward the audience—this black hole, an undistinguished mass of cheers—you just couldn't see it without wanting to cry.

I wanted to be up there, holding hands with those beautiful strangers, smelling their sweat, touching their arms, feeling as exhausted and exalted as they all did. I felt my throat tighten, and my eyes moisten. At the time, I was moved by seeing Isabella on stage for the first time, but now I know that her happiness was the beginning of a new kind of loneliness for me.

Tomas was in the dance company, an American guy of Cuban descent, dark straight hair falling over one side. He had a way of tucking it behind his ear and tilting his head sideways.

I had watched his body move across the stage, flip and jump like an acrobat. At one point he had turned his head so fast, that a spray of sweat radiated from his hair like the fine spray of a fountain. The first thing I felt, when I went backstage that night, was this incredible heat emanating from his body, and his musky smell. He came out of the dressing room wearing only a pair of loose jeans, his bare torso muscular and lean. He had a towel thrown around his neck, his hair still wet.

"Are you coming to dinner with us?" he asked, with a thick American accent.

I couldn't believe Isabella had spent so much time rehearsing with someone like that and never mentioned him. On the way to the restaurant I asked her about him.

"Oh, Tomas. He's our choreographer He's very, *very* smart. He studied with Grotowski in Poland."

"How come he lives here?"

"I think he grew up here because his father had a job with the embassy or something. Anyway, he *hates* America," she said somehow proudly. "He says he'll never go back."

We sat outdoors, around the table of a trattoria in a small square in the back of Campo dei Fiori. It was a cheap place, one they could afford, paper tablecloth, greasy food. It was thrilling, to be sitting at a table with ten people barely older than me who ordered their food, lit each other's cigarettes, drank wine, talked of politics, books, cinema, just like grown-ups.

Those guys had nothing to do with the pretty boys, the harmless teenagers I had made out with so far in my school in the posh part of town where we'd been secluded. The romantics who preached revolution from their parents' terraced penthouse and told me I should read Marx (I tried, wanting to please them). I had made love to a couple of them because I was determined to find out what it was like. Sex had turned out to be much like my lovers themselves: sweet, harmless, somehow unexciting. It was more like a physical exercise my body had at some point required, something that needed to be performed. I thought it would change me, that I would wake up feeling like a completely new person. Instead, I woke up just the same.

But what came from these young men was totally different. I was startled by their tangled long hair, the ropes of veins that streaked their forearms, the round muscles in their legs, the loose shirts they wore. There was a sense of danger, and of freedom, about them that I had never felt before.

The girls, too, all looked similar, as if they had been exchanging their vintage clothes, dangling earrings, and lovers for some time. Something about their appearance—maybe the tousled hair, the bruises on their legs, the rips in their dresses—made them look as if they had just survived a hurricane. Although Isabella was the youngest of the lot, I could see that she was going to look just like the rest of them, once she'd put on the dark-red lipstick, the bangles, and smudged some kohl around her eyes. It was obvious, how she already belonged to their tribe.

Suddenly it hit me: I had been left behind. There I was, in my bland clothes, my flat shoes, my stupid *Charlie's Angels* layered haircut. With my upper-class lovers in their secondhand army jackets and desert boots, my pile of unread Marxist texts.

I sat back, jealous of their intimacy, of what they had been sharing. I watched how hands nonchalantly touched arms, grabbed wrists, brushed shoulders. How close they were, how fearless their bodies were to touch one another. Even off stage, they were still a unit, a single organism, dancing, moving with grace and confidence. Like the ripple of a wave.

I ached to be part of it. And I couldn't believe Isabella had managed to keep this away from me for so long. Clearly this must have been her little secret plan, to join their tribe and leave for good.

Tomas, already in his mid-twenties, was the oldest of them. He obviously was the underwater engine that activated the wave, the one to set its rhythm. He sat quietly at the center of the table, everyone reaching for him, turning to him, carefully feeling his beat. All the girls must be madly in love with him, I thought.

"Alina"—he turned to me—"what do you do?"

"Nothing," I said, as proudly as possible, realizing how uninteresting I was going to sound. "I'm still in high school. It's my last year."

He stared at me, waiting for more. I held his gaze, I didn't say anything else but felt I must be blushing.

"You look like someone I know," he said, and from the sound of it I knew he was thinking of a lover.

He scutinized me.

"Right here," he said and brushed his shoulder and upper arm. "It's amazing. And your hands, let me see your hands."

I gave them to him across the table. Everyone noticed. He held them, looked closely at my palms and fingers as if he were searching for a particular mark, then turned them upside down. Then he dropped them.

"The way you move them. Identical."

He reached for me across the table and stroked his hand hard through my hair.

"You're beautiful."

I felt my blood shoot up, pulsing at my throat and temples. The table had gone quiet, the girls pretended to look the other way. They must have watched him do this a million times—close in on a new prey—and they knew to retreat slowly. He obviously didn't like anybody to be in his way.

He tore a piece from the paper tablecloth and scribbled something on it. Then he pushed it into my palm. *Come home with me tonight.*

I felt Isabella's stare. I knew it had turned cold, I could feel it on my skin.

I followed him that night to his place in Trastevere. It was cluttered, messy, clothes and books scattered all over, piles of greasy dishes in the sink. There were big beautiful paintings on the wall. Light watery colors, soft round shapes, reminiscent of clouds, beaches, shells.

"Who painted these?" I asked.

"A girl who used to live here," he said and then stretched his arm toward me. "Come."

He led me into the dark bedroom. There was a tall window that gave onto the garden of Gianicolo, from which one could see a clear winter sky hanging over the silhouette of the trees. He lit candles and incense around his bed, then took off my clothes, piece by piece. He methodically undid buttons, hooks, zippers, holding his gaze on me as I stood in the center of the room, my arms drooping sideways like a child in front of a doctor, embarrassed to be so naked. I watched him unbutton his jeans and take them off slowly, so that I would see his hard-on while he kept staring at me. Then he pushed me on the bed and, as he started to slowly kiss my breasts, he slid a hand between my legs.

Sex so far had been a sweaty, anxious affair done in haste in the afternoon, one of my panting schoolmates on top of me. Half-dressed, hands frantically searching for warm skin under woolly clothes, trousers and panties twisted around the ankles, keeping an eye on the door. It had been like a marathon, something exhausting one had to go through in order to get to the other end safely.

Now I realized lovemaking was an art. As Tomas kept moving smoothly on top of me, I tried to think what to do, how to respond to his hands. But I knew I lacked the experience. He made love to me slowly, moving inside me with exaggerated languor. He stopped and started again. Then I almost fell asleep and he came back inside me, stirring a surge of desire I had no idea could still be there. But he was the infallible engine of this new amazing mechanism.

Of course he knew what he was doing: this was Tomas, the Choreographer of Sex.

We fell asleep for a couple of hours, huddled together, my mouth pressed on his hair, his arms around me. I woke up to the sound of screaming seagulls and I knew it was almost light. I slipped out of the bed and searched for my clothes on the floor.

He didn't stir and I didn't wake him. I was anxious to be alone now, in order to analyze every little alteration that had occurred in me. I wanted to search on my own body for the evidence of what had happened.

Outside, the light was a pale blue and everything was still. I could hear my own footsteps echoing in the cobblestoned alley. I crossed the river on the old Ponte Sisto, the cupola of St. Peter's on my left like a watercolor against the lightening sky, the thick canopy of plane trees along the river's edge reflected in the water. A bus went by, like a shot. Its interior lights were still on and I could make out the few passengers—sleepy workers on the way to their jobs, their heads dangling next to the window.

I crossed Piazza Farnese, Corso Vittorio, Piazza Navona, feeling weightless. Only birds, stray cats, and myself, sprinting like an antelope across the empty squares. It was so pristine, the city still asleep, the shutters still closed, I wished it could freeze like this forever, stay so fresh and untouched.

I felt a pang of hunger and walked inside the first café that I saw open. It was crowded with people going to work, smelling of aftershave, drinking their first coffee, smoking their first cigarette of the day. Their skin shone from cheap soap, their clothes were freshly ironed, the papers they read still crisp. I was sure none of them had spent a night like mine.

I ordered a cappuccino, bit ravenously into a croissant, and caught my reflection in the mirror across the counter. My hair was a mess, I had put my shirt on inside out. I felt a wetness between my legs, and I could smell Tomas all over my skin. I smiled at myself in the mirror and thought, *Remember this face.*

I tiptoed into the house just before seven-thirty, holding my breath.

I thought I could smell sleep behind each door. But I was wrong.

Isabella was sitting up straight in her bed. She didn't smile when I sneaked into our room.

"Did you sleep with Tomas?" she asked me right away.

"Yes."

"I knew you would."

I sat on my bed and faced her. I didn't want her to snatch this new feeling away from me so quickly.

"What is it? Did I do something wrong?"

She gave a strident laugh and clapped her hands.

"God forbid. No, it's perfectly natural that you should meet him for the first time in your life and go to bed with him, just like that."

"I didn't know you had a crush on—"

"I didn't say I did."

"Well, then, why are you making a scene?"

"This is *not* a scene," she said and looked at me hard.

"What is it, then? Come on, say it." I took off my shoes and sat cross-legged on the bed. Then gave her a nasty grin.

My hair a mess, my shirt inside out, damp between my legs. Proud.

I felt nothing could touch me now. I had just learned something new, something that had to do with being selfish, and with one's own pleasure.

"They are *my* friends, that was *my* show," she said slowly, pressing on each word as if she had been rehearsing the speech during a sleepless night. "You can't come in just like that and tramp all over the place."

I faked an outraged laugh.

"Oh, come on, Isa. *Tramp all over the*—"

"I don't want to always have to share everything with you," she cut me off.

"There you go," I said, as if I had finally caught her with her hands in the jar. "But guess what?" I held a pause and then I challenged her. "Neither do I. *Particularly*."

That moment was our final split, when we each went our own way. Over something as irrelevant as the body of Tomas.

"Fuck off," she said softly. "You're just as selfish as everyone else in this house. I hate you."

"*You* fuck off," I answered, like a soldier unloading the rest of the magazine on one man, hoping the noise will scare the rest of them off. "When things don't go the way you want them to, all you can do is hate. It's pathetic. You just don't know how to live."

I was shooting all my bullets off for the sheer sake of the noise. She was the kamikaze, the one who dies for the cause. The one who silently aims her last shot, who kills and in the end is killed.

It was 1977, the apex of the student movement in Italy, but I was no longer interested in the Revolution.

My friends from high school had turned into serious political activists by then, and we pretty much shared a single credo. We had been taking upon ourselves the pain of the whole planet and were committed to healing it. There was no time to rest for any of us: every day there was another injustice, another iniquitous war, another attempt to restrict someone's freedom. In the early seventies, myriads of revolutionary groups had sprouted—they called themselves *extraparlamentari,* which meant they were more left of the most left-wing Communist sitting in the Parliament—and each one was specifically committed to a favorite cause. One could tell just from the militants' wardrobe: some wore the keffiyeh, the Palestinian red-and-white scarf, around their neck; others had the Maoist blue cap, others a Che Guevara beret. There were enough plights one could choose from, since everyone was under threat: women, Palestinians, the working class throughout the world. It didn't matter how far from us, the dictatorship of capitalism was looming everywhere.

The activists in camouflage jackets and desert boots kept ringing me up. They wanted me to join their meetings, join their groups.

"We're turning into a Fascist state again," they warned me. "Come tonight. It's extremely important."

By now their urgency was beginning to make me feel guilty and annoyed at the same time. I could tell they already considered me a traitor, since I had ceased to show interest in the class struggle.

They were right, I wasn't motivated. I didn't want a cause anymore. I just wanted to spend time with Tomas, smoke pot, have sex.

Soon after the Tomas incident, Isabella left his dance company. The two of us stopped speaking. We kept it to the bare minimum necessary for two people who share the same room. We pretended we were no longer interested in each other's lives. I knew she had moved on—new voices on the phone for her, a new attitude and different clothes. She had started attending architecture classes at the university. She was wearing baggy trousers and men's shirts these days and was reading all the Marxist books I had abandoned.

Tomas was the one who told me.

"Your sister said she's tired of dancing. She wants to be an architect."

He grinned.

"She said our concept of theater is hinged on a hedonistic and bourgeois aesthetics."

I said nothing.

"I wonder who suggested that to her."

I still said nothing.

"Maybe her new friends from the university. Sounds a lot like them," Tomas insisted.

I detected a pang of jealousy in his voice, and for the first time I wondered if he had ever been interested in her sexually. Or maybe it was just his insatiable vanity: it just bothered him that she had dared to rebel against his control.

"She says she needs to feel useful," he scoffed. "To the proletariat!"

So that's what had been happening. She obviously couldn't stand my following her tracks so closely. She'd rather exchange places and take over my abandoned path. For the first time I felt like I had stolen something from her, but looking at Tomas, naked in front of me, a joint in his mouth, I knew it was too late to give it back to her now.

So I said nothing, but something hurt.

Where is Alba in all this?

Where is Alba while our bodies grow till they can fill her clothes, our feet stretch to fit her strappy sandals? Has she taken the time to even look at us?

Alba is asleep in her bed until noon. These days Alba locks herself in the bathroom to color her hair. She takes Valium with her scotch. She says she needs it or else her heart goes funny, it scares her. She says it's like having a fluttering bird trapped in her ribs.

She hardly ever calls her father in Casa Rossa, and whenever she does, her conversations are short. As she listens to him—he tells her about his X-rays, complains about the frost—she scribbles furiously on a little pad next to the phone, nodding with her eyes fixed on the paper. Does it make her sad—or does it irritate her—that her father, the giant, is turning into such a frail old man?

Her friend Angelica no longer comes over to share secrets with her on the sofa. Now she's just her sister-in-law who knows too much about her. So Alba has a new circle of friends, but we no longer know who they are. She meets them for lunch, she never brings them to the house. They sound different, these new people in her life, more sophisticated than Bruno and his sister. Every now and again she'll say this friend of mine took me to see a Japanese film playing at the Filmstudio. This friend says Robert Redford might win an Oscar. I'm reading this wonderful collection of short stories. This friend gave them to me for my birthday. She never tells us their names.

She has a new life, somewhere. Maybe a new lover, who knows. Outside our house, once again.

Within the four walls of our apartment she has slowly retreated into a silent resentment that finally reached the stage of contempt. She despises Bruno, but she won't walk away from him. Her victory is her hatred, her strength is that at last she no longer loves him. But she needs to stay close to him, in order to wield her lack of love as a weapon.

Therefore, one could say, in a sense, that Alba is nowhere.

Isabella found a new friend.

Enrico was skinny, aloof, unhealthy-looking. He belonged to a leftist revolutionary group, Autonomia—an antireformist movement, a militant counterculture that had positioned itself way to the left of the Communist Party. Autonomia called the Communist Party a lackey to the bourgeoisie, accused it of having betrayed its Leninist ideals, and pledged itself to working in alignment with the Christian Democrats. That is to say, where once the PCI—the Italian Communist Party—had fought fascism with rifles in hand, it was now collaborating with it. By the late seventies, Autonomia exuded a sexiness that other student movements found hard to match. They had become famous for their guerrilla actions: they beat up union leaders, wrecked machine tools, they forcibly took food from grocery shelves without paying or ripped out bus fare boxes, calling for proletarian expropriation. They joined rallies, masking their faces with bandanas and waving P38 pistols in the air, chanting gloomy slogans about the death of the state.

Lately, Isabella and Enrico—who had met at the university—were inseparable: they spent hours discussing politics, writing communiqués, going to meetings, and attending rallies. Sometimes I would find one of their leaflets lying around our bedroom. The language was always the same: militaristic, threatening, repetitive.

The only thing this state can guarantee is exploitation, unemployment, misery, and prison. The needs of the masses and the proletariat are inexorably and violently denied by a type of power whose only concern is its own survival. Only the full use of revolutionary war will destroy the bourgeois state and construct the Communist society.

By then, heavily armed security squads had become the rule at left-wing demonstrations, and often rallies ended with shoot-outs between masked pistol-carrying activists and the police. Early one morning I watched Isabella get ready to go to a demonstration. She was in the kitchen, cutting a lemon in half. She slid it into her pocket.

"What's that for?" I asked.

"Tear gas," she said, blasé, tying a bandana around her neck.

I went to aswer the buzzer. It was Enrico on his Vespa. He'd come to get her. I could hear his exhaust pipe blaring through the intercom.

"Does he actually carry a gun?" I asked her as she strapped her leather campesino bag across her shoulder. It was thick with leaflets.

"Don't ask stupid questions," she said and left me without a clue.

One day, out of the blue, Isa announced to Alba that she was moving out.

"Enrico and I have found a place we can share. It's cheap."

"How come you only tell me now when everything's already been arranged?" Alba took it as a personal affront. "What's all this secrecy? I mean, couldn't you discuss it with me? We're a family, after all."

Isabella made a face.

"Are we? I didn't get that impression. Anyway, I'm twenty years old, I don't need to ask permission for every single move I make."

The day Isabella moved out, Alba sat on the sofa, her legs crossed and slightly bent sideways, a glass of scotch between her fingers. I remember the way her foot was shaking while the rest of her kept perfectly still, as Isabella moved out boxes, clothes, her bed, her desk lamp, a couple of paintings, with Enrico's help. Alba sat on the sofa like some head of state who is being interviewed on camera, showing all the poise and authority the situation required. When the door finally closed behind Isabella and her unattractive friend, she looked at me, arching an eyebrow.

"Excellent. You must be very happy now."

" Me? I had nothing to do with this."

"Yes you did. Stealing her boyfriend, what's-his-name, and all the rest of it."

"Listen"—I sat in front of her and took a deep breath—"you don't have a clue about what's going on here. Why do you bother to talk if you don't even remember a single name?"

"It's immaterial, I'm not interested in his name."

"Exactly. You're never interested in anything. Maybe that's the reason she left. Because she was tired of your not being interested in her."

Alba laughed. A dry, spiteful laugh.

"Whooh! And how did you come up with this clever little analysis, may I ask?"

I just shrugged. I had recently become aware of how much I resented her. And it no longer scared me. In fact, I was actually rather proud of feeling so distant from her.

"I think she'll be better off away from here," I said. "This place is insane." And with that I stood up and headed for the door.

"You can leave it whenever you want," she said, before I left the room. "I'm tired of seeing you both sulk, sulk, sulk."

I walked out of the room without replying.

"You don't lift a finger to help me clear the dishes," she said to my back, "but you're so worried about saving the masses. It's pathetic."

That night she came into my room. She sat on my bed. She looked at me without saying anything, just stroking my hair. I could tell she had been crying.

"Alina," she whispered, "I love you so much. It kills me that you don't believe it."

"But you never say it."

"I know, my love." She hugged me and pressed her face to my neck. "But I do, I do, I do. It's just that . . . so much has happened. Sometimes I feel I've failed completely."

She looked at me and grabbed my hands. I knew she wanted my reassurance, but I couldn't find anything to say.

"It's been my fault," she said. "Don't think that I don't know. But I've been so unhappy. You know, when you're unhappy you have no strength left to take care of others. But it doesn't mean you don't love them."

She pointed with her chin toward the door, and her gaze hardened.

"*He* is the biggest mistake I ever made, but I couldn't see it at the time. You'll understand me when you're older. Then you'll see how men can blind you. And I mean *blind* you. To the point that you're no longer yourself."

"I know that already," I said calmly. I wanted to believe her and sympathize, but I couldn't help feeling she was doing her drama-queen number on me.

"I know I made a mistake, Alina," she whispered, "and I know that you and Isabella haven't forgiven me for it. I wish I could just push a button and go back to the time before he came into our lives. To just the three of us."

"But you *can't* just push a button," I said, and I felt angry again. What was she doing, curled up on my bed, talking about pushing buttons? Wasn't she ever going to turn into a dependable human being, accountable for her actions? Or was this going to go on forever—her making all the mistakes, then her crying and begging for forgiveness?

"But one day you will," she said.

"What?"

"Forgive me. Because you'll understand me. And you'll see that I have always loved you. More than anything else I've ever had."

I felt tired. I wanted her to go away.

"Go to sleep now, Mamma," I said and I patted her shoulder. "You look so tired. Don't worry about it. It's all right, I love you, too."

Alba's own personal concept of motherhood. Hang in there. Stick around. One day they'll make the same mistakes you made, and you'll be buddies again. You'll see, they'll come back to you.

CHAPTER FIVE

A ring of tiny flags crowns the new Gulliver Supermarket, an imposing blue shoe box that sits on the highway just outside Tricase. They're flapping madly in the breeze, but they're drowned out by the pop music blaring from a bank of speakers. Everyone from the area has gathered for the grand opening. The lot is crowded with muddy pickups, battered trucks, old Fiats. I am watching the trail of matrons in flowery frocks as they march up to get a shopping cart. They each grab one and pull it out, then push it carefully, respectfully toward the entrance with the most intent expressions—almost religious. The husbands, middle-aged farmers in their Sunday clothes, follow them, two steps behind, with a mix of awe and discomfort, as the automatic sliding doors open and swallow them, one couple at a time.

Inside, amid the confusion of gaudy colors, ugly ads, cheap graphics, and bright fluorescent lights, I recognize many of the faces I see floating down the aisles with enraptured smiles. I watch their weathered faces, wrinkled by too many years in the sun, their hands hardened by farming, as they study a box of chocolate-flavored cereals, a jar of low-fat mayonnaise, a can of lemon or strawberry iced tea. I see their eyes twinkle: this is such an improvement in their lives, to have access at last to all the stuff everyone else has, all the stuff they've seen on TV. They can stack it in their cupboards and refrigerators now and feel part of the larger world.

It feels like light years away, that time when Stellario thought of the rest of the world—the space that stretched beyond his trees and goats—as a vast, useless place where people did things that didn't make a difference to him.

"Alina!" I hear someone call my name and turn around. I see a big man in a pale-blue uniform come over to me, waving.

"Ntoni! I didn't even recognize you under that hat. What's this you're wearing?"

Ntoni is the youngest of Stellario and Celeste's sons. He must be in his forties now, a stocky man like his father—same blue eyes, same broad smile. He shakes my hand vigorously.

"I'm working security here," he tells me and pats his right hip. I see a kind of old-fashioned gun stuck in his belt. He looks proud, like someone in a costume who has just won a prize.

"Wow," I say, "is it loaded?"

"Of course." He laughs. "This is the real thing."

Suddenly I have this urge to run away. I hate to see how childish they all look now, these people who all once seemed like oaks to me.

"The *Baronessa* is here," says Ntoni. "I saw her this morning at the Caffè Sport. She was asking about you."

The *Baronessa* is Rita, of course. Out of respect for the Sanguedolce family, here in her homeland nobody dared bat an eye when she showed up as a woman. If they whispered behind her back, all they had to do in public to acknowledge the change was to add an "a" at the end of her title.

"Is she? I'll give her a call." I glance at my wristwatch. "I must go now, Ntoni, I've got so much to do."

"Okay, give my regards to your mother. When is she coming?"

"I don't know, she's busy."

He looks genuinely surprised.

"You mean she's not coming to say goodbye? To close the door of her own house?"

"I think . . . I think she's"—and I realize I don't know what to say, so I throw my hands up in the air. "You know what she's like, right?"

When I get home I find a message from Rita on the answering machine.

"Alina, I'm here, I've come to see my sisters. Alba told me you are still here packing. Honey, I was thinking of coming over for dinner tonight if you still have a working kitchen. Otherwise we can go have a bite somewhere. Actually I was thinking of spending the night at Casa Rossa, if that's all right with you." She lowers her voice and chuckles. "You know how I always underestimate the effect my so-called ancestral home has on me. See you around eight, my love?"

This is wonderful, to have Baroness Rita Sanguedolce over. She loves to hate this place. She can't say enough bad things about it. Provincial, hopeless, stifling, you name it. She's adamant on keeping a negative attitude about life in the country.

I need her sarcasm in order to squeeze the spleen out of this move.

In the seventies, Beniamino enjoyed great success as Rita.

He was the first Italian to undergo a sex-change operation and turn legally into a woman. As such, Rita became quite a celebrity. She began to appear on controversial TV talk shows—in blond curls, fake eyelashes, and miniskirts—where she would describe her calling as a woman from an early age. Throughout the years, her makeup became more subdued, her skirts longer. She ended up with bifocal lenses and a Glenda Jackson haircut, decked out in faux Chanel, and in the end everyone forgot she had even been another gender. This dignified, handsome woman had turned into a committed militant who fought on behalf of every minority group on the planet.

First it had been the consuming campaign for divorce, then came abortion, and after that gay rights. She crusaded for freedom of speech, the liberalization of drug laws, for pornography and against child abuse, and was devising how to create a union and a pension plan for prostitutes.

Hookers loved the idea of being championed by such a prim and austere-looking aunt on TV. It was a dream come true: respectability without hypocrisy. Soon enough the streets at night were full of Brazilian transvestites dressed up as Rita clones, haircut and glasses included.

But to Isabella and me, Rita had always just been family.

We had grown up seeing her come around the house, bringing chocolate eclairs for Sunday lunch. She and Alba talked on the phone at least once a week, exchanged birthday presents; Rita always sat at the head of the table at our Christmas Eve dinner. The fact that she had once been a man was a total abstraction. To us, she was our delightful frumpy aunt with a satchel full of causes.

She marches into the house, a chubbier version of Queen Elizabeth II, clutching a light-blue handbag to her chest and clad in one of her brightly colored woolly *tailleurs*.

"Holy Jesus, what chaos," she sighs, taking a look around what used to be the kitchen and is now a messy stack of boxes. "I guess we'll have to eat out."

Then she starts pacing, holding her wineglass like a scepter.

"I envy you, believe me. I wish we could get rid of that hideous palazzo. What a relief that would be!"

"Do you really mean it?"

"Are you kidding? It's the gloomiest place on earth. They handed it down for four hundred years, and each generation kept adding more ugly stuff. I mean, you can't imagine the clutter. And look at my sisters now. They sit in these rooms without a purpose. Just holding on to what they own. It's pathetic."

She shakes her head and gulps down the wine.

She holds her glass out as I pour more into it. I notice how her teeth are smudged with red lipstick. There's always at least one detail in Rita that reveals her imperfection. She somehow keeps just missing the mark.

"I mean, did you see that horrid supermarket?" she asks with a frown.

"Mm-hm."

"There you go. Eventually Domenico's store will have to close down. That'll be the end of buying your groceries and having a proper chat. You know? That hello, good morning, how's the weather, who's getting married, who's gotten sick, and so forth—it's the end of village life. *Basta,* it's over."

Later, in the car as we are heading to the restaurant in the piazza, she can't help herself.

"You'll feel so much lighter once you move out of this place. Too much has happened here. Casa Rossa has turned into an albatross for all of you. Let me tell you, nobody knows better than me."

I know Rita is right. And I think I know why she's so relieved we're leaving this house. She can't get over the fact that she played a big part in what happened later on, right here. I know she feels guilty for being in such denial at a time when she was so close to Isabella and knew exactly what was going on. And did nothing to prevent it from happening.

That albatross belongs to her as well.

It was March '78, still early in the morning. Tomas and I were asleep. I had cut school and gone to see him. We had gone straight to his bed and had sex, then he rolled a thick joint. The sirens woke us. It sounded as if the whole city were on fire. Helicopters started hovering over the center of the city with a menacing sound. Tomas jumped out of bed.

"This is bad. Sounds like a bomb exploded or something."

He switched on the radio in the next room. I detected an anxious tone in the voice of the newscaster.

I heard Tomas mumble, "Holy shit!"

"What is it?"

I sat up and tried to listen. I made out "Red Brigades . . . prime minister . . . Aldo Moro . . . bloodbath . . ."

I heard him turn the television on and I ran into the living room. We were both standing naked in front of the screen now. The anchorman looked shocked, on the verge of tears.

"They kidnapped Moro," Tomas said slowly, without taking his eyes from the screen. "Killed his escort . . . it's fucking crazy."

The city was under siege, the sirens kept screaming, their wails crossing one another incessantly. Then an eerie silence descended. A stunned, ominous silence.

In the early seventies the Red Brigades staged some astonishing kidnappings: they had seized and then released—after a brief "proletarian trial"—a right-wing union secretary, the personnel director of Fiat, a director of Alfa Romeo. The student movement regarded this clandestine group with admiration and enthusiasm: in the eyes of the students, and of the extreme left, the Red Brigades were Robin Hoods, and their actions symbolized proletarian justice. But by the mid-seventies the group's activities were becoming more and more brutal: first they had taken to shooting dozen of industrialists and politicians in the legs; then they started to bomb police stations. Eventually, in 1976, they were assassinating judges, police officers, journalists. Every day in the papers there was a photograph of a body lying on the ground, a pool of blood beside it. Many among the left-wing militants strongly opposed their adoption of violence as a tactic. The "revolutionary" movement was now split in two: there were those who were committed to following the Red Brigades' example to "take the struggle to the military level" and those who flatly opposed the use of arms.

Now the Red Brigades' campaign of terror had reached its zenith: Aldo Moro, twice our prime minister, was an untouchable, one of the most powerful men in the government.

"I'd better go home," I said and quickly put on my dress, then searched for my underwear under the bed and collected my schoolbooks. Tomas nodded vaguely and started rolling another joint, crosslegged, stark naked, his eyes fixed on the news.

At home I found Alba in front of the television, too. She was still in her nightgown.

"Thank God you're back. Did they close the school down?" she asked. "This is just too horrible."

"What, are you crying?"

"Well, yes. I'm . . . I'm shocked," she said, wiping her eyes.

I didn't know what to feel. In my recent militant past, I had always identified Moro, the leader of the Christian Democrats, as one of our main enemies. But suddenly, seeing his photo on the screen, his famous white hair streak that had been so widely caricatured, his poised stance, and his conservative gray suit, he just looked like an old-fashioned professor. A frail, pedantic man who goes to church every morning. I saw the footage of the aftermath. The car windows shattered to pieces. Blood on the seats. The photos of Moro's bodyguards, who had been machine-gunned in the attack. Only three hours earlier, when I was ringing Tomas's doorbell, they had all been alive.

I felt something cold catch me in the chest. This was not another step in the escalation of violence: this was a full-scale declaration of war.

A couple of days later I came home and found Isabella rummaging through her closet in what used to be our bedroom, lots of bulging plastic bags lined up on the floor. I hadn't seen her in a couple of months at least. For a split second I thought she had come back to live with us.

"There are police blockades everywhere," she said. "They are really freaking out big time."

"Of course there are. After what happened."

She turned to me with a grin.

"They got that pig. It's fucking amazing, isn't it?"

I stared at her, unable to answer.

"The whole world is talking about it," she went on. "They just can't figure out how they did it. Flawless military action. Pretty cool, isn't it?"

"Yes. It's unbelievable." I paused, then asked her, "How come you're here?" I was anxious to get off the subject.

"I've come to collect the rest of my stuff," she said. "We're moving into another apartment."

She looked pale, thin. Where was she eating these days?

"Who is *we*? You and Enrico?" I asked.

"Yes. Rita found us a place."

"Rita did? And where is it?"

"Across from her, same landing. It's only a one-bedroom, it belonged to a friend of hers who used it as . . ." She smiled, somehow proudly. "It was a call girl's pied-à-terre. Apparently the whole building is like that. Hookers' Colony, they call it. But I don't mind."

She stopped doing whatever she was doing and lit a cigarette. It had been so long since the two of us had had a talk in our bedroom. She squinted as she pulled a drag and gave me a hard look. I, too, had changed. I had taken to wearing her vintage clothes, dangling earrings, had lots of bangles around my wrists.

"You look pretty," she said quickly.

"Thanks."

"You can come and see me, if you feel like," she said, then turned her back to me again and started stuffing thick sweaters in the plastic bags. "It's a long way, though. Three buses."

She didn't sound exactly encouraging, but I had missed her badly. I wanted us to be close again. So I made the trip, a week later.

It took me hours to get there, till the strawberry ice cream I had bought began to melt and started dripping on my lap. The bus struggled through unknown parts of town. Ugly apartment buildings, hideous architecture, sad shops. Even the passengers on the bus got sadder and grayer as we got closer to Isabella's new neighborhood.

Hookers' Colony was in a new so-called residential area, built on the model of a cheap suburban condo. It had ugly little balconies with curly Spanish-looking balustrades and arched windows. *Zorro* had definitely been a major inspiration in the design, at least judging from the amount of black wrought-iron fixtures, the uneven plastered walls, and the terra-cotta Mexican-style floors. Inside, the lobby smelled of damp, the carpets were stained; plastic ivy vines were covered in a thick layer of dust.

"Isn't this just great?" Rita greeted me from her wide-open door. "Come, you must come and meet Maurizio. He's making lasagna. Your sister is taking a shower at my place, she'll be ready in a minute."

Maurizio lived on the same landing, between Isabella and Rita. The brass plate on his door read "Clairvoyant, Astrologer, and Tarot Reader." He was in his late fifties and hugely overweight. His hair was dyed a raven black, and he perspired profusely. He was wearing an apron that had the headless naked body of a woman sprawled across it.

His tiny flat was all trinkets, plastic Buddhas sitting on top of the television, oversized Spanish paper fans on the walls, lacy curtains, and plastic flower arrangements. He showed me the round table covered in black brocade where he read his deck of tarot cards, did charts, and called spirits from the "other side," as he called it, for his séances.

"I have some very important clients who talk to their dead relatives through me," Maurizio said, holding the pan of lasagna he had just extracted from the kitchenette's oven. "People who died suddenly, carrying some pretty big secrets to the other side. If you only knew the sort of heavyweights that show up at this table. The things I come to know.

Unbelievable stuff. I could write a book that would turn this country upside down, sweetheart."

"Tell her the story about the guy from the Vatican Bank," Rita said.

"Rita!" Maurizio feigned reproach, but was thrilled to be in the spotlight. "Are you indiscreet or what?"

He winked at me.

"What do you expect? She's a Libra with the moon in Gemini. They'll betray you for a plate of fries."

Then I was dragged to inspect Rita's flat. Her identical living room cum kitchenette was so cluttered with papers, magazines, books, one could hardly move through it. On a small table, next to the couch, I noticed some photographs framed in silver. Rita's mother, the Baroness Alearda Sanguedolce as a young girl in a very elaborate evening dress, looking like a film star from the forties. A black-and-white photo of all the Sanguedolce children on the beach right after the war: the five sisters and Rita—still Beniamino, a fat, curly-haired, boisterous little boy. The bedroom had a rather sumptuous four-poster bed covered in fake fur, a cheap Japanese screen, and a large gilt-framed mirror opposite the bed.

"This is where I work," she explained, "so I have to keep it traditional. A sort of Shanghai meets Madame Pompadour kind of thing. They have to smell sin in order to come."

She poked me in the ribs with a naughty expression.

"And you want them to come as quickly as possible, believe me."

Maurizio was laughing hysterically, but I was beginning to feel awkward, if not depressed.

Isabella appeared from the bathroom, a towel wrapped around her head.

"Oh, you're here," she said without smiling. "Food will be ready in five minutes. But we need to borrow a table and Maurizio's chairs."

Enrico came in and helped us move table and chairs, hardly acknowledging me. I took in his unwashed, stringy hair, his pasty complexion, and the particularly ugly handknit scarf he wore around his neck. He looked like a ravenous mouse and smelled of nicotine.

Their flat was essentially empty. There was no furniture to speak of. Only books on the floor and a couple of cardboard boxes. It was much colder than Rita's or Maurizio's, as if it had no heating. As if it had no life at all. Isa didn't seem to have plans to improve the decor.

"It looks a bit bare in here," she declared, "but we only come here to sleep."

I glanced at a stack of leaflets that filled a cardboard box. I rapidly scanned the first paragraph: *". . . the imperialist use of mass revisionism in a neofascist way mobilizes the masses and places them at the service of the State apparatus. The Communist Party has turned into an informer's network and an anti-left thug army."*

I turned my eyes away, wearily.

We all sat down, pretending to feel comfortable and cheerful. Enrico didn't say a word. He kept studying me, as if I were the enemy he had been hearing about and needed to devise a strategy fast. He was one of those people whose tactic is to hold back and let the other make the first move. But I knew better. I tried to be as passive as possible.

Isabella wasn't particularly friendly, either. She looked bored, as if she were sitting at someone else's dinner table and was planning on going home early. I couldn't help wonder why we were having this dinner at all. At one point both she and Enrico disappeared into the other room.

"I think they had a fight earlier on," said Rita.

"He's weird," I said.

"He's very . . . strict," Rita conceded.

"A bit in the extreme, if I may," added Maurizio.

"What do you mean, 'strict'? Strict about what?" I asked.

"Well, you know. He's very committed," Rita said somewhat cautiously.

"He goes out at four in the morning in order to get to the factory gates by six-thirty. To hand out leaflets," Maurizio whispered, with a mix of awe and fear, "or just talk politics to the workers."

"So what is it they fight about?" I asked. "Ho Chi Minh?"

"Possibly," Rita shrugged. "More likely than sex, that's for sure."

"Sex?" said Maurizio. "I mean, *please,* not if you have to wake up at four in the morning."

The idea of that ratty man having sex with my sister in that single bed made me nauseous. The squalid flat, the bad wine, the stale stench of cigarettes, the bags under her eyes. Her sullen expression. Could that be love? There was no happiness there, that much I could tell.

We waited a bit longer, and then, as they still hadn't come back, we cleared the table and went to Maurizio's to watch a pop-music show on television. Both he and Rita knew all the songs by heart and sang along, discussing everyone's outfit thoroughly. At some point Isabella and Enrico reappeared, as if they had been gone only five minutes and didn't need to explain.

"I must go to bed," Isabella said, yawning. "I have to get up very early tomorrow. Thanks for coming."

She kissed me, fleetingly, on the cheek. Her chapped lips felt rough. I hugged her and she let me hold her a second longer. But she didn't look at me as she moved away. Enrico gave a vague nod, without a sound. I felt too exhausted to take three buses to go home, so I asked Rita if I could spend the night on her couch.

It was still dark when I heard the door across the hall slam, it must have been before five. I heard their voices on the landing, Isabella coughing, and then, a couple of minutes later, the engine of a Vespa starting in the street below.

It must be freezing, I thought, and I pictured the two of them, holding on to each other against the cold wind with those long knitted scarves around their necks. Could that be love, I asked myself again. No, to me it felt more like punishment.

"Here, lick this one," said Tomas.

"Which one?" I asked.

"Mickey Mouse."

What a concept. Acid disguised as a cartoon character. I stuck my tongue out and Tomas placed the paper square on it.

"Good girl." He grinned. "That's the way to go."

We were sitting on his unmade bed, on a Sunday afternoon. I watched him, in trepidation, lick his Snow White portion. I looked at my watch. Two-fifteen.

"We're off."

"It'll take a while," he said.

I was nervous: I had heard so many stories about acid. Pretty frightening tales, mostly. People who had lost their minds, nearly killed themselves because of a bad trip. It was a catalogue of nightmares, the outcome of other people's acid trips.

"It's as if your head splits up into a thousand brains, and each one is working parallel to the others," Tomas had told me once. "It's pretty intense."

I wasn't sure I was going to like it, but I knew this was an inescapable test. Tomas wasn't going to hang out with some kid who had no balls to take LSD.

"Don't worry, you're going to be fine. You're with me," he'd said when he announced we were going to drop acid together. "I'll guide you."

Somehow I wasn't so confident he would.

During the next forty minutes, I kept checking for signs, for something to tell me this thing had started to do its job, but I felt absolutely nothing new.

"Don't be nervous," Tomas said, lying on his bed, a cigarette dangling from the corner of his mouth. "You'll know when it hits you. You'll know for sure, baby."

"Are you feeling anything?" I asked him.

"Beginning to."

That made me restless: I couldn't stand the idea of being left behind. I wanted to be right there beside him with all my thousand brains at work.

"I need to get something sweet at the corner," I said. My automatic reaction: seek refuge in something else as soon as I sensed any form of distance between us.

"Come on. Just sit here. It's going to hit you, I promise."

"I'll be right back. Really. It'll just take me a second."

I took the elevator down and out on the street. The light was blinding and it made my skin feel prickly. I walked into the café on the corner and looked at the ice cream counter. The colors seemed exceedingly bright.

Then it hit me like a club, in the back of my neck. I felt the heat spreading into my blood vessels, tingling, prickling into every nerve. I raised my eyes and met the eyes of the girl behind the counter who was wearing a bright-red uniform and holding an ice cream cone like it was a gun.

"What flavor?" she asked in a strangely metallic voice.

The red of her uniform was so thick, so dense, so unbelievably red it hurt my eyes. Every particle of the fabric seemed to have been drenched in a solution of pure red that had the depth of an ocean. One could dive into it, drown in it, and never reemerge. I looked away and lowered my gaze, slowly, hoping she wouldn't notice.

The yellows, the acid greens, the fluorescent pinks of the ice cream flavors barked at me like angry dogs. Chemical, monstrous, poisonous colors.

"No, thanks," I said, "I'll . . ."

I could hear every sound in the café, the spoons tinkling in the espresso cups, the steam hissing from the mocha machine, the buzzing of the refrigerator, as if each one of them was on a separate Sensurround soundtrack.

I ran out into the street, and the sky had gone silver. It felt scary to be without a roof over my head. So much atmosphere, too much air.

Back in the building, I ran for the elevator.

Mistake.

The tiny wooden box immediately closed in on me like a coffin, pressing on my lungs. The graffiti scratched on its walls said things I couldn't understand. These must be messages they left before they died in here, I thought. Before they ran out of air. I had to persuade myself this was an elevator and that it was actually going to take me up to the fourth floor, but I could hardly believe it ever would.

"Breathe," I said out loud, "and don't scream. You need the air."

I lost track of where I was and where I was going.

Tomas, Tomas.

I knew I had lost him, and I had a very slim chance of finding him again. Finally, after what felt like an hour, the elevator stopped and I got out of the coffin. I rang the door and when it opened I felt like I had been hit in the face by a ton of water flooding out of the apartment.

Tomas looked totally different from when I had last seen him.

"Hi, babe," he said, "you were gone for ages."

(When? Where had I been? Why was I there?)

I could tell that he, too, could turn into something scary, unless I did something, and fast.

"Are you feeling it?" he asked.

This is Tomas. You know Tomas, he's your friend.

"What is it? Are you all right?" I heard him say in slow motion.

I knew he had seen my fear. It was written all over my face. The terrible thing is that I knew this was never going to stop. The way I was seeing things now was how the world *really* was. This is how his room *really* looked: sordid, dirty, shabby. The crumpled sheets on the bed, the bare lightbulb hanging from the ceiling, the dishes in the sink.

"Are you all right?" he said again, and put a hand on my head.

I couldn't answer, because I knew that if I named my fear, it would grow a thousand times bigger and would wipe him out, the only relatively familiar figure left in this terrifying picture. My fear was like a giant vacuum cleaner that could suck me in.

"Come, baby."

He dragged me onto the bed. I didn't like lying on those dirty sheets.

Air.

"Let's get out," I whispered. "This is . . . too much."

"What?"

"Let's walk," I said very slowly. "I think we should walk. Now."

"What a great idea," Tomas said. He was having a good time.

We walked outside and the world was restored. The sky was lavender, and we both looked up at the same time, just as an airplane ripped the immaculate lavender pool with a white trail of foam. It exploded in slow motion into a bubbly tread. It was simply amazing.

"It's fine, babe. It's going to be fine. I told you," he said. I knew he meant it now.

We walked into the Botanical Garden.

How could we have been so foolish to think of green as only one color?

We got lost in the intricate design of leaves. The pattern of their veins was the same as the one on the back of our hands; there was no difference in the way they pumped chlorophyll and we pumped blood.

We sat under a gigantic oak. Soon we could hear the whole park creak, rustle, squeak. We listened as the seeds sprouted, buds popped, sap surged, leaves unfolded, flowers bloomed, branches stretched, roots pushed and blasted rocks underground. We couldn't believe the intricacies of the overlapping sounds. This was some genius symphony.

"We have to come back with a tape recorder," I whispered. "This is too unbelievable."

"You won't be able to hear it later," said Tomas.

Then he turned to me slowly. He gently pulled me down on the grass and lay on top of me. His body was warm, I could feel his blood streaming under his skin. He pulled up my skirt.

"I need to make love to you, *now*," he said.

I looked up at the oak's canopy against the sky while he slid inside me. Yes, this is what making love was really about.

Veins, blood, sperm, sap, pollen, lymph, chlorophyll. Seeds. It was all the same, we were all part of the same system.

He came inside me and I could feel the seed he left there. I saw it unfold, grow, take shape. I saw the whole thing in slow motion, as it would look in a documentary, with some great classical music score. The tiny baby floating in the womb, turning around slowly, his—or her?—head the shape of a bean sprout.

"Wow," I said and took a very deep breath.

I had just got the point of the whole thing.

Coming down was an interesting part. It was like seeing Planet Earth approaching after a long journey in the galaxy. We headed back slowly, strangely relaxed. I felt tired, like my body had been a hundred different places and was coming back in bits and pieces, not all of them on the same schedule.

When I finally got home that night, I had lost all sense of time. I found Alba stretched on the couch, reading a book in her nightgown, under an extremely yellow light that pulsated like a heartbeat.

I sensed that she had been waiting for me. I could almost touch her loneliness, it filled the room like a scented vapor.

"Hey," she said, pushing the book away gently, "where have you been?"

I curled up on the pillows next to her.

"Hanging out with Tomas," I said, stretching my neck and arms like a cat. "Had a wonderful day."

I could feel my body still giving off sparks, like fireworks dimming in the night. She must have sensed the faint trail of lights around me, because she smiled.

"It shows." She brushed my hair with her fingertips. "You look so pretty. So alive."

Then she pulled herself up and sat straight, shaking her head as if to shake off her mood.

"Tell me, what was so wonderful about your day?"

Suddenly I saw something new in her, something I had never understood before. Her breasts and hips and mouth were round and full again, her colors were intense, her eyes shining. It was something strong, and raw, that she had never lost and that now I wanted her to keep. I saw her with the eyes of a man, and felt almost the same attraction they would, as if I weren't her daughter but just a pair of eyes.

I think what I saw was her selfishness, her will to survive. How it streamed through her, brightening her up, like a string of Christmas lights. It was exactly that selfish will that had pushed her to mate, reproduce, give birth, survive, be my mother. I saw it in her, as a scientist would see the will of a cheetah, and I realized I wanted her to cherish it and like herself the way she was.

Nature, it dawned on me, can be cruel, but it makes no miscalculations. Alba, therefore, must be a perfect mechanism just the way she was. The trick was to have faith in that—in her.

This drug, I saw, was like a laser beam that cut through all the unnecessary complications.

Tomas and drugs. Neither was ever as good as the first time. But I kept at them, hoping they would surprise me again.

Tomas fed me all sorts of pills, pot, hash, then he switched to powders, all paid for with the money his father sent him from the States so he could be a choreographer and not have to worry about the bills.

We constantly increased our doses, tried different combinations, switched to new dealers, always in the vain hope of achieving the chemical satori. We began spending more and more time indoors, indifferent to the changes in the weather, oblivious to the crisp morning air, either dozing off or jabbering away all night, depending on what we were high on, waiting for the phone to ring or the drugs to come, eating erratically and taking baths at the oddest hours.

But it was never that good again.

I never saw things so clearly as that first time under the oaks. In fact, what happened after that felt more like getting used to a fog.

I took my final exams in high school on a cocktail of speed and painkillers. Several professors listened gravely to my tirade on the Industrial Revolution and on Pier Paolo Pasolini's body of work. They mistook my high for exuberance and thought me a passionate student. When I blanked on a couple of questions, they thought me wired from too many sleepless nights and forgave my temporary loss of memory. I passed with pretty high marks, and at the time it didn't even strike me as lucky how I had managed to fool them: I felt invincible with all those chemicals dancing around in my body.

Alba watched me come and go, growing thinner and paler, more and more secretive about my wanderings. We both agreed I was looking so bad because of keeping late hours for school. After the last exam I blamed the weather.

"Can't sleep or eat in this heat," I said when she asked what was wrong with me.

She packed up to go to Casa Rossa for the summer, leaving Bruno in the city. She said Lorenzo needed her, especially as Stellario and Celeste had both died, one after the other, just a few months earlier.

"Come," she asked, "you need a bit of sun. It'll do you good. And your grandfather will be so happy to spend a bit of time with you."

She was the one who needed company, I thought. She didn't want to go by herself.

All I wanted was shade, darkness, silence.

"No thanks, I love the city in August. It's the best time of the year, when it gets so empty." I couldn't come up with any better excuse.

That summer I lost track of everybody. Including myself.

In the apartment, Bruno and I crossed paths only at random moments, like perfect strangers. Without Alba, we could finally stop all pretense of being a family and act out our indifference without a shade of guilt. We never even tried to plan a meal together. We went about our own business, using the house as a laundromat, a place to wash and change, exchanging brief greetings and scribbling messages on a pad by the phone. He was seeing other women—I heard their cautious voices on the machine—and he probably listened to Tomas's poorly coded messages about his drug score of the day.

I asked Bruno for money now and again, and he never inquired what it was for. We performed this transaction always in a hurry, by the door, without looking one another in the eye, as if it were a bribe we were both ashamed of. Whenever I felt I couldn't ask for more cash, I slipped a few bills out of his wallet when he wasn't watching.

It didn't feel like stealing, more like taking something I needed.

Nothing felt wrong or illicit in those days. I never had a sense that I was sliding down the wrong direction. Heroin made everything acceptable and smooth.

Tomas and I had started to smoke it, then we began to snort it. It was better than anything else I had ever tried before. It was soft, warm, it smoothed the edges. It made me curl up like a baby floating on feathers. Sometimes, if it was too strong, I got sick and had to throw up immediately, but even the nausea was delicious. Nothing could touch me or rip the film between me and reality.

Alba came back from Casa Rossa in September. She was tanned and had gained a little weight. I was green in the face and my ribcage stuck out.

"I hear you've hardly spent a night in this house," she said dryly. I could tell she was feeling resentful. Maybe it was the prospect of having to face another gloomy winter with Bruno. She had had the whole summer to ponder her life so far. The result must have been pretty unsatisfactory, and here she was, back, and full of angry claims.

I shrugged. She didn't even register. She couldn't have said or done a single thing to upset me, wrapped as I was in that invisible film of indifference.

"Alina, it's me." Isabella's voice over the phone sounded rushed. "I need to ask you a favor."

"What is it?" I could hear the sound of traffic in the background. She must be calling from a phone booth.

"Can you meet me tomorrow at the train station? Track twelve, at six?"

"What happened?"

"Nothing. I'll tell you when I see you."

Something in her voice sounded alarming. As if someone was pressing a gun to her temple."

"Okay," I said.

The phone call made me strangely anxious. I hadn't heard from her in months. Now this. It didn't sound good, that much I could tell. Before getting on the bus to the station, I quickly snorted a line of heroin. It shut me off immediately. I went to meet her as if I were sealed in an airtight bag.

The Termini station smelled of urine and stale sweat. As I walked under the high, pitched ceiling of the main hall, the departure announcements echoing gloomily throughout the length of the place, I felt an overwhelming wave of nausea: my forehead was covered in a cold sweat and I felt like throwing up. I didn't like the idea of seeing my sister—and there, of all places. The interior of the station was squalid, its gray concrete pillars streaked with dirt, the old linoleum peeling off the floor. And so many of the people crowding it looked sad, seedy, or just lost.

Isabella was waiting at the front of the platform. She looked weird.

Her hair was cut short, without a shape, as if she had chopped it herself. But what was even stranger was the way she was dressed. She was wearing a gray two-piece suit with a skirt that fell below her knee and see-through nylons with flat brown shoes. And she had a black fake-leather handbag strapped across her shoulder.

"Hi," I said. "Jesus, you look strange."

She obviously didn't care for my little remark because she gave me one of her hard stares and didn't kiss me.

"You're fifteen minutes late."

Travelers with suitcases were rushing onto the platform, pushing past us to catch their trains.

"So, what is this all about?"

"I'll tell you. Let's go over there." She pointed at a plastic bench in the midst of the crowd.

"Can't we go somewhere quieter?" I asked.

"I don't have a lot of time," she said, frowning. "But . . . okay. Somewhere close, though."

I followed her out of the station. We sat inside a brightly colored fast-food place across the square. There were giant photos of pizza slices and melting cheese plastered on the wall. It was deserted, except for two Polish-looking men drinking milk shakes in silence. Isabella bought us two Cokes and a basket of fries.

"It's ages since I saw you," I said, feigning lightheartedness. "What have you been up to?"

"Not much." She looked carefully into the paper basket and selected a fry. "The usual."

I realized I didn't even know how she was surviving, if she had a job, how she and Enrico managed to pay the rent.

"Have some," she said, licking ketchup off her fingertips.

"No thanks."

"You look skinny. How come you've lost so much weight?"

"I'm not very hungry lately, that's all."

She looked at me, squinting slightly, as if she didn't particularly trust me. I could tell she wanted to get to the point.

"This is strictly between you and me," she warned. "I want your word."

"You have it," I said, but her attitude was beginning to irritate me. "Come on, Isabella, what's this about, anyway? Why are you dressed like a flight atten—"

"Sshh! Keep your voice down, you're screaming."

"I'm not."

"Yes you are."

Then she said quickly, lowering her voice, "I need you to do me a little favor."

"So you said. What is it?"

"I want you to buy something for me. I'll give you the money."

"What sort of thing?" I asked cautiously.

She put her plastic handbag on the table and unzipped it. She started fumbling inside and pulled out a wad of cash. I don't believe this, I thought. Don't tell me this is about drugs.

"Something stupid," she said and stretched her lips in a fake attempt to smile. "A wig."

"A *what*?"

"See that place across the street on the corner that says 'Antoine'? There is a dark-brown wig with long hair in the window. Try it on, as if it's for you. Then buy it."

I went silent.

"A wig? Why don't you go and buy it yourself?" I said.

"I wouldn't ask you to do it if I didn't have a reason, would I?" She pushed the money across the table toward me.

"Wait, wait . . ." I placed my hand on hers and stopped her. "I don't think I'm getting this."

"You don't have to *get it*."

I stared at her. Although nothing could really touch me, I felt a coldness like water swell inside me. A draft from a window giving me a chill. I wouldn't let go of her hand on the table.

"But why do you need a wig?" I heard my voice slur slightly. It had a muffled sound, like the rest of me.

"Don't ask questions. Just do it."

I could tell she hated to have to do this. To beg me.

I shook my head.

"This is too weird, Isa."

I pushed her hand with the money away.

"I don't like what this is for."

"You don't *know* what this is for." Her eyes had turned cold. She looked so much uglier than she was, in her sad, proper outfit.

"I doubt you want a wig just for the fun of it," I said.

"Why not?"

"Fun doesn't seem to be one of your priorities, if you ask me," I said, forcing a smile.

"So you are not going to do this?"

I shook my head again.

"I didn't say that. I just want to understand what you're going to do with—"

"Oh, shut up already!" she cut me off, shoving the money back into her bulky black leather bag. "I don't need to discuss this. I knew you were going to be useless."

Right. I wasn't being *useful*. She couldn't *use* anything I had to offer.

"And stop rubbing your nose!" she snapped.

My eyelids felt incredibly heavy, I was struggling to keep them open.

"You're stoned," she said. "Look at you. I can't fucking believe it."

"I'm *not* . . . ," I stumbled, "what are you—"

"For God's sake"—she gave a short, shrill laugh—"who do you think you're fooling?"

"I had to take a very strong painkiller after the dentist and I'm feeling a little groggy. All right?"

I saw her clutch her bag and stand up. Her chair screeched.

"You look pathetic. But it doesn't surprise me one bit to see you like this. Typical you—to choose anesthesia over facing the truth."

Her words didn't touch me. They rolled on the floor like droplets of rain off a water-repellent surface. She didn't even irritate me. Yet another me, trapped inside somewhere, was kicking to rip the airtight bag open and come out. I watched that other me trying to tear the plastic, but I couldn't do anything to help.

Then I saw her march off like a Prussian officer toward the glass door in her gray uniform, dripping anger, judgment, disgust. I ran after her and clutched her arm as she was pulling the door open.

"Wait."

I feared somehow that I would never see her again. That this was to be our last chance to warn one another. We both knew this, of course. Otherwise why did she choose to ask me—of all people—to buy a wig, and why did I make sure to show up stoned? Wasn't the purpose of this meeting to inform each other of the path the other one had taken? And weren't we supposed to be stopping one another before the road fell away?

"Wait!" I shouted again. In slow motion I saw my hand pull her shoulder toward me, her face turning slowly, hair swaying, eyes widening.

I knew I only had a second, but I felt sick again. I pressed a hand on my mouth, feeling my blood drain to my ankles and a wave of nausea choke me.

"What?" she said slowly, her voice echoing.

"Don't go. Let's talk. Please." I wiped my mouth with the back of my hand. "Sorry about this. I'm not feeling too well."

"I'm not talking to you in the state you're in. You're completely fucked up."

"No I'm not," I insisted.

"Get a life, Alina."

She pushed me away and slipped out the door. She disappeared instantly in the grayness, like a chameleon on a branch, her ugly suit fading into the drab crowd outside the train station—a sea of faceless people, just bodies pushing and struggling in the dim light of a winter afternoon.

I walked out and made my way through the crowd. I felt as if all the beauty in our lives had been killed, forever. And we both had been responsible for murdering it.

I couldn't weep because of the plastic film still wrapped around my heart. I felt like crying for not being able to cry and not being able to run after her. Instead I retched again on the corner of the street till my eyes finally had tears in them. I looked up and saw a Nigerian hawker selling cheap sunglasses give me a knowing look.

To him I was just another junkie.

Tomas lay in bed, not knowing which day of the week it was, nor what time of day. By then he had pretty much lost his looks: he was too thin, his complexion had turned pasty, his hair greasy and limp. He hadn't been working for a while.

As I walked into the room he started dialing a number on the phone and didn't even acknowledge me.

"Where the fuck is he?" he yelled to the wall, slamming the receiver down after many rings. I knew he was trying Carlo, our latest supplier.

"He's not picking up. I bet he's too fucked up to hear the phone. Jerk."

I said nothing and looked around the room. Everything looked stale and hopeless. The blackened tinfoil on which we burned and smoked the brown sugar, the stinking ashtrays, the dirty clothes on the floor.

"Do you have anything on you?" he asked.

I shook my head and collapsed next to him.

"Christ, look at you," he snarled. "You're as high as a kite!"

"There was only a tiny line left," I said.

He threw the phone on the floor and got up from the bed, cursing. I heard him rummaging in a frenzy through the bathroom cabinet.

This is what we had become: greedy, mean, either completely indifferent or ready to jump at each other's throats for a line. We no longer touched or felt like making love; feelings and physical attraction were issues of the past. We had become partners of another sort: now we shared addiction and guilt.

I knew perfectly well it was only a matter of time: shooting up was going to be the next leg of this trip, a difficult one to avoid.

I could see it looming ahead. I had seen Carlo do it many times when I was at his place to buy a gram. I hated the whole procedure, the spoon, the flame, the tourniquet, the syringe. My stomach turned every time I saw the needle go into his ravaged forearm and his blood drip.

Tomas came back from the bathroom, sipping from a cough syrup bottle. The smell was familiar and revolting at the same time.

There was no kindness in his eyes.

"You are such a little shit. I can't believe you snorted the whole thing yourself."

I didn't move. My eyes felt heavy and started closing again.

"Go to Piazza Santa Maria," I heard him say. "See if you can get some from that German guy who hangs out at the café on the corner."

"No," I said, "I'm not going anywhere. Just leave me alone."

I closed my eyes and turned my back to him. I knew this was going to be my last sleep on a cloud of warm feathers. I was going to wake up on a bed of nails in few hours. But I had made up my mind.

I heard Tomas slam the door and go out to score on his own. I curled up under the duvet and tried to picture what it was going to be like to go off smack just like that. To peel the film off and be scolded by the high temperature of all that surrounded me. To feel sad and angry again, to feel spikes, sharp corners, and claws bite into my skin once more. To bleed.

I'd like to be able to say that the whole process of getting clean was heroic and revealing, but in fact it turned out to be just sickening and depressing. My whole body ached, my skin burnt and shivered. A mere draft of air hurt like a million needles. But the agony was unenlightening, because it had no object, and there was no real redemption at the end of it. It simply led me back to square one. There was no gain, only pain, and I felt like I had learned nothing. I shut myself in the bedroom and told Alba and Bruno that I had caught a bad flu and I needed to rest. Except for the occasional knock at the door and warm soup on a tray, they didn't interfere with me too much. Whatever they had figured out about my condition, they were keeping it to themselves.

Once the physical suffering finally subsided and my body had reassembled its bits and pieces, I woke up to find out that during my one-year absence someone had broken into my psyche and had destroyed everything I had left in there. I felt like a convalescent who finally comes home from the hospital only to discover the house has been torched and is left standing among charred, unrecognizable belongings. That was the hardest part of all.

Heroin had been the raging fire in my backyard. I was eighteen and already felt like I had to start my life all over again.

I remember sitting for an entire morning in a café, watching people come and go, sip their espressos and cappuccinos at the counter, munch happily on croissants and sandwiches, leave tips on the tables, light cigarettes. Most of them came in pairs and were engrossed in conversation; nobody looked around or seemed to have time to spare. These were people who had things to do and could only take a quick break between pressing assignments. I felt that my life could no longer resemble theirs. I had no place to go, no friends to see. I felt the damage irreparable, and this realization made me almost suicidal.

The first hint of my rebirth came a few days later, when I found myself enjoying the taste of sugar in my tea. I was at home, sitting in the kitchen, and the April sun coming through the glass was warming my shoulder. The smoky tea was a dark gold in the thin china cup. I closed my fingers around it, feeling the warmth and the flavor. I opened the window and could smell something sweet in the air. The trees below were in bloom. Soon it would be Easter.

"We should buy some bulbs for the terrace. And a jasmine creeper," I said when Alba came into the kitchen.

"Funny, I was just thinking the same thing. We could go to the nursery today," Alba said and checked her wristwatch. "In fact, why don't we go right now?"

"Yes. That would be fun," I said.

We got in the car, and as she turned the ignition key, we smiled at each other, proud for having managed such a task so easily.

"I need to pick up Bruno's raincoat at the cleaners. It'll take a sec." Alba double-parked in front of the dry cleaner. "Just beep if anybody needs to get out, okay?"

"Sure."

I turned on the radio and started humming a silly song. *"Piccolo grande amore . . .tu sei un piccolo grande amore."* Suddenly there was a tap on the window. Two armed carabinieri, holding what looked like machine guns.

"Get out!" Their tone was nasty.

"Documents."

"I . . . I don't have any."

"Turn around. Raise your hands and place them up on the car . . . here."

I felt their hands pushing me hard against the car, then patting my arms, my pockets, all along my legs. One of them kicked me hard in the back of my leg. Something pressed in the middle of my back. I felt my knees weakening.

"I'm waiting . . . I'm waiting for my . . . my mother is in the—"

"Shut up!"

Then I heard Alba's voice.

"What are you doing? This is my daughter."

"Documents," the same hard voice ordered bluntly.

I didn't even dare turn my head and look at Alba. I heard her high-pitched protest as she followed one of the carabinieri over to their car. The other one kept pressing that cold thing into my back. I could feel his hatred on my neck. It seemed an eternity before they confirmed Alba's documents over the radio and decided to let me go, without apologizing. We saw them take off, tires screeching, the blue light turned on and the angry sound of a siren echoing behind them.

"This has become a police state," I said to Alba once we were back in the car. "I don't think this is constitutional. They can't just stop somebody like that and treat you like you're a criminal."

"I shouldn't have left you in the car," she said. "Young people like you look suspicious if they're sitting alone in a car these days."

The previous May, Moro had been found dead in the trunk of a car parked near the Christian Democratic Party's headquarters, his body wrapped up in a filthy blanket, like a homeless man. Italy was in shock. Almost a year later, the tension in the city was still unbearable.

"Fuck, no!" I said. "How is it I look suspicious? On what basis, excuse me? They just enjoy terrorizing people."

Alba shrugged, like she didn't want to get into the subject.

"That's just how it is now, with all that's been happening. These groups . . ."

She lowered her eyes and turned the key in the ignition.

The nursery was a big place, acres and acres of potted plants all lined in rows, cars roaring by along the wire fence. A cold *tramontana* wind started to blow, clouds were sliding fast across the sky. Alba walked close to me as we strolled along the rows of trees. We kept walking amid the frostbitten plants, arm tucked under arm, shivering.

We walked into a greenhouse and the warm moisture clogged our throats. We took off our coats and lingered among the ferns, touched the thick leaves of the African violets, smelled the damp mulch of wild orchids. We were both thinking hard. I could almost hear the buzzing of our brains.

"Do you think Isabella will come for Easter?" I asked. I hadn't seen her since that day at the station, a couple of months earlier. After that run-in with the carabinieri I couldn't help wondering where she was. I knew Alba had been thinking about her, too.

She shook her head.

"I don't know," she said. "I haven't heard from her in almost two weeks now."

I kept brushing the light fuzz on the back of a leaf. There was a moment of suspension.

"I don't understand what she's up to," Alba said. "She's disappeared."

"I think it's her boyfriend. He's so weird."

"Is he?"

I nodded. We both liked the idea that it might be all his fault. That if it were up to her, she would show up with a basket of hand-painted eggs and lots of chocolate.

"Call her," I said. "Tell her we all want her to come."

"I'm not even sure *where* she is, actually."

She hesitated, and looked at me cautiously.

"Rita told me she's hardly ever there."

We exchanged a meaningful glance.

"Does Rita ever talk to her?" I asked.

"A little bit. I think they had . . . they had like, a bit of a falling out."

"Why?"

"Oh, I don't know. It's just an idea I got. Rita is a bit elusive whenever I ask about Isabella. Maybe it's nothing."

I didn't press her any further. I guess I didn't want to spoil that moment of warmth inside the greenhouse. I wanted to enjoy it just a little bit more—that intimacy, mother and daughter planning to plant tulips and hyacinths on the terrace—before getting out again into the noise, the gray, and the chilly wind.

It was Bruno who came up with the idea.

Maybe he and Alba had discussed it privately. Or maybe, after so many years of silence and distance, he finally had decided it was time to make his move, the surprising move that decides the course of a chess game, just to show that he, too, had been a player in our life all along.

It was May. Isabella had neither shown up nor called over the Easter holiday, and we had all decided to pretend this was perfectly normal. I had gained a bit of weight and gathered some strength but was still convalescing.

Lorenzo came up to stay with us for a week. He looked old and frail now, like glass that could break at any moment. He kept talking about how many olives they had lost to the frost, and about the new pesticides he didn't trust. He talked about Stellario's granddaughter, Adele, the oldest daughter of Rosa, who was going to marry a magistrate from Lecce.

"This fellow, Lo Capo, is going to have a brilliant career. They say he'll end up in the Supreme Court. . . . Imagine what it would have meant for Stellario and Celeste—their granddaughter marrying a judge!"

We all nodded, only half-listening. We didn't care about the olives, we had no opinion about the pesticides, we didn't care about young girls marrying decent men with a future. He felt our distance and couldn't wait to get back to Casa Rossa.

Then one night Alba and Bruno had gone out and we had dinner, just the two of us. I noticed that he kept looking at me as I was clearing the dishes from the table.

"You have the same hair as your grandmother," he said finally, with a half-smile. "The color is just like hers. But she hated to have it so curly, she was always straightening it."

"Really?" I wanted to hear more. He hadn't mentioned Renée in years.

"Yes. She always spent hours in front of the mirror. She was very meticulous about the way she looked." He shook his head disapprovingly, although I could tell he still had that half a smile. "But don't get me wrong, she was a very intelligent woman, your grandmother."

"I know," I said, and realized that it was actually the first time I had heard someone use that adjective for Renée, the first time I could remember him smiling like that about her—or at all. Beautiful, dodgy, unscrupulous: this is how she had always been described. But intelligent—never.

"Good night now. I'm tired," Lorenzo said, as if he had said too much already.

"Good night, Grandpa," I said and kissed him lightly on the cheek.

Maybe that's what happens with age, I thought. All your life you force yourself to forget people who have hurt you, but as you get older and weaker their memory surfaces again, like a bubble in water. You have to surrender, because you feel too tired to fight it and push it down again. And maybe, unexpectedly, you find out that, instead of revamping your anger, those memories produce an unexpected sweetness.

After Lorenzo left and the house was quiet again, I finally threw the

Easter basket full of broken bits of chocolate eggs away. Alba kept complaining she had gained too much weight and didn't want to be tempted anymore.

As for me, the parenthesis was over. Now what? Now where?

I had enrolled at the university a few months earlier. I'd signed up for history and literature courses but never bothered to show up to a single lecture yet. And now I felt it was too late to try and catch up.

Tomas phoned every now and again, asking me to come around. I could tell from his voice he was high. I pictured him on the bed, surrounded by burnt tinfoil. Each time I found an excuse not to go. I was scared. I knew it would have been so much easier to get high: all it would take was one drag and I would stop feeling like a failure.

Bruno was about to leave on a business trip to New York. He had to place orders with a furniture factory in Brooklyn, attend a fair, and look at new things for his catalogue. I overheard all this in a conversation between him and Alba at the dinner table. I never paid much attention to Bruno, I wasn't interested in what he did. But this time, after a short silence, he raised his eyes from his soup and said to me:

"I was thinking of taking you along."

"Me?"

"Yes, why not? You could walk around, go to museums while I see the people I need to see, and then at night we could go to the theater, go listen to jazz in the Village, stuff like that."

I looked at him, speechless. Bruno cleared his throat.

"You could look into some schools, too. If you liked it, I mean."

Alba and he exchanged a quick glance. She gave an imperceptible nod, as her sign of approval to the way he had presented the proposal.

"Schools?" I asked.

Bruno wiped his mouth with a napkin and looked more confident, now that he had laid his cards on the table.

"I don't know, it's just an idea. I thought it might be good for you to have a change."

He waited for me to say something, but I kept perfectly still, wanting him to say more. I wanted to get this right. I tried to look encouraging, I didn't want to scare him off.

He shrugged, grasping for the right words.

"You don't seem particularly happy here, it seems to me. And I'm worried about you not going to university. That's why I thought, why not take a look at some opportunities in America."

I was stunned. That this should come—of all people—from Bruno.

"Yes," I said, finally, "I'd love to come."

"Okay, then," he said and smiled. It was a boyish smile, a smile I had never seen. "I'll book you a ticket."

As Bruno and I took off in the taxi for the airport, a week or so later, it occurred to me how uncomfortable we were at the idea of spending two weeks alone together. We needed to reinvent our relationship, and fast. Make up a brand-new one that would match the spirit of the trip. He ordered champagne for both of us as soon as the plane took off. We got pretty drunk right away and quickly established this one rule: that all rules were to be broken. We were starting fresh.

New York appeared in my life like one of those children's pop-up books, where with each page you turn a new intricate world springs up suddenly.

The skyline appeared magically, as we drove into the city from the airport, propped against the spring sky, its pinnacles and glass towers clear-cut against the cold. A last ray of sun brushed the tip of the Empire State Building with a reddish glow. I never thought one could fall in love with glass, steel, and concrete, bridges and ramps, but by the time we had reached our hotel in Midtown I was shaking with excitement.

That first night, Bruno and I ate in a deli across the street from the hotel. We sat in a red plastic booth next to the window. I couldn't take my eyes off the people who kept flowing by, the yellow cabs, the clouds of white smoke that puffed from secret holes in the ground. The constant speed of the city hypnotized me, a never-ending waltz constantly replacing its dancers.

Everything surprised and attracted me instantly. The way the middle-aged waitress in a brown apron and bleached hair called me "honey" and kept pouring weak coffee in a mug (refills were free!), pulling a pen from behind her ear to take our order. How Bruno struggled in his English and ordered pastrami sandwiches with fries. I could tell he was excited and intimidated at the same time. He looked younger, lighter, and I liked this new shyness I saw in him.

I felt greedy: I wanted to taste everything, and I worried that my hunger could not be satiated that easily.

"Thank you for bringing me here," I said, raising my mug in a toast. But Bruno didn't smile back. He looked almost sad.

"You shouldn't live with us, Alina," he said. "It's not good for you."

"Why do you say that?"

"Your mother and I . . . we've been going through a difficult period, you know that. I know it's not a good atmosphere in the house."

I didn't say anything. It was scary to hear him speak with me so frankly.

"I've been watching you over the last few months. I wanted to tell you that I knew you were taking drugs."

"Did you?" I was surprised that he decided to be so blunt.

"I'm not stupid, you know." He took out a pack of cigarettes and offered me one. "But, on the other hand, it's not easy for me to say what I think, to ask, to act like . . . like . . ."

"My father."

"Yes, a father," he agreed and pondered over the word. "That's not my role with you and your sister."

I paused.

"What about Alba, then?" I asked, and I felt anger swelling in my voice.

"What do you mean?"

"Why doesn't *she* ever say anything? Why is it she pretends she never understands what's going on around her?"

He looked into his plate and started fiddling with what was left of his sandwich.

"It's not true. She knew about . . . what you were doing. We've been talking about it, and that's why—"

"But why didn't she ever talk to *me* about it?"

"Alba is the way she is. Sometimes she finds it more convenient to ignore what's really going on. You better stop trying to attract her attention or you'll really get hurt one day. You'll get run over by a car, hoping she'll notice you."

"And what about Isabella? What does she think is going on *there*?"

He shook his head slowly.

"I don't know what exactly is going on with your sister, and I'm not even going to ask you if you don't want to talk about it . . ."

He stared at me and I didn't flinch.

"Although I have a feeling that she's gotten herself in a pretty messy situation," he said, shaking his hand in the air. "But I think *you* still have time to do something good with your life. You have a brain. You should use it, find something you like to do. Study, get a job. I can help you—in the beginning, if you want. Just until you settle down. You might as well at least try."

I sighed. Things were happening so fast, I couldn't keep up. Now I could see why he had taken me all the way to New York. To drop me off on this undiscovered island with enough supplies so that I could survive for a while. In a place where I had to figure everything out by myself. Basically what he was saying was that he was willing to come back and rescue me if I didn't make it, but that I had a better chance of surviving on my own here than at home among my family.

"I don't know. It frightens me a bit," I said and tried to smile. "But, sure, I see what you mean."

This was the very first time anyone had ever actually taken the time to study a problem I was having and really try to figure out a solution.

I looked around the tables in the restaurant: Who were all these people sitting across from each other in the booths, where did they live, what were they talking about? The young black girl in the corner with plaits and round glasses, the beautiful white-haired woman in the Chinese silk coat, the fat man with the baseball cap and faded jeans, the middle-aged gay couple in leather jackets. I couldn't tell much from their clothes, I couldn't really place them, but I could feel the buzz of all those lives crossing each other, meeting each other in an endless dance.

I might as well try to have a go on the dance floor.

Rita and I have eaten way too much, as usual.

Vito, the owner of the trattoria on the piazza, keeps bringing from the kitchen dishes we haven't even ordered. Now he's back with a huge plate of fried mussels.

"Just a tiny bite," he insists as we begin our protest. "Maria made this for the Baronessa because she never comes to visit us, and this is her specialty." He sets the plate down next to the marinated red peppers, the fried zucchini flowers, the octopus salad with potatoes, and the chickpea soup with pasta.

Rita shakes her head disapprovingly.

"Have they never heard of cholesterol?" she whispers as she reluctantly picks up a fried mussel between her fingers and swallows it. "This food is *barbaric*."

Vito comes by our table to watch her eat. Only when she gives him a groan of appreciation does he retreat back to the kitchen and dutifully report to his wife.

It's too chilly to eat out in the piazza under the trees, so we have taken a table inside. Vito's trattoria is almost empty—it's off season. The interior is lit by stark fluorescent lights, the walls are covered with large posters of local football teams, old torn Pirelli calendars, photos of Vito's family and friends toasting and smiling. Through the open kitchen door I get glimpses of Maria, Vito's wife, working at the stove, pale, exhausted, wiping sweat from her brow with a thick white cloth. The wine and the heavy food have made me suddenly sleepy.

"You know, considering what happened," I say, "it's amazing how they still treat us like family in the village."

She raises one of her penciled eyebrows in a slightly defensive arch.

"Oh. They've put all that story behind them by now. And in any case, you and I had nothing to do with it." She raises her eyes to the ceiling and puffs. "I mean, not *directly*."

I tap my finger lightly on the rim of my wineglass. She watches me.

"Right. But still . . ."

"What?"

"I think they have been very generous in their forgiveness."

Her expression becomes so serious that for a moment it's as if her features are of an entirely different mold. I see a handsome middle-aged man staring at me from beneath the Glenda Jackson haircut.

"Yes," Rita says, "I think so, too. It's a good lesson we all learned from them."

Our mood has shifted now. But I think this was the direction the evening was bound to take.

"Rita, when she . . . disappeared. Did you have any idea they would be coming here? Did she ever discuss the possibility with you?"

"Not really." She looks up at the ceiling, squinting, then shakes her head. "She never openly *said*."

"But you had an inkling."

"I did. I don't know why. Maybe she had mentioned something about Casa Rossa. I don't remember. But, yes, I did have an inkling."

She sighs and looks at the chickpea soup.

"This is my absolute favorite dish in the world."

"And did you have an inkling of the *reason* they had decided to come here?" I interrupt her.

"No—" she looks at me, dead serious—"I don't think you understand."

She leans across the table and grabs my hand.

"Alina, they didn't discuss their plans. Ever. Okay?"

I nod.

"And even though I had been covering their ass from the police and stuff, I wasn't . . ." She hesitates. "I wasn't part of their group."

"Yes, I know that."

She picks up a roasted pepper in her fingers, and then, as if having a second thought, puts it down.

"But if your question is, did I know they had guns, did I think they were prepared to use them, the answer is yes."

"Right. I had a feeling."

We're groping our way, cautiously, pausing between each sentence. Testing how far we can go. It's the first time in all these years we're addressing the issue so candidly.

"It doesn't mean I agreed with their ideas of . . . violence," she says as she pours more wine in her glass, "But I wasn't going to run to the police to tell them what was going on next door to me, either."

She takes a slim cigarette out of her pack and lights it slowly, savoring the warm smoke in her throat.

"Thinking about it now, it was madness, really. But at the time I had no idea what was at stake. How dangerous a situation she and Enrico had gotten themselves into."

I nod, and brush the bread crumbs off my side of the table.

"The truth is, we all knew it," Rita says. "You and I, too, one way or another. But we all had decided to sit still, even when the fuse started burning—no?"

Yes. Ears shut, eyes closed, waiting for the blast.

CHAPTER SIX

I had moved into a one-bedroom on Elizabeth Street. I was working for Raimonda Morrison at her gallery on Greene Street. It must have been the Monday following Thanksgiving, my second one in New York. I remember how lovely all that orange autumn stuff looked—the sweet potatoes, the acorns, and the butternut squash and how delicious pumpkin pie tasted . . .

The phone rang before daybreak. My brain flashed a red alert and I sprang up. This was a bad ring, I knew it. Too early, too dark, and too cold outside for this ring to bring any good news.

"Hallo?"

"Alina, sorry to wake you, love. It's me—Mamma."

"What's happened?"

"They arrested Isabella."

At first my brain let the phrase slip away, as if it were a sound in a foreign language. Then it caught up with its meaning.

"What? Arrested—why?"

"I don't know. I don't even know where she is right now. Oh, darling, it's been such a nightmare. It's all over the papers, everywhere. They'd been hiding in Casa Rossa. The police apparently found an arsenal in the well."

"Wait, who are you talking about? Who is 'they'?"

"You know, her political group. They call themselves 'Proletarian Revolutionary Units,' and they say Enrico is the leader. Can't you get Italian papers over there? It's on the front page everywhere."

"Mamma, just try to explain a little bit. Why were they arrested? On what grounds?"

"We don't know yet. They were all interrogated by the magistrates last night, there's no way I can get in touch with her, but we'll know more in the next few hours. I mean, I'm in such shock, I can't even . . ." Then she burst out in tears.

I kept breathing into the receiver. Squeezing in another second of limbo.

"The papers say they are the commando group that shot Lo Capo."

"Who's that?"

"You know, the magistrate from Lecce."

"No, I don't know."

"Yes, you do." She paused, and her voice tensed. "He's the one who married Adele. Remember Lorenzo was talking about him when he came last Easter?"

Adele. Stellario's granddaughter.

"And he was killed?"

"A few months ago"—she let out a puff of air—"on the road to Parabita, by the mill. He was working in this antiterrorism unit. He was a . . . a target. A commando of six people with machine guns ambushed him. They shot him and his bodyguards."

There was a silence. We both listened to it. It was so eloquent that we had to break its spell.

"But of course this is just the press," Alba went on. "The lawyer said we have to wait for the charges once the magistrates have completed their preliminary inquiry, or whatever they call it."

"Of course."

"I mean, this could be anything. They could have framed them. Who knows."

I kept silent. I just didn't know what to say.

"It doesn't look good, though." She hesitated. "You know, they found all these guns and ammunition."

"In the well?"

"Yes, under the almond tree."

I heard the siren of a fire truck whining across Houston Street.

Somewhere, on the other side of the ocean there was a garden with an almond tree and a well that Stellario and my grandfather had dug so many years before. It seemed impossible that such different places could exist at the same time.

Lorenzo had died only a year earlier.

I hadn't gone to the funeral. I had a good excuse, being so far away and so broke. I couldn't bear the thought of all those hours on a plane, and the theme of the entire journey being the end of our family. Without Lorenzo in Casa Rossa, I felt that Isabella, Alba, and I had to accept once and for all that we were lost and had lost each other. I took a long walk by myself. I went all the way across to Brooklyn, my eyes fixed on the ground as I crossed the bridge, concentrating on every little memory of Lorenzo that I could remember. I went through each one, like someone making a neat inventory.

Now, in the same ground where Lorenzo was buried, "they" had buried their guns.

"Sorry, Mamma, this is very difficult to digest," I said after a long silence. "It doesn't even register."

And we hung up just like that, without another word.

Later that morning I walked all the way up to Rizzoli's bookstore on Fifty-seventh Street and got copies of *La Repubblica, Il Corriere della Sera,* and *La Stampa.*

There they were, six of them, under every headline, looking like ordinary criminals in their fake ID photos. LO CAPO'S KILLERS CAUGHT IN SOUTHERN ITALY HIDEOUT; ARMS CACHE MAY LINK GROUP TO OTHER KILLINGS, MAGISTRATES BELIEVE; DEATH BLOW FOR CLANDESTINE CELL: LEADER ENRICO PIERSANTI CAUGHT WITH OTHER FIVE. Isabella stared coldly at me from every page, her features flattened by the flash. She looked older with dark hair. It must be that wig—the one she wanted me to buy for her that day at the Termini station.

It was warm inside the bookstore, sounds were muffled by the wood paneling and carpeted floor. Haydn played softly in the background. A tall woman wrapped in cashmere from head to toe was flicking through a coffee-table book on Japanese gardens. I felt like screaming or throwing myself on the floor, but instead I smiled politely at the girl behind the register.

"Would you like a bag for these?" she asked

"Please."

"Here you go. Have a nice day."

"You, too," I whispered.

I took the subway back downtown. I needed to be at work at the gallery by eleven. I couldn't make myself read the papers in front of all those people on the train. I felt like a thief, hiding stolen goods inside my green-and-white Rizzoli bag.

I sat behind the desk in the white pristine space of the Morrison Gallery. I had picked up my usual large cup of coffee and croissant at the French bakery on the corner, and bought a bunch of fresh white tulips for the week to put in the big vase we had at the entrance. Raimonda insisted we have only white flowers. The answering machine was blinking. I transcribed the messages. A museum curator from Brussels; the Brazilian artist we were currently showing; a woman from *Artforum* magazine. Everything looked and sounded quite ordinary, but nothing was the same. Raimonda came in around noon, cloaked in black, her blond hair tied in a neat bun, her lipstick tragically red. She was skinny as a chopstick.

"Anything urgent?" she asked, going through the bills I had stacked by the phone.

"Not really," I said.

She fell on the chair and sighed.

"I'm feeling like shit today. I don't think I can handle much. I feel like going right back to bed."

"Why?"

"Oh, the usual. Josh and me. It's just exhausting."

She and her husband were dancing around the subject of divorce. She talked about it nonstop. She had a lover, an artist. Younger, good looking, Mexican, the son of a famous writer. What else.

Raimonda Morrison was in her early forties, a sophisticated Italian woman. She had moved to New York from Milan in the seventies, had married Josh, an architect twenty years her senior, and opened her art gallery in SoHo. Bruno had introduced me to them when I first arrived, two years earlier—I think he and Josh knew each other from business—and she had immediately hired me as her au pair. I lived in the Morrisons' loft for the first nine months of my new life in New York, looking after their five-year-old daughter, Clara.

It was an easy beginning, a shielded life. My English, when I first arrived, wasn't terribly fluent. I remember watching the news on TV and not being able to make out what they were going on about, or staring at a waitress in a coffee shop, unable to figure out what exactly was the special of the day. Raimonda and I always spoke Italian around the house, so during the first weeks she acted as a buffer between me and the new sounds bombarding me outside. She pushed me to run errands for her, dragging little Clara along.

"New York is like a bull: you have to take it by the horns," she pronounced, with the proud display of aphorism and the hint of sadism one enjoys with a newcomer.

Eventually I found my way in the Gristedes's, with its foreign-looking foods, made sense of the subway map, and, through Raimonda's heavily Italian-accented English, I came to master the language. Till I could get the jokes on *Saturday Night Live.* By the end of the first summer I began to feel at ease and bored with my job as an au pair. I hadn't come all the way to New York to be a baby-sitter, after all. Just as I was about to leave Raimonda's house and look for a job as a waitress, she offered me a job at the gallery.

"As what?" I asked.

"As the pretty girl who answers the phone and greets the visitors. And then you'll learn the rest. It's not that difficult."

I did. And I quickly became good at was I was doing. I scheduled her appointments, sent the invitations, talked to the printer, to the freight company, faxed our press releases to the magazines, dealt with caterers for the openings, booked her manicure, and lied to her husband whenever he called looking for her.

Raimonda eyed the Rizzoli bag.

"Missing Italian news?"

"Uh . . . there's . . . there's a review I wanted to read. A friend's show."

"Can I see them when you're through?"

"Sure. Oh—you have to call *Artforum*. They need to know about the ad before one o'clock."

I grabbed the papers while she was on the phone and hid them in the closet under my coat. I wasn't going to say a word about Isabella to anybody.

The headlines stuffed in the bag made me feel like those guns were mine.

A few days later, I learned, Isabella was taken to Voghera, a maximum-security women's penitentiary in northern Italy and put in solitary confinement. Alba was finally granted permission to visit her, and as soon as she came back from her forty-five-minute visit (after nine hours on the train), she called me. She could hardly speak; it was as if she had no words to describe what it was like. I felt as if a cold slab of lead had descended upon both of us, leaving us no space to breathe.

Alba tried to describe the building—a square concrete box in the midst of a muddy plain, surrounded by an electric fence—the metal doors, the armed guards, the dogs. She said she had been allowed to see Isabella through a sheet of thick glass, and they had to speak through an intercom. But I couldn't get a clear picture out of her, nor any meaningful information. She didn't even remember what they had talked about. But she said Isa looked calm, and that she had received my telegram and was going to answer soon.

My sister and I hadn't talked since that day at the train station, almost three years earlier, and I feared our silence might have lasted too long, our distance grown too wide for us to reconnect. I panicked, and wrote her three weepy letters in two days, full of regrets, apologies, and longing.

When her first letter finally arrived, I held the long narrow envelope in my hand for a few seconds before opening it: the magic in a piece of paper that travels so far. From that cold place to sunny Elizabeth Street.

> *Dear Alina,*
> *I was so happy (yes, it's still possible to use this word) to receive your*

letters. They all came this morning, and I've spent the whole day reading them over and over. It means so much to me to see your tiny crooked handwriting again. I need every single bit of proof that the world outside hasn't ceased to exist, or I would go completely crazy in here.

Once you visualize the space I fill, you can be sure that no detail is ever going to change, so that you'll always know where to find me, any time of day or night. In a cubicle with no windows, where every piece of furniture (bed, small table, chair, sink) is nailed to the floor so that nothing can ever change its place. I'm not allowed to have books, nor a stove to cook my own meals. They keep the lights on day and night so that one loses sense of time. At night they keep waking me up by banging loudly on the metal door. Once every two days I get to walk (strictly by myself) in a circle for thirty minutes inside a concrete courtyard, surrounded by tall, thick walls. It feels like pacing the bottom of an empty swimming pool. I haven't seen the shape of a mountain, of a tree, since I've been in here.

Although I'm not allowed to see them, I know there are five other women in solitary confinement on this floor. I hear them banging against the metal doors of their cells at night. I bang back, like a pygmy answering a call in the rain forest.

They call it maximum security but it's annihilation. They call it solitary confinement, but it's more like being buried alive.

Everything we will write to each other will be censored, keep that in mind if at times you find my tone impersonal. There will never be a private exchange between me and another person as long as I'm in here. In fact I'm no longer a person. I've lost all my rights, even before they begin to try me and prove me guilty. This kind of repression is no surprise to me: in fact, this imperialistic system is the one I have been fighting against. I always knew, when I started, that the possibility of detention was included in the price.

This is not a case of mistaken identity, you better get that straight and make Alba understand. It is me they want, Alina. I know they will want to keep me in here for as long as they can. As you probably know by now, my comrades and I have been charged with armed insurrection against the state, manslaughter, armed robbery, everything down to possession of arms, insult to a public official, and God knows what else.

They have no interest in speeding up the procedure. Once they managed *to lock us up, and keep each one isolated from the others, they were in no hurry to give us a trial. The technique is pretty simple: they wait till they hear from the guards that you have begun to bang your head against the wall, that you've stopped eating, or that you're talking to yourself all day long. Then they fly in like vultures and offer you a deal.*

They say they'll move you out of solitary, into a regular jail, in a cell shared with others, where you can even watch television and get to see your visitors in a room without the glass. By then, the thought of being able to touch someone is like a mirage in the desert. You realize how starved you are for any form of physical contact.

All they ask of you is what they tastefully call "a bit of cooperation." A couple of names, some dates, who was where, when. A little memory aid, to help the judges do their work.

In exchange, you get a discount on your sentence. A state-approved, end-of-season, final sale. Prices reduced by up to seventy percent! That's why they are taking it so easy. Time is on their side. The longer the clock keeps ticking, the easier it will be to close the deal. At least this is what they must assume.

They have come up with a proper name for this dirty deal, it's a brand-new law, fresh from our legislature. They called it the "Repentant Law." Only in Italy could they come up with such a brilliant concept: to substitute the word repentant for informer. To give Judas respectability.

But enough about me for now. Tell me about yourself, it's so hard for me to picture this life of yours in New York. What do you do all day? What do you see from your window? Tell me stories, draw me pictures, feed me with images. I'm thirsty, I need to drink up some life. I love you too.

Isabella

I had mixed feelings about almost everything she said.

Clearly, from the way she wrote, she wasn't concerned that her letters were being read and censored. She wasn't going to deny her role as *"combattente rivoluzionario,"* and certainly wasn't interested in maintaining her innocence. She and her comrades had declared themselves political prisoners, which meant they were accountable for whatever actions they had decided to take. They simply were going to keep their mouths shut. Their silence was the only weapon they had left, since it left the investigators in the dark and unable to prevent any further strike the "proletarian revolutionaries" were plotting against the "system."

Yet there were so many things that I—as her sister—needed to know but was afraid to ask. I was too scared I might lose her again if I did.

So I held on to what I had and didn't question it.

Alba and I talked on the phone twice a week. She'd give me her reports, now punctuated with obscure legal terms. We had stopped speculating, or asking each other questions about what had happened. We talked about Isabella as if she were a terminally ill patient in intensive care; we'd been assigned to keep track of her temperature, weight, heartbeat, tiny improvements. We avoided talking about the causes that got her there in the first place. We stuck to our job, which was simply to keep her breathing.

Meanwhile, I walked around New York City feeling like an impostor. Someone who had a cool job and not a worry in the world.

As Christmas approached, Raimonda's mood plummeted.

Her young lover, the painter, had gone to Mexico for the holidays with his friends, and without him she didn't see the point of celebrating anything at all.

"All this syrupy music greeting you everywhere you go," she huffed. "This pretense of joy and warmth, it's making me suicidal. No matter how much I search within me, I have no desire to give anyone a gift."

Nevertheless, she gave me a list and I did her shopping, at Saks. It was an unimaginative list—though pricey, in order to counterbalance its lack of warmth—and I went through it, crossing each item off like a scientist conducting a test. I selfishly enjoyed her unhappiness, it made me feel less lonely.

She invited me to her Christmas Eve dinner party. It was terrible.

She and Josh hardly spoke to each other, only exchanged snappy remarks that seemed more like measured bursts of poison gas. The child, Clara, started howling at eight, with a ferocity I had never seen back when I used to take care of her, and she was put to bed. The food was bad, the guests were visibly uncomfortable. After everyone left I helped her clear the table and clean up. Josh had gone to bed without even saying good night.

Her life seemed a mess to me, just like the floor of the living room, which was strewn with lots of torn paper and empty boxes.

"Let's have another bit of this bubbly stuff," she slurred, opening another bottle of champagne. She was swaying on her chopstick legs and her lipstick was all smudged.

We ended up completely drunk. I suddenly blurted out my secret: that Isabella was in a high-security prison and was risking a life sentence. Her eyes bulged.

"She's a terrorist? Is she affiliated with the Red Brigades?"

"No. No. Of course not. Hers was a small group. I'm sure you never even heard of them." I tried to make them sound like dilettantes. "The 'Proletarian Revolutionary Units,' I think they call themselves. She was part of a commando group that's been accused of shooting a judge and his security men. He was someone vaguely related to my family," I said as I gulped down another glass.

"You mean she *knew* this man?"

"No. Not personally. But she knew the place where he lived, the shortcut he took to go to work. We sort of grew up around there. Which makes me think she might have had a big part in masterminding the whole thing. Along with her Svengali boyfriend."

As I heard myself say it, I started crying. In Raimonda's high-tech steel kitchen—the moonlight shimmering on the Hudson perfectly framed in the window—my sister's fate seemed utterly unbearable and no longer possible to ignore.

She fished for her bag underneath a bundle of cashmere coats in the hall and scribbled her signature on a check for a thousand dollars.

"This is my Christmas present, okay? Alina, I want you to buy yourself a ticket tomorrow. Go see her. Come back after New Year's."

"Wait . . . I . . . I don't know if—"

"You must go, she's your sister. You must go home, be with your mother at a time like this. Plus it's Christmas, for God's sake!"

She suddenly looked totally sober and in control. I guess my problem had made her feel like she was a responsible family member again. Perhaps my unhappiness was my Christmas gift to her.

———

I bought the ticket, flew to Rome for a week. Just like a jet-setter.

Alba came to pick me up at the airport. She had let her hair go gray and kept it tied in a loose bun. It struck me, how suddenly she had begun to look old. How her skin had gone slack around the bones.

We got in her car, which was dented and scratched. Lots of old yellowing newspapers piled in the backseat. It smelled stale and the ashtray was overflowing.

"What's this? Don't tell me you're smoking now."

"I took it up since this thing with Isabella. It gives me something to do when I get anxious."

"At your age it's kind of stupid, isn't it?"

She shrugged as she adjusted the rearview mirror and pulled out of the parking lot.

"Everything looks stupid past fifty."

We drove in silence for a while.

"By the way, Bruno's away till the end of next week," she said. "He's sorry he missed you."

"So am I."

"Actually, I'm happy to have you all to myself. Plus it's such a relief when he's away. I can't bear to know he's in the next room, even."

I looked at her askance. She didn't return my look. She kept driving with her nose slightly tilted upwards, her face a bit too close to the windshield. She was getting more and more nearsighted but wouldn't give in to wearing glasses.

After two years in New York our neighborhood struck me as hopelessly tame, with its cherry trees lining the sidewalks, the newsstand on the corner, the ugly church built in the sixties on the piazza. Inside the house, everything looked neglected, cracked, as if a musty patina shrouded the familiar rooms and nobody had opened a window in a long time.

I put my bag in my old room, the one I used to share with Isabella. It was like walking into a wax museum. Some of the clothes we'd worn as teenagers were still hanging in the closet, put away with old junk Alba had forgotten to throw away. I stared at the clothes—a long army coat, a tartan skirt, a pair of brown corduroy jeans. They looked like ghosts from another century. I opened the drawer of the desk where we used to do our homework. Among the jumble of half-used rolls of tape, broken pencils, and old sets of keys, I found a pad with notes scribbled in Isabella's square handwriting, from God knows when. There were names and phone numbers, lists of things she needed to do. *Buy shampoo, pick up shirt at the cleaner's. Buy Alina's present.* Obviously none of it had been interesting enough for the police to take away with them when they searched her room for evidence. I shut the drawer as if something had burnt my fingers.

Alba and I spent the whole next day in the kitchen, cooking. It looked like we had organized some kind of a party once we had all the food laid out on the table, wrapped in tinfoil. A tin of timballo di maccheroni, roast beef, tagliatelle with smoked salmon, meat balls and ossobuco, tiramisù. We packed everything in a bundle and then at ten o'clock that night Alba put me on the train to Voghera.

"If you get lonely, go to car number five. The others always ride in the same car, to keep each other company," she said.

"What 'others'?"

"You know, the relatives. They take this train every Tuesday night. They're very nice people."

Number five sounded like the saddest car on the train. But in fact the opposite was true.

These women made this nine-hour trip once a week in order to be at the prison gate at nine o'clock sharp every Wednesday. Visiting day.

Some of them had been doing it for years. They were mothers, mainly, whose daughters were convicted of political crimes, and they all knew each other well. They all carried gigantic bundles similar to mine. They were excited, chatty, like they were going on a trip somewhere fun.

"Hi, I'm Laura. My daughter, Silvia, is in solitary confinement too." The heavy woman in her fifties, her hair streaked with gray, smiled at me. She had taken her shoes off and was massaging her swollen feet.

"I'm Gabriella," a thin, pale woman in a cheap gray track suit said as she stretched her hand. "You're Isabella's sister, right? Would you like some water?"

"Thank you."

"My daughter tells me about her." She unscrewed a bottle and handed it to me. She smiled encouragingly. "They all know each other, even though they're not allowed to spend any time together. They have a way to talk to one another by banging on the bars. They use Morse code."

"Your mother stayed home?" asked Laura. "This trip is so tiring for her, it's good you can take her place so she can rest." While she spoke she was fumbling around inside a big plastic bag. "Here, have some fruit."

"She's a nice lady, Alba," another woman interjected. "So where do you live in America?"

These women were mostly working-class and probably struggled hard to pay for lawyers and for these long trips on the train. Some of them came from small towns around Rome and probably never had a lot of schooling. I'll bet none of them had any idea what a penitentiary or a judicial proceeding was before this had happened to them. But by now they had become competent, even belligerent. Not only did they exchange the names of guards and the phone numbers of liberal lawyers along with recipes, but they were discussing the latest bills to pass the legislature, the so-called Special Laws that had come into effect since the beginning of terrorism. These women knew the penal code inside out, they had the terms, the law sections, even the riders, down to perfection.

They warned me.

"Is this your first visit?" Laura asked. "Then prepare yourself. The first time is always a shock."

We got off the train at dawn. We were suddenly quiet, grave. It was foggy, wet, muddy. We huddled together on a bus, and rode silently, engrossed in our own thoughts.

Now, as I sat in that bus heading toward the prison, I wondered if this was when I was supposed to ask Isabella exactly what it was she had done. I wondered whether she was expecting me to do so and was preparing herself to answer my question. Wasn't that what lawyers did in movies? Wasn't there always a scene where they needed their client to tell them the plain, unadorned truth?

I watched the mothers and sisters sitting with me on the bus, clutching their parcels of food and clean clothes. I envied their confidence. I wondered if every one of them had, at one time, sat down in the visiting room, looked their daughter or sister in the eye, and said:

"Now, tell me the truth, because I need to know. Are you guilty? Did you actually pull the trigger? I will be on your side no matter what, but you'll have to tell me."

I realized I didn't know what I was supposed to feel, how I was supposed to act. All I knew was that I was scared.

I thought of Oliviero. Of the way things would have been completely different had he been with me on that ride. He would have known how to handle it. I closed my eyes and fantasized that he was sitting next to me, in his threadbare corduroy jacket, looking out the window into the fog through his black-rimmed glasses.

Don't worry, monkey face, I'll talk to her.

And I dozed off, lolled by the dream and the swaying of the bus.

Finally, after a long ride, we arrived at a gloomy concrete cube in the middle of a field. Inside, it was sterile in a terrifying way. Metal doors, electric fences, and at every turn, something either locked, clanked, or shut behind us. It was like walking inside an industrial freezer. A deadly place, if you stayed too long.

The guards made us wait four hours inside an empty room with no windows and no seats. They had locked us inside; we weren't even allowed to go to the restroom. I was hungry. All I could think of was the food I had packed for Isabella. Then one of them finally appeared and yelled out our names, one by one. And in we went for the "inspection."

First they checked the contents of the food we had brought.

They placed every item on a scale, scanned it with a metal detector, and then poked it mercilessly with a sharp knife. They stabbed my timballo and the roast beef. They mashed the tiramisù. They cut everyone's food till it oozed, dripped, crumbled—till it looked like a bloody mess. All that work we had done in an attempt to infuse it with a bit of our love, and now it looked like something retrieved from the garbage.

Gabriella, who was standing in front of me, raised her voice as the guard started piercing her beautiful fruit tart with a knife:

"Don't do that! You don't need to do that!"

"Shut up or I'll send you back," he said without even looking at her. He cut even deeper into the tart, till all the juices started dribbling out.

They scanned every bag, checked every pocket. They searched each one of us and took away any metal object, even wedding rings. Because I was new, they took particular care in searching me and going through my things.

"Follow me," the guard who had destroyed the food parcels said and pointed to a door.

I looked at the other women. I didn't like the idea of being separated from them.

One of them nodded as if to say, "It's all right, don't worry."

The guard took me inside a tiny empty room.

"Wait here."

"What *is* this? Why?"

"It's the procedure. Just wait." He closed the door, and I heard him lock it. They had taken my wristwatch away, so I had no idea how long they left me in there. By the time a fat woman came in—short gray hair, tight lips, smelling of Listerine—I was almost hysterical.

"Remove all your clothes," she said.

I saw her put on a plastic glove.

"What's that for?" I asked, and I felt my throat tighten because I already knew the answer.

"Vaginal inspection. Open your legs."

"I have . . . I'm having my period."

"Doesn't matter." Her lizard eyes didn't even flick. "If you have a tampon, pull it out."

"Listen, I can't do this. *Really*"—my voice was shaking now.

"Fine. Then you can go home. Those are the regulations," she said and crossed her arms on top of her fat belly.

You Nazi pig, I thought, and felt like hitting her in the face.

When she finally let me out of the room—only after I had done as she wanted—I was led again into the waiting room with the other women. They immediately surrounded me. They had obviously been worrying about me.

"What did they want?" Laura asked, frowning.

"Did they search you?"

178

"Vaginal inspection?"

I nodded. I was mortified.

"The cunts," Gabriella hissed. "They usually do this to new visitors in order to discourage them from coming."

"But it's totally illegal to search you like that. You must report the guard to the authorities," Laura said. "Did you get her name?"

They were all outraged and insisted that I should file a complaint with the magistrate.

"You have to react right away. You have to show them you're going to bust their ass, otherwise they'll keep on doing this to you," said one of the younger women, lighting a Marlboro. She had a giant black panther tattooed on her forearm.

"It's all right. I'm going back to New York the day after tomorrow. I wouldn't be able to follow this through," I said feebly.

They looked at me and shook their heads. I think I disappointed them by wanting to drop the issue so fast. After only a few hours inside that giant freezer, my sense of dignity had crumbled.

The guard called our names again, and let us into the visitors' room.

I've tried many times to remember the details, but that room has vanished from my memory. I remember nothing: not the people, not the guards who crowded it. Not even the tables or the chairs.

All I saw was this tiny person behind the glass.

She looked different from the last time I saw her, at the train station. She didn't look anything like her photo in the newspaper, nor like the Prussian officer in gray uniform with a cold stare and a gun in her handbag. There she was, this bony waif, her blond hair longer than I remembered, dark circles under her eyes, specks of gold swimming in the blue of her irises. That blue vein I knew so well, crossing her white forehead. She tapped on the glass and pointed to the intercom. I saw her lips say "Push the button." I did. Her voice came through the intercom. Crackling, completely distorted, as if it were coming from another galaxy.

"Hi, *bambina.*"

She flattened her palm over the glass and I placed mine on hers. But all I felt was the cold surface.

She had turned back into the old Isa, the sister I used to play detective with in Via del Babuino. The older sister with whom I used to pick glass pebbles on the beach.

"You look . . . you look good," she said, and I smiled awkwardly.

"So do you." She smiled and pinched her cheeks—rosy. At last.

I don't remember what we said. Forty-five minutes in that room felt like an out-of-control roller-coaster ride. Up and down, up and down, my stomach twisted in a knot. It was impossible to slow down, concentrate, savor anything. I was too busy holding on tight. There were a million things I wanted to ask her and I couldn't remember a single one. I was too terrified of the minutes slipping by. Isabella was strangely poised. She kept asking me very specific questions. She wanted to know what my apartment in New York looked like, what exactly I had to do for Raimonda. Then she pointed at my sweater.

"Where did you buy that?"

"What? This? Oh . . . in some secondhand shop in New York, why?"

"I like it."

"You can have it. I'll send it with Alba when she comes next time."

I smiled at her. Maybe I could buy more pretty clothes, spray them with perfume so that she would have something nice to smell in that freezer.

"You know," she said suddenly, "this is going to take a very long time, *bambina*. I just want you to understand that."

"Like how long?"

"I don't know. Years," she sighed, and her breath came through the intercom like a diver's from underwater.

I tried quickly to make out what she meant by that. Whether she meant she didn't trust the judges and expected them to convict her, regardless of her innocence, or that there was just too much evidence against her and she knew she had no hope of getting out. I held my breath and waited for her to explain herself, but she just looked at me.

I panicked as I realized the time had come to ask the question I had been dreading. I knew I had only this one chance. It wouldn't make sense to ask her any later, it was either now or never.

"But *why* years?" I pleaded.

I detected a shift in her gaze. A hint of alarm.

And suddenly I remembered the day we met at the station, over a year earlier. Her cold stare, her gray military outfit. How her hardness had scared me. How I then thought *she could be capable of anything.*

I realized that I wasn't going to ask that question—and that I never would, for purely selfish reasons.

Because I didn't want her to turn into that stranger again. Not now that she was back as her old self, that she had smiled and had called me *bambina*. Not now that she wanted my sweater. Not now that she needed me again.

"They're going to keep me in here as long as they can because I'm not going to make this any easier for them," she said, calm.

"You mean you're not going to turn into a *pentita*?"

She shut her eyes tight, as if she had swallowed something bitter.

"Don't even say that word. It makes me puke."

One of the guards entered through a metal door behind her and announced that our time was up. He didn't even let us finish what we were saying. I realized I was actually relieved we had run out of time right at that moment. She turned to me just before he closed the heavy door behind her and waved, smiling. As if she were in school and had to go back to class.

Then we were all back on the train, the women of car number five. If on the trip down we couldn't stop talking, and sounded like a flock of geese, now we were silent, totally deflated. I watched the same women look out of the windows, their heads tilted on the glass, staring in silence at the gray countryside rolling by. This herd of silent women on a train, wrapped in a coat of sadness and physical exhaustion. Each one of us thinking about the person we had left inside that concrete cube.

As I began to doze off, the conversation in the compartment slowly resumed. The women were starting to plan their visits for the following week.

"Don't bother with the fruit tart again, Gabriella," said Laura. "They'll just destroy it, it's not worth it."

"I was thinking of spinach lasagna. It keeps well and they can eat it cold."

"Great idea. No meat, right?"

"No. Ricotta, and a pinch of nutmeg."

It made me feel better that they were obsessing about the food again. I suddenly had a feeling that these women had, just like me, evaded the questions I was haunted by. Their daughters, the same little girls they had raised with such discipline, dragging them to church every Sunday, for whom they had baked birthday cakes, put ribbons in their braids, were now charged with murder, manslaughter, conspiracy. How could these mothers grasp it, come to terms with it? In order to be able to function and be there for their daughters they needed something they could control, something familiar. Something they were good at. Preparing their meals was a way to scale the inconceivable down to domestic proportions.

It reminded me of how I felt after Oliviero died.

I had been left with no instructions on how to deal with that pain, but I had figured out a way to do it, by reducing his death to a missing place mat. Now, once again, I had no clue how to deal with the possibility that my sister might have killed someone—and I needed to shrink it to a size I could live with.

I would simply do what all the women in the sad compartment five did: make sure she got clean clothes, and lasagna that would keep well and could be eaten cold.

And I would let the rest of Italy—the press, the judges, the jury, public opinion—deal with the questions I couldn't ask.

The minute I got back to New York I started resenting everything and everybody with a passion. Everything enraged me: the issues people debated on television or in the paper sounded ludicrous. Even a film review irritated me. It all sounded so irrelevant—the ozone layer, kids taking crack, the Grammy awards.

"Stop it. You're beginning to feel sorry for yourself," Raimonda said when I came back to work and tried to explain to her how I felt. "You're just going to drive yourself crazy."

I pouted and swiveled my chair around, showing her my back, pretending to be sorting out the paperwork. The desk at the Morrison Gallery was covered with mail, unanswered faxes, unopened bills. It was shocking how much stuff managed to pile up in only a week.

"You chose to live here now," I heard her say, her voice too mellow. "You should try to live in the present."

"Did you get that in your yoga class?" I snapped.

"Alina, I just don't want you to start resenting everybody, or to feel guilty for living a normal life. It's not your fault that your sister ended up in jail."

"I wasn't going to. It's just . . . I'm just a little shocked to be back in here"—I waved my hands around, indicating the clean white space, the perfectly fresh flowers in the Venini vase, the pile of correspondence— "and all these people worrying about paintings and catalogues."

"Life goes on"—she took the receiver and started dialing a number, quickly checking the state of her manicure—"that's the beauty of it. *Inutile piangere sul latte versato.*"

Raimonda felt reassured by her own clichés and wanted to make sure that the moral standards of people around her wouldn't make her seem a lesser person. Although she had the power to irritate me like nobody else, I couldn't help liking her.

Life did go on, as she said. Soon after that, I found myself worrying once more over brochures, trasparencies, international couriers' bills, and artists' bad tempers.

But I had a parallel life, and its weight was constantly pulling me down.

It was Isabella's life; it flowed parallel to mine somewhere underground, in a dark place. It unfolded everyday in the same loop, round and round between a bed and a table inside a cubicle, between the rounds in the courtyard—the empty swimming pool where she could delude herself she was outdoors—and the weekly walk to the visiting room. Onto this narrow stage I kept playing out her day, over and over. I made her walk up and down, I improvised her monologues. I staged the contents of her letters. It was like having kidnapped a doll and trapped her in a dollhouse.

I never lost track of what was going on inside there.

Taylor Davis walked into the gallery unexpectedly one early spring day. I was standing on top of a ladder, repainting the walls after we had taken down the previous artist's exhibition. I had come in at eight in order to do the job before opening time. Taylor Davis was a large man in his mid-fifties. Powerful and handsome in a very rugged way, there was something of the mastiff in his face. We were going to mount his show in the fall. It was Raimonda's highlight of the season. Taylor Davis had produced some phenomenal paintings in the sixties and seventies, but art collectors and museums only realized it in the eighties. He was big.

"Alina," he said, looking up, puffing a cigarette.

"Oh, hi." I held my brush in midair. "I was just . . . just . . . we're not open yet."

"Raimonda said you'd be here early. I need to read the fax from Webster. Those people in London."

"Oh, right. Absolutely."

I stepped down from the ladder and started looking through my incoming mail pile on the desk. I could feel his stare, like he was X-raying me. Davis always made me feel uncomfortable. There was something out of control about him. He didn't bother to play the part, he never wore the black costume of the pseudo-bohemians who tended to come to our openings. This man was not afraid of looking old-fashioned. Maybe Jack Kerouac had looked something like Taylor Davis, I thought. Clean-cut and deranged.

"Interesting pattern. Like aboriginal dot painting," he said slowly.

I didn't get it. Then he pointed at me. I was completely covered in tiny specks of paint. It was all over my clothes, my skin.

"Yeah, I still can't figure out how to paint a ceiling without getting this messy," I said nervously. "Here's that fax."

He looked at me askance, naughty. Then he pressed his cigarette hard in a glass. Didn't even bother to ask if we had an ashtray.

"See ya," he said and walked out, stuffing the sheet of paper in the back pocket of his jeans.

Two days later, I was watching David Letterman and eating ice cream when the phone rang.

"Taylor Davis wants to talk to you about something," Raimonda said with a mysterious tone. "His assistant is going to call you tomorrow morning, early. This is, like, *important*."

"What do you mean?" I asked. I didn't like the way he had looked at me. He terrified me.

"Listen, Alina, he's not going to eat you alive, don't get all nervous"—and she hung up.

Taylor Davis's assistant, Julian, rang me at eight sharp the next day. He said that Mr. Davis had decided to start doing portraits, and he was thinking of doing mine as his first.

"He's never done people before, you see." Julian's voice went down an octave, as if he were letting me in on a secret. "So this could be a very significant turn in his work. Something about you standing on that ladder really inspired him and he would like to try you out as a model."

"Well . . . I mean . . . I don't know if . . . you know, I work at the Morrison Gallery from eleven to seven."

"Mrs. Morrison knows about this. She's very excited. I don't think your working hours are going to be a problem," he said, slightly condescendingly. Clearly, I wasn't getting how unimportant my work was, or how extraordinary this opportunity was.

"Well . . . okay . . . if she has no problem . . . then . . . I mean, I've never done this before."

"You don't need to do much. Just sit still. Could you come to the studio on Thursday at nine?"

"Fine. What should I wear?"

"Wear? Oh, well, I don't think it'll make any difference." He paused. "Actually, I don't think he was thinking *clothes,* you know."

I ended up standing stark naked on a ladder in Taylor Davis's studio in Brooklyn, covered in paint.

"Do you mind?" Taylor asked, once he had positioned me on the ladder and proceeded to spatter drops of paint on my body by shaking a thick brush.

"No. Go ahead."

He stepped back and looked intently at one of my thighs, now covered in dripping blue and brown.

"*Hommage* to Pollock," he said to himself and chuckled.

Up on the ladder, after Julian had made me some hot tea and put on a Callas tape, I slowly relaxed.

I liked the concentration, the trancelike state Taylor was in. He kept smoking cigarette after joint after cigarette after joint, leaving the burning remains everywhere. I could almost feel the vibrations of his thoughts as he searched on his table for a brush or a color. I became enraptured by his quick movements. I liked how economical he was. Every now and again I was allowed to step down from the ladder, put on a soft robe, and stretch, drink some coffee.

"You know," I said to Taylor, who was chewing a pastrami sandwich Julian had ordered from the deli, "my grandmother posed in the nude for years for my grandfather. I think there must be hundreds of his portraits of her around somewhere."

He grunted something, like he wasn't really interested. I could tell his mind was still on the painting.

He was rough, in a way that made me feel more at ease, like we didn't need to fuss about much. I wasn't a person to him, I was just a surface.

I stood up on the ladder for days. It was quite an interesting position to hold, up there on the top. I had the advantage of the view from above. I saw the beautiful younger lover come and go, her arms full of expensive-looking bags. She nagged about something wrong with their platinum card and never once said hello to me. I saw an art critic, a hyper brunette on stiletto heels, look at the canvas, nod pensively, decree in a husky voice, "This is just wonderful, Taylor. This is the beginning of something entirely new."

I saw the shiatsu masseuse (Korean, tiny), the chef (Californian, gay), the drug dealer (Iranian, bulky), the best friend (a musician, depressed). They all came, did their thing, and left. They all looked at the canvas and said:

"Taylor this is amazing."

"Wow."

"One of your best works."

"This is really something."

I started enjoying it, up there on the ladder. I began feeling epic. It was a combination of things: the arias, the smell of paint and turpentine, the breeze shaking the trees outside the large windows. The first hint of spring. My heart was in bloom.

Then the buzzer rang again.

"It must be Daniel Moore," Julian said, "the guy from *The New Yorker*."

"Shit," said Taylor, "I had forgotten all about that."

He grinned and coughed hard.

"He's writing something on me," he said. "Like there's anything new to write about a painter in his studio."

Daniel Moore did absolutely nothing to disrupt my mood. He simply politely introduced himself and sat down in a corner. He watched everything with great concentration. He took quick notes, asked Taylor what was playing on the stereo, and if he knew what the title of the painting was going to be. Taylor Davis grunted, as if the questions annoyed him.

"Hey, man," he said, shaking his head slowly as he passed his brush to Julian, "I never remember a painting of mine by its title."

He stepped back and looked at the large canvas, propped against the wall, tilting his head to the side. Although my silhouette had become one thing with the dots and drips of the background, you could definitely tell that it was me.

"This one, for instance, it's all about this blue right here, see?" And he pointed to a cluster of blue sploshes, almost caressed it with a gentle movement. "That's what's interesting. That's what this painting is *about*. The title doesn't matter."

Daniel Moore scribbled something on his pad. Suddenly I became completely self-conscious. The spell of my calmness up on the ladder was broken.

"What is your name?" he asked me gently.

"Alina. Alina Strada."

"Italian?"

"Yes."

"Lovely name." Then he turned to Taylor. "Isn't it?"

Taylor ignored him and kept on painting. I caught Daniel Moore smiling at me. I smiled back, trying to overcome the fact that I was completely naked and suddenly wished I wasn't. They talked some more, but it was a struggle. Taylor just didn't seem to want to be civil to him. It took a while, but by the end of the afternoon, after a couple of glasses of vodka—neat—he finally gave in and loosened up. He told a story about a Braque painting of two pears and some bread. He first conjured up the thick gray background, then the two pears, and then—just by pronouncing the word, slowly rolling the *r* in his mouth, moving his hands in a small circle—he put the bread next to the pears. Daniel Moore and I saw it happen. We both laughed, as the painting had just materialized before us, and we looked at each other, like two children who have just seen a magician do his trick. It was brilliant.

That was my last sitting, and before I left, Julian handed me an envelope with some money.

"Hey, thanks," I said and quickly hid the envelope in my jeans without even looking at it. It embarrassed me to be paid in front of Daniel Moore.

"There's a car waiting for you downstairs," Julian said as he handed me another piece of paper, "and this is a gift certificate for the Kyoto House. You could go straight there if you want. They're open till nine."

"What for?"

"The Japanese spa?" he said. My lack of knowledge was beginning to bore him.

The writer was listening to this exchange, and I could sense his amusement, over my shoulder.

"They'll scrub every speck of paint off your skin and soak you in the hot tub, give you a proper shiatsu. That kind of stuff," Julian explained.

"Do you always send your models to the Kyoto House at the end of a sitting?" Daniel Moore quickly interjected, pad in hand.

"Well, Taylor *loves* that place. You know, it's the ultimate pampering, especially when you have to get a lot of paint off your skin," Julian replied, still in his robotic, professional mode. "But, no, this is the first time Taylor is using a model, so you couldn't really say that. No, that wouldn't be accurate, would it?

I ran for the elevator. Daniel Moore followed me. He kept his eyes on me and maintained a friendly smile as we descended the four floors. I pretended to ignore him. As we came out of the building I saw a white stretch limo waiting at the corner.

"Oh, shit," I whispered, "I'm not taking *that*."

"Why not? It'll be fun. And you could give me a lift uptown," he said. He was beginning to get on my nerves, with his tone of voice that always implied he was smarter than you.

"If you don't mind, I'd rather take the subway," I said. "You can take a ride in the car."

I left him at the corner. I don't know whether he eventually took the limo or whether I had succeeded in making him feel stupid about it.

I didn't care that much, either way.

That evening I sat at my tiny kitchen table, waiting for the kettle to boil. Isabella's letter lay open on the table, next to the gift certificate for Kyoto House. I had picked it up from my mail box, its white corner jutting out, as I walked past it quickly, dreaming of a hot bath.

Nothing matched, nothing added up.

Yet there they were, two parallel worlds unfolding at the same pace.

I played out, once more, the contents of her letter, adding a few variations from my previous staging. Different wardrobe, a few additions to the dialogue. I was getting good at this.

It's visiting day. Alba walks into the room, dragging her feet. She looks shabby and untidy, as she has of late. She's taken to wearing these long flowery skirts that make her look like an old hippie. For some reason it annoys Isabella to see her like this.

"How are you?" Isabella asks as she presses the button of the intercom.

"I'm exhausted. That train ride kills my back."

There's a pause.

"I don't think you should come again if it makes you so tired," Isabella says, and right away she realizes this is a mistake.

"Don't start with this," Alba snaps back, "there's no point in always being so destructive. I just said my back hurts, that's all."

But this is not a good beginning.

They talk about the usual things, what the lawyer said, the persistency of Isabella's migraine, a letter from Alina. They both feel uneasy and keep shuffling their feet and moving back and forth on their chairs.

Then Alba changes the subject. She says there has been something on her mind for some time and that she has decided it's time they talk about it.

Isabella narrows her eyes, like a cat suddenly alert.

"You know, I've been sorting out some of your stuff . . . old things I found at home in your room. Clothes, things you left in the drawers. I packed it all away in a big box. Well, I came across a journal you wrote when you were about thirteen. And I thought that since it was a child's journal, it would be okay to read it. You know, after so many years."

Isabella's back stiffens. She cannot believe what is coming at her, the rush of water through a dam that has given way.

So there she is, Alba, now wanting to confront "her horrible fabrications."

"I mean, did you really hate me that much as a child? Because the words I read . . . it wasn't even resentment, oh no, it was pure hatred."

"Alba . . ."

"No, wait! I mean, to go so far as to imply that I had something to do with the way your father died . . . What monstrosity is this, to insinuate something like that?"

"Listen . . ."

"That I *killed* him?" She claps her hands and gives out a shrill laugh, pretending to be amused by such a preposterous proposition. "That I pulled the trigger and shot him?"

She's almost screaming. One of the guards turns his head.

"I refuse to discuss this in here like this," Isabella says through the intercom. "You're the one who's being destructive now." She's speaking calmly, like a doctor to a patient.

"Oh, now she doesn't want to talk about it!" Alba raises her eyes to the ceiling, as if talking to God. "How come you get to decide everything? And how about *my* feelings for once? They don't really matter, I guess. Right?"

"Listen. Please. These are the only forty-five minutes in a week I get to see a familiar face other than the guards. I won't see you again till next week. I can't face this now. Not like this, not behind a sheet of glass. *Please.*"

"It's not my fault if you're here behind glass."

Isabella gives her one of her frozen stares. She hardens. She lacks the strength to say what Alba needs to hear. She knows exactly what it is that she's supposed to say. That it was only a child's sick fantasy. But at this point in her life the fantasy has sunk so deep within her that it has settled with time and has slowly turned into a truth.

Whether or not Alba actually pulled the trigger of that gun, she *did* kill him. She's the one responsible.

So she decides to confront her. She sighs deeply, like an athlete before a high jump.

"All right, then, if that's what you want. I'll tell you what."

"What?"

"Why don't you tell me the truth, once and for all?" she challenges. "Come on, just tell me exactly what happened that day when Oliviero died, and we'll put this behind us for good."

Alba recoils.

"You're crazy."

"No I'm not. I'm simply saying it's your turn to reveal something."

"I don't need to answer any of your questions."

"Then why did you bring it up if you're not ready to answer?"

Alba is white with rage. Her lips have tightened.

"You know what your problem is? You've spent all your life feeling betrayed, from the time you were a little girl. First by me, then by the whole world," she says with contempt. "And look where it took you."

She looks around the room, she looks at the guard with the machine gun, at the bars on the window.

"And anyway, if there's anybody here who has to answer questions, I believe that's you."

Isabella pulls the wire from the phone, the communication is interrupted. *Fuck you,* her lips say. She stands up, calls the guard, and asks to be taken back to her cell. She doesn't turn back to look at her mother again.

I rang Alba first thing in the morning.

"I sent her a telegram. I said I won't be going to visit her for some time. I think it's better for both of us, at least for the time being," she said.

"You're joking!"

"No. Not one bit," she sighed heavily. "I need time to sort this thing out."

"But she needs to see *someone*. We can't leave her alone in that—"

"*You* can come back and visit her," she interrupted me. "She's your sister."

"I can't believe we're having this conversation."

"You better believe it. Do you realize she had the nerve to ask me to tell her the truth once and for all? It's absurd."

"I know, I know. She wrote me that—"

There was a pause. We listened to the crackling on the line.

"She's too hard, Alina." Suddenly her voice sounded so sad. "Your father died from his own unhappiness, you know it perfectly well. But your sister has always been so manipulative: since she was small she was always twisting facts so that she could put the blame on others. . . . I mean, wanting the truth from *me*? Considering where she is, and why. It's absurd, that she should play the victim. I won't have it."

We had finally gotten to the core of things, a stripped-bare core that I couldn't handle either. So far I had only been able to look at it for a few seconds before everything started to hurt so much that I needed to close my eyes again.

"Plus, I'm getting a divorce. *Plus,* I'm getting older," she went on. "It's a lot, Alina. It isn't just the two of you and your problems in my life. I need to take care of myself as well."

I just wanted to get off the phone as quickly as possible. I was tired of having to hear the same thing: how it was always too much to ask, how nobody had the strength to help anybody.

"I have to go to work, Alba. We'll speak in the next few days."

It would have been fun to tell her about Taylor Davis, the portrait, and the stretch limo. But it never seemed to be the right time with her for those New York kind of stories.

Every now and again, whenever I happened to be running an errand in Midtown, I would pop into Rizzoli's and browse through the Italian newspaper section. There was always at least one headline on the first page with the word *pentito* on it, or *terrorista*. The stories were about either new terrorist actions—attacks, killings—or arrests. The *pentiti* were increasing in number, and, thanks to their information, the police were finally getting their hands on the underground groups that were responsible for the bombings, kidnappings, and killings. The gloomy season of their trials had begun and Italy was getting ready to witness the just punishment of the killers. The liberal papers objected that it didn't add up how those killers who volunteered to cooperate would eventually walk away free. Then again, in a Catholic country, that kind of hypocrisy about repentance was the least one could expect, they said. The relatives of the victims were interviewed on the news and in the major newspapers. They felt that the state, by introducing such laws, had betrayed them and the memory of their dear ones and were doing more for the killers than for them.

I read what I could standing there, quickly scanning the columns on the first page, pretending to be only mildly interested; but often I couldn't resist and had to get a copy in order to read the whole story. I could hardly believe my country was going through such a drama, and yet there was hardly a trace of it on the American news.

Every time I took one of the newspapers home and read it thoroughly I felt like I had just given myself a fix of something I wasn't allowed to have. More often I felt a distinct pang of guilt, for allowing myself to be so far removed from it all.

Shortly after my call with Alba, Bruno came to New York on another of his short business trips. He had a big meeting with buyers at Macy's who were interested in Italian sofa beds and lamps. He phoned me at the gallery from his hotel. He had read an interesting review of a new southwestern restaurant in SoHo in a magazine, he said. I liked the way his taste turned instantly adventurous the minute he set foot in Manhattan.

I held the receiver in my hand and motioned at Raimonda, who was sitting across from me, reading the Arts and Leisure section of the *New York Times* with her shades still on. Her boyfriend had not called in days and it was driving her crazy.

"Can I take a normal-size lunch break? It's Bruno. He's only in town for a few days."

"Only if he takes me out, too. I need some distraction."

We ended up in a booth in what seemed a gigantic Frida Kahlo shrine—aluminum-framed mirrors, plastic flowers, lace, murals, pictures of the Virgin of Guadalupe, Mexican music from the forties—with three gigantic Bloody Marys and a mountain of corn chips, guacamole, enchiladas, and chile rellenos in front of us. The clientele—chic, downtown, black-clad—seemed to be fairly amused by the pretentious kitsch. They had all probably read the same review as Bruno and were enjoying acting like old-timers in the newest fashionable venue.

"It's fun, this place," Bruno ventured, looking around the room, slightly intimidated.

His beige suit and blue tie made him look totally out of place. Golden Rolex on hairy wrist. He could never lose that look, no matter how much he tried.

"It's like a theme park," I said, vaguely irritated. I didn't want him to feel inadequate. "It's like you have to wear a costume to go to a restaurant in this town."

"It's New York," Raimonda said, gloomily sucking her Bloody Mary through a straw, shades still on. "And no matter how much it may annoy you, you won't be able to live in many other places after this."

"Oh, that's bullshit," I said and realized I sounded unnecessarily hostile. "I mean, I don't believe I'd be bored if I ended up in a place where people were a little less obsessed by what's cool and what isn't."

Raimonda ignored me and turned her attention to Bruno, slightly flirtatiously. They had known each other a long time and acted like old friends. I was surprised by their degree of intimacy; I never would have expected Raimonda to be close to someone like Bruno. I thought her too much of a snob.

"Alina says you're getting a divorce," she prompted him.

He nodded as he swallowed a big chunk of chile relleno.

"Yes. There's really no reason for us to be together any longer," he said, wiping his mouth. "We're going to divorce amicably. We just want our lives back, that's all."

"Lucky you. If I ever manage to get my divorce, mine will be *bad bad bad*," Raimonda said, shaking her head slowly and picking a minuscule piece of chicken from my enchilada.

Bruno looked at me.

"Your mother is going through a difficult time. I can't really understand what it is. It has to do with your sister. With her mother, her father. It's, like . . . all coming back."

"How do you mean?" I asked.

"I don't know, she won't talk to me about it. She's retreated into her shell. Door closed. You know what she's like when she gets like that."

"She said she's not going to visit Isabella anymore."

"I know. I went to see Isabella last week." He took a long sip of his drink and kept his eyes in the glass. "You know, I figured she might feel a bit lonely without a visitor."

"You went all the way to Voghera?" I couldn't believe it.

"Sure. I drove. It was a little awkward. Your sister and I never had . . . much to say to each other." He smiled timidly. "I don't think I'll go back, though. She didn't really know what to make of my visit."

There was a short silence, during which I felt Raimonda's eyes on me through her dark glasses, studying my reaction. I took a deep breath. Suddenly it had made me incredibly anxious to hear how Bruno had attempted unsuccessfully to play the father. Anxious for him, anxious for Isabella.

"Jesus . . . I don't know what to—"

"You don't have to do anything for the time being," he said. "Really, Alina, there's nothing you can do to change anything."

"You're not Mother Teresa," Raimonda said. "You've just pulled *yourself* back together and can barely stand on your own feet. Your mother will need you for five minutes and then won't know what to do with you."

"I'm thinking of Isabella."

Raimonda took off her glasses and leaned forward across the table, squinting slightly as if she needed adjusting to the light.

"Would you leave New York and move back to Italy just so that you can see her for a few minutes once a week? Don't you think it's better to wait till after the trial before you consider such a big move?"

Bruno nodded. I wondered if those two had already spoken about this. Judging by their downcast eyes, they had.

A couple of weeks later I was coming back from the printer, loaded with boxes of invitations, when I saw Daniel Moore on Greene Street, peeking through the gallery glass door. He had his nose stuck to the glass and a hand screening the light from his eyes.

"Hello," I whispered behind his back. "I'm just now opening."

"Ah, there you are!" he said, as if we had a date for which I was late. He followed me inside and sat on the chair at Raimonda's desk, totally at ease. He watched me hang my jacket inside the closet and place the boxes in a drawer, and kept swiveling right and left with the chair, hands in his lap and head tilted slightly backwards.

"Yes?" I asked, my head still in a drawer. "Is there anything I can do for you?"

"I'm writing that story on Taylor," he proclaimed.

"Yes, I know."

"I was wondering if I could ask you a couple of things."

"Like what?"

"Would you mind if I used your name, and the Kyoto House story?"

"What story? There's no story."

"You know, how he sent you in a limo to the Japan—"

"He didn't *send* me anywhere. Plus, I never took the limo."

"All right"—he raised his hands in surrender—"I mean, would you mind if I mentioned he *offered* you a chauffeured limo and a gift certificate for a spa? Would you mind if I quoted your name?"

"I don't know." I shrugged and looked away. "Maybe not. I mean, yes. Yes, I would mind."

"Why?"

"I just don't want you to make Taylor look like an asshole, that's all."

He stared at me, surprised. That made me feel stupid and I blushed.

"I like Taylor," I said, lowering my eyes.

"Well, so do I," he said. "A lot. I'm not writing this piece against him, you know."

"Okay, then."

He fiddled for a bit with a pen he found by the phone, tapped it a couple of times on the desk.

"Have you known him a long time?"

"A few months. We're having his exhibition here next November."

He stared at me, deadpan.

"Are you lovers?"

"Excuse me?"

"Do you mind my asking you?"

"Yes."

"It's off the record."

"Then why do you need to know?"

Daniel Moore smiled. A large, happy smile.

"Because I would like to ask you to dinner."

I didn't say anything. I remained perfectly still.

"I just want to make sure I'm not overstepping," he said and stuck the pen in his mouth. He began swiveling again in the chair.

"What a crazy idea," I said.

I couldn't really look at him, because I wanted to stay serious and I felt like laughing all of a sudden.

"That's good, then," he said and stood up, as if the interview were over. "Then I'll call you here. How about classical music? Do you ever go to concerts?"

"No."

"Would you like to go? The Bach Suites, next week? A new young Hungarian cellist."

I didn't know exactly what he meant, but I nodded.

"Whatever," I said. "Just call me some time and we'll make a plan."

Isabella's letters kept coming regularly. Thick envelopes, the blue *ESPRESSO* stamp always on the left side, my name and address in her tiny handwriting always perfectly centered. One was an exact replica of the other.

In the last few weeks she had taken to writing meticulously about her life with the "group" after they had gone underground.

I guess that, on one hand, she wanted to fill in the gaps for me—I couldn't remotely imagine what her life had been like during the years when we had drifted so far apart—but I also felt she needed a witness now that she was totally isolated, unable to communicate with any of her comrades. She had to tell the story out loud again, in order to keep the memory of those days fresh. After all, that was all she had left to hold on to.

It was her legacy, her identity.

Every time I held another envelope in my hand I couldn't resist tearing it open immediately. I would read her long letters on the run, if need be—on my way to work, on the subway, sometimes at the French bakery where I had my *café au lait* before opening the gallery. I'd have to stuff the sheets back in my pocket and continue to read as I ate my lunch, stain the pages with grease from my sandwich. Those fragments haunted me all day, like a song that got stuck in my head and wouldn't leave me alone.

Try to picture us: a small group of people who never felt safe, wandering from one rented flat to the next, always farther out, deeper in the outskirts of the city. We always jumped if the door rang, if a policeman looked at us in a certain way at a traffic light. There have been many moments when I would have liked to be able to pick up the phone and hear a familiar voice. I thought of calling home so many times, but I couldn't, because it wouldn't have been safe. I knew the phones were tapped.

This is how it happens: one day you wake up and you realize you have slid underground. It's not a decision you make overnight, somehow it just happens gradually. Till one day you are forced to admit your whole life has become a clandestine affair.

So I follow her instructions; I picture it.

It's 1982. Rome has become too dangerous and they decide to move to Casa Rossa. It's Isabella's idea. Lorenzo has just died and the place is empty.

For the rest of them this is just another hideout. A safer place where they can live for a while. But for her it's harder. She'll realize only later what a bad mistake it was, to mix her past with her present.

Does she resent the way they pay no heed, the way they break the good crystal wineglasses, put out their cigarettes in the china, put their muddy feet on the couch, use the place like it means nothing to them?

As she opens a drawer, she invariably stumbles upon familiar objects, small things that spring from her past like a jack-in-the-box. An old ladle, a mended tablecloth, Jeanne's sewing kit. She holds the object in her hand, frozen, while fragments of an Easter lunch, the memory of her birthday celebration when she was eight years old, attack her from nowhere, till someone shakes her out of her reverie with a question.

Enrico is increasingly paranoid, he feels the circle is tightening around them. He decides, for their own security, that Isabella should be the only one allowed to go out. The others have to remain within the house.

Isabella goes shopping for groceries. She shops at Domenico's store on the piazza, discusses the freshness of the cheese, takes her time deciding whether to get capers in salt versus the ones in the jar.

"I'm here for a little vacation," she says.

"All by yourself?" Domenico's daughter-in-law has taken over the place now. "Don't you feel lonely?"

"No. I actually love it," she says and forces a smile. "I needed a rest. I read a lot and go for walks."

In order not to raise suspicions she buys a little food in different places in the area, so that nobody wonders why she needs so much. Sometimes she stops at the *pasticceria* and has an ice cream cone by herself, sits outside at a table, watching people stroll in the evening light, kids play, young couples coming back from the beach, sand still sticking to their feet.

When she comes home with the groceries, the others are usually sitting around the table, looking at maps, chain-smoking, discussing the political articles they've read in the papers. Sometimes raising their voices. A Beretta on the counter, next to the bread basket. They sweep off the maps from the table, they stop arguing as soon as she comes in.

"What shall we have tonight?"

"Carbonara?"

"I bought clams."

"Great," Enrico volunteers, "I'll go pick some fresh parsley in the garden."

They pour themselves some wine, and as they wait for the water to boil, they slide back into being like an ordinary family. Puttering around the kitchen, discussing the best way to get rid of the sand in the clams.

After dinner they play cards, and enjoy teasing one another. They joke with Enrico, they tell him he sucks at this game. He laughs as he slams his cards on the table.

"Fuck off," he chuckles. "I know exactly what I'm doing. Just wait and see." Isabella loves to see him like this, his eyes shining with laughter when he wins the hand. He has been so tense, lately. At night in bed, he jolts in his sleep.

Enrico and I were the oldest couple of the group. The others tried different arrangements. Couples broke up and re-paired all the time. Sex was our only outlet, physical contact was the only release we had from all that tension. I'm sure you can see why we've been extraordinarily close all these years, in a way that is difficult to describe. What bound us to each other were the choices that cut us off from the ordinary.

Now they've made sure we're as far apart as possible, and all our mail has been suspended. If I could see him, or even receive his letters, I think even this concrete pit would be more bearable. The last time I saw him was the day we were caught. It's also the last memory I have of being outside.

They have been hiding in Casa Rossa for three months now.

The worst has passed.

They have been watching the news religiously every night, always holding their breath. The carabinieri have been following the tracks of the commando who shot Lo Capo, and they suspect the group is hiding somewhere in the North of Italy. They don't even think of looking so close to where it happened. Then, as weeks go by, the top news stories change. Other terrorists' actions in the North are taking the heat off that particular story. Police special forces, antiterrorist squads, are mobilized all over the country, but they complain they need reinforcements to carry out their investigations and searches thoroughly. The country cannot cope with all that is happening. In a way, there's a feeling these armed groups have succeeded in their aim: to attack and seize the heart of the state. To show Italians, and the rest of the world, how just a few organized fighters can paralyze an entire country and bring it to its knees.

They feel a sense of relief, as if they are beginning slowly to come down from the monstrous tension they have endured till now. They alternate between a sense of elation—they keep reassuring one another that they are winning the war—and a feeling of doom, which they keep to themselves. Deep down none of them believes they will ever be able to get away with it.

Enrico feels it's time to move on. He has another action in mind. Planning this one will take even longer. They need money, new arms. A new hideout.

It's hard to admit it, and they don't talk about it, but each one of them, in his or her own way, dreads having to start the process all over again.

Autumn in the south still feels warm, it's a beautiful breezy afternoon. They stir with longing as they watch Isabella get in the car for another shopping expedition. They all feel like they deserve a break before they move on.

"Come on, let's all go," says Enrico. "Just for an hour, before sunset."

Maybe he needs to reward them, to prepare them for the job ahead.

The four doors of the car are flung open.

"Yes! Let's go—four in the back, two in the front!"

They squeeze into the car, laughing like children on vacation.

And they find themselves sitting on the steps of the church of Santa Caterina in Pisignano, basking in the golden light, licking their ice cream cones of *stracciatella e cioccolato*. Starlings cutting the sky, kids running after a soccer ball in the square. Familiar, soothing sounds. Their arms resting across one another. There's that stupid love song they've all heard all summer on the radio, coming from some car's radio. Isabella gives in and hums the irresistible chorus.

Then a screeching sound of tires, hysterical screams, men in uniform, guns leveled mere inches from her temple, a rush of adrenaline, a weakness in her knees. Dust in her nostrils, the smell of metal, sweat, fear. She turns to Enrico, his face is frozen, suddenly he lookes fifty years old. He looks at her and shuts his eyes for a second, as if to say, *Let go . . . It's over, don't even think of taking the gun out of your pocket.*

She's holding her arms up, almost without realizing it, the ice cream cone still clutched in her hand. Then she feels the chocolate slowly trickling down her wrist. Warm and sticky. She keeps trying to rub it off her forearm once they have pushed her inside the car, but she's hand-cuffed and it's hard to reach.

Although Isabella had rehearsed this scene a hundred times in her mind, the day it actually plays out before her eyes, she realizes how un-prepared she still is. She knew this was coming, she only wishes she had had a little bit more time.

Everything about Daniel Moore came in waves, with no date attached. There wasn't a beginning, a middle, and an end.

I'll have to describe him from a distance, as if it wasn't me, the one standing next to him. Smiling like a fool.

I discovered how much I liked him only the second time we went out. After I sloshed down two large margaritas, he finally ceased to in-timidate me and I allowed myself to notice his sandy blond hair curling at the back of his neck, his strong freckled forearms. I watched the way he moved his hands and felt like touching them. His oddly threadbare clothes. Missing buttons, crumpled shirt collar. Thick woolen sweater mended at the elbow. He smelled good.

Daniel took me out to see things he loved. The Syrian shops on Ocean Avenue, the lobby of a great building in the West Forties from the turn of the century, a view of the five bridges, the old Russian baths in the East Village, that Hungarian cellist. As I listened to the Bach Suites next to him, I started to cry. Without even turning his head, he put his arm around me and drew me closer. I started sniffing in his sweater, not knowing if I was crying because of the music or because I was so close to him.

He kissed me in the cab after the concert. He kissed me slowly, lightly, like we had all the time in the world. It made me feel faint. I had not been touched by a man since Tomas, and that felt like light years away already.

"I've wanted to do that for some time," Daniel said and then told the driver to pull over at the corner in front of a restaurant.

A first kiss is the demarcation line: the same information that a mo-ment ago felt private, all of a sudden seems unfair to withhold. And with that exchange came more.

We were in Chinatown, in a small restaurant filled with smoke and clatter.

"I was married for four years. Her name is Maya. She fell in love with someone else, and we got divorced a few months ago. She's living in Los Angeles with him now."

He said this matter-of-factly, carefully rolling sesame noodles around his chopsticks. I waited and gulped down more green tea.

"I've been brokenhearted," he said, looking at me, intentionally, like he wanted to make sure I got the message. I nodded and stared at the greasy cloth. "I suppose that's why I've been acting so cautiously." He wiped his mouth with a paper napkin.

"Of course," I said, as if this were superfluous information, something that didn't really concern me. "I totally understand that."

"I'm attracted to you, Alina. But I'm going to have to go slowly."

Daniel didn't seem afraid to call things by their name. I nodded again. A man with a broken heart. What a tricky inheritance to accept.

For a split second I played with the idea of standing up right there and saying something on the order of "Sorry, I don't need this, not now." But then I thought, *You want him. The rest is fear, pride. Uninteresting feelings. Stop being difficult.*

So I made myself smile, and offered him my hand across the table.

"I love being with you," I said.

He reached for my hand and held it for a few seconds. It made me feel like I had achieved something.

We didn't talk about Maya again that evening. He didn't seem to be avoiding the subject; it was more like he had exhausted whatever he felt was necessary to say and had moved on to something else. A book he was reading, a place in New Mexico he would like to show me someday. His confidence, his lack of awkwardness calmed me.

I decided to trust Daniel Moore. This is a man who's not afraid of telling the truth, I thought.

Then came August and its blinding light on the beach. I remember those days as blue. Vibrant, deep, windy blue. Daniel asked me to come out to Long Island for the weekend.

"This is my little shelter," he said as he showed me his wooden cabin on stilts on the dunes.

"I want to spend some time alone with you," he'd said over the phone. I could tell this was part of his experiment. Checking if his broken heart was mendable.

As I stepped on the verandah the sun-bleached planks creaked under my feet. I peeked inside the glass door. Just a big white bed in the center of the room. A tiny desk by the window. A flower in a glass. My heart nearly burst. I was so desperate to sleep with him by then.

"It's perfect," I whispered, more to myself than to him, since he already had his head inside the kitchen drawers.

I watched him fiddle with fire and coals in the fading light, chop onions, slash open the belly of the fish and pull its guts out. I looked at the shells and the driftwood he had collected, scattered on the windowsills, on the mantelpiece. I could imagine him sailing in a windbreaker, then walking with his trousers rolled up to his knees on the jetty. I kept an eye open for a picture of him and Maya on that same beach, but didn't find any.

We ate, barefoot, on the verandah, under the stars. There was a feeling of sumptuousness to the way he fed me. The small table was cluttered with glasses, expensive bottles of wine, dripping candles, and all the food we could eat. Then, when all was eaten, and nearly all was drunk, I found myself telling him about Casa Rossa. I wanted to conjure up images of my own past that would stay with him so that he could fall in love with my life as well. The beautiful part of my life, which I had almost forgotten. I told him about the smell of oregano and mint in the fields, of the shape of the *furneddhi,* the color of the sea beneath the crumbling tower at San Emiliano.

"You would love it. You have no idea how much that place would move you."

And suddenly, for the first time, I understood how much I missed it. He smiled.

"I love the way your hands move all over the place when you talk," he said.

"Do they?"

"Yes. A lot."

"Such an Italian cliché. So, were you listening at all or were you just watching my hands fly around?"

"Come here."

That shut me up.

"Let's make love," he whispered in my ear.

"I was hoping we'd get to this at some point," I whispered back, and we both laughed.

His skin was softer and whiter than I expected, his smell was sweeter than I remembered, and we found our way out of our clothes and into each other without obstacles.

I woke up wrapped in a knot of sheets and legs. I didn't stir, till he moved closer and threw his arm across my chest with a short moan. I watched the light filter through the wooden Chinese shutter and let him sleep a while longer, trying to practice breathing at his pace to give myself something to do.

We came back to the cabin every weekend till the end of the summer. We would swim very early in the morning and make love in the afternoons, falling asleep into thick sound sleep filled with dreams and sweat.

During those weeks, we were careful to exchange only tidbits of information about our lives, so as not to flood each other with our pasts. I, of course, had a pretty good reason not to: I felt it was too soon to overwhelm him with my family's history. It felt safer to stick to the present. It made us feel more open to each other, like there was no tomorrow and we should enjoy what we had.

Nevertheless, at times I caught myself rehearsing a little speech in front of the mirror, where I tried to explain to him that Isabella had been charged with murder and was locked up in solitary confinement. But invariably I would stop somewhere in mid-sentence, frightened. It was an untranslatable feeling that I simply couldn't bear to express, a coldness that was hard to shake off: each time, it stuck to me like wet, heavy snow. I had designated him to be the happy part of my life, and I was unwilling to taint him with that.

At the beginning of September, the days shifted from blue to silver. One morning we woke up to a rainstorm.

"Let's stay in bed," Daniel said as he felt I was about to move and start the day. We were going back to the city that evening. Somehow it felt like it was the end of something. Maybe the beginning of something new, but nevertheless there was a hint of death I could smell in the air. We both felt the spleen of that first rain. When he made love to me I felt like crying, but I turned my face so that he wouldn't see it.

Later, as we were sitting around a warm pot of coffee, he looked out the window, biting a piece of toast.

"It's going north. There will be an amazing light in half an hour. We should go for a hike."

"I love you," I heard myself say.

"What?"

He turned his head quickly, his mouth full of toast. Surprise in his eyes.

I cleared my throat. "I love you." The repetition had made me hesitant, I no longer felt so bold.

Daniel smiled.

"Good. That's very good."

That's all he said.

I kept writing all of it to Isabella. I guess I wanted to keep a record. I thought maybe one day—when she would finally be released—I would get the letters back, and it would have all been there: the serial novelization of my love for Daniel Moore.

I said I have to talk about Daniel as if it weren't me, the one next to him, smiling like a fool. Because now I cannot bear to think we were ever that close.

Not only can I not bear it, today I actually find it impossible to believe it.

It's a good thing I can never read those letters again.

Then came the fall.

We were back in New York, back at our jobs. Daniel would come and spend the night on Elizabeth Street. The letters were lying everywhere, around my kitchen counter, on the desk, by my night table.

Daniel couldn't help noticing them. The narrow envelopes kept appearing without fail.

"I always meant to ask you," he said one day, holding one of the envelopes between his fingers. "Who are these from? Should I be jealous of someone back home?"

His tone was light, his eyes smiling. I froze. I wasn't going to say anything till it became unavoidable.

"It's my sister, Isabella," I said nonchalantly, and went to the fridge to pour myself a glass of water.

"She still lives in Italy, right?"

I nodded.

"I thought maybe this was your Italian boyfriend or something," he chuckled, relieved. "What a coup de théâtre that would have been."

I shook my head and tried to look amused.

"What does she do, your sister?"

"She's . . ."

Then I knew the time had come. I could no longer keep one life separated from the other. And I also knew this was going to be a head-on collision, I could hear the crash coming.

"She's writing me from jail."

Something collapsed in Daniel's face. All my planning for how I'd tell him had come to nothing. I had no choice now: I told him the story I had long dreaded having to tell. He listened quietly, without interrupting me. I could sense his horror when I told him about the murder, or the alleged murder, as I rushed to add. It was as if his silence at that precise moment had turned hollow, as if my words were bouncing off his body and were falling down on a hard floor.

"But *why?*" he asked me.

"Why *what?*"

"Why kill people like that, at random? Why this magistrate?"

I recoiled. I didn't want to be the one to explain. I realized how little I had explained it to myself.

"I don't know. Because he was investigating terrorism, I guess. These groups . . . they attack like that, they choose different targets that are part of the system, in order to destabilize the country. They use these expressions, like *attacco al cuore dello stato*—'to attack the heart of the state.' "

"But what does that *really* mean?"

I sighed, anxiously. All of a sudden I felt the enormity of our distance.

"I don't know, either. It's like a . . . a . . ." I spread my arms and shook my head. "A civil war. By spreading terror they are keeping the whole country under siege."

How was I going to explain that many of those people had been my schoolmates? That it was my generation—people like me—behind those bars? Although Daniel was a journalist and an avid reader, he knew only what the *New York Times* had bothered to write about terrorism in Italy. Moro and the Red Brigades had made the front page in '78, but nobody really had a clear picture of what was happening after that. Of the complexity of the situation.

"You have to understand, there are dozens of different clandestine revolutionary organizations," I tried to explain, "and not all of them have resorted to"—I searched for a better word, but couldn't find any—"killing."

He didn't say anything. He nodded pensively.

"I hope this isn't going to freak you out too much," I said, in a whisper. He looked at me in a kind of stupor, then shook his head.

"No, of course not," he said. But his voice was strained, as if he were answering just out of politeness.

Later that night, as we lay in bed before falling asleep, I sensed that Daniel was still thinking about Isabella.

"You didn't tell me the most important thing," he said.

"Which is . . . ?"

"*Did* your sister actually kill this man?"

I felt the words land, one by one. I flicked the light on and sat up.

"She's declared herself a political prisoner. All of them have. They refused to answer to the interrogations. But I think she'll agree to say something at the time of the trial."

"Yes, I understand that. But what did she say to *you*?"

My throat locked.

"She . . . she and I . . . have never discussed it."

He stared at me, stupefied.

"You haven't?"

"No."

I looked at him defiantly and heard myself give a shrill, quick laugh. Out of fear and embarrassment.

"Because . . ." I struggled. "Because . . . I never felt like . . . like confronting her like that."

"Confronting her? But Alina . . . it's a very relevant question, isn't it?" he insisted.

"Yes, of course."

"I mean, it's *crucial*. I don't see how you can"—he pulled himself up and sat up straight, alongside me—"how you can *avoid* asking this question."

I was exhausted. My eyelids felt like they weighed a ton.

I was wishing he'd let go so we could go to sleep. But Daniel was looking at me, still waiting for an answer.

"It's harder than you think, to ask a question like that," I said, without being able to suppress the hostility in my voice. "I hope for your sake you'll never have to."

For a few seconds he didn't move. He kept staring at me with that serious expression. Then his eyes softened.

"I'm sorry, baby," he said, "you're absolutely right. I didn't mean to upset you." And he held me close to him without speaking, just stroking my hair.

We didn't talk about it anymore.

He took me to his parents' house in Connecticut for Thanksgiving. The place was just like I had imagined it, comfortable and unpretentious, full of family photographs, warm and slightly untidy. Daniel's mother, Elizabeth, was a handsome woman with a thick mane of gray hair. She had been a teacher at Juilliard. There was a certain sadness about her that I liked. His father, Peter, was a big redheaded man, almost too tall to be good looking, a giant with disarmingly blue eyes. They had had five kids, Daniel was the next to oldest, and they were all coming to spend the weekend.

"Elizabeth and I *love* Italy," Peter pronounced, as he leaned against the kitchen counter, uncorking the bottle of Brunello I had brought. "We go as often as we can."

"We were in Siena two summers ago," Elizabeth said as she bent down to check the turkey in the oven.

She stood up again and wiped her forehead.

"We were thinking of going back again in October. There's a cooking course they give in this wonderful castle near . . . where is it exactly, darling?"

"Arezzo? Or maybe Pienza—I don't know, I'd have to look."

Peter handed me a glass of wine, then handed one to his wife. Our three glasses touched lightly in a toast.

"We're victims of that phase that hits you when you retire," he said, giving me a conspiratorial little smile. "You know: wine, gourmet food, cookbooks. Epicurus. We read only restaurant reviews these days."

"That's not true, darling." Elizabeth elbowed her husband jokingly. "We also go to museums and see a lot of art when we go to Europe."

"Have you ever been to the South of Italy?" I asked, slipping into in my well-rehearsed rap. I did that automatically in America. I called it my "southern pitch." "Tuscany is beautiful but a bit too tame for my taste," I began.

"Oh. Are you from the South?" Elizabeth inquired somewhat suspiciously.

"My mother's side of the family is from Puglia. It's a stunning region—cactuses, olives, strong light. Pretty harsh compared to Siena and those green hills."

"No, we never have. But maybe you should tell us where to go," Peter said politely.

Daniel entered the kitchen. He was pleased to find me chatting with his parents in such a relaxed manner, glass in hand.

"Alina says there's also a lot of amazing architecture in the South," he said, perhaps to reassure his parents that my mother's birthplace had some cultural appeal other than horseflies and women with hairy armpits.

During dinner I tried to play the part of the nice new girlfriend as best I could—helping with the turkey and the cranberry sauce in the messy kitchen—and managed to blend in with the other boyfriends, girlfriends, wives, and husbands of the several siblings who crowded the house. There were so many of them I couldn't even get their names straight. Daniel kept staring at me throughout the meal, pleased to see me there, merging with his clan.

"Where does your family live, Alina?" Peter asked me.

I stiffened slightly.

"In Rome, mostly."

"Do you have brothers or sisters?"

"A sister two years older than me."

I tried not to intercept Daniel's gaze, but I felt it on me.

"Is Thanksgiving a big holiday over there?" one of the younger brothers' girlfriends asked. She was eighteen, pretty, wearing too many different pastels.

"Oh, no, we have no Thanksgiving at all in Italy," I said, grateful for a way to change the subject. "Actually, I don't really know what this day is about. Who is it we're thanking here?"

"The Indians," Daniel said, holding up his glass, "for letting us take over their land and their harvests."

After dinner I glanced at a photo from Daniel's wedding on the mantelpiece. I had been trying to give Maya a face till then, and there she was at last. Beautiful, of course. She looked strong and intense in a champagne lace dress with white flowers in her hair. She could have been Latina, Mexican maybe. I tried to look at it again when nobody was watching. She and Daniel were running on the lawn, holding hands. They were laughing so hard the flowers were falling from her hair.

Before Daniel and I left, I stressed to Elizabeth and Peter they should feel free to call me anytime in case they planned another trip to Italy, that I would be glad to help. I boasted I could find them a house to rent on the beach if they wanted to explore the South, or the perfect bed-and-breakfast in Tuscany.

"Anything, really. Anywhere you want."

"That would be really wonderful," said Elizabeth emphatically. "I'll get your number from Daniel and maybe we'll go over some options together."

Peter nodded, his arm around his wife's shoulder. They waved on the doorstep, till we reversed out of the driveway.

"Great parents you have," I said.

Daniel pretended to dismiss my comment, but I could see he was pleased I liked them.

We drove back to New York in a drizzle. It may have been the rain on the pavement—sadly reflecting the headlights and neon signs—it may have been the turkey stuffing and the Brunello still running around my bloodstream, but I felt a wave of spleen overcome me, a dark, heavy feeling, pressing around my chest.

I knew I had passed the test. I could now count on endless plans and complications with the Moore clan. I was the Italian Girlfriend, the one who knows how to cook a perfect risotto, knows the titles of the relevant Renaissance paintings.

But that's not who I was. And I felt like a fraud for not saying the truth.

I rested my head on the window and followed the droplets of rain as they streaked across the glass. Daniel sensed the quality of my silence.

"Tired?"

"A bit. I feel like taking a hot bath and watching a movie on TV."

But the truth was that I felt even worse for being there with him, driving on a country road in Connecticut, having celebrated a festivity that meant absolutely nothing to me, pretending to be family with a bunch of strangers, speaking a strange language, warping my *r*'s, deluding myself that I could be this other person.

I kept seeing Isabella's face, asleep—it was just dawn in Voghera.

I was strangely quiet during the following weeks. It was as if I finally had allowed myself to sink a little deeper into myself and look into all the things I had abandoned somewhere in there. I needed the stillness and the concentration: I was getting ready, like an athlete gathering momentum before springing. I phoned Daniel.

"Let's meet for a drink after work. I need to talk to you about something."

"You worry me."

"It's kind of serious, and I . . . I don't want to talk about it over the phone."

I was sitting on a stool at the bar when he arrived. It was snowing lightly and I could smell the flakes on his wool scarf and the cold air on his cheeks.

He looked at me for a couple of seconds as he untied the scarf from around his neck. He brushed his cold finger on my hand as he hopped on the stool next to me and ordered a glass of wine.

"What's wrong?" he said.

"Listen, I've been thinking a lot. . . . I don't even know how to say this."

"My God, what is it?" he laughed, nervously. "Is this one of those 'I've met someone else' conversations?"

"No, of course not, but listen," I grabbed his hand and pulled it close to my chest. "This has been on my mind a lot in the last few months. It's about my sister."

His expression shifted. He looked concerned.

"Ultimately, I don't think I would be here right now if it weren't for you, Daniel."

He stared at me. Then arched an eyebrow, surprised.

"Really?"

"Yes."

"And?"

"And now I'm beginning to think that this isn't fair, that I'm being selfish and unrealistic. I got a letter from her last week. Her trial is about to start. It's . . . it's a big deal. It's going to be all over the news. It's going to be *huge.*"

"Yes, of course it will be. When does it start?"

"Soon. Next month, I think. Isa didn't know for sure yet, but she'll let me know."

We paused and each took a sip of wine.

"I need to be there," I said.

"Of course," he said again.

He sighed and ran his hand through his sandy hair a couple of times.

"How long is the trial going to take?"

"I don't know. Long."

"Approximately how long?"

"It could be months."

Daniel stared at the bottles lined up on the shelf against the mirror, pretending to read the labels.

"Wow. This is a surprise," he said softly.

"I know. But I've thought this through and I have no choice. I need to deal with this. I can't just pretend that . . . it's not happening. She's my sister."

He turned away and looked out the window. I followed his gaze and watched the flakes of snow float in the orange light of a streetlamp.

"Well, I guess it's the right thing for you to do," he said, turning back to his wineglass.

"Yes. I think it'll mean a lot to her to know that I'm there. We'll be able to see each other every day in the courtroom. Though she'll be behind bulletproof glass."

He shook his head slowly.

"Unbelievable."

"What?"

"The whole thing: you . . . going to a trial . . . the bulletproof glass. I can't even begin to picture it."

"Don't try to picture it. It's too sad."

He looked defeated.

He loves me, I thought.

"I'll miss you," he said.

"I'll be back."

But I couldn't say when.

That night, we slept together at my place, but something was different. We were both slowly retreating into silence.

In the following days I noticed how Daniel had stopped making plans and using the pronoun *we.* He no longer mentioned places he wanted to show me, or things he wanted to do with me.

"I'll be going to California for Easter," he announced, "to see my old friend Jeremy."

I nodded. But I feared California: it was Maya's home.

Just to torture myself some more I began to improvise what he was going to tell his parents when they asked him about me.

*She's gone back to Rome to attend her sister's trial. What? Didn't I tell you?
She's a terrorist, charged with murder.*

But what also infuriated me was how far back in my family the history of deception and betrayal went. Perhaps even murder.

Renée first, then Alba. Now Isabella. How was it possible, I asked
myself, that that history could be handed down so quietly, from woman
to woman, like it was an inheritance, something we simply had to get
used to?

That's what I was thinking as I watched Daniel's naked body moving
in the shower. I could almost visualize his past, sculpted in his straight
back, in his perfect proportions, reflected in his flawless skin. Mine, instead, felt like it had been twisted in my curls, obscured by my olive
complexion, hidden under my foreign accent.

In the next few days I dreaded to look into the mailbox, dreaded
finding the next white envelope, the one carrying the date of my departure.

I watched the snow melt and turn to slush. Before I knew it, it was
almost March, and it was time to go.

The minute I got off the plane in Rome, I was back as if I'd never left,
never learned, seen, or experienced, anything new.

It hit me suddenly, like a wave of some familiar smell, right in
the face.

Every man I set my eyes on—the guys in the baggage-claim area, the
dodgy taxi drivers offering a cheap ride to town, the road workers tearing up asphalt—every one had a cigarette dangling from the side of his
mouth. They all had thicker hair on their arms, as if displaying their
menacing hormones, overtly sexual body language. I hadn't seen these
men in America.

The streets, as I approached the heart of the city, looked dirtier, covered in dog shit and cigarette butts, the cobblestones uneven, bumpy. I
noticed the weeds and wildflowers sprouting among the cracks on the
pavement, between the terra-cotta shingles on the church roofs. I nego-
tiated the noise and the crowd, fascinated by the faces coming my way.
I had forgotten the stray cats and dogs feasting on the piles of unat-

tended garbage, the bleached blondes in outrageous fur coats and Bulgari bangles, the bearded beggars playing violin, their gypsy children begging shamelessly for money. I passed through the open-air market and watched fishmongers gut fish and wipe the blood on their aprons, old women in woolen caps cleaning muddy watercress they had just picked along the riverbank. I was amazed by the physical, the manual, the plants, the shit, the birds, the dirt, the smells.

The city didn't blink an eye, ignored me, and went on minding its own business, like it always had. This place never stops, I said to myself, contemplating the circus unfolding before my eyes. This place has been baking bread, selling fish, this place has had to drink and to eat, and has had sex, for thousands of years without a break. There hasn't been a single day when this city has been still or quiet, not even through the Dark Ages. It just kept moving on and on, baking its bread, yelling the price of fish, wanting to drink, to sleep, to fuck. It didn't matter what it took, it just went on and on, pushing through, resilient, like a root pushing through the stony ground. Bargaining, making deals, taking different routes, never stopped by wars, barbarians, invasions.

And suddenly I saw that, just like everyone else, I had been shaped by the particular geography I had grown up in. In Rome every street ended in a curve, in a twist, in a cross, sometimes a dead end. I saw that I'd grown up inside a labyrinth full of amazing surprises. You never knew what was around the corner, you could never see very far ahead in a straight line. There was no north or south or east or west. Just this constant turning around in a circle.

In the grid of Manhattan were predictable numbers and a cross streets, and you always knew exactly where you stood.

CHAPTER SEVEN

—◆—

I'm up at six-thirty.

I can hear Rita snoring loudly as I pass by her bedroom door.

The rest of the house is eerily silent, almost as if it were holding its breath. I tiptoe downstairs into the kitchen.

I sit at the marble-top table and unwrap some bread. I wait for the coffee to bubble in the espresso machine.

Suddenly the phone rings.

"Alina, it's me," Alba sounds unusually cheerful. "Were you asleep?"

"No. I'm making some coffee."

"I know you're an early riser. I called to let you know that I'm on my way. I'm almost at Caianello."

"You're on the highway?"

"Yes, I started out at five. I should be there by lunchtime."

I laugh. I like the way she enjoys being adventurous, turns a trip into a mission.

"Perfect. Oh, by the way, Rita's here, too. She spent the night."

"I know. That's why I decided to come, I thought we should have a proper family reunion and close the door of the house together. I'm bringing a bottle of champagne, so you better unpack the flutes."

Immediately after I got back from New York—I had only been back a couple of days—she asked me to go to Casa Rossa with her.

"I haven't been there since Lorenzo's funeral," she said. "The police were the last ones there, when they arrested Isabella. None of us has been back since. I have no idea what we're going to find. I really don't want to have to go alone."

When the house appeared at the end of the tree-lined driveway, Alba's face twisted in a grimace.

"Oh, God."

Its red had turned into a bleached pink, the paint on the shutters was peeling off, the wood was rotting, the garden was wild and overgrown. It looked like it had been abandoned for twenty years.

We opened all the windows, let the spring breeze blow in, and blow through our hair, as we carefully pulled on plastic gloves, like surgeons before an operation. Alba didn't want to ask anybody in the village to come and help us.

Let them clean that place up by themselves, they must have thought behind their closed shutters when they saw Alba and me coming out of the grocery store with soaps and detergents.

So we began.

First we started brushing off the dust from the furniture till we were covered in a white coat of powder. Then we knelt down and scrubbed the floors, and threw buckets of hot water onto the stone tiles to rinse the soapsuds. We washed the windows, waxed the tables, the chairs, the windowsills. We worked for three days without a break, till our backs hurt so much we could hardly bend.

On the fourth day, I started working in the garden, pruning trees, weeding, and cutting back the bushes. Alba went to the store and came back with flour and yeast.

"Fresh bread," she explained as I walked into the kitchen and found her kneading the dough, her apron dusted in a light coat of flour.

In the quietest hour of the afternoon, I came back from a walk and found her on the sofa in the living room, her book on the floor next to her shoes, her breathing thick with sleep. I entered the kitchen and peeped under the clean towels laid neatly over the terra-cotta bowls. The dough had turned into airy balls, the pungent smell of yeast tickled my nostrils.

That night Alba and I sat at the table and ate our soup with crunchy bread and cheese, smiling, the fragrance of firewood and freshly baked bread still warming the room.

The next morning she took a long bath, straightened her hair, and pulled it back in a tight bun. I watched her as she carefully put on makeup. I knew she must have a plan.

"We are going to see Rosa," she announced to her image in the mirror, spraying a whiff of her perfume on the inside of her wrists.

"Rosa?"

Stellario's daughter, the mother of Adele, lived a couple of miles away, in the next village. After Stellario and Celeste had died, their little white house—the one where Alba had seen the tarantula dance—was turned into a car workshop that sold Toyota spare parts.

"What about Adele?" I asked.

"She might be there too."

"Right."

I felt something contract in my stomach. The idea of facing any of them terrified me.

"Does she know we're coming?"

"She knows we're here." She clipped her pearl earrings onto her lobes. "*Everybody* knows we're here, by now."

"I mean, don't you think we should call first? Maybe we shouldn't just show up like this."

"It's all right."

She gave me a look.

"We don't have much choice in any case, do we? She can spit in our faces if she feels like it."

She was nervous, just like me. But she must have been tormenting herself with these thoughts for God knows how long. Till it had become impossible to postpone the visit any longer.

We drove in silence to Rosa's house. The weather matched our state of mind. It was an uneven morning, ridden by gusts of wind, clouds traveling fast across the sky, alternately obscuring and revealing the light. Nothing was still, the trees were swaying in the mistral, skirts flapped against our legs as we walked across the empty square. A single loose newspaper page rose, twirled in the air, and plummeted.

I remember Rosa's face as she opened the door. The surprise—it was almost horror—passing across her eyes, froze her.

"Oh, my God . . . Holy Jesus," she invoked like she had had an apparition.

There she was, Alba's childhood playmate, the scrawny hairy monkey, the young girl who danced like a spider, possessed by the tarantula. Now she looked more like a weary grandmother, a golden crucifix around her neck, in felt slippers and a housecoat. Her body had lost its shape, her hair was short, badly cut.

"Come in," she said.

We entered the small living room where everything looked polished, varnished, spotless. There were white crocheted mats on every surface, thick crystal vases filled with plastic roses on the table. A huge television set stood across from the flowered sofa. It didn't seem as if anybody ever sat in this room, or moved any of the objects around.

"Have a seat." Rosa whispered, as if we were in a church. "Just a minute, please."

She disappeared behind a door, dragging her felt slippers on the shiny tiled floor. I heard the muffled sound of her voice in the next room. Hushed, weepy. Alba and I exchanged a nervous glance. She closed her eyes and reopened them to reassure me that everything was under control. Then Rosa came back.

"I told Adele you were here. She'll be here in a minute."

We sat across from each other, Alba and I on the sofa, Rosa on the chair. Rosa's husband appeared. A small man in an undershirt with gray hair and a farmer's tan. He pulled up a chair, after shaking my hand and Alba's. Then a teenage girl, wearing thick glasses, a cheap gray track suit, and furry slippers, sneaked into the room.

"This is Teresa, my youngest. Teresa, this is Signora Alba and Signorina Alina."

Teresa nodded. She looked at Alba and me with an expression of terror, slid slowly on the armrest next to her mother. The three of them stared at us, perfectly still, hands in their lap. I felt uncomfortable and shifted in my seat. I couldn't bear the way Rosa had addressed us as *Signora* and *Signorina*, using the same deferential tone her family had always used with us.

"Adele lives in Lecce now, with the little one," Rosa said. "But she comes to visit every Sunday."

"Good," said Alba in a whisper.

We all felt the silence deepening in the room, but nobody had the heart to break it.

I looked at Alba: she had leaned across the table toward Rosa. Their heads were very close now. I think Alba had grabbed her hand or something. I could tell, by her body language that Alba felt more at ease than I did in that awkward polished living room. She knew these people, she had grown up with them. She knew the smell of their houses, the eeriness of those silences. When all you hear is the ticking of a clock.

The door opened and in came Adele. She was tiny, thin as a bird, a mane of tight black curls crowning her perfectly white face. She looked like one of those Madonnas modeled in wax you came across in the South. Her skin was moist, covered in a film of sweat. She looked at us as if from a distance. I noticed the dark circles under her eyes.

"Thank you for coming," she said, gravely.

Alba and I stood up, and Alba hugged her. I saw Adele close her eyes and take a breath. She looked at me.

"Alina."

We had known each other as children, just as my mother and hers had. I had let her dress and undress my Barbie doll endlessly, and she and I had lost over and over again to Isabella playing Monopoly and Scrabble during the summers we used to spend in Casa Rossa.

I felt her skinny body quiver slightly between my arms.

We all sat down again. Adele placed her hands neatly on her knees and I noticed her manicured hands and dark nail polish.

"We received your letter last year," she said, "but we didn't know how to answer. It was too soon."

Alba nodded. Adele cleared her throat.

"It's been very difficult to say anything. But we've never stopped thinking about you. About all of you."

There was an awkward pause.

"When the one who can forgive can no longer grant forgiveness, one must learn to bear the silence," Adele said, as if quoting a line from somewhere. She sounded solemn, ponderous, like an old-fashioned professor.

Rosa began to cry, unable to stand the tension anymore. Her tears rolled down without a sound, and Alba stood up, crossed over to her, and held her. Rosa strained to find the right words, then gave up and shook her head.

"I know, I know," Alba handed her a tissue she found in her bag.

"It was God's will. Only He knows," Rosa said and lowered her eyes. "Yes."

Alba kept holding Rosa's hand as she blew her nose.

I felt Adele's eyes on me. Did she expect me to say something on behalf of Isabella? Our mothers had done their thing. But for us it was different. There was no *Signora* or *Signorina* between us. I couldn't make myself talk

She cleared her throat. Again, she sounded almost as if she were reading, as if she had rehearsed the words over and over again.

"There are things we will never understand. No matter how much we torture ourselves. I've been asking myself so many times how it has been possible that . . ."

She let it hang in the air. Then I realized she couldn't go on.

". . . how it was possible that the person I loved more than anyone else lit no spark of humanity in those people . . . You know, when they met his eyes and had their finger on the trigger? . . ."

Her mother looked at her, stunned. Perhaps she was worried that we might feel insulted. That her words might be too blunt.

I couldn't help thinking there was something about Adele that bordered on the grotesque. The manner she had adopted to impart these statements, like a bad imitation of a prophetess. I don't know why, but my mind was playing some weird tricks on me.

"But, you know . . . for you . . ." She was staring at me now. "I'm thinking that for you it must be just as hard. To realize that this person you love, who you know since you were born, the sister you grew up with . . ."

She looked at Alba.

". . . your daughter. This tiny baby that you brought into the world. That she could have turned into that cold-blooded murderer. It must be just as unthinkable."

I felt like standing up and saying *Stop lecturing us, will you? We're here to pay our respects, that's all. We had nothing to do with it.*

Suddenly, Alba broke into sobs, eyes shut tight, tears rolling down her cheeks. I guess that that was the whole point, the reason she had wanted to come. She had dragged me to hear Adele give out the verdict we had to live with. Till then nobody in our own family had dared pronounce the word.

Murderer. It did make a difference to hear it, as if a spell had been broken.

Nobody said anything. I shifted again in my seat, listening to the silence, broken by the heavy ticking of the clock and of my mother noisily blowing her nose.

Rosa brought a glass of water for Alba and whispered something to her.

"It's okay. I'm fine. Really."

Then, after what seemed an unbearably long time, we finally stood up to leave. We kissed and hugged at the door, tighter and longer than was required.

"It's a good thing you came. It's a relief," said Rosa. The husband nodded, so did Teresa.

But Adele looked at us silently, without smiling. She closed her eyes and then opened them.

"You must keep praying," she said, then she squeezed my arm, hard. "Even when you think you're going crazy. Even if you're angry with God because you don't understand. You must always keep praying."

"Yes, yes," I said quickly and wriggled out of her grasp. She scared me.

I gave myself permission not to like her and felt almost proud in succeeding to do so.

We got into the car and didn't say anything for a few minutes. Then Alba let out a puff of air.

"That was something," she said.

"Mm-hmm," I paused, but then I couldn't restrain myself. "She's a bit . . . I don't know."

" Who, Adele?"

"Yes. . . . It's all mixed up now with the tragedy, so it's hard to separate her pain from her madness. But I'm telling you: she's *weird.*"

Alba didn't say anything. Probably she didn't feel it was right to distance herself from Adele. She needed to savor her tears without hindrances.

"Anyway, I'm glad we did this," she said. "It was haunting me, the idea that we couldn't come back to Casa Rossa. I couldn't bear to think that we lost the right to be in our own house, because of what happened."

Maybe one day it will be possible to walk again with our heads up, I kept thinking. To draw a line between us and what happened. Maybe one day it will be possible to hold on both to our past and to Isabella at the same time. Maybe. Maybe not.

I want to try to describe the glass cage now. How it felt seeing it for the first time.

Eventually we became so used to it, it no longer affected us. In fact the whole country got used to it; it was shown on the news and photographed on the papers countless times. It became a common sight and soon lost its meaning.

You have to picture a large nondescript room lit by fluorescent lights. The jury and the judge are sitting behind a long table, center stage. Flanking the table are two bulletproof glass boxes, like empty fish tanks. One is smaller—it has been built for the defendants who have chosen to "cooperate." The other is large and will contain the majority of the defendants: the ones who call themselves political prisoners and have refused to name names, reconstruct facts, implicate others. They are not supposed to mix—the ones who "repented" and the ones the press have labeled "diehards."

When we—the audience—showed up for the first day of the hearings, we entered the room, holding our breath. We were intimidated by the coldness of the place, the dark cloaks of the judges and lawyers, and by the procedure that awaited us. We took seats on the wooden benches, as in a church. We were nervous. Scared. We kept checking each other anxiously, hugged the ones we knew, waved to the ones we vaguely recognized.

Then, there was a sudden stir. A group of armed carabinieri walked in and surrounded the empty glass tanks, swiftly, like dancers taking their position in a well-rehearsed performance. And there they were: a group of about fifteen young people, huddled together. One by one they offered their wrists, and were freed of their handcuffs.

Only two young men entered the smaller cage. They took their seats, and waved at some familiar face they recognized on the benches.

In the big cage it was chaos: smiling faces, intertwining arms, kisses, hugs, laughter. They were all standing, oblivious to the rest of the room, grabbing, patting, hugging, stroking each other. These were men and women who had been lovers, comrades, accomplices, finally reunited in such a small space, where they could touch, feel, smell each other again.

I watched Isabella fly into Enrico's arms. It suddenly hit me that they hadn't seen each other in nearly two years. I kept my eyes on her hands, they way they clutched onto his shoulders, and then didn't let go of his hands.

They were intoxicated by the physical closeness. It took a good fifteen minutes before their excitement subsided and they finally managed to settle down and turn their heads toward us.

They all looked exhilarated. I looked at Isabella, at her dazzled smile—how she squinted, trying to make out where I was sitting in the room. It reminded me of the scene I had witnessed many years earlier. When she had walked center stage, holding hands with the rest of the dancers, bowing before the audience, her eyes blinded by the lights.

In the following weeks, reality began to shift.

What had seemed surreal became more and more familiar. What had seemed impossible to adjust to, when I first pictured it in New York the night I told Daniel, had now become my daily routine.

I started to get used to my bus ride to the courthouse in the early mornings. To the cold fluorescent light in the long halls of the building, to the empty room that filled up slowly with lawyers and their assistants. To the way they lit their first cigarette and started exchanging greetings or quickly read the newspaper headlines, like teachers waiting to begin a class. To the way the "group" made its entrance every morning after the long ride from prison to the courthouse in the armored vehicles—we could hear the sirens grow louder and louder, and stop outside, just before they were led in. To the way they scuttled into their fish tank, waving their handcuffed hands in the air to us. Us, who showed up every morning and took always the same seats, as if returning day after day to the same absurd matinee.

The minute they came in, each one of us started waving to the person we had come for. Like mothers waving at their children in a school play, as they peek into the audience before the curtains parted.

We're here, darling.

Nice sweater. You look so well.

I received your letter yesterday.

Giorgio didn't come?

He's in bed with the flu. He sends his love.

Have you cut your hair? I like it.

We all exchanged these lines in sign language, because no sound passed either in or out of the fish tank. Poised middle-aged women, young men in tweed jackets and round glasses, graying fathers in suits— our hands moving deftly around our faces, squeezing ears, crossing chests, cutting the air with our fists. We must have looked like a herd of monkeys, unaware of the pathetic sight we made. An army of deaf and dumb, not paying the slightest attention to the jury, the lawyers, and the judge as they began their daily routine: reading out from their papers, listing the accusations, the charges, the names of the defendants.

As reality kept shifting, what I had just left behind—the streets of Manhattan, the apartment on Elizabeth Street, my desk at the Morrison Gallery—began to feel like it all never existed.

Daniel Moore.

I was terrified at the idea that he might begin to fade away, too. Every day I began to write a letter to him, trying to explain how it felt.

I tried to explain how, through all this—the surreal cage brimming with smiling faces and young bodies—the legal proceedings remained a kind of background noise. How the legal aspect of this trial had become secondary. As if we were all sitting in this room facing each other for the purpose of spending time together, like a proper family should, for that's all that was registering. There we were, mothers, fathers, and siblings, discussing what the person behind the glass wanted us to cook for them next week—carbonara? risotto con porcini?—and we didn't even bother to listen to the prosecutor and his accusations. As if it weren't their names he was calling out. Again, nobody wanted to hear. We had adjusted to the consequences, but we wanted to ignore the cause.

I tried to explain all this to Daniel because I wanted to make it real for myself as well. But every time I tried to write it all down, I ended by tearing the letter up because I feared he would never understand what I was talking about unless he saw it with his own eyes.

But the truth was I didn't really want him to see that. I had designated him to be the happy part of my life: cabin on the dunes, New York in the snow, Thanksgiving dinner in Connecticut, Bach Suites, and making love in the afternoon. That's where Daniel belonged in my mind. Not to that cold room, among those sad faces. Yet each time I started a letter and tore it to pieces, I knew I was putting more distance between us.

It wasn't a conscious act. More like swimming and drifting slowly away because of an undertow pulling me the opposite direction. I didn't even realize how strong the current was until I lifted my head and saw how far I had been dragged away from shore.

Rita was one of the first witnesses to take the stand. She had been subpoenaed as Beniamino Sanguedolce, and when this chubby middle-aged lady—properly decked out in one of her legendary *faux* Chanels—made her entrance and sat down on the stand, the audience couldn't help tittering. She tipped her glasses down her nose and politely addressed the judge.

"It's actually *Rita* Sanguedolce, Your Honor. My status was officially changed in 1975. It should be stated on those documents somewhere."

There was a bit of a stir among the jury, the prosecutor, and the judge. Rustling of papers, nervous coughing, more muffled laughter. It was finally agreed that the witness was to be addressed as a female and that the prosecutor's interrogation could proceed.

"I'm reading from a transcript dated 25 October 1981. This is the transcript of a telephone conversation that took place between Sanguedolce Rita and the defendant Strada Isabella at the time when Strada had just vacated the apartment across the hall from the witness. More than vacated, she had in fact disappeared without informing the landlord."

The prosecutor cleared his throat theatrically. He wanted to make sure he read the transcript with the proper inflections.

STRADA: Rita, hi, it's me.

SANGUEDOLCE: Thank God you called, I was going nuts. Did you hear the news?

STRADA: What news?

SANGUEDOLCE: They came yesterday, looking for you. *(Silence.)* Are you there?

STRADA: Yes. Did they have a warrant?

SANGUEDOLCE: No, just questions. They asked lots of things of me and of Maurizio.

STRADA: And?

SANGUEDOLCE: No, it's all semi under control. But you have to come and take your dogs.

STRADA: What are you talking about? We took them already.

SANGUEDOLCE: No, my dear. You took the big ones. You left the other ones. *(Pause.)* The poodles. Two of them.

STRADA: Oh, I see what you mean. Okay.

SANGUEDOLCE: Listen, I want you to come get them today, I can no longer keep them. They're too messy. Neither I nor Maurizio can look after them anymore.

STRADA: Rita, today is impossible.

SANGUEDOLCE: Then send someone.

STRADA: Like who? For God's sake, Rita, don't start. They are only poodles, you can dump them in a trash bin, can't you?

SANGUEDOLCE: I'm not going anywhere with those poodles. They're not mine, I don't want to carry them any-where. You promised you would—

STRADA: All right, just stop hammering me. I've got enough to worry about. I'll be over this evening.

"Now, Miss Sanguedolce, it turns out that nobody in your apartment building has ever seen these poodles that the defendant and yourself were discussing. No dogs whatsoever, neither small nor big. So what was it exactly you two were talking about that day?"

The prosecutor's question hovered in the air for a handful of seconds.

Rita kept her gaze fixed on him and curled her lips into a somewhat less friendly smile.

"I don't see how I can be held accountable for what my neighbors fail to notice, sir. All I know is that I had two filthy poodles in the house who shat all over my carpets."

In May the hearings were suspended for a few days to allow for a long weekend. I went down to Casa Rossa by myself. I needed the time alone. Away from the fish tank, the prosecutor's monotonous voice, the sad relatives, the headlines in the papers.

In Puglia I found the triumph of spring: the fields had exploded in bright patches of wildflowers and poppies. Bushes of wild yellow *ginestra* were scattered everywhere. A cold wind—the *tramontana*—started blowing; it scrubbed the air till every tiny silver leaf on the olive trees was clear and visible from a distance. Every curl of foam on the sea. Every feather on the breast of a seagull.

Everything became sharp, impossible to ignore.

I sat down to write a letter to Daniel Moore. This was an easier letter than all the others I had planned to send him. I wanted to tell him about Casa Rossa and the beauty of the change of season. I wrote how I knew he would love it there. I begged him to come over during the summer as Isabella's trial was likely to drag on till early fall. I finally gathered the strength to tell him that we shouldn't let too much time come between us. That I feared we might lose each other. That I couldn't bear that to happen.

I took a ride on my old bicycle every evening in the rich six-o'clock light. I liked to wander through the labyrinth of the dirt tracks, skirting along stone walls and cacti. The smells were still sharp and distinct in the cool weather. Once the summer took over, the heat would melt everything into a sweet, pungent scent and it would be impossible to distinguish the mint from the wild roses from the almond trees.

My rides got longer and longer, and I ventured farther and farther away. One day I found myself on a narrow winding road. I don't even know how I got there.

I saw the cross planted on the ground.

It was covered with plastic flowers; their original color had faded under the sun and they were covered with dirt. In the center of the cross was a small image of the Virgin, sealed under clear plastic. Someone had written "In memory of" and a date. The letters had faded, but I could make out his name—it came first—followed by the names of his bodyguards. An aluminum vase beneath it was filled with fresh wildflowers.

Right on the corner, across from the blue sign that said "LECCE 15 miles." Just before the junction for the highway.

This was it. The shortcut. The exact spot that had been mentioned over and over in the courtroom. I got off my bicycle and sat down on the ground next to the cross. I touched the fresh flowers. Did Adele bring them? Or were they from the people in the village?

And finally it sank in for me. That it had actually happened! Right there where I was sitting! Screaming, shooting, blood on the ground. Masked commandos firing guns. Lifeless bodies in the car.

I heard a lizard jumping on the ground from a rock. It looked at me, uncertain, before running into a crevice in the wall.

She knew this shortcut. She knew every single stone in this labyrinth, just like I did.

It had been *her* plan, *her* idea. Who else would have known?

A week later Daniel called me.

"I got your letter today," he said.

"Oh."

I waited for him to tell me how the letter had moved him, how he was missing me just the same and couldn't wait to come. But the tone of his voice was flat. He paused.

"I think it'll be difficult for me to come in the summer. I'll be working."

"Can't you find a couple of weeks, even?"

"I don't know. I have two big assignments, both of them are New York–based stories. I'll have to do a lot of research."

"Oh. I see."

There was an awkward silence. Then I heard him fill his lungs with air. I heard it all the way from across the Atlantic. I knew that sigh.

"Maya and I have been speaking lately. She wants to come out east in the summer. I think she wants to see if our relationship is reparable."

I didn't say anything. My silence had the depth of a black pit, and I felt like I was tumbling into it. A long black flight, in slow motion.

Another transoceanic puff of air reached me.

"I didn't say that we were back together, or that this is what *I* want. I'm just informing you that she'll be coming out here to stay with friends of hers. And that she has asked me to see her and to listen to what she has to say."

"Oh. Thanks for the information."

"Alina"—his voice snapped and went up an octave—"*you* are the one who has been away for nearly three months. You called me twice and said you were going to write because you hated speaking on the phone. Fine. Letters never came. I've been waiting to hear what's happening over there and what's happened to our relationship—for something like ninety days now. Then you finally send a letter all about flowers in bloom and expect me to pack a bag and board a plane and go hiking in Puglia. I mean, how do you—"

"I don't *expect* you to do anything," I said harshly. "I only *asked* you."

"All right, whatever. But it doesn't change the substance of what I said. I'm confused by your behavior. I'm not saying I'm angry at you or that I don't want to see you. All I'm trying to say here is, had you been in touch with me a bit more maybe I would have made different plans. I don't know."

"I'm sorry. I hate the phone. I think talking on the phone fucks everything up. Even now, this conversation we're having, it's—"

"Why can't *you* come here instead?"

His question, so simple, so direct, put me in a panic. At that point I so much feared his distance that I needed to put even more of it between us.

"I can't. I mean, I don't think it's possible. Not immediately."

We both paused, waiting for the other to come up with something.

"What's happening with your sister?" he finally asked.

"Nothing much. The prosecutor is making his case now. Then it'll be the turn of the defense lawyers. It'll take months."

"Can't you leave even for a week or so?"

"I don't have the money to come and go like that, Daniel."

I heard him sigh. I could feel his frustration.

"What about you and Maya, then?" I asked hesitantly.

"I told you. I just thought you should know that I agreed to see her when she comes out here."

"Right."

He didn't say anything else, so I forced myself to go on.

"Thanks for letting me know. I would have hated to find out any other way."

But I didn't feel like thanking him. I felt like calling him all kinds of names. He heard it in my voice.

"I was hoping you'd be back in New York by the summer," he said, "so that it would be more clear—not only to Maya, but to me—that you're still in my life."

Daniel Moore was a man who always told the truth. Who was not afraid to call things by their name. I should have remembered that before asking any question.

Looking back, I think it must have been a fatal combination of fear and arrogance, mixed with an attraction for the void, that allowed me to let go of him.

It was like a scene in a film where one person is dangling off the ledge of a building and the other is holding him desperately by one hand. I watched his hand slowly slide away from mine till I lost my grip. I could still see the look of reproach in his eyes before his fall.

I know I could have done any number of things.

I could have phoned back right away, or I could have boarded the first New York–bound flight. In other words, I could have reshuffled my priorities and made him my number one.

But instead I sat there, listless, watching him disappear in slow motion into a fog. Persuading myself that it was already too late to do anything. That it would prove impossible to retrieve him from whatever he was fading into, especially now that Maya had made up her mind and was on her way.

That's what it is, I thought. I love him but he has never become familiar to me. Nor have I for him.

So I turned back to the bits and pieces of my own broken family, making that U-turn my mission. Back to the courtroom, to the glass box. Back to visiting hours in jail, back to cooking Isabella's favorite dishes, back to buying her lipstick, hair conditioner, and cologne so that she would smell good next to her lover in their cage.

In order to attend the hearings, all defendants had been transferred from their high-security prisons to the Rebibbia jail, on the outskirts of Rome.

For Isabella, this Roman sojourn—which was going to last at least six months—was almost like a vacation. She had been taken out of solitary confinement and now shared a cell with two other women; and they were allowed to cook their own food on a small camping stove, visit with other inmates, play basketball in the courtyard. And what was more, there was no glass or intercom in the visitor's room. We could sit across a table from each other and hold hands in a crowded room full of screaming children, gypsies, West Africans, young women with tattooed arms and bulging veins. It was a noisy circus, Rebibbia, compared to the frozen atmosphere in Voghera.

It was almost two years since her arrest, and I was getting used to Isabella's life as a detainee, to the point that I could hardly remember that she'd ever had a life outside. I realized I couldn't picture her walking on the street again. I watched the way she nodded to other inmates, how she addressed the guards, calling each one by name, how confidently she moved within those walls, the electronic doors, the locks. That place had ceased to be just a prison, it had started to become home to her. What was painful for me was to see how she had begun to erase the outside world in order to make that confining one tolerable. She asked me less and less about places and people she used to know. She had to suffocate her memory in order to stop missing them.

By the end of the summer, pictures of the trial and of the glass cage hit the front page of the newspapers as the scandal exploded: one of the defendants, a small redheaded girl named Livia Monti, five months into the hearings, was looking visibly pregnant.

The press was obsessed with the story.

SEX IN THE CAGE! PRISONERS HAVE INTERCOURSE WHILE ON TRIAL!

The captain of the carabinieri squad that had been patrolling the courtroom claimed he had been unaware of anything unusual going on.

"They have obviously been shielded by the others. There are fifteen people in that glass cage. It's easy to conceal anything," he said to the press.

Isabella shrugged when I saw her on the following visiting day, already weary of the subject. She must have been sick of hearing about it by then.

"Come on. It's all we think about. By the time we got to the courtroom on the very first day, every one had pretty much figured out a way to do it."

"You're kidding me.

"No, I'm serious. It's not *that* difficult. All you need to do is to sit on someone's lap. It only takes a few minutes."

The image was so grim. I shook my head.

"Jesus. How sad."

"Not so sad if that's all you can get."

"Yes, but . . . how can you . . . I mean, what about this child now?"

"I don't know. Maybe it's wrong. But maybe you would think differently if you were locked up in here, in this totally sterile universe, and then you were given the chance to give life."

"Yes, but—"

"Maybe you, too, would feel that selfish and decide to go for it. You'd think you'd love this kid so much that it wouldn't even make a difference he wasn't free. You'd think he would get so much love and attention that he wouldn't miss running around in a park like other children."

"Come on, Isabella, it's nonsense. This poor baby is going to have a miserable life, no matter what. I can't believe Livia hasn't thought about it."

"Maybe. But I guess she has decided she'll be accountable for bringing her child into the world like that. I don't know. I'm just saying it's not easy to judge her. Everything's been taken away from her while she's still in her prime."

She's the one who took it away from herself, I felt like saying, but I restrained myself. It was as if Isabella and her comrades had forgotten why they were locked up in the first place. The past seemed to have no connection with their present situation. They only saw themselves as prisoners, and perceived freedom as a right that had been unfairly taken away from them. It was as if they'd forgotten they were there because they were paying a price for what they had done.

These were the times when I felt our distance widen the most. To her, we who lived outside had become members of a different tribe, and the more she felt separated from us, the more she clung to her own tribe. It had a painful and irritating effect on me.

"You have no idea what could happen to you in a situation like this," she went on vehemently. "Your body would make its own decisions, make moves that might look totally irrational."

"Like what?"

"Your body *takes over.* It's like a forest, it just grows, covers ground, doesn't ask whether it's doing the right thing or the wrong thing, it simply takes what it needs in order to live."

"What about you? What does your body tell you to do?"

She blushed, then leaned back on the chair, suddenly defensive.

"Have Enrico and I done it in the cage—is that what you're asking?"

"Well, yes."

"No." She reached for her cigarettes on the table and looked off into space as she lit one and exhaled with exaggerated force.

"My body has shut down," she said. "I haven't had my period in eight months. My body is dead."

I looked at her without being able to say anything. She shook her head and forced a smile.

"It knows there's no hope. Unfortunately mine is a rational body. It doesn't waste energy on a lost cause."

"Yes but . . . I mean . . . don't you feel like making love now that you're physically close again?"

Her eyes were watery, but it could have been the smoke of her cigarette.

"Lately he's been, like . . . I don't know . . . distant."

The guards signaled our time was up. We kissed hurriedly, and she turned one last time, waving her hand, before she disappeared behind the door. I hated having to leave always like that, each time with the same image printed in my head: her tiny body next to the bulkier one of the guard, her childish smile as she waved her hand one last time, just before the guard pushed her gently through the door. Impatiently. The way she let him do that. The clank of the door.

Once outside, the city swallowed me back in a second. There was no transition, I was allowed no extra time to climb out of the dark place where I had been. Scooters and cars, ugly ads, women carrying their groceries from the market, everything passed me by in a mix of unpleasant sounds and smells. I would find a seat on the bus, surrounded by a group of boisterous teenagers on their way home from school. Nobody paid any attention to me.

At the end of the summer, after the state's witnesses were heard, it was the defendants' turn to sit in front of the jury and give their depositions, but all expectations were disappointed. One after the other they came out of the cage and read a brief statement from a single piece of paper. Each one said essentially the same thing:

"We do not recognize the authority of the Italian Fascist State, and we consider ourselves political prisoners. The only criminals we recognize in this society are the Christian Democrats and the defenders of capitalism. As of today there are thirty-five thousand proletarians in prisons and more than three thousand comrades held in concentration camps. The struggle will go on within the prison walls. Beware!"

The newspapers ran pictures of them, on the stand and as they walked back into their cage, with raised arms and clenched fists. On the eight-o'clock news, they showed Adele on the doorstep of her house in Lecce, surrounded by a mob of reporters. She held her baby, the fatherless child, in her arms.

"How do you feel about these people who still throw their fists up in the air, showing no signs of remorse?" they asked.

The harsh lights exaggerated her eerie pallor. She looked like a Caravaggio as she emerged from the shadow, holding the baby close to her chest. Alba and I watched her, frozen in our seats, as we were eating our dinner in front of the TV. Adele looked straight into the camera and spoke in that unsettling, prophetic way she had.

"I'll have plenty of time to think about my husband's death. I have this baby to remind me everyday of what he was like. And they . . ."

Her voice broke. She took a second, swallowed hard, and tried to calm her heaving.

"And they will have a long, lonely time ahead of them. If they don't want to be judged by the jury, then it will have to be their own conscience."

The next day it was Isabella's turn to be interrogated. I watched her step out of the cage. Once out of the glass, she hesitated before reaching the defendant's chair in front of the jury. She tucked a strand of blond hair behind her ear, cleared her voice, and took a piece of paper from her pocket. I cringed and instinctively closed my eyes. I felt so anxious, fearing what she might read, that I actually managed to absorb only fragments of her statement through the metallic reverberation of the mike.

". . . it is this regime that is violent and barbarous. It's the Christian Democrat gang and their lackeys who are bloodstained. . . . We won't submit ourselves to be interrogated by Fascist magistrates. . . . We believe in armed proletarian power, and firmly believe that the full use of revolutionary force will destroy the bourgeois state."

I opened my eyes and saw her raising her fist. She stood there for a moment, closed her eyes briefly, and then shouted—

"Forward to victory!"

The next day I went to speak to Sergio Tommasi, Isabella's lawyer. A kind, well-mannered man in his mid-forties who wore tailored tweed jackets and smoked a pipe, he spoke with surgical precision, never allowing a second interpretation to his words. Sitting across from him in his office, I asked him if that harsh declaration had worsened Isabella's position. Dark wooden shelves dominated the walls, English hunting prints in the spaces between them.

"No. Technically speaking," he explained to me, "nothing has changed. The defendants are not pleading guilty, they are just refusing to negotiate."

"But it makes them look like a bunch of heartless killers." I sighed and looked around the room uneasily. "The tone of those statements, it's so harsh . . . so remorseless. I mean, did you look at the jury when Isabella called the magistrates a bunch of Fascists? They were horrified. And you saw the way they got slammed by the press."

Tommasi lowered his eyes to his perfectly manicured fingertips as he kept screwing and unscrewing the cap of his Mont Blanc.

"They're not looking to get good press, Alina. Theirs is a clear political stance. They will not answer to the magistrates. It's like in war. Actually, this *is* a war, and they consider themselves prisoners. This is happening all over the country, in every other trial that involves acts of terrorism. There are those who decide to cooperate with justice, and those who stand their ground. I knew from day one that Isabella had made her choice."

Then he looked at me. Provocatively.

"Are you surprised? You didn't expect her to change her mind and turn herself in, did you?"

I blushed.

"Of course not."

I knew Tommasi respected Isabella. I had noticed how he nodded to her as she had walked back into her cage, after reading her brief statement, holding her head upright.

Then it was Enrico's turn. They had kept him last, the alleged leader of the group. His was to be the grand finale.

When I saw him come forward and sit in the chair he looked smaller, thinner than I remembered him. His shoulders were drooping. He wore a suede jacket and a light-blue shirt.

His words cut straight through the silence. As if he had made up his mind and wanted them to be as sharp as possible, so that he wouldn't need to be long.

"In all these months spent in detention I have come to realize it's necessary to make a choice between justice and truth. We"—and he gestured with his head toward his comrades in the glass cage—"all fought a war because we believed in a different justice than yours."

This was not the formal statement we'd been hearing from everyone else. This was different. We held our breath, unsure of the direction he was going to take, alarmed by the emotion that cracked his voice.

"The concept of justice is subjective. We called ours 'proletarian justice,' and we went so far as to kill in its name. Truth, on the other hand, is objective: there's only one truth, only one way to tell the way things went. And I believe that although the truth will not bring back the dead, it will release them from silence. Only truth can mark a new communal starting point, make a clean break from the past."

The silence of our suspended breath, the thump of our hearts filled the room. The air thickened, solidified. All of us, at exactly the same instant, understood.

He's going to talk.

"Today I am able to say that we have been wrong, and I think we must acknowledge the wrong we did if we want to build foundations of justice for the new generations to come."

There was a long silence, then we heard a shuffling of papers, and someone coughed nervously. It was the prosecutor, who stepped forward, like an executioner ready to begin his job.

Thus the sad litany began.

The prosecutor's questions were specific, focused, and to the point. Enrico's answers were just as concise. He named new people, explained in what way they had been involved with their group and what roles they covered in the "military actions"; he told where they had hidden more caches of arms, revealed ties between one group and another. He re-created the map of their underground days, filled in the gaps, provided the missing links. Until all questions had their answers.

We witnessed his body progressively bend, deflate, his voice give in under the weight of this necessary, objective truth.

This truth that had no honor, no righteousness. This truth that was shameful because it was forged from the names of people he had shared his beliefs with. Isabella's face behind the glass looked like it had been carved in ice. Then her name came up.

"No," he said, "Isabella Strada strongly opposed our decision to execute Lo Capo. She didn't participate."

"Why? Hadn't she shared all your decisions up to that point?"

"Yes. But she refused to have anything to do with Lo Capo's execution. She didn't take part in the action."

"What was her reason?"

"She said she couldn't live with the idea. Lo Capo was married to a woman she knew from childhood. In a sense he was like family to her. She cried the night before. She begged me to think it over. But it was too late."

I looked at Isabella. She was frozen, like a statue. She kept her eyes on Enrico as, at the end of the interrogation, he stood up and walked into the other cage, the small one across the room built for the defendants who had decided to "cooperate." The way he crossed over to the other side—it was like a crossing of the Styx. She watched him slump on the bench, without even acknowledging the other two, who long ago had made themselves available to the magistrates. A gloomy trio they made.

That was it, he had crossed the threshold. He would never come back into their cage, they would never speak, or be close again.

That was the end, and both of them knew it.

He looked at Isabella, but she turned her face. He had marked her with his words the same way he had marked the others. She let him know that she despised his lies as much as his truths. That she didn't want to be spared. Not by him. Not like that.

Then the judge announced a coffee break. The spectacle of a man going to pieces, losing his dignity, must have been hard for the jury to watch as well.

We all went out into the corridor, smoked a cigarette, unable to comment.

The truth—that one and only version of the story Enrico mentioned in his speech—had vanished once again under the skillful touch of a magician. One moment it was there, for all to see, and then it was not. Gone, like a card in a trick.

Enrico *had* to be accountable. That was what the new law specifically required before granting its discounts on his sentence. The magistrates couldn't pick and choose which statements to believe. The truth-for-sale had to be bought in bulk.

Therefore Isabella *had* to be innocent, whether she liked it or not.

That was the gift he had left with her before stepping out of their cage. His last gift to her—and one she didn't want. A Gordian knot more likely, impossible to undo.

Once Enrico had offered his truth, we all had decided to settle for it. The jury, the relatives, Isabella. It seemed far less painful than to keep torturing ourselves with further questions.

Her alleged innocence, her estrangement from the acts of her friends, was a new burden she had decided to bear. But to do it, she had to shut herself off even more. She stopped coming to the hearings: defiantly, she said it was because of a bad flu. She stopped eating, she lost weight. She chopped off her hair. She looked like a young boy. A saint.

A Joan of Arc.

CHAPTER EIGHT

———◆———

Rita staggers into what's left of the kitchen of Casa Rossa around nine. She's wearing a cheap polyester kimono splotched in dragons, her hair a mess.

"I need coffee," she says, clearing her throat. "I don't feel human till I get my first shot of caffeine."

The harsh morning light doesn't do her any favors. She looks old, untidy, her makeup—yesterday's—smudged around her eyes and mouth.

"Alba is on her way," I announce as I prepare another pot of coffee. "She'll be here by lunchtime."

"*Will* she? Typical of her, to show up at the last minute. For the grand finale."

"We'll have a picnic in the garden. It should be warm enough."

"Mm-hmm. . . . I might have to get on my way right after breakfast." She looks out the window with a somewhat suspicious expression. "Actually, I'm in a bit of a hurry to go."

"Are you sure? Why do you need to go?"

"I've got lots to do back in Rome. This was a bit of a hit-and-run kind of trip. I've done all I needed to do here and—"

"What was it you needed to do?"

"Oh, well . . ."

Rita smiles. There's a palpable awkwardness. I sit across the table from her, as I wait for the coffee to bubble up.

"It's funny," she says with forced nonchalance, "but I think I wanted to give this place one last chance. For a moment I thought, what the hell, that's where I came from, maybe that's where I should end up. You know, sometimes one believes in the power of symmetry."

"I thought you said you would never live in your family home again."

"Oh, that dreadful place. No, of course not."

She produces a pack of slims out of her kimono pocket and fumbles with a lighter.

"No, I wasn't thinking of moving back here *like that*. I came here to . . ."

She takes a long drag and coughs, stretching her lacquered fingers in front of her mouth. I can tell she's reluctant to talk.

"I came to have a chat with the Dominican Sisters of the Convent of Santa Caterina."

"Why?" I sense something's up.

"You know my mother has been one of their greatest benefactors, right? Well, I thought, since they know the family so well, they would be the best choice I had."

"Choice for *what*?"

She stares at me, feigning surprise.

"Didn't you know I was a believer?"

"No, honestly I didn't know. I always thought—"

"Ah, well"—she waves her hand in the air to disperse the smoke—"people always *assume* all sorts of things about me. I've always had faith. In a sense you could say I've always been searching. I mean, you could say that I began as a child, when I started searching for the real me and I came across this little girl waiting to be let free, right?"

I go to the stove to turn the coffee off and keep my back to her, waiting for her to say more. I feel slightly embarrassed by the direction the conversation has taken.

"Then I searched for love and came across mercenary sex. I kept searching further and found politics and commitment. Now," she sighs, as if exhausted by the list, "I'm over sixty and I'm getting tired of running around like a chicken with its head cut off."

She looks at me, with a slightly conspiratorial expression.

"I want to retire. Rest."

"Right. But what can the Sisters of Santa Caterina do for—"

"Vows," she says, "taking my vows."

I'm standing by the stove, frozen, holding the hot coffeepot in midair. I can hear the tap drip in the sink.

"You're kidding."

She shakes her head slowly, closing her eyes.

"But this is totally insane," I say.

I put the coffee back on the stove and sit back on the chair across from her. She tries a smile.

"But why? All I want is to be able to pray to God in peace in His house. What's wrong with that?"

"All right, but this is so *drastic*. You don't need to lock yourself up in a convent to pray! It's not your vocation, it's not your style!"

"Who says so?"

"Come on, Rita. Plus, you would hate having to wear those clothes."

She frowns for a second, then shrugs, annoyed.

"Well, it's perfectly useless to worry about it at this point, since it's not going to happen. Technically speaking, as far as the clergy is concerned, I'm still a man. That's what God made me, they say, and that's what I have to endure. According to them."

She scans her red fingernails.

"No sex changes allowed within God's Kingdom."

There's a part of me that would like to burst out laughing and at the same time something about her hurt expression deeply moves me. *This is wild. She's still a man according to God,* I think. Why can't they let her be what she wants now? And who am I to tell her that God or the rigors of convent life aren't her *style?* I look at her and I cease to see her as a wretched hybrid: the whore, the frumpy aunt, the aging southern gentleman all mixed into one. All of a sudden it looks like a wonderful gift and a great power, her ability to be everything at once without ever betraying her nature.

"I thought we were having coffee," she reminds me, pointing a finger at the stove.

"Yes. Coffee. Sure."

I hand her a small cup.

"Maybe you should look into Buddhism," I say. "They seem to be less fussy about the body you inhabit in this particular life."

"Buddhism, huh? I don't know about shaving my head and wearing orange robes. Actually I was thinking more like crucifixes, processions, incense, and self-flagellation. But maybe you're right. Maybe I've turned into too much of a conservative with age."

She goes to the window and looks out at the field of hay. It's a clear morning, the wind has changed and has washed the sky clean like a sheet of glass. I hear her sigh.

"It's interesting. You know, this concept of symmetry that I came up with? Going back to the place where one started?"

She turns toward me, and she's smiling now. She looks beautiful now.

"It's total bullshit."

In 1985 Isabella was sentenced to twenty-one years for "armed insurrection against the state" and for moral responsibility in the assassination of Lo Capo. Her sentence was milder than those of her comrades; thanks to Enrico's deposition she had not been found guilty of first-degree murder like them. He had turned her into something of a lesser terrorist, I guess.

Nevertheless, I stopped counting.

Numbers were too cruel: I didn't want to add up twenty-one more years to her age. I didn't want to picture her walking through the streets with gray hair.

I also stopped counting the days, the months that went by without me making a plan, buying a ticket, talking about going back to New York. I just let time slip by. It wasn't a decision, but more like giving in.

For almost three years I had thought of New York as my home. Now I let Elizabeth Street fade, Raimonda, her gallery, and of course the voice and the reality of Daniel. I let it fade slowly, till I was no longer able to conjure up smells or sounds, anything that might stir a longing for my previous life. Till I had suffocated it with a pillow and felt it lie still beneath it.

After the verdict, I waited a few weeks, moving as little as possible. I felt like someone who had been in a car crash and needed to recover from the shock.

Then I rang Peppino Esposito. His secretary put me on hold. There was a funny Muzak on the line, some modern arrangement of *La Traviata*. I waited for a while, expecting her to come back and tell me that he was held up in a meeting.

"Alina Strada?" Esposito's hoarse voice roared into the phone.

"Yes. Hello, how are you?"

"Still alive! Which in itself is an achievement. Yes, dear, what can I do for you?"

"Well, it's a bit of a . . . I . . . I was wondering if—"

But his impatience overcame me.

"Shall we do lunch?" he leapt in. "Let's see. . . ." I heard a shuffling of pages. "No. Lunch looks difficult this week, and then next week we're off to Cannes. . . . I'll tell you what, come over here tomorrow evening at seven. It'll be a slightly quieter time, comparatively speaking."

Once I was ensconced in his elaborately designed Zen meets Palm Springs–style office and had taken in the way he had aged (so beautifully, turning more and more into an old lion), I realized how he had always been more of an icon than a real person to me. He had that unique flair, that manly confidence only men who had lived in the fifties had (his Creed Cologne scent, the way he poured himself a scotch and swirled it around the ice cubes). It hit me right there and then: he was my only remaining link to Oliviero. This near stranger, of all people, was the only one still willing to talk to me about him.

"I remember the day you were born. I had my driver take your mother to the maternity clinic. Oliviero rang me at seven in the morning, frantic because he couldn't find a taxi." He was looking at me sideways, tapping a pen on the open palm of his manicured hand. "One could say I'm partly responsible for your existence in this world."

I felt that Oliviero, had he lived into his seventies, would have looked something like him, which of course was ridiculous. But Esposito had taken on all his attributes, at least in my frustrated imagination.

"How can I help you, my dear?"

Adopt me. Take me under your wing, I wanted to plead.

But instead I blushed and said that I had decided to move back to Italy after a period of time working in New York and that I—

"I read about your sister," he said, cutting through my limp preliminaries.

I nodded. He took a sip of scotch and kept his eyes on me as he tilted his head back and gulped it down.

"Very difficult," he said, placing the glass on the desk slowly and turning it between his fingers.

I nodded again

"Twenty years, right?"

"Twenty-one."

I felt as if the sheer sound of it had produced a crash inside that plush room, a room where movie stars came and went, sat on the padded sofa and discussed scripts and their astronomical fees, where assistants brought silver trays with Evian water in crystal pitchers and smoked salmon canapés. Within the reassuring luxury of those wood-paneled walls—was it cherry? rosewood?—"twenty-one years" sounded simply outrageous.

"I've decided to stay here in Italy so that I can be close to her," I finally said, and it was like spelling it out for myself as well.

"Of course, of course." I saw his bushy eyebrows converge in a frown. But he lit up again after only a few seconds. Esposito was a man who would rather find a solution than dwell on a sad note.

"And we have to find you something to do, right?"

"Well . . . I . . . yes. I'm looking for a job, yes."

The phone rang.

"Excuse me, dear, I have to pick this one up. It's Los Angeles."

He started barking into the receiver in his appalling English at someone called Jack about a script. Just for the fun of it I pictured Jack Nicholson at the other end of the line, wearing Ray-Bans and eating his morning cereal by the pool, grinning. Esposito's accent was so atrocious that I could hardly understand what he was saying, and I wondered how much this Jack was making out of the conversation, but there was certainly something disarming in his confidence.

He kept looking at me throughout the conversation, making faces every now and again, as if he couldn't wait to get off but was tied up with something urgent. Then, without any warning, he simply dropped Jack, as if he had to run somewhere else.

"Very good, my friend, very good. We'll talk next week. And give my best to Deedee." Then he put down the receiver, and without a pause he pressed the button of the intercom. "Elisabetta? Could you bring me the scripts we were going to give to Mr. Federici to read?"

He turned to me and leaned across the table as if to reach me.

"I have piles and piles of stuff they send me everyday. I always meant to have a little team of readers—right now I only have one person, and I'm not very happy with his comments. You know, I need someone who really has a sense of what can work and what is completely hopeless."

I didn't understand what he meant but I nodded. His speed confused me, yet it felt good. I needed the energy. And I desperately wanted him to like me.

Elisabetta, clad in a tight red leather skirt, entered his office, holding a pile of scripts, which she deposited on the desk. Esposito slid them over to me, like chips across a roulette table.

"One page, max, for each. A synopsis, and a final comment. Two categories: 'hopeless,' and 'worth taking to the next stage.' Easy, right? Elisabetta, take Miss Strada into Aldo's office to discuss her contract. The same as Federici."

He stood up and hugged me.

"Let's take it from here and then we'll see. Give my best regards to your mother. And a hug to your sister, when you get a chance."

"Yes, thank you. I will."

"I still remember the two of you, when your father used to take you to Cinecittà, on the set. Such pretty little girls. And so well behaved."

He looked at Elisabetta and said, "They sat behind their father for hours on end, so still, you didn't hear a squeak. Never even asked for a glass of water. Not like the horrible spoiled brats you see today. Ah well . . ."

He omitted to mention to Elisabetta what had become of one of those girls—the prettier one, with the pale pale eyes.

Suddenly it was Isa's sixth year of detention and she turned thirty in jail.

Alba and I would go to visit her once a week. By then the guards had ceased to appear like the villains in a nightmare and had turned into real people doing their job; we knew them by name, waved hellos and goodbyes. The steel doors and the metal detectors no longer intimidated us. Before we knew it, we had turned into old-timers.

Bruno had grown a belly and lost his looks.

He had divorced Alba and moved in with Federica, a much younger woman, someone pretty and uninteresting who didn't stir up any new trouble in his life. He got her pregnant right away and they had twin baby girls. I saw him rarely, but whenever I did, I still felt we had a connection.

Alba had remarried.

Giorgio Carlei was a neurologist almost twenty years her senior. They had met on a Greek island at a conference on dreams held by a famous American psychoanalyst. She had decided to attend on the spur of a moment, after seeing the ad in a literary magazine. I guess that, especially after her divorce, she found herself in serious need of interpretation, and Jung had come as a great discovery. Apparently it had been love at first sight. At the wedding—a brief, cheerful ceremony—Giorgio held up a glass of champagne and called her "the first of my dreams to come true."

I, too, had a new life. I had gone back to live in Casa Rossa, by myself.

I had proven successful as a reader for Peppino Esposito. After trudging through so many hopelessly bad scripts, I grew bolder and started writing witty remarks, just to let him know that I was not without a sense of humor. I wanted him to think of me as something more than a needy orphan who could sit still for hours on end without even asking for a glass of water.

He started calling me up more often and we shared quick laughs. He was amused by my reports in the "hopeless"category, and appreciated my suggestions regarding the "worth taking to the next stage" scripts. He had me meet the writers and discuss their script problems with them. Slowly, from reader I had turned into script-doctor and he began to commission me to do rewrites for scripts he wanted to develop.

These were mainly commercial films—mainstream thrillers, action movies, nothing very exciting—but plunging into their imperfect twists was a good training. I realized I had a sense of rhythm. I could tell when the story "sat down," when it skipped a beat, missed a turn. I had an ear for dialogue, I knew what felt artificial or contrived. Mine wasn't talent, it was simple craftsmanship: I snipped, cut, inserted, altered, as a seamstress would with a dress. Although I never did anything particularly creative to them, the plots always worked better when I returned the scripts to Esposito.

He started paying me a decent salary, and I began to use it to restore Casa Rossa.

I fixed the roof, replaced the pipes, redid the wiring. I repainted it a fresh deep red. I planted a new bush of rambling roses, which started to climb up its façade. I adopted three dogs that followed me closely on my evening walks, always running after birds and lizards.

I went to Rome only when it was necessary—to see Isabella or to confer with Esposito. Otherwise I spent more and more time by myself in Casa Rossa, working on the house and writing.

I didn't know I had it in me, this gift for solitude.

My new life had become increasingly simple, filled by small tasks that needed to be attended to every day in the same way. And each task filled me with a sense of well-being. Making my first cup of coffee early in the morning, waiting for its fragrant aroma to fill the room as I rekindled the fire. Feeding the dogs, watering the potted plants. Filling the bathtub slowly, closing my eyes as I slid into the hot soapy water. Changing into my clothes and tying my hair in a bun. Sitting at my desk in front of the window on the second floor.

Things around me sat quietly through the night, and I found them as I had left them the next morning. There were no other hands to alter their position. The stack of papers and scripts to go through. My notes scribbled on the margins. The empty cup of tea with its dry bag. I was welcomed by the same repetition of sounds. The radio always tuned on the same station, the same birds chirping away on the same branch.

My universe had folded into itself. I had turned it hollow, restrained it, so that my longings and my needs could subside. In a way I thought my day paralleled Isabella's. I, too, now was trapped inside my own dollhouse.

In the evening I lay in the grass crackling with grasshoppers, feeling the shiny silk stems rustle in the breeze. The sweeping plains, the warmth of hay in my nostrils. The honey-colored sandstone. I persuaded myself I needed nothing more.

This is my landscape. This is what I'm made of.

This I love.

I was at Fiumicino Airport, waiting to catch a flight back to Puglia. I had to be in Rome for a meeting with Esposito and he had treated me to a round-trip ticket. He didn't mind the extra expense, he always liked things to happen fast.

I was early, and was aimlessly browsing through the new *Vogue* at the newsstand, when I felt someone staring at me. I lifted my gaze above the fashion spread and I met Enrico's eyes.

He was wearing a crumpled beige raincoat. His hairline had receded and showed some gray at the temples. His Ray-Ban shades were far too big for his face.

"Alina?"

He moved closer. I noticed he was holding a briefcase. Everything about him looked stale, as if he had slept in his clothes.

"I thought it was you," he said and smiled. A perfectly friendly, innocent smile.

"I . . . I . . . didn't recognize you. Sorry."

I shoved the *Vogue* back into its slot and stuffed my hands in my coat.

"Where are you going?" he asked.

"Bari. Back to Casa Rossa." I stared at him. He lowered his eyes. A film of sweat covered his forehead.

"Do you have time for a . . .would you like to sit down for a minute?"

"Jesus, Enrico, I don't know if this is—"

"Please."

Right next door there were a few plastic tables, people eating prepacked sandwiches. We sat facing each other. He lit an extra-mild cigarette.

"When did you get out?" I asked.

"Almost a year ago. It was all over the papers. I thought you knew."

"I didn't see it."

There was a pause. He rolled up the sleeves of his raincoat, letting his wrists show. He was wearing a thin gold bracelet.

"I live up north now, in Bergamo. I went to stay with a cousin of mine. I just started working with him. In fact I came to Rome for a short business trip."

"Good."

"He's helped me out a lot. We produce grids. I do the accounting."

"Grids?"

"Metal grids. Building materials. For gates, roads." He chuckled. "We probably make the bars they use in jails as well."

I didn't laugh. He turned serious again.

"It hasn't been easy, Alina. And it still isn't."

"I bet."

I wanted to feel angry and show him my contempt, but I couldn't. He looked destroyed, limp.

"At least you're out. You can start a new life," I said. I wanted to reach a conclusion as soon as possible, so that I could leave.

He shook his head.

"You get out and you realize it's even worse. Your comrades hate you because they think of you as worse than Judas. For the rest of the people you meet outside, you'll always be . . . you're a criminal. You've lost everyone's trust. You gave up your past but you can't buy into the future. So you're just stuck in no man's land." He drew on his cigarette and closed his eyes.

"Do you ever regret . . ." I hesitated before pronouncing the word— "testifying?"

"You mean do I regret regretting?"

He took off his glasses and rubbed his eyes hard. They looked red, shiny.

"No, I don't. I chose to do it. Not because of the advantages they were offering. I realized we were defeated way before we got arrested. Right after Moro was killed I thought, 'This is over.' I could see that the whole idea of armed struggle was doomed. It was the lowest point. We should have stopped right then and there."

I was startled that he wanted to talk about all that, so openly. He and

I had never exchanged more than a quick, uneasy greeting in the whole time I knew him.

"Really? And what prevented you from stopping? Before . . ." I hesitated. I found it hard to pronounce that name in his presence. "Before Lo Capo."

He took a last drag of his cigarette and then stubbed it out in the saucer of an empty coffee cup.

"I'll tell you why." He didn't look at me but kept twisting the butt in the saucer, as if he wanted to disintegrate it. "The more you realize you have lost, the higher you raise the stakes. Who knows? Maybe, subconsciously, we wanted to get caught so that we'd have to stop. How's that?"

"But . . . wanting to put an end to it didn't necessarily mean you had to turn into a *pentito*."

He pressed both his hands on his temple and closed his eyes again.

"You know, Alina, I made that decision knowingly, aware that I would carry a weight around for the rest of my life." Then he stared straight at me. "But Isabella—I knew she never would have."

"Why not?"

He smiled bitterly.

"Because of the way she is. Because admitting that she was—that we were—wrong would destroy her."

I straightened up in my chair, determined to meet his gaze. "Maybe the difference is that Isabella has enormous integrity," I said. "She's carrying her burden, too, but without any of the advantages."

"There are no advantages, I told you," he said and grimaced. Then he touched my hand, which was lying on the table. "When you see her, would you please tell her that—"

"No, I won't. She doesn't want to hear from you. Don't ask me that."

He raised his palms in the air, as if resigned.

"Fair enough."

I stood up to leave.

"I have to go now."

He remained seated and looked at me.

"It was good seeing you. It made me feel better that you and I could talk, if only briefly."

"Good luck, Enrico. I hope things work out for you in the future."

"You look good, Alina. You look happy."

I walked across the hall without turning back, feeling his eyes still fixed on me. Once I took my seat on the plane, I kept my eyes glued to the window. I went through every single word we had exchanged, scanning their meaning, one by one.

Everybody has lost. There's been only pain.

I couldn't stop thinking about Isabella, how she had lost her faith, her identity, her lover, and now was losing her youth, all because of remaining faithful to her idea of integrity. And how she hadn't managed to change anything, or make the world remotely a better place.

And I couldn't help thinking that I had come back to live in Italy and decided to stay for a reason. Maybe it was just a delusion, but I wanted to change something, too—to break that cycle of betrayal and pain. My family legacy. I wanted the pain and the silence to end, but I feared I didn't know how to stop it.

I came home that evening and I found a note scribbled on the pad next to the phone. Carmela, the woman who cleaned for me once a week, had taken down a message in her loopy handwriting.

Daniele Mur. He'll call again.

I held the piece of paper and kept staring at it, in the vain hope that some more information might materialize. But it was impossible to just keep staring at that name, so I picked up the phone and called Carmela, even though it was kind of late and I knew she was probably about to go to sleep.

"Carmela? It's Alina. Can you remember exactly what the man said on the phone?"

"I don't know, he was speaking in English. He was looking for you."

"What did *you* say?"

"I said you were out. I told him you'd be back later."

"And then what exactly did he say?"

"Nothing."

"Carmela, please, he must have said *something.* Please try to remember, it's very important. And tell me *exactly.*"

"He said his name, and then, when I told him you were not in, he said, *'Va bene.'* "

"In Italian?"

"Yes."

"Are you sure?"

"Yes."

"But he doesn't speak any Italian."

"He did. He said, *'Va bene.'* "

I immediately called his number in New York. I got his answering machine. Just hearing his recorded voice gave me a shock.

"Hi, you have reached 891-2847. I'm out of town, but feel free to leave a message after the tone."

Where on earth are you?

I sat by the phone as the house grew dark around me. I started speaking to the gray box, soothing it.

Please ring.

I held it next to me as I slipped into bed.

Please, please, please.

I woke up at six and went downstairs to make some coffee, let the dogs out, water the garden. Except nothing felt the same again now that I knew Daniel was looking for me. I looked at the clock. It was only seven. The whole evening ahead of me, and this horrible wait. I paced around the house, trying to calm down.

This is nothing, I kept saying to myself. This means absolutely nothing. You just keep on with your life and all the things you need to do.

I tried sitting at the desk. All I could think was that the phone was not ringing.

What is it I need to do? Is there anything important I need to do?

Then I heard the ring and I flew into the next room.

"Alina?"

"Yes."

"Hi. It's me. It's Daniel."

"Daniel."

I repeated his name slowly as if I needed to learn it all over again. I filled my mouth with its sound, feeling my tongue against my palate.

"I'm in Naples."

"You're not!"

So close. It shocked me.

"Oh but I am," he said, proud to surprise me. "I've been in Italy for a few days now, but I only got hold of your number yesterday. It hasn't been easy to track you down."

I swallowed hard. My mouth felt dry

"Really? I'm glad you succeeded."

"Oh, Jesus," he said, and I could tell he was smiling.

"What?"

"Your voice. Hearing your voice again."

We both paused and took a deep breath.

"Alina . . . um . . . listen, I don't know what your plans are, or what you're—"

"I have no plans." I cut him short.

"Okay, then. I'd like to see you, if that's possible."

I let it hang in the air, trying to absorb the implications slowly. There was no point in skimming over the surface of this conversation. Better get right down to the core as fast as possible.

"Who are you with?" I asked.

"I'm by myself."

I paused again.

"I don't know. . . . Can you meet me in Lecce?" I must have sounded impatient.

"Yes."

"When?"

"Is this evening too soon?" he laughed. "I could drive down, I've rented a car."

"No." I couldn't help laughing, too. "That *is* too soon. I need to sleep over this and do some deep breathing. Tomorrow afternoon, at five o'clock, on the steps of the church in the main square."

"Will I find it easily?"

"Yes, of course. You can't get lost. On the steps, at five."

"*Va bene,*" he said. "*A domani.*"

You wait a thousand years, unable to move—a body buried deep in ice. Perfectly preserved. Hair, skin, nails, clothes, and jewelry, everything whole, everything in place.

Not dead, not asleep. Just silent.

256

Then . . . the sound of one voice—is that all it takes for this iceberg to thaw? For breath, tears, saliva, blood, to begin to circulate, stream again through your veins? Bring color to your cheeks, luster to your hair, warmth to your skin? Your body stirs, your fingertips want to touch, your lips want to kiss. And all it took to perform this miracle was the sound of that one voice. The only possible explanation is that you've been in love all along. Keeping still under the slab of ice.

With this kind of clarity I walked through the Corso in Lecce, and turned into the main square at five in the evening. As someone who had been hibernating for so long and could easily slip back into that frozen stillness without making much of a fuss.

I had taken the whole day just to play the scene of my reunion with Daniel Moore in all its possible variations. There I was now, off to play the final version.

And there he was, a small figure sitting on the steps of the church, across the windswept stage of the square I knew so well. I took a moment before I started moving toward him, just to take him in while he was still unaware of me—a long-legged man in baggy jeans and sneakers reading a book, his sandy hair glowing in the orange light. The only unexpected detail was the dark red of his cotton shirt. I had never seen him wear red before. It suited him, such a bold, rusty color. He saw me—the square was so empty, the two of us seemed like two actors walking on a stage—and he immediately stood up. We held each other tight, we attempted a kiss, I smelled his hair. All I remember is that my heart was suddenly throbbing in my throat and my hands felt shaky.

"I need a drink," he announced.

"Thank God for alcohol," I said, as vodka infused my veins only a few minutes later. It helped accelerate the thawing process, the production of sounds in my dry throat. I tapped with my finger on the soft white skin of his forearm.

"I'm so happy to see you."

"So am I."

And we just sat there, drinking and beaming at each other.

This scene was definitely the least exciting one among the many I had played in my mind, and it had the worst lines of all.

But it was the most real.

Later that evening, we were sitting under the vine trellis of a trattoria, in the dimly lit corner of a piazza in the old part of town. A bare bulb was swinging over the table as the night breeze rustled in the palm trees planted in the square. In front of us sat the sticky leftovers of a massive grilled fish. The head, the tail, messy chunks we couldn't eat. Two empty bottles of *rosato*. I kept flicking the ashes of a cigarette onto the gluey fish bones. I just had to have a smoke, I was too agitated. We had talked incessantly, interrupting each other all the time, not even paying attention to what the other one was saying, just to keep the conversation going in order to avoid dangerous pauses. By the end of the second course we had reviewed all the people we both knew in New York. I had meticulously asked about each one of them, even the ones I couldn't care less about, he had given me a pretty punctual update on Raimonda (how the young Mexican artist had dumped her and she was desperately trying to make things up with her husband). We had skimmed the plots of books we had been reading, my new job with Esposito, Isabella's approaching appeal. By the time the waiter put the grappa on the table we had run out of subjects.

Suddenly he leaned over and touched my forehead lightly, pulling a wisp of hair behind my ear. I instinctively turned my face sideways.

"You are beautiful," he said, and he was grinning, unfazed. Somehow his unending confidence irritated me.

I turned my head back to him and blew out the smoke.

"So, what about you and Maya?"

He didn't flinch, I guess he knew this needed to be addressed at some point. The sooner the better.

"She moved back to New York right after you and I"—here he hesitated, looking for the right words—"stopped communicating. By then I knew you were not coming back. That it was pretty much over between us."

He paused and brushed some bread crumbs off the table.

"I was feeling pretty miserable, in fact."

He looked at me, I nodded but didn't say anything. He went on.

"So when she asked me if I was willing to give it a try, I said yes, and she moved back in with me for a couple of months. But it didn't work. We both knew it deep down, but I thought we owed it to each other. Another chance, I mean."

Again, I said nothing and waited for him to say more. I felt he now owed it to me, to make this issue absolutely clear.

"It's really over between the two of us," he said. "We both know it now."

"Right."

I called the waiter by name and asked for the check. I felt strangely sure of myself. Maybe because our encounter was taking place on my own turf. The language, the rules, the landscape: it all belonged to me this time. Daniel pulled out some cash.

"Let me take care of it," I said, lightly brushing his hand.

There was no fear in me, strangely. It seemed almost absurd that I had ever been afraid of losing him to someone else.

"And what about you? I mean, are you . . . attached? Is there anybody—"

"No. There's no one." It embarrassed me to have to answer that question. It was torture having to stumble our way like that. Like two strangers on a blind date.

"All this time I've been trying not to think of you," I said. "Which I guess is the equivalent of saying that I've been thinking about you all the time."

I didn't even take the time to check how this had landed on him. I turned around in my chair, grabbed my jacket, my handbag, and stood up.

"Let's go," I said. "It's about twenty-five minutes to Casa Rossa from here."

His car followed mine down the dark country roads. It was pitch black, once we got outside of town, and I was sure he was marveling at how poorly lit the place was. I smiled into the rearview mirror, checking his headlights behind me: I knew exactly what sort of things Americans noticed.

As we crossed the bridge and took the sharp turn by the Madonna shrine, the silhouette of Casa Rossa appeared against the starry sky. Its bulky, solid profile. The wooden gate, the long driveway lined with trees planted by my grandfather and Stellario sixty years ago. The sweetness of jasmine, the familiar night song of crickets, the barking of dogs.

"What a place," he said, getting out of his car. "This is incredible."

As he said that, I looked at the house as through his eyes, and it appeared so big, so impressive. A place I always took for granted, as something that had always been there and always would. I'd never needed to assess it in any way. We came through the back door into the kitchen and he stopped to look at the high vaulted ceiling, the imposing stone fireplace, the sink carved in sandstone.

"And you've been living here all by yourself all this time?" He smiled as he gestured vaguely in the air.

"Yes."

"I always pictured this place as a country cottage sort of thing. I mean, this is a *mansion*."

"Actually, this is a farmhouse. It was originally built and lived in by people who worked in the fields and had animals, stored grains in the barn. Simple people."

"Sure," he said mockingly. "Anyway, this place is amazing. No wonder you always used to talk about it."

I realized how excited I was that he was seeing Casa Rossa at last.

"You have to see it in the daytime. You'll see the view. I'll take you for a ride in the countryside around here. I'll show you some other amazing houses like this one that have been left to crumble."

It dawned on me that for the longest time I had been compiling a mental list of things for Daniel to see. I had been adding new entries to the list for each season. The sweet smell of figs in August, the yellow stains of wild broom in May, the taste of *orecchiette con le cime di rapa* in the fall, that particular clarity of light over the sea in December. Until that moment I wasn't even aware that my list still existed somewhere, that I hadn't lost it or discarded it along the way. It was surprising how I had been holding on to it. Such an act of faith.

So I felt like everything had fallen into place at last.

This must be my reward, I thought. For having had the willfulness and the endurance to keep waiting in my austere solitude. There was something too miraculous—Daniel Moore showing up out of the blue, right on my doorstep—for me not to think that this was obviously meant to be. That this must be the right time and the right place.

Everything had found its slot, but the balance was still too shaky. I didn't want anything to fall off and shatter. So I didn't ask how long he was going to stay, or what his further plans were. I didn't want to worry about him having to leave already.

Suddenly we were quiet. We stared at each other across the room.

"*Vieni qui,*" I said, and I stretched my hand out.

I led him upstairs, into what was now my bedroom and once had been Lorenzo and Renée's. Then Lorenzo and Jeanne's. A bedroom with a big brass bed and a broad window over the sea of olives: a room that was never meant to be for one person only.

Lovers find their path into each other like blind people do. No matter how long they have been apart, they immediately recognize the smell, the shape, the texture of the other body and find their way. Nothing needs to be learned again.

I felt Daniel's hands lingering on my hipbone and caressing it, then sliding between my legs. The taste of his mouth, the way my fingers pressed the back of his neck, then brushed his collarbone.

And when he asked me what it was I was laughing about, I shook my head.

"Nothing," I said. "I'm just deliriously happy."

"I've taken a sabbatical," he announced the next morning, spreading his buttered toast with a thick layer of apricot jam.

I had laid the most lavish breakfast table imaginable.

At six-thirty, while he was still asleep, I had run out to the garden and cut fresh roses and branches of ivy to put on the table. I had fished out the old handmade plates painted in ochre and black. I had ransacked the cupboard and found the most delicious preserves from the previous summer. I had laid the table with silverware and an old embroidered linen tablecloth that I believe Jeanne used only on special occasions, like weddings or Easter Sunday lunches. But I was feeling extravagant.

"Which is to say . . . ?" I asked.

I could hardly swallow my coffee. My stomach was tied up in a knot of expectation and euphoria.

"Which is to say that I've been given a grant to write a book. I'm writing one last assignment for *The New Yorker*, which is the reason I had to come to Italy, but that's going to be my last story for a while. I'm taking a year off."

"Off from what?"

"From everything. I've sublet my place in the city." He smiled triumphantly and stretched his arms. "I'm a free man. I can write my book wherever I want."

I could tell he had been waiting for the right moment to release this piece of information. I stared at him in a stupor, holding my cup in midair.

"You're kidding."

"No, I'm not."

So, there you go, I said to myself. He's letting you know you two could have another go. I just couldn't believe he still trusted me and was ready to throw himself like that into my life again, so fearlessly. But that's what I loved about Daniel: his unending confidence that people would always make room for him in their life. His assurance had a naïve but endearing quality. Not like me, who would move out my bags and boxes even before I had unpacked them. Me, who would leave out of fear of being in the way. But this time around I was the one in place and he was the one with the luggage.

"What's the magazine assignment you're here to write?"

"A piece about this Russian choreographer, Leonid Massine. He worked in Paris with Picasso and Cocteau. Then he came to Italy in the twenties and built himself a house on top of a cliff on a tiny island across from Positano. Actually it's not even an island, it's more like two rocks, one next to the other."

"Yes, I think I've heard his name somewhere."

"Around that time there was an entire Russian community which gravitated around the Amalfi Coast. Lenin and Trotsky were in Capri, Nijinsky and Diaghilev with Massine in Positano. Apparently he had built a gigantic ballroom where he practiced. Can you imagine"— Daniel was obviously in love with the story—"this mad Russian dancing alone in a ballroom built on top of a rock in the middle of the sea? No electricity, no water, nothing?"

I smiled. His romanticism moved me. Maybe he felt it was time to break away from his Anglo-Saxon mold and come to Europe to be a bohemian. Resuming our affair on my turf must have been part of this plan.

Yes, this was exactly what a romantic American would be seeking. A truer lifestyle, less sheltered, less contemporary. A place where a Russian dancer would come to build his ballroom on top of a rock.

"I have to go to Rome early next week," I said. "I have to visit my sister, and I have a meeting with Esposito."

"Right," he said, a whiff of disappointment as I mentioned going away already.

"Would you like to come with me? We could take your car and stop along the way—somewhere beautiful, of course."

I wanted to make sure not to lose sight of him, now that he had rematerialized. I wasn't going to fuck it up again because of my fear. Things don't come back more than once in your life, I said to myself.

But everything turned out to be surprisingly easy.

We drove up north, crossing the plains right above Benevento, those vast, sun-scorched plateaus that look like what I imagine Mongolia must be like. We ate juicy slices of *mozzarella di bufala,* tomatoes and oregano on freshly baked bread, in the cafeteria of a small service station on the way. We both were astonished at how good it tasted. Daniel insisted on learning the Italian name for everything he touched, and repeated it out loud, relentlessly. His urge to instantly blend in, to acquire the know-how, was almost bombastic, like the impatience of a child allowed to take all the rides he wants in Disneyland.

We got to Rome, booked into the Locarno Hotel, made love in the afternoon, and ordered chilled white wine from room service.

I gave him the "Rome for Beginners Grand Tour." I was proud to be able to show him my favorite places, like he had for me almost five years back, in New York. We walked through the gardens of Villa Borghese to Villa Medici. He looked down at the view from the top of the Spanish Steps. The uneven skyline of red roofs, cupolas, domes, rooftop loggias. We came down the steps slowly. I showed him the house where Keats died, then the three thin palm trees across from Babington's Tea Room, covered in a golden light. A feast of yellows and oranges, blue sky against the pink of the buildings.

"*So* Edith Wharton," he said.

I should have known that he would have felt at home here. At home with his aspirations, his desires, his own projections. He already possessed all the knowledge necessary to decode and familiarize my country for himself, at least on a literary level. I should have known that he was always meant to come here and that he would learn this language and make it his without a problem.

Most of all, I should have known that I had been less of a stranger to him than I thought I was.

From Piazza di Spagna we turned into Via del Babuino.

"This is the street where I was born," I said.

There it was, the building where we lived as children with Oliviero, the café across the street where I had my lattes before going to school. I had a sudden urge to take him inside our old building. Its large door was open. The old marble staircase, the black banister, the wrought-iron lift, nothing had changed. Even the smell inside the elevator had stayed the same, a mix of wood and dust. I pressed the button number five.

"I just want to take a look," I said to him. "I've never been back here in all these years."

He nodded. Everything to him was worth doing. I recognized the whistling noise of the old-fashioned elevator, like a musical score I'd heard all my life. The gate clanked with the same sound when I closed it behind me.

I stepped up to the door of what used to be our old apartment. It bore a big brass plaque.

Laboratorio Analisi.

The door was ajar. I couldn't help pushing it open.

I saw a counter, flooded with fluorescent light, a receptionist with a computer screen in front of her. What used to be our hall—the large room where we kept our bicycles and hung our coats—was now a waiting room. Ugly office furniture, cheap sofas, women absorbed in medical magazines. A gray carpet on the floor covered the old uneven tiles.

"Can I help you?" asked the girl behind the white Formica counter.

I looked over her shoulder, to where the L-shaped corridor made a bend. I knew that right behind that bend was the room where Isa and I used to sleep. Then the living room. At the end of the corridor, there was the small studio where Oliviero used to work.

"Madam, can I help you?" her high-pitched voice insisted.

"No, I was just . . ." I looked at her as from another planet. "I used to live here."

She didn't register my words.

"Do you have an appointment?"

"No. I just came in to take a look. I lived in this apartment as a child," I said, somehow proudly.

One of the women raised her eyes from the magazine she was reading. Another gave me a cold stare. I had the feeling I was getting on their nerves. These women were there to get their blood and urine tested.

The receptionist looked nervous. She tapped a pencil on a pad. I smiled at her, before she could say anything else.

"It's all right, thank you. Goodbye," I said to everyone in the room.

No one responded.

I introduced Daniel to Alba and to her husband, Giorgio Carlei. They took us out to dinner at Nino's, an elegantly old-fashioned restaurant on Via Borgognona where neither the menu nor the waiters had changed in thirty years.

Daniel and Giorgio got on very well, they couldn't stop talking, bouncing from international politics to opera, from Salman Rushdie's new book to edible mushroom species. I sat back, watching Daniel deal with this new situation with his usual ease. For my part, I had always found Giorgio slightly intimidating. He was an interesting-looking man, always perfectly groomed, with an impressive mane of white hair, thin oval-shaped glasses worn in the middle of the nose. He had a very particular way of selecting his words, making the longest pauses in between, which always made me shift in my seat uncomfortably. But Daniel looked totally relaxed, and truly interested in what Giorgio had to say.

Alba smiled at me, with a brand-new gratitude. For once I was making it easy for her. Showing up with such an interesting man, who could hold the attention of Giorgio Carlei, notoriously impatient with ordinary people.

"Your mother is gorgeous," was the first thing Daniel said as we climbed the stairs of the Hotel Locarno. "She's great fun. And I liked your stepfather a lot."

"He's really more my mother's third husband than my stepfather," I said. "I've spent hardly any time around him. But he does seem to make my mother very happy, which is great."

He fumbled with the key and we entered our chintzy room.

"I expected your mother to be more difficult. I don't know why, but from the few things you've told me, I thought of her as more . . ."

"Hard work?"

"Yes, exactly."

His willingness to embrace my history, and his eagerness to decipher it, disoriented me. Suddenly I realized that what scared me was this new proximity, where he could see for himself where I came from, what I was made of. He could draw his own conclusions now, he was smart enough.

I realized that it was much easier to be in love than to be close.

The next day I left Daniel to look at paintings at the Galleria Doria Pamphili and went to visit Isa in jail.

She sat across from me, smoking a cigarette, her ash-blond hair cropped like a boy's. She was wearing a striped long-sleeved T-shirt and a pair of loose black jeans. She had been exercising a lot, her body looked skinny and hard, like an acrobat's. She had been biting her nails to the quick and I noticed a deep line furrowing her brow.

I love her, I thought. *She's like a stray dog.*

Maybe that's what we really were like, Alba, Isa, and I. Stray dogs, sniffing for food and warmth.

I told her about my visit to our apartment in Via del Babuino. She wanted to hear every detail, asked all kinds of questions, in her old detective fashion.

"Did you look to see if Olga's name was still on the buzzer?"

"Yes, I did. It wasn't."

"You know, she might be dead. She would be in her nineties now."

Olga. The Russian lady who lived above us and always gave us tea and cake. She took care of us the day Oliviero died.

"The minute I walked into the building I immediately recognized the smell. Especially inside the elevator. Remember that, a mix of wood and dust?"

"Yes, I do." She closed her eyes for a second. "I can't believe our apartment has become a lab. You should go back and pretend you need a test, just for the hell of it."

"Oh, I don't know. I'm not sure I'd like to go back. It already feels as if someone has wiped off the picture I had in my mind, and I kind of want to hold on to it. I want to remember it the way it was."

The furrow in her brow deepened.

"Sometimes I think that when I get out of here, nothing will look the same."

There was a short silence.

"Casa Rossa still looks exactly the same. Nothing has changed at all," I said, eager to offer her a way out. "If the city is too much to take, you can always come and live with me there."

She didn't respond. I gave her an awkward smile and looked at my nails. We always felt uneasy whenever we had to conjure up the future. Twenty-one years, a hundred, it really doesn't make that much difference when you're only thirty.

Daniel was determined to plunge deep into a new life.

Once we got back to Casa Rossa—although we had never had a specific conversation about it—it was clear that he was there to stay. At least for some time. He had set up his working desk in a small sunny room on the second floor and had started making notes for his book. I puttered around the house like he wasn't even there, working on my rewrites for Esposito, talking on the phone to the writers, feeding the dogs, watering the garden, pretending to be too busy to notice what he was doing but always making sure I kept an eye on him.

He was too excited by the surroundings to sit and concentrate for long. Any excuse was enough to send him out of the house—to shop for food, get the paper, get the car washed—so that he could attempt conversations in the village and practice his poor Italian.

It was as if he had dropped all his baggage from the past and was ready to absorb anything that came his way. His new lightness—this euphoric, momentary loss of memory—almost frightened me. I feared that any day I might wake up to see him drifting off into the air.

He had bought a *Teach Yourself Italian* book and was constantly asking for clarifications about past and future tenses, gender declensions, the subjunctive.

Suddenly my own language, dissected by his rational mind, sounded like this perverse and treacherous maze, impossible to negotiate.

"What does *'periodo ipotetico della irrealta'* actually mean?" He would walk into the kitchen holding his book in his hands, without even lifting his head from its pages.

"Let's see . . . something like 'hypothetical period of unreality.' "

"Sounds interesting"—he would grin—"which . . . when you translate it into normal English, means what exactly?"

"Something that you assume but it's not going to happen. Like, 'I would finish cooking lunch if you didn't interrupt me every five seconds with silly questions.' "

He'd shake his head and start back to his desk.

"You guys have such grand expressions for very simple concepts—I love it."

People in the village, after their customary initial mistrust of anyone so fair-haired and foreign, took to him, and to his kind manners. Carmela, the woman who came to clean, would bring homemade eggplant parmigiana or lasagna she had especially made for *Signor Daniele.* The woman who sold newspapers at the back of the *"tabacchi"* shop ordered English papers for him and kept them aside with his name neatly printed at the top of page one. The man who sold fresh vegetables from his pickup truck on the road had put aside some *cime di rapa* for *l'Americano.*

"No money," he would say, shaking his head. "I explained to him what he has to do with these. I told him to fry some anchovies and olives with the garlic. You know, that's how we make them at home."

I would dutifully bring the gift to Daniel and watch him cook according to the local instructions. I was proud of him, of the way the whole village called him by name. Our life together had no hard edges, no tensions. It was almost too smooth for me to get a grip on it. Sometimes I felt like I was sliding on glass, I couldn't hold on to anything.

This is what happiness is like, you idiot. You're just not used to it, I kept thinking. But sometimes a little voice taunted me: *Isn't this more like a parody of happiness?*

Sometimes I woke up in the middle of the night and felt like shaking him and asking, "What is this between us? Is this just another stretch of life, or is this going anywhere? Can you name this for me, please?" But I never did, I just watched him sleep, breathing so peacefully, and reminded myself that I should stop obsessing.

Sometimes, if during the day I'd been working on a script for too long, I'd worry about what Daniel would be doing, and I would rush to his study to check if he showed any signs of boredom, any little spasms of restlessness. But he was too busy loving his new life. I would peek in the room, and there he was, at his desk in front of the computer screen, smiling.

"Hi, baby. Do you feel like taking a break?" he would ask.

Everything mattered to him, every walk we took, every person I introduced him to, every new word he learned.

He bought books written by American political analysts who had lived in Italy and were fascinated by the muddle of Italian politics. Like many other foreigners, he, too, fell in love with its convoluted twists, its devilish principal characters, its perpetual ambiguity. He loved the melodrama, the lies, the tricks. It got to the point where Daniel knew more about what was going on in my own country than I did.

"You must read this article on Andreotti!"—and he would flop the *Herald Tribune* down under my nose, excitedly—"I can't believe he's getting away with this. This man is too clever and perverse!"

He often asked me about Isabella. He wanted to understand that part of my life which I was still trying to keep underground. It no longer seemed so distant and hard to believe now—the maximum-security prison, the bulletproof glass cage, Isa's sentence—especially now that he had seen the photos in the newspaper. He even had me translate some of the articles I had clipped at the time of her trial. He avidly read any article related to the many terrorism trials that were going on in the country. By then he was beginning to have a clearer picture of what had happened during the *anni di piombo*—"the years of lead." That was the media's name for the horror of the previous years, after Moro's killing.

"Show me a recent picture of Isabella," he asked me one evening. I was packing a small bag, getting ready to catch a train to Rome early the next morning. I was going to visit her and come back the following day.

"You know, it's crazy, but I don't have one. All I have is the two of us as children."

"Really? Your mother must have one. Maybe you could ask her and bring one back."

"No, I know she doesn't have any. Isabella destroyed all her pictures before she went underground. You know, for security reasons."

"Every existing photo?"

"Yes. I don't know how she managed that. Alba told me. I think she raided her house first, and then when she moved here with the others they—"

"They lived here?" He looked at me, totally surprised.

"Yes, I'm sure I told you."

"Yes, you're right. I had forgotten all about that. Sorry." He furrowed his brow lightly. "When was that?"

"I'm not sure exactly, but it was a couple of months before . . . the thing with Lo Capo happened. Anyway, when they were here, they were pretty clandestine already. I think she hunted up the family albums and took out all the photos of herself."

He sat on the bed and watched me fold a shirt.

"How many of them were here?"

"I think about six of them."

I felt uneasy. I knew what he was thinking.

"In which room did she and Enrico sleep?"

I stopped and looked at him.

"I don't know. I never asked her."

He shook his head, puzzled.

"It's funny—you never ask the things I would think of asking."

"We must have a different concept of relevance . . . But I can ask her, if you'd like," I said.

He stood up and went for the door.

"It doesn't matter. It was just a thought. Come down when you're finished, we'll have a glass of wine outside. The light's beautiful."

She took a drag and held the smoke in her lungs a while before blowing it out. Her eyes were two light-blue slits. She was thinking hard.

She slid a piece of paper across the table over to me, coughing.

"Here," she said, "read it and tell me what you think."

It was another document, one of the many she had masterminded in all these years. They spent entire days, she and her comrades, considering the meaning of each word, weighing the consequences of an adverb. To me, these pamphlets always failed to communicate much because of the convoluted, blurry, political lingo they used. Concepts were suffocated by ideology, their meaning strangled. It had been years, and I was still struggling to really grasp what it was she was trying to say.

"This is important," she stressed. "It should be published on the front page of *La Repubblica.* Tell them this is crucial."

I had passed many of these documents to the press before. In the beginning I had dealt with fervently committed young reporters who with time were promoted and turned into jaded senior editors. Over the years, I had handed these pages to magistrates, to the members of the antiterrorism commission, to talk-show hosts who had a soft spot for left-wing militants. Over the years, I learned their faces and they had begun to recognize mine.

As time went on, I found it more and more difficult to get their attention. After the initial horror and shock, Italy was eager to move on, to disentangle itself from the legacy of terrorism. Newspapers were looking for brighter stories, I was told. Readers and TV viewers were apparently sick and tired of terrorists.

But I had joined the sad family who had to trudge on—the family of women I had met on the train to Voghera that first time—and we were the only ones left to deal with the loose ends of the tragedy the others had been allowed to forget.

For us there was no moving on to brighter news.

"Isa, I doubt they'll publish it," I said after looking it over. "They don't want to hear about amnesty. It's too soon to bring this issue up."

"Who the hell says *amnesty*?" she snapped immediately. "It says 'political solution.' Look!"

She showed me the paragraph, pointing with her finger at the words. I obediently read again, then shook my head.

"Yes, but, ultimately, that's what you're asking for! When you invoke a 'political solution to create grounds for reconciliation,' you're asking that everybody forgives, forgets, and moves on."

"Not exactly. I'm not asking for forgiveness. We admit we have lost a war and we're just asking to be treated like prisoners at the end of a conflict."

"Whatever. Maybe I'm just being overcautious, but I don't think they'll publish this the way you want. Not on the first page."

She glared at me. I was perfectly aware that I was irritating her.

"Just take it to the internal affairs desk, to that guy, what's-his-name . . . the one who came to visit us in here three weeks ago."

"Marco Sestieri?"

"Yes, him. He'll know what to do with this. He's keen on this issue, believe it or not."

"Okay."

She took the piece of paper, folded it neatly in four, and pushed it over to my side. We sat facing each other with a certain awkwardness. It was part of the deal of our restored intimacy, the way we managed to get on each other's nerves.

She tapped with her fingers on the table. I grabbed her hand. Its skin felt rough.

"You need hand cream," I said. "Do you want me to bring you some?"

She nodded and remained silent. She left her hand in mine and checked my short, clipped nails.

"So, are you happy with your American?" she asked me without smiling.

"Yes."

"Has he moved into Casa Rossa with you?"

"I don't know if he has 'moved in.' He asked me if he could work there for a while. He's writing a book. He got a grant to write it, so he can live off that money for some time."

"So he's staying till . . . when?"

"We haven't really discussed it yet. I think for the summer. Then we'll see."

"That's good. I didn't like the idea of you being all by yourself there."

I noticed the way she thought of Daniel more as my bodyguard than my lover. But I had already noticed how the subject of men in the last few years had become a difficult one to touch. It was as if she no longer wanted to acknowledge their existence. She hadn't seen one in years, save for her lawyer and the occasional journalist or politician who showed up to visit them in their special section.

"Would you like to see what he looks like? I have a photo."

I wanted her to acknowledge him; I wanted him to have a face for her. Also, I wanted Daniel to know that she had seen him. It was a way for them to meet somehow.

She nodded and started biting her thumb furiously.

It was a photo I had taken just a few days earlier, while he was writing at the computer, the desk covered with books. He looked completely absorbed. His hair had grown a bit longer, his light skin had a healthy shine from the southern sun.

She studied the picture carefully.

"Is this in Casa Rossa?"

"Yes."

"Which room is this?"

"The small room upstairs, where Mamma used to sleep. I've turned it into a studio."

"You've painted the walls green?"

"Yes. Do you like it?"

"I love it."

She handed the photo back to me as if it burnt her fingers.

"He looks beautiful. And so serious."

"He's not. He has a great sense of humor."

But somehow I sensed that was enough. I could tell she didn't want to discuss my love life any further.

Marco Sestieri belonged to the tiny category of political reporters who would never turn into a jaded chief editor. He wrote a political column for *La Repubblica,* and his articles showed a sensitive, ever contrarian point of view and an unusual complexity.

Like many others his age, he had been an ardent radical in his university days who, later on, when many of his peers were joining ultra-leftist groups and were considering the use of arms in order to "defeat the system," had opted for a moderate route. Nevertheless, he still believed that his generation—and the left in general—bore a cultural responsibility for the explosion of terrorism. A skinny man in his early thirties, after two kids and a divorce, he was still searching for an answer to what had happened in the seventies. He wanted the wound to heal—not because he had a relative in jail like I did—but because he felt he deserved to live in his country feeling at peace, with a clear conscience.

"This is very good," he said, tapping Isabella's document with his fingertip.

We were sitting inside the tiny cubicle where he worked at the paper, a million phones ringing all around us, loud conversations, a steady buzzing of computer printers.

I had gone to see him at the paper, straight from my visit with Isabella in Rebibbia. I was in a hurry to hop on a train as soon as possible and head back to Casa Rossa. Although I knew this was important, I didn't want it to delay my return.

"Let's go for a cup of coffee," Marco said and stood up to grab his Burberry coat from a hanger. "There's too much noise in here."

I reluctantly followed him downstairs and across the square to an ugly café. We sat at a table on the sidewalk, on white plastic chairs, and ordered two espressos.

"I think your sister's document makes a lot of sense," he said, "but it's too soon to present this issue. We spoke about this already when I went to see her in Rebibbia, three weeks ago. I was there as part of a group of journalists and television people."

"Yes, she told me briefly about it. She said she liked what you had to say."

"Oh, did she?"

"Yes. She doesn't say that about a lot of people. I think she trusted you."

He smiled, pleased. I could tell she had made an impression on him.

"She's like a wounded animal," he said, shaking his head. "I wish she could express herself with less belligerence. The press, the judges, they all think of her as this fierce creature. She's so different in person."

"She was never good at pleasing others."

"And she's paying a high price because of it. I'm convinced the High Court should revise the Appellate Court's verdict. It's outlandish that she ended up with a sentence of twenty-one years, considering they found her not guilty of the actual murder, but only of conspiracy to commit murder. Which, in fact, they should have never charged her with, since Enrico what's-his-name testified that she begged him not to kill Lo Capo, that she tried to dissuade him, was in tears, and so forth. Am I right?"

He clearly had studied her case with care.

"I know. But I don't think the jury entirely believed Enrico's testimony insofar as Isabella was concerned," I said cautiously. "I think they were convinced he was trying to shield her. Because of . . . you know . . . their relationship."

"But that's absurd!" He threw his hands in the air heatedly. "That's just the point I'm making: if the jury considered him a reliable source for whatever concerned the rest of the defendants—and they did sentence people on the basis of his information, right?—they cannot make this exception. If he's reliable, then they have to accept his story entirely."

He drew a straight line in the air with his thumb and forefinger.

"It's a judiciary principle. As simple as that."

"Well, perhaps. Yes, I guess so."

"Any court of appeals with a sense of justice would have nullified the verdict. All the evidence is circumstantial, with regard to her conspiracy-to-commit-murder conviction."

"I know."

He stared at me, disconcerted by my lack of outrage.

I straightened up on the chair and tried to look more upset.

"But it's difficult to single her position out," I said. "She never once agreed to talk, to defend herself. It's almost as if she wants to stay to the bitter end, like all the others in her group."

"Yes. But why, do you think?"

"She hates the idea that she got a slightly lighter sentence than the others thanks to Enrico. She doesn't want to owe him anything. She despises anything coming from him."

Mario Sestieri looked into the bottom of his empty espresso cup and shook his head.

"I don't know. It may have been like you say until a couple of years ago. But I have a feeling she's had enough of being a martyr by now."

"I agree. But it's kind of too late now, isn't it?"

He looked somewhere, his eyes went out of focus for a couple of seconds.

"I'm convinced now she would be willing to talk. Maybe not to a judge, but to someone like me. That could help. Times are changing: politicians know they have to 'adjust the picture,' even if only slightly. Her case would be the perfect excuse."

"And *will* you do anything to help her?"

I was surprised at my own audacity. But I had faith that this man could actually do something. He could translate for others what had been impossible for me to translate all these years. That she had paid enough. That it didn't make sense that Enrico and many others who had shot and killed had been released and were walking around free as a reward for turning their comrades in. That it just didn't add up. That this had nothing to do with justice; it was merely a deal the government had struck in order to win a war. And that now that the war was won, it was time to forgive, reconcile, and move on.

Maybe this young man with glasses, hairy hands, an aquiline nose could make that clear.

"I think I can," he repeated, "by writing about her, by singling her out, as you say. If she agrees to come forward and let me interview her, then maybe I could bring attention to her case specifically, before it's examined by the High Court. It's the last chance she'll get."

He looked at me expectantly. I sensed he'd been thinking about this. I sensed he'd been thinking about *her*.

For a man like Marco Sestieri, to fight against the injustice he perceived in Isabella's judiciary case was an act of catharsis. He so much wanted to heal the wound which had infected the country that almost any wound would do.

"All right. I'll write her a letter and ask her what she thinks about speaking with you," I said. "Maybe you should write her as well, since she seems to trust you so much."

He smiled and blushed lightly.

"Okay. I'll do that, if you think it'll help."

I looked at my watch.

"I have to go now. I have to catch a train."

We stood up. I stretched my hand out to shake his.

"Listen . . . thank you so much for taking an interest in her case. I really appreciate it."

"She doesn't deserve to sit in jail till she's fifty. And there's no need for her to turn into a spy in order to get out, if that's what she fears. Make sure she understands that."

He's falling in love with her, I thought fleetingly.

Marco Sestieri smiled as he shook my hand, sealing a new sense of kinship. Now we were together in this.

And he succeeded.

Marco Sestieri wrote about Isabella in his column with such poignancy and attention, with such respect for every party involved, that the article immediately created a sensation. The photo of Isabella in the courtroom, her fist up in the air in the witness stand, her eyes turned upward, like a saint seeking the light of God, was still vivid in the national memory; now, almost five years later, she appeared to be a deeply transformed person.

A few days later the weekly magazine *L'Espresso* decided to follow up and do a bigger story on Isabella. It turned out to be a pretty detailed profile: they had gotten hold of some of her old school friends, they got a couple of quotes out of her teachers, they had managed to fish out the review of one of her performances choreographed by Tomas. The writing was cautious, but Isabella's portrait was dignified and benign. The way the story was told clearly showed that she had come from a sound family background, that she had had a good upbringing, great opportunities, artistic aspirations. She's not a monster, the article basically said. She's one of us. She could have been anybody's child.

The talk-show host, Serena Mancini, a former foreign correspondent turned TV personality, caught the drift and phoned me at Casa Rossa. She announced that she wanted to interview Isabella in jail for her show. I had never seen her program and had only the faintest idea who she was.

"I don't know if she'll do it," I said.

"But my show has ratings through the roof. She'd be crazy not to. It's really in her interest."

"I don't know what she thinks her interest is," I said, "but I'll ask her."

Isabella wasn't thrilled when I told her that Serena Mancini wanted to tape an interview with her. The articles in *La Repubblica* and *L'Espresso* were already more than she could cope with.

"I don't particularly want to be on TV. I received a stack of letters this high only within the last three days," she said to me when I went to see her the following week. "People I knew from school, convicts from all over the country . . . perfect strangers who say they want to come and meet me . . . sex maniacs. It's crazy."

"I know, but . . . hey. So what do I tell this woman?"

"Forget it. I'm not discussing my political position on some fucking TV show. Does she expect me to say I'm sorry, or I'm guilty? I mean, I refused to speak in court, why should I talk now, in front of the whole country—in between Pepsi and laundry detergent commercials, while they're gulping down their dinner?"

"She said she won't ask you anything political. She just wants a portrait of you, she said. 'As a woman.' A kind of personal—"

She waved her hand, annoyed, to stop me.

"I have nothing to say 'as a woman' " she sneered. "I don't even know if I *am* one anymore."

I knew she was scared of stepping forward, of coming out of her shelter.

Marco Sestieri went to visit her the following week and persuaded her to accept.

"How did you do it?" I asked him.

"I told her that she embodies the perfect case for political debate. That it has the potential to ignite a discussion in Parliament about a general amnesty, reconciliation, and all the rest of it. So, basically, I pointed out to her that she'd be helping every prisoner who was convicted on the same charges and has never collaborated."

He smiled. "In other words, I laid some guilt on her."

Serena Mancini called me back at Casa Rossa as soon as she heard Isabella had agreed. She sounded nervous and suspicious of me before I was even able to say hello, as if she was convinced I was going to withhold critical information from her.

"I need some background in order to prepare the interview. You know, about her upbringing, the family history, memories of your childhood, and so forth. I usually have an intro that gives the viewers a little background on the guest."

"Right," I said cautiously.

"We show some photos. We'll need at least five or—"

"There *are* no photos. She destroyed them all."

"You mean you have no pictures of her at all?" She sounded deeply annoyed.

"Just a few, of her as a child," I sighed. It just sounded so menacing, every time I had to explain this business of Isabella having wiped out all record of herself.

"We need to have *some* images. I'm interested in the *personal* angle," she stressed, as if I were being purposely uncooperative.

"Yes, I understand. I'll be happy to help you with whatever I have."

"All right, then. I'll be there tomorrow evening. I'll call you from the hotel."

Daniel volunteered to cook dinner while I went to pick her up at the hotel in Lecce. Serena Mancini, in her late thirties, could have been good-looking, but she was overweight, overly neurotic, and clearly not happy with herself. She was wearing an extravagant frilly dress, flashy and unbecoming. As we drove to Casa Rossa she bombarded me with questions and started taping everything I said, while chain-smoking, without even bothering to open the window.

"So your grandfather came from a wealthy family? Marble, right? Well, there was quite a lot of money in marble in those days. So actually you and your sister come from a pretty bourgeois background, right?"

"I don't know," I said and shrugged. She bugged me. "I don't think *bourgeois* is the word. Nobody in the family was really a professional, or had a steady income."

When we finally got to the house, she sized it up, suspiciously.

"Don't tell me your grandfather bought this with his paintings. It must have been family money."

"Actually you're wrong. He bought it by selling some of his work to a French banker in the twenties. Back then this was a ruin nobody wanted."

By this point I had begun to dislike her deeply. She was like a dog hunting for a bone to chew on. She seemed particularly obsessed by the subject of money, as if that was the key to the mystery of Isabella's destiny. This Catholic, punitive bullshit, I thought, which in this country, has translated into sheer resentment for anybody who was raised with their plate full. She probably had her little story plot figured out in advance: rich girl turns terrorist in her search for salvation—or, worse still, to escape a meaningless existence. I regretted ever having talked Isabella into doing this. I didn't need anyone else to tear to shreds whatever was still left of my family.

We sat in the living room and I dutifully showed her the family photos I had found and set aside for her. I pulled out a snapshot of Isa and me. The colors had faded somewhat and gone all yellowish. We must have been eight and ten. The skinny shrimps. Long ruffled hair like two shaggy dogs. We were each holding a small basket full of colored eggs.

"It was the Easter egg hunt. Jeanne, my grandfather's second wife, she always painted the eggs and hid them in the garden, right there.

They were so beautiful. Look . . . we never wanted to throw them away."

"Is this her?" Serena pointed at Isabella.

She was holding her egg basket toward the camera like a trophy, her eyes shining with excitement. She looked like a crazed angel.

"Mmm . . ." Serena flicked the photo between her fingers. "This one may work."

She had picked up a photo of Oliviero in black tie, holding the Nastro d'Argento award in his hands.

"Who's this?" She looked at me suspiciously, as if I had been hiding something from her again.

"Our father. That was when he won the award for best script. For *The Summer of Alina,* this film he wrote back in—"

"He *wrote* that film? I didn't know he was . . ."

She looked up as Daniel walked into the room. He was holding a bottle of wine. I introduced them.

"Dinner is on the way. Have something to drink first," he said as he poured us some red wine.

Serena excused her poor English, but I noticed how she blushed and instantly became more animated. Obviously the unexpected presence of an attractive man had put her slightly off balance.

"Do you live here also?" she asked him.

"Yes, I do," he said and I felt my heart speed up when I heard him say that. I sat close to him on the armrest of the sofa, so as to establish that she had to deal with the two of us from here on. Serena lit another cigarette.

"And what do you do?" she went on in her inquisitive fashion.

"I'm a freelance writer, mostly for *The New Yorker.*"

That shut her up. She rolled her eyes.

"*The New Yorker?* My absolutely favorite magazine."

He smiled at her, unfazed.

"You know, I've read about your show. It sounds very interesting. Unfortunately my Italian isn't quite there yet for me to follow it on TV."

He lifted his glass, in such a way as to suggest a cease-fire might be in order.

At dinner Serena drank quite a few glasses of wine, took two help-ings of pasta, devoured the fish, the potatoes, and the almond pastries. She staggered on with increasing confidence in her broken English, try-ing to win Daniel's approval. Now that she was in the presence of an-other journalist, she stopped acting like a cop in search of evidence in the house of a fool who doesn't know her rights and started to behave more graciously. Daniel kept her at bay without her knowing it. He kept steering the conversation in directions he felt were more meaning-ful. Serena Mancini relaxed, seemed less concerned with her hunt for a sensational angle on the story and seemed more interested in discover-ing something real about my sister.

"What do you think it was, ultimately . . . I mean, what was the trig-ger that turned Isabella into a terrorist?"

"Oh, I don't know. I've often thought about it." I felt both her eyes and Daniel's on me. I swallowed hard. "I think she believed . . . that she was miserable because the world around was unjust."

"Yes." Serena squinted, slightly impatient again. "A lot of people felt that way, all over the world, in the seventies. But not everyone used guns. That's taking it to a whole different level."

I had never discussed Isabella's motivations with anybody before, and it didn't feel right to have a stranger pushing me into coming up with an answer. With my fingertip I fiddled with the crumbs of the dessert in my plate.

"Why was she so angry? Did she feel betrayed, perhaps?" she pressed me.

"Betrayed . . . by whom?"

"For instance by your father's suicide? The way he disappeared from one day to the next? Why do children turn into angry adults? I don't know. I'm trying to conjure up a psychological background. Something to work with in the interview."

I stared at her, speechless.

"What I mean is, do you think she was seeking some kind of emotional retribution? A new family?" Serena went on, unphased, un-aware of the horrified look on Daniel's face. "I think the group, the comrades . . . they became a sort of substitute family for a lot of people. Don't you?"

"I don't know. Maybe."

"Maybe she needed an enemy," she suggested. "She needed to see the world in black and white in order to give herself the power to judge others and come up with a verdict. It's a very powerful feeling."

"Looks like you've got it all figured out already," Daniel interjected.

"I think she believed she was fighting a war to dismantle a repressive system so that people could be free," I said, louder than I intended, and a note of anger entered my voice, "and not because she needed to find a lost father or get back at my mother in some creepy Freudian scenario."

"I didn't mean to ascribe her motivations merely to—"

"All I know is, she's no longer that person today," I interrupted her.

"You really don't think so?" Serena asked, not eager to placate me.

"No. But I also think she has too much integrity to say that she wished she'd never done it. And, basically, that's why she's still in jail."

I stood up and began clearing the dishes.

When we finally dropped Serena Mancini at her hotel after midnight, I felt relieved.

"Thank God that's over. She wiped me out."

"She's not so bad."

"Oh, *please.* She's relentless. And so fucking neurotic."

"No she's not. Just a typical magazine writer stressed over her assignment."

Unlike myself, Daniel Moore loved to be fair.

When I saw the interview on TV a couple of weeks later, I sighed with relief. I watched it on the old-fashioned TV set we had in a tiny room downstairs at Casa Rossa. Daniel, sitting next to me, held my hand throughout.

When Isabella appeared on the screen, in the small bare room where inmates usually met with lawyers, I squeezed his hand hard and my heart started beating furiously. She was wearing her long-sleeved striped shirt. She bit her nails a couple of times before answering some of the questions, and the line on her forehead deepened before she spoke. I was surprised by her poise, her soft tone of voice, by the way she paused before answering each question. There was a vulnerability in her that I hadn't expected to see. She showed up without armor, almost offering herself. Serena Mancini showed none of that preconception that I in my

283

paranoia had detected. She wasn't trying to be provocative or to push Isa up against the wall.

"What is the first thing you would want to do the day you'll walk out of this place?"

"Have a child," Isabella answered without hesitation. She looked straight into the camera, without blinking. "Give new life."

She paused and then smiled. Her eyes lit up.

"I'd want a child, because I would love him or her unconditionally."

"One last question." Serena Mancini leaned over, closer to Isabella, with a particularly grave expression. "After all these years spent in silence . . . do you ever feel the burden of . . ."

Isabella's eyes turned cold, I saw her face harden. Serena hesitated, cleared her throat, but then decided to go for it.

"I mean, to put it simply . . . does your conscience ever come back to haunt you?"

I stiffened in my seat and squeezed Daniel's hand again, hard. Isa took a long pause. Then she turned her eyes away from the camera and looked to the side. She shook her head.

"It's not my conscience that comes back. I never lost track of my conscience. I think what comes back to trigger the pain is something different. . . ."

She paused again and took a long breath. Her voice cracked slightly, and I realized that she was fighting back tears.

"It's our good side. It's the side that we tried to suppress in order to carry out what we believe we had to do. That's what keeps coming back, whole and untouched . . . to remind us of a life that"—and she turned her face down and quickly, lightly, wiped something from her cheek with the tip of her finger—"that could have been, and never will be."

Although he didn't understand it all, Daniel sighed with relief as the interview ended.

"Jesus," he said, "that was *powerful*."

I felt totally drained. In a way, I still wished she hadn't had to do that. To have to come out of her den and reveal herself like that.

The next day, the papers wrote about her appearance and compared her to Jean Seberg.

She didn't look like a film star to me. She looked like my sister. Too thin, too pale, worn out by too many years of jail.

Daniel and I had gotten used to going to bed early. It was the country, after all. So, the night when the phone rang around midnight, I jolted out of bed and ran downstairs to pick up the receiver.

"Hi, it's Marco, sorry to call so late."

"Marco? . . . Who?"

"Marco Sestieri. But it's important."

"Yes, Marco, of course. What is it?"

"The ruling. They announced their judgment two hours ago. The High Court has amended the verdict of the appeal."

"And?" I was suddenly wide awake.

"She got eight years. Which means, basically, she's out."

"When?"

"*Now.* Counting good conduct and all, she's *out.* She's served six years already."

"Please, don't tell me this unless you're absolutely—"

"I'm sure. I know it for a fact. She's out. Free to hop on a bus and leave."

"Swear."

He laughed.

"I swear. I double-checked with Tommasi. Call him now, he'll tell you. It'll be all over the newspapers tomorrow. You'll read it in *La Repubblica.* We're printing it on the front page."

I started giggling hysterically. I just couldn't stop. I kept saying, "Swear it's true! Swear it's true! . . ."

He kept on laughing at the other end of the phone.

"Would I be kidding you?"

"Okay, I'm gonna call Tommasi," I said. "I'll call you back—are you at home?"

"Yes. But you don't need to call me back. Let's speak tomorrow. After you read it in the papers. It'll feel more real then."

I hung up the phone and just stood there like an idiot, stark naked in the middle of the dark living room of Casa Rossa. I could hear the crickets outside. My heart thumping, singing. I started dancing. I jumped up and down, I screamed.

I ran upstairs to wake Daniel. I rolled him over gently, till he opened his sleepy eyes and looked at me.

He had been sleeping next to me for a few months by then. At night, even in my deepest sleep, I never forgot that he was there next to me. *I love this man,* I thought as I bent over to kiss him lightly and whisper in his ear.

"Isabella. She's coming home."

He was the first person I could say those words to. The words I had silently rehearsed for years.

I wanted to thank him, for being there to listen to them, for being so close.

"When?" he asked, blinking like a little boy.

"Soon. Tomorrow, the day after tomorrow, next week. Now."

"Do you want to go to Rome?"

"Yes, I'll call Tommasi. I'll find out exactly when they'll let her out."

He held me and kissed me.

"I'll come with you."

"Of course," I said.

Of course, I said.

But what else was I supposed to say?

Nothing would have stopped it from happening.

CHAPTER NINE

———◆———

Of the much awaited scene—the scene of Isabella's return—I remember nothing.

I don't remember her expression, her first step into Alba's living room as she came through the door.

I don't remember our first hug, the first words she said. I don't remember Alba's face when she saw her daughter walk through the door, whether they cried or laughed or both.

Nor how Isabella looked around and took in this new place—Alba and Giorgio's new home—the luxury of the leather sofas, the pillows, the dark mahogany bookcases, the thick oriental rugs.

That is all gone, blurred.

All I remember is that she looked out of place, that I had the distinct impression she didn't know what to do with her body, she didn't know how to sit down, nor how to hold a glass.

That she looked more frightened than happy.

It reminded me of the time when she and I were children and we had brought home a tiny puppy from the pound. We were so proud to have freed him from his cage, but all the puppy could do was look at us with his big liquid eyes and hide under the table, trembling.

It's odd how time had dripped like a leaky tap all those years she spent in jail. And then, from the moment she walked through that door, time burst forward and I could hardly keep track of what was happening.

But I remember clearly the minute Daniel appeared in the room (he had decided to join us for dinner, to give us some time alone as a family). If I close my eyes I can still see it happening.

The way their eyes locked.

And instantly it was as if her fear had dissolved, and something entirely new had taken over her. A resolution, a desire, something so powerful nobody could shake it from her. I could see all the muscles in her body sprinting forward, the tension of this forceful longing arching her back. Her eyes shimmered, glazed by the wine and by this new drug spilling slowly into her blood.

There was nothing I could do but sit back and look at the two of them. Two absolute strangers, two people who didn't even speak the same language. Who were now scanning each other, hungry to learn more, as fast as they could.

Alba and Giorgio were too excited to notice anything, too busy opening bottles of wine, lighting candles, making toasts. This was the one family party nobody was allowed to spoil.

We were sitting around the table by then, and I felt like getting up from my seat and screaming.

No. Please don't. You can't do this.

But it had already happened.

Over the next couple of days, Isabella avoided me.

Maybe I should say we were avoiding each other. It was subtle, but we both knew it was happening. In those first few days after she had come home, we never attempted to be alone in the same room, we never found a moment to be just the two of us, to laugh or cry or simply give each other a hug.

All that closeness, that intimacy we had regained slowly over the years, letter by letter, visit after visit. It was gone.

Not only couldn't I rejoice that she was home at last, but I felt threatened by her presence. It was shameful.

It made me curl back, nauseous, but I couldn't help it, and I couldn't talk about it to anyone. The fear had made me hollow, mute. The failure.

People spoke to me, asked me questions, phoned to congratulate us over the good news. But I couldn't hear a thing. It was as if I had fallen into deep water, into a different realm, where everything was silent, and all I could hear was the sound of my own breathing.

I searched for air, but my lungs, my throat, my tongue, everything felt dry. My body temperature, too, had dropped, and I was cold.

We celebrated her return nonstop for two or three days. Alba and Giorgio's house was full of people coming and going who wanted to greet Isabella. I lost track of who was who. I came across faces I hadn't seen since our school days, faces I knew from the hearings. Laura, Gabriella, and the other women from car number five showed up with flowers and homemade fruit tarts. Their daughters were still sitting in Voghera, and they toasted Isabella's release with tears in their eyes.

"It makes us so hopeful to see you here," they said, hugging her tight.

There was always food on the table for the unexpected visit, always more than we needed. We made such an odd mix, this group of people who had become familiar in the cold waiting room of a high-security prison, in the corridors of the courthouse, in the second-class compartment of the train going to Voghera and now were sunk in the plush cushions of Giorgio Carlei's living room holding a glass of champagne in their hand.

I knew it was going to be hard to mask my true state with such a festive mood all around me. I walked around the apartment like a zombie, spending as much time as I could in the kitchen. Somehow, cutting vegetables or washing dishes calmed me down. Whenever I had to sit in the living room with the guests, I was seized by this new terror, which turned me deaf and dumb.

I couldn't keep my eyes off Daniel and Isabella, had to check each time they made eye contact. They hardly ever spoke, his Italian was too tentative and her English was nil, but somehow they communicated by quick gestures, awkward smiles. He never lost touch of where she was in the room. He didn't seem to feel uneasy in the least among this unlikely crowd. On the contrary, he looked alert, interested, eager to be helpful and to talk to anybody who could understand him. He acted like he was part of the family.

"What is it? You seem tired," Daniel asked me. He had come into the kitchen to get some clean glasses.

"Too much confusion. I'm not used to it."

"It's only for these first few days. It'll calm down."

"I know. But I miss the quiet . . . the silence of Casa Rossa," I said.

He looked at me with slight reproach.

"Do you? I thought you wanted to be with Isabella as much as possible."

"I do. But not with a million people around."

"Yes, I can see that. It must be very tiring for her as well."

Everything he said stabbed me.

"Did she tell you that?" I asked.

He looked at me, surprised.

"She told me she had a headache. I gave her an aspirin."

"Oh. Okay."

I had to leave the room, and lock myself in the bathroom.

Jealousy is a disease, it's like a poison, I kept saying to myself. You are going mad, you must stop. You must shake it off.

You are imagining it. Nothing is happening.

I looked at myself in the mirror as I kept repeating these words, like a mantra. But I didn't believe them. I didn't feel better.

Marco Sestieri came on the third day. He had waited, he said, because he wanted to give Isabella a bit of time to adjust to the confusion of the world outside.

I suppose he had hoped to come after everyone else, because he didn't want his face to be muddled together with all the other faces and loud toasts. He had been patient because he wanted his encounter with Isabella to be a special one.

He looked shy, expectant, like a man in love. He had brought her a book. She read the dedication and blushed.

"Thank you," she said, "that's very kind of you to say."

He sat next to her on the couch, with adoring eyes. I think he had expected to be welcomed like a hero, the man who had orchestrated her freedom. Maybe he had fantasized that Isabella would run into his arms and be moved to tears.

He must have been disappointed by her grateful yet cool response.

"Would you like to go out for dinner?" he ventured. "I thought I'd take you to eat out on Via Appia, under a trellis."

"No, thanks. I'm still a bit nervous," she said. "I don't think I can face a restaurant yet. I have to take this one step at a time."

"Of course. Maybe next week you'll be ready," and he laughed clumsily.

"Maybe," she conceded. Then she realized she had sounded too dismissive, and forced a smile.

"Why don't you have dinner here with us? It's only us, the family. Daniel is cooking a leg of lamb. He's a wonderful cook."

It pained me to hear his name on her lips. And when we sat once again around that family table, and when Daniel brought the meat out on a plate and carved it for everybody, I saw Marco Sestieri's gaze, I saw the way he evaluated Isabella's smile as she eagerly accepted her plate from Daniel's hands and thanked him. He, too—I saw it— could feel the current between them. He sunk back in his chair, defeated.

Then everything changed. It took only seconds, like a rip in a cloth.

It's useless to linger and dissect, to try to separate one expression from another, to single out the gesture, the phrase that was the most telling.

But by the time I got back to Casa Rossa with Daniel, I knew I had lost him.

Although he was sitting at the same desk, in the little room upstairs, in front of his computer, although he kept on working steadily on his book, reading and making notes, although he would come into the kitchen and drink wine with me when I had finished my work and was making dinner, although he would ask about my day like he cared, everything had changed.

His silence had a different quality. His quietness concealed a restlessness. And so did mine.

By then we only made love in the dark, without looking into each other's eyes. Lately we had been doing it in the same way: quickly, silently, without ever changing the order of our movements, as if this was going to be the only way to love each other for the rest of our days. I always fell into a thick, dead sleep, from which I always woke up exhausted.

Then one day Isabella phoned.

"I'm going mad here," she said.

"Why?"

"It's all so difficult . . . getting adjusted. I feel like I'm in everybody's way. I feel totally useless."

"No, you're not. You just have to take it easy. It'll take some time. You can't expect to—"

"I know, I know. It's just that . . . here there's too much of everything. Too much traffic, noise, people. I'm overwhelmed. I need some peace."

"I was thinking maybe you should sign up at a gym. You should keep on exercising."

"*Please.* This is not about exercise."

"No, I know. I was just trying to—"

"I want to come to Casa Rossa."

There was a silence. I felt as if her words had slid and sunk in a bottomless pit. I cleared my throat.

"Why?"

"Because . . . I'd like to go and visit Rosa. I want to ask her if I can speak to Adele."

I said nothing.

"It would mean a lot to me," she insisted.

"Yes, but"—and I realized I didn't know how to stop her. "I mean, why don't you let me speak to her first? Let me test how she—"

"She wrote me a letter. I got it yesterday."

"Who did?"

"Rosa."

"Really?"

"Yes. She says she was happy to hear I was out. She said something about God's will."

"Oh . . . well . . . that's great, then."

She paused and then I could feel a surge of excitement in her voice.

"How's the weather? Is it still warm enough to swim?"

I looked out at the warm afternoon light. It was early October.

"Yes. It's still warm enough. We went for a swim on Monday and it was beautiful."

"I don't think she realizes," I began.

"What?" said Daniel. We were eating dinner downstairs in the kitchen. I had lit a fire, the first of the season.

"I mean, how awkward this is going to be, if she comes here. It took me years to . . . fix things. To make everybody comfortable again about having us back here."

"But you said that Rosa actually sent her a note. That means she's welcome."

"Yes, I guess so. I don't know. I just feel that it's a bit too much, to show up here so soon. And this thing of going to see Adele, I think is mad."

"Why?"

"Because . . . I mean . . . I don't know how Adele would feel about this. She never came forward, she never wrote or said anything in all these years."

He lifted his eyes from his plate and looked at me.

"But Isabella is innocent."

I stared back at him and said nothing.

"Adele might not be so convinced," I said.

"How do you know? And why wouldn't she?"

"Because . . . oh, please, let's drop this. It's a bit too much, really."

There was an awkward silence as we continued to eat. I had never felt so uneasy with him. He had never seen me so aggressive.

"I think you should let her come, if that's what she wants," he said as he poured more wine into my glass. "This must have been a plan she's had for God knows how long."

"What do you mean, 'I should let her come'?" I snapped. "I'm not in charge of issuing permits around here. She can do whatever she wants now. This house belongs to her as much as me. I just don't think it's respectful."

He looked at me, and just as he was about to say something, he shook his head, as if to say, forget it.

I went to pick her up at the station in Lecce. She was overwhelmed. She said the train ride had been beautiful and she had cried when she saw the sea, near Brindisi.

She insisted on stopping in the old *pasticceria* outside the old walls of the city, near the railway station, before we headed for Casa Rossa, to have one of their *pasticciotti con la crema.*

She said eating them had been one of her most recurrent dreams in jail. She had two of those, a cappuccino, and a chocolate eclair.

She was ravenous.

In Lecce people recognized her. Some remembered who she was because they knew our family or had met us as children. Others knew her face from the articles or that TV show.

The alleged killer of Lo Capo.

The young Jean Seberg.

Most people ignored her, but some kept staring. A few came forward and shook her hand.

"We saw you on television. It's a good thing they revised the verdict. We're happy to see you back here."

When we stopped to buy the paper at the newsstand across from the *pasticceria,* the woman in the kiosk, a short and stocky bleached blonde in her mid-fifties, leaned over and spat in her face.

"*Feccia!* You scum," she hissed. "Don't you show your face here! Assassin!"

Isabella wiped her face with the back of her hand and didn't flinch.

She grabbed the hand I had rested on the gearshift as we crossed the bridge and turned by the Madonna shrine. There was the house, perched on the gentle slope, its color faded slightly.

"Oh my God," she said. She had tears in her eyes.

Daniel was standing at the front door to greet us. They hugged, quickly. He had set the table, arranging a cheerful plate of figs and grapes in the center.

"It looks so beautiful," she whispered, as if she were entering a church.

Then suddenly she leaped forward with two big steps and flew across the dining room into the living room, jumping up in the air, doing a perfect series of pirouettes, her arms rounding above her head. Graceful, precise, like a prima ballerina. She stopped and broke out laughing, her eyes shining, as Daniel clapped his hands.

"Alina? Pick up, it's Esposito, I have something urgent to—"

I heard his voice on the answering machine at eight in the morning. I rose from bed, picked up the cordless, and swiftly closed the door behind me, in order not to wake up Daniel.

"Yes, yes, how are you?"

I passed by Isabella's bedroom. The door was ajar. I saw her unmade empty bed. She must be down in the kitchen already, having breakfast, I thought.

"I read your second draft," Esposito said bluntly. Displeased.

"And?"

"And I think it doesn't work. I had a long talk with Jacques last night from Paris. He's kind of perplexed as well."

Jacques was the young French director who was supposed to be shooting the script I had been working on. It was another silly script, about a good cop and a drug-addicted teenage girl in the slums of Rio.

"It's too clichéd, too rushed. And the ending doesn't work. It feels like a TV movie."

I would have paid a million dollars not to have to think about that ridiculous story again.

"I know," I said feebly. "I've just had a pretty hellish two weeks. My sister has—"

"We need to have a meeting," he interrupted. "Let's see . . . he's coming on Tuesday, so we could meet on . . ."

I heard him take a drag on his early-morning cigarette as he checked his diary.

"Thursday at three?"

"Okay."

"But don't make plans to leave right away, because you and Jacques might want to have another session on Friday. He's coming especially for this, and he's really concerned. He wants this script to be absolutely right, he's not going to take a chance with this."

I detected a menacing tone I had never heard before. I needed to straighten things out with Esposito right away. I couldn't afford to lose his trust.

"Don't worry. I'll be there, and I'll work with him as long as we need to. I'll fix it."

But I knew it was like a death sentence, my having to leave.

Isabella had been at Casa Rossa for nearly a week, but she hadn't paid her visit to Rosa yet. She had been speaking about it to the parish priest in the village. The priest was very close to Rosa, and he had said it would be a good idea to leave things in his hands. These were delicate matters. There were rumors that Adele was seeing someone at last, seven years after her husband's death. A doctor, apparently. Even for her, as for the whole of Italy, the possibility of a new life—a release from the *anni di piombo*—was beginning to take form. The priest trusted that with a little bit of time, she would agree to see Isabella and grant her forgiveness.

"I trust him, he's a very nice man," Isabella said. "He'll tell me when it's the right time."

So, in the meantime, she was hanging around the countryside, patrolling her childhood territory, learning again how to move her body in the open space. Savoring smells and colors long forgotten. We went swimming together under the crumbling tower of San Emiliano. She shrieked with delight when she first jumped into the clear water. It was touching, to see her swim underwater, like a fish released back into the sea.

"When's the last time she was here?" Daniel asked me. He was lying on a rock next to me, aimlessly turning the pages of a book.

"Almost seven years ago."

He raised his eyes from the book and looked at her for a while, a dark silhouette, cutting through the water with a forceful crawl.

I went to Rome and went through my meetings with the French director and Esposito like someone walking on hot coals. I couldn't wait for it to be over. It seemed impossible to concentrate and listen to what Jacques or Esposito had to say, to care about the story, to believe in the characters. It all sounded so artificial, so removed. Why couldn't I just get up and scream that I didn't give a damn about this idiot cop. Why couldn't they leave me alone and let me go back home?

Two days later I finally managed to get on a train back to Lecce. Daniel and Isabella were waiting for me on the platform of the train station. They could have been brother and sister, I thought: both of them fair, slender, almost the same color eyes. I noticed she was wearing my red sweater. It annoyed me that she would go through my drawers like that, without bothering to ask.

Driving back home, they related each detail of how they had spent those forty-eight hours without me. They said they had gone to see the frescoes in the church of Santa Caterina. Isabella had showed Daniel the ruins of a medieval castle where we played as children, not far from Casa Rossa. They had discovered a new *gelateria* in Borgagne. They both sounded nervous.

"We must take you there," Daniel said. "They make your favorite chocolate. Bitter like you wouldn't believe."

"Yes, we should go. Maybe tonight after dinner," Isabella echoed.

"No thanks," I said, curtly. "I'm too tired to go out. I'm really exhausted."

They followed me around the house like two children who had done something wrong. They helped me cook and set the table, carefully avoiding looking at each other.

When we started eating, the conversation suddenly lagged. By then, the illusion that we would come out unscathed was over. Each of us was deeply entrenched in the vision of what was going to come next.

It was only a matter of minutes for all this nebulous matter to fit into a phrase, slip into a clear question.

"You fucked her, didn't you?"

I heard this voice—metallic, hard, not mine—formulate the question while he was brushing his teeth in the bathroom.

He waited to rinse his mouth, then came out of the bathroom, shirtless, barefoot.

"Alina, please."

"You fucked her today, didn't you?"

He didn't raise his voice, he didn't look at me with reproach. He sighed and slumped on the bed next to me.

"Why do you ask me like that?"

" Why? Is there any other way to ask?"

"Yes . . ." and he let all the air out of his lungs till he was deflated. "Maybe not. I guess it doesn't matter."

He kept his eyes down on the bedspread as long as he could. Then he had to raise them to meet mine.

"Yes. We made love. It was impossible to avoid."

"Oh. You *made love,* did you? And tell me, please, how come it was so impossible to avoid?"

"Because . . . ," he began, but then he had to stop.

Even Daniel Moore, the man who always told the truth, couldn't bear the weight of it.

"Because I wanted to," he admitted.

That shut me up. It was the unexpected punch, the one that grounds you. You have to catch your breath to overcome a blow like that. But when you are back up on your feet again, you're not the same fighter.

"Why?" I asked. I'd lost all my bravado.

"Because I'm in love with her."

"You can't be," I whispered.

He didn't answer me. He kept looking at me, shaking his head slowly.

"You can't," I repeated, raising my voice. And I hit him hard in the face.

She was waiting for me, with a cigarette between her fingers, pacing up and down the room, just like she had paced her cell. She must have heard me thrashing the room upstairs, throwing everything off his table, flinging all his books and anything that had come my way.

"You came here because you wanted to fuck him!" I said, bursting the door open.

"No," she said. Then she raised her chin and gave me a challenging look. "But I was aware I was attracted to him."

"You should have stayed away! Why didn't you?"

"He wanted it, too. It wasn't just me."

"It's your sister you're doing this to."

She turned her back to me and went to the window. She opened it and let some cold air in.

"Do you hear me?" I shouted. "It's your sister you're doing this to!"

Everything that up until a few minutes earlier had been hollow, mute, came tumbling down. Rage and blind fury were racing through me.

"How can you?" I shouted at the top of my lungs.

She turned toward me slowly, biting her lower lip, but kept her gaze leveled.

"I'm not in a position to be thinking of other people right now."

"And why the fuck not?"

"I can't afford to, Alina. I'm sorry."

"I hate you," I said, "and I wish you were dead."

She didn't move.

"I want you out of here, both of you," I said. "I never want to see either of you again. Pack up your stuff and get out."

The house went silent and empty, and I found myself lying on the floor.

It was good to lie down, curled up in a knot. It felt like I would never be able to stand up again.

But everybody rises from their pain at one point or another.

After I don't know how long, I got up. I looked at my face in the mirror, saw how rage had changed it. I was going to stand up on my feet, yes, but I was determined not to let go of my fury.

Alba phoned.

"What the hell is going on there? Can you explain to me, please, what you and your—"

"Shut up, Alba!" I snarled. "I have nothing to explain."

"Alina, please, calm down. Just let me understand, so that I can—"

"There's no happy ending to the story and there will never be one. That's all you need to understand. Now leave me alone."

And I slammed the phone down.

I cheated the pain by drugging it with some pills I wheedled out of the *farmacia* in the piazza.

I diluted it, I exchanged it for sleep.

I bought myself time.

I woke up late, narrow bars of bright light falling across my face. I didn't dress, I just watched the sun move across the house from east to west and then fade. I waited in silence till the silence made me so brittle that anything could shatter me.

Carmela showed up with a tin of eggplant parmigiana. I came downstairs barefoot, in my rumpled nightgown, and said I didn't need anything. That she should come back another day, that I couldn't eat.

"Can I do something for you? Should I call the doctor?" she said.

I shook my head. She looked frightened.

"*Santa Vergine,* Alina, you take care of yourself."

I rang Esposito, I told him I was sick, that there was something wrong with me, probably hepatitis. That I needed to rest.

I enjoyed lying to him.

I thought of Lorenzo when, fifty years earlier, Renée had gone and left him with the baby girl. I thought of the silence that must have wrapped the house then. It must have had this same quality, like the silence of a well. Deep, thick, black.

He, too, must have wandered from room to room, half-dressed, groggy, maybe even drunk. He, too, must have spent hours gazing at the ceiling from the same bed where I was lying, watching the thin bars of light slowly crawl up his body, till they reached his face. Till they came to rescue him and took him away to Switzerland.

Days went by and I started talking to myself. Loud and animated. I made all sorts of different speeches, I rehearsed each one of them thoroughly. So that I would have all my lines ready, just in case.

But the phone didn't ring. And no taxi showed up at the gate.

In mid-November I got a letter from Daniel, posted a couple of days earlier in Rome, written on the letterhead of the Hotel Locarno.

It was a cautious letter, the words painstakingly chosen, so I wouldn't misunderstand their meaning. I read it over and over again.

It was a brief, honest message. It said he didn't expect to be forgiven, and that he was well aware of the pain he had inflicted on me. He knew the devastating implications of his betrayal. He was wondering if I would be ready to meet him in the near future and attempt to talk peacefully, because he felt that in my rage, which he totally understood, I hadn't given him the chance to explain himself.

None of the words I had been waiting for were there.

There was no ambiguity in the letter, yet I must have misread his carefully selected adjectives; I thought I detected a note of melancholic longing.

I got on the train to Rome, without even calling him.

I took a taxi straight from the train station to Piazza del Popolo and drank two Campari-and-sodas on an empty stomach at the Caffè Rosati. Then I walked one block and stormed into the fake art noveau wood-paneled lobby of the Locarno with a bunch of flowers I had picked up at a stand on the corner, feeling slightly fogged.

I felt a certain buoyancy.

"I'm here to see Mr. Moore," I said to the concierge a bit too loudly, waving the flowers.

He nodded, smiling. I figured he thought we made a good couple.

I stormed into his room like a bank robber, brandishing my tulips like a shotgun.

"I forgive you," I announced.

He looked at me dumbfounded. His face turned white.

"I've been thinking," I went on. "I cannot live like this. It's only pride."

"What?" he whispered.

"I want you to come back. I don't care what happened. I said I forgive you."

He didn't move. He stood perfectly still in the center of the room. I crashed on his bed and I pulled him by the wrists till he lost his balance and fell over me.

"Let's make love." I was on the verge of tears. "Please."

"Stop it, Alina. Don't do this."

He tried to disentangle himself, but I wouldn't let him.

My legs were bare, I had no stockings. I was wearing sandals and a light silk dress even though it was the middle of November.

"Come, hold me. I'm cold," I begged him, and I pulled him harder toward me.

"Let go, please, let go." He bolted back.

He was scared to hurt me, but he knew how to be professional with pain. He touched me without passion, like a doctor would touch a patient. He held me from under my armpits, sat me up like a child.

"Come, Alina, sit here, calm down."

He was handing me water.

I think I was sobbing. Saliva, tears, the bitter taste of Campari—I felt everything melting, a sticky taste in my mouth. All that composure I thought I had regained, that new quiescence, my well-rehearsed lines. It was all being washed away, like dirty water in the gutter.

"Then you must go back to New York," I cried. "You can't stay here, you have to disappear."

He sat on the other side of the bed, giving me his back and hiding his head between his hands. I saw his back shake, like he couldn't bear it any longer. Like he, too, was crushed.

"Alina, listen to me," he said, keeping his back turned.

Something in his voice moved me. I think I felt he was about to break down, too. I had never seen him like that. We had never allowed ourselves to be that emotional with one another, I realized. I went to the bathroom and washed my face. The coolness of the water woke me up.

I pulled a little flowery armchair in front of the bed and sat down facing him. Maybe, I thought, one had to try and be reasonable. Act like a mature, grown-up, responsible person.

"Okay, I'm listening. Go on."

"Isabella and I . . . we are going to . . ."

He stopped. He rubbed his eyes with the back of his hand, hard.

"Isabella is pregnant."

"She can't." I said it quickly, coldly. "She's lying."

"I know this is very hard for you to—"

"She hasn't had her periods in years. She can't. I'm telling you, *she's lying.*"

"She told me about that. I *know* about that." He raised his voice slightly.

He took a sip of water from the glass on the night table. Then he placed his elbows on his knees and waved his hands slowly, slightly leaning over me.

"We went to see a doctor yesterday. He said that things like that happen, it's psychological. Her body has somehow . . . started to function again."

Didn't I know about this? Hadn't I heard it all before? The body that had been shut down had now been let out.

It was like a tropical forest in a downpour. It needs to cover ground fast, strangle smaller plants, suck their sap. It doesn't ask whether it is doing the right or the wrong thing. It just takes whatever it needs in order to grow.

"And?" I asked.

"And . . ." He spread his arms in a pathetic, helpless way. "And she's going to have the child. And I'm going to be the father of this child."

I stared at him, perfectly still.

"I'll marry her," he said and let his arms fall down.

I stood up from the chair. The shock had somehow defeated the alcohol and I was lucid again. I grabbed the tulips and held them close to my chest.

We stared at each other for a few seconds.

"You're crazy," I said. "You have no idea of what you're doing."

"I've been thinking this through."

"You don't even know who she is."

"You're wrong. I think I do."

I gave a short, bitter laugh.

"The romantic American marries *la bella terrorista*? Come on. What is this? Are you buying yourself a new biography? Something extreme, something to write about?"

He looked at me coldly now, with complete hostility.

"I'm in love with her."

I walked to the door and put my hand on the knob.

"You don't know what the fuck you're doing. You're marrying a killer."

That was it. I had spoken the unspeakable.

I had kept those words locked inside me for so long, to the point I didn't even know they were there, and now they had pushed their way up. It actually astonished me how easily they had surfaced and burst open.

But at that point nothing should have surprised me: all the rules had been broken. This was anarchy, pure chaos. A landscape where everyone can just go ahead and say or do whatever they feel like.

I walked back into the Caffè Rosati, my wilted bunch of tulips pointing downward.

"A chamomile, please," I asked the same barman who had served me a Campari soda only an hour earlier.

I slumped into a chair and realized I had no place to go back to, after this. That my whole life had come to a halt right then and there, in that very café, the same one where my father as a young man used to close his film deals and flirt with girls. Way before he started drinking by himself and weeping at the counter till the barman had to gently show him the way out.

I called Bruno from the pay phone by the rest room.

"Hey, Alina," he said cheerfully. "Are you in Rome?"

"Yes, at Rosati's. Listen, this is important. There's something I need to ask you."

"Tell me, what is it?"

"Something about you and Alba."

"Yes, go on," he said, somewhat more cautiously.

"When you started to . . . when you and she became lovers—*when* was that exactly?"

I felt a long silence at the other end.

"Alina, come on, why do you ask me this? I don't—"

"There are things I need to know once and for all," I said emphatically.

"Hang on. I'm getting in the car now. Just wait there, it'll take me five minutes."

I felt better when I saw him step into the café in his worn-out raincoat and come over to my table. I liked the way he handled the waiter, handed me a tissue, ordered a couple of *tramezzini*.

"What is this all about? You look terrible," he said.

"It's a horrible day. It's one of those days when you could do something crazy."

"Like what?"

"Like . . . I don't know."

I looked straight back at him and laughed nervously.

"Like kill someone—or kill myself."

I felt like saying just about anything. Using words I had never used. Push them to the limit of decency. I was scared and I wanted to scare.

"Don't be ridiculous," he said, unimpressed. "Are you drunk?"

"A bit."

I fell back on the chair and closed my eyes with a sigh.

"This is one of those days I'll never forget."

"All right. But what does this have to do with me and your mother, may I ask?"

"It has to do with betrayal," I answered promptly.

He stared back at me calmly.

"I see. All right, then. Shoot."

I fiddled with my sandwich, ate a tiny piece of the bread.

"Did you and she start having an affair before Oliviero died?"

"Yes."

"Did Oliviero know about it?"

"Yes, he eventually found out."

"And . . . what happened?"

"He begged your mother to stop. She told him she wouldn't. Then he came to see me. At the store."

"Did he hit you?"

"No, of course not. We had a pretty civilized conversation. I told him that ours wasn't just a sexual affair. That I wanted to marry her."

"And what did he say when you told him that?"

"He said he would never agree to it, because of you two. But, you know, the truth was that your father simply couldn't conceive of ever losing Alba. He told me. Straight to my face. He said, 'I can't and I won't live without her.' "

He stopped and started patting his pockets in search of a cigarette. He lit one and scratched his head. I was surprised by how willing he was to answer my questions, as if he had always expected we would have this conversation one day.

"It was hard for Alba and for me, after what happened to your father. Although we were still very much in love at the time, you know. We couldn't help feeling that our relationship had been . . . I don't know how to put it."

"Tainted?"

"Yes, in a way. I think both of us kept wondering if we'd been too selfish. But, you know, I've come to the conclusion that the most selfish of all is the one who chooses the role of the victim."

We stared at each other.

I never thought that it would be him—he had been a stranger for such a long time, someone I couldn't envision ever getting close to—the one to talk to me about my father like that.

"Your father . . . Oliviero . . . he took the emergency exit," he said. "You see, today your mother and I are—we're these two middle-aged people, who've made way too many mistakes. In the end, you see, Alina . . ."

He flicked the ash carefully and shook his head, his gaze on the remnant of my sandwich.

"Passion—eventually it cools. And here we are, your mother and me, still wondering if what we made everyone go through at the time was worth it. You know, Alba was always convinced that our relationship . . . your father's suicide—that it was all part of the reason why Isabella had taken . . . that path."

I shrugged, showing some irritation, like I wasn't interested in that kind of analysis. He went on.

"Anyway. Oliviero is forever fixed like a desperate young man with a broken heart. That way he has erased all possibility, in anybody's mind, that he might have gotten over it one day. Remarried, had more children, whatever. Gotten on with life, like the rest of us. Probably today it would be him, sitting here in front of you. He should be the one to help you deal with your horrible day, right?"

He spread his arms, as if begging me to see the logic of his reasoning.

"I mean, just think. What a terrible waste."

I took a drag off his cigarette.

"I didn't think you smoked," he said.

"I don't. Only in desperate situations."

No more waste, no more debris left for the others to clean up. I want to take care of myself, I thought, I'm not going to leave another mess behind.

"Can you give me a lift to the station? I think I want to go back home."

"If you want. Otherwise you could come to the house and have dinner with us, spend the night if you like. Federica likes you so much, and the twins would love to see you."

I had a sudden urge to close my eyes and go to sleep. I needed to rest, I needed my energy back. I didn't know how to get it, but I desperately wanted to.

"Yes, that sounds nice, Bruno. I'd like that."

He paid the bill and we stepped outside. Suddenly the light on the square felt too harsh, and the noise of traffic too overwhelming. His car smelled of leather and alpine deodorizer. I closed my eyes as I slid back in the passenger seat, fighting a wave of nausea.

"You know, I think you're right about my father," I said, keeping my eyes closed. "That he took the easy way out and left you and Alba to deal with the guilt."

I heard his Zippo snap again and smelled the smoke.

"But, on the other hand," I continued, "I was thinking that love sometimes makes people ruthless in a way that not even hatred can. When it comes to love, nobody thinks it's a big deal to stab someone in the back when they're not looking."

He kept on driving and didn't answer.

After that day at the Hotel Locarno I walked around like a person with a hole in her chest. I had cut both Daniel and Isabella out in one surgical go. I felt like someone with a heart condition, who couldn't take risks. I never answered the letters she sent me, nor to the many messages she left on my answering machine. I chose to be the bad one in the story for a change. The one who doesn't forgive.

I went back to Casa Rossa and buried myself there, deaf to the world outside.

Then came a day when everything hurt, as if it had shrunk a size and had become too small: the life I had been so used to no longer fit, no matter how hard I tried. I knew I had to move on, but I still didn't know where to.

That's when Esposito phoned. As usual, very early in the morning.

"You know, dear,"—he was never big on preambles—"I need to talk to you about something important."

"What is it?"

"I'm not going to tell you over the phone. I booked us for lunch at the Bolognese tomorrow."

"Ha. Sounds pretty official."

"It is. You'll see. You can catch a train around seven tomorrow morning—you're an early riser, aren't you? I'll see you at the Bolognese at one."

"Fine."

"Yes, but, you know . . . before I put you on this thing, I need to . . ."

He cleared his voice and then raised it an octave. I could almost see him propel his body forward, like he always did when he wanted to get a message across.

"I mean, what's the story with you still living out there? I need you to be here if you want to start working on big projects like this one. I can't send a director to work with you in some godforsaken farm out in the middle of—"

"I know. In fact, I was—"

"You really have to move back to Rome, be available to come to the office for meetings—do you see my point? You have to choose, dear: it's either writing films or growing lettuce. This business of you living in the middle of nowhere can't go on. It's just not practical."

"All right. Don't scream at me like that, you scare me. I get it. I have to look for an apartment, is that what you mean?"

"Exactly. So get your ass over here and we'll talk about the project I have in mind."

The Bolognese Restaurant in Piazza del Popolo, right next door to the Caffè Rosati, had seen more movie deals being closed in its plush wood-paneled dining room than any other restaurant since the fifties. Esposito, of course, was the undisputed god there, as well. In fact, whenever in his company, one had the impression Rome belonged to him. The impeccable gray-haired waiters had known him for thirty years and worshiped him. The maître d' came personally to greet us and didn't stop blabbering about how happy he was to see him. Esposito nodded to him a couple of times without smiling.

"But you're going to have to let me smoke, my friend," he interrupted him curtly. "Otherwise I'll simply have to stop coming."

"Of course, *Dottore,* for you we always make an exception"—and the maître d' showed us to the best table in the room, by the window.

Once we were done with ordering and were left alone, Esposito finally pulled out a wrinkled yellowing script and slammed it on the table.

"This is what I've been thinking about. I want you to sell me back the rights," he said with a mischevious smile.

It was Oliviero's script. The story of Lorenzo collaborating with the Ovra and then pinning the blame on Renée.

"While you were hiding in your Casa Rossa, doing whatever it is you were doing all this time by yourself"—he gave me a knowing look—"I reread it and realized this story is like a bottle of good wine: it has only improved with age. With only a few adjustments it'll make a sensational film."

He took off his glasses and leaned across the table, closer to me. He whispered conspiratorially, "I'm talking about an Oscar-winning film."

I stared at the cover sheet: *Where Truth Lies,* a story by Oliviero Strada.

"Originally it was called something like *The Sleep of Memory,* but I gave it a new title," he said. "This one is more appropriate. A little melodramatic, pehaps, but it works better for the times. You know, with all this business of terrorism, truth, penitence, and whatnot, I think this story of your grandfather and his wife under the Fascist regime has become incredibly . . . what's the word I want?"

"Emblematic?"

"Exactly, yes. Of course, it needs a little reshaping, and I want you to do some work on it. It needs to be put in context. I have a great director in mind for this. But I'm not going to tell you who until you agree."

"Wow. This is kind of unexpected."

"You'll finally work on a meaningful project. It's time."

"What makes you think this story will still be interesting today?"

"I'll tell you exactly why." He lit a cigarette, savored the first drag. "Let's see. Do you have any idea why I have become so rich?"

"No. Yes . . . because you have . . . you have—"

"Because at the end of the war, we all wanted to forget really fast, that's why. We couldn't wait to put the guilt behind us, the sense of ambiguity. We were desperate to move on, pretend it had never happened—how we had been fighting side by side with Hitler and Mussolini—you get it?"

"Yes, but what does that have to do with—"

"Even your father. Oliviero. The liberal, Socialist Oliviero. He had to go into the army and fight on Germany's side, like everyone else. Did you ever think about that? We all bowed our heads, whether we liked it or not. They were only a small minority, a comparative handful, the ones who fled or went up in the mountains with the partisans to fight fascism."

I nodded, like a student who was following a lecture.

"And when people want to escape, what do they do?" He smiled triumphantly and spread his arms. "They go to a movie and forget their misery. When the war was over, the whole of Italy needed to forget recent history. They were only too happy to plunge into Technicolor. The reason why *La Dolce Vita* was the most brilliant title ever was because it came after such *bitter* times. And I was lucky enough to be right there and ride the wave."

The waiter placed our main course on the table and started grinding fresh pepper on my fettuccine. Esposito tasted his consommé and handed the plate back to the waiter.

"Too much salt. Please, Alfredo, are you trying to kill me? My high blood pressure."

"Of course, of course, *Dottore.* I will speak to the chef."

Esposito turned to me again.

"In Hollywood they've already begun to deal with their Vietnam guilt. Here in Italy we haven't managed to deal with the shame of our duplicity forty years after the end of the war. That's why I think this script will make a wonderful film, an important film."

I stared at him. There was always something so irresistible about his enthusiasm.

"Look," I said, "I want to think about this. It's not just me involved. I'm thinking of my mother."

Esposito started carefully rolling some of my fettuccine around his fork.

"Yes, of course. But here's what I think, my dear, and here's what you have to bear in mind—God, this fettuccine is sublime. Just one more tiny bite. At my age, eating well has become practically illegal."

He swallowed another bite and wiped his mouth.

"Here's what you have to understand, Alina: this story is not about your family anymore. This is about all of us—my generation, how we fell unconscious and then woke up and called it a bad dream. It's about those of us who said, 'It wasn't me, it was all the others.' It's about the collective amnesia this country so loves to fall into every now and again. Your father saw it. And it pained him. That's why he decided to write about it."

The waiter came back with a steaming bowl of consommé.

"I'll tell you what, Alfredo. I think I'll have the fettuccine after all."

"As you wish, *Dottore.*" Alfredo swiftly took the plate away.

I pushed my fettuccine toward him. I wasn't hungry anymore.

"Have some of mine in the meantime."

"Are you sure?"

I watched him scoff it up.

"I see what you mean," I said, "but Oliviero wrote my grandfather's story exactly as it happened. He didn't change a thing."

"But that's exactly what all good writers do!" he said triumphantly. "They steal! They're brutal, they're remorseless. They take from their pasts to bring things into focus, brutally sometimes, in the present. And we have to thank them for being so callous."

He smiled, totally satisfied with himself, and winked at me.

"Telling the truth can be a dirty job," he proclaimed with a smile and rolled more fettuccine around his fork.

It took me just one afternoon to pack my things and move out of Casa Rossa. I paid Carmela to come and take care of the house. She gladly took the dogs with her, thank God, so I could close the door behind me without remorse.

That's how I changed my life: I stepped out of it like a stripteaser from her dress. In one elegant and swift move, which left no room for second thoughts, I was gone.

Once back in Rome I found a little one-bedroom apartment in the center of the city. The whole place was roughly the size of the kitchen of Casa Rossa, but I didn't feel I needed more space. I wanted small, easy, manageable tasks.

Alba and Giorgio invited me for lunch every Sunday. They scrutinized me; I could feel they kept checking on me, to make sure I was coping. They made sure never to mention Isabella and Daniel around me, as if they didn't exist. This was the advantage of my mother having married a neurologist: she, too, had to learn how to handle people with care now.

Although I knew it was coming, it shocked me when I heard Isabella had the baby. The reality of it—this tiny being who carried their genes so perfectly mixed together, who had sealed their union forever—hit me in the face like a punch. I shut myself in the house and didn't pick up the phone for a few days.

Giorgio called—something he rarely ever did—and on my answering machine offered to prescribe me some antidepressants. I picked up and declined.

The baby had somehow pushed a button, and I was obsessing all over again.

How could this be possible? They don't even understand each other properly, I kept saying out loud. They are two strangers, they don't even have the same tastes.

Then I had an epiphany.

I had been madly in love with Daniel, of course. But by being so frightened of scaring him away with my family history, I had always kept him slightly at a distance, hadn't I? I made sure that things between us always ran smoothly. I recalled that funny feeling I had, of not finding an edge, of sliding over, without being able to get a grip—the parody of happiness.

I wanted him to feel that he would always be safe with me. That had been my aim.

But, obviously, that was the last thing he wanted. Otherwise, why on earth would he have decided to come and live in Italy, choose to move in with me in a crumbling farmhouse surrounded by cacti and deafening cicadas in Puglia, a region he knew nothing of, had he not been looking for some kind of adventure? For the possibility of risk? Had he not been longing for some form of emotional disruption, something that would turn his well-ordered, pragmatic world upside down? Had he not been seduced by drama, irrationality, and passion, desiring secretly to be contaminated in some way? He didn't need a smooth surface where everything just glided over. Daniel Moore was looking for permanent scars.

Did Isabella know any of this? Did she care to figure it out? To share his opinions on books or films, or different performances of the Bach Suites? Did she envision cooking gourmet dinners and drinking wine under the stars? She had no time for any of that.

It had been her neediness, her desperation he had fallen in love with.

When the second baby was born, Alba rang me.

"Why don't you go and see her? She's in the hospital for another two days."

"No."

"But, for God's sake, you haven't spoken to her in three years now. You can't go on pretending she doesn't exist for the rest of your life."

"I'm perfectly aware that she exists and that she keeps having babies. I'd just rather not see her. I don't want to know."

"It worries me, this thing between you two. I think she really needs you. She'll never admit it. But of the two, you can be the one to rise above it. Go to see her. She—"

"She doesn't *need* me. She has plenty of people around her."

"You're wrong. I think she feels very lonely." I heard Alba sigh heavily. "She's talked to me about it. You know, Daniel is a great father, and I think he's a good husband—responsible and all—but at times he—how can I explain it—he seems so distant. Who knows, maybe he has—"

"Mother," I interrupted her, "I'm not the right person to talk to about their marital problems. I don't want to know."

But I did, I always did. By erasing Isabella and Daniel from my life, I made sure they would become my obsession.

I knew they had moved into a house in the country outside of Rome, where it was cheaper to live. I also knew that Daniel never got around to writing his book, because he couldn't afford the luxury, with a wife and two babies on board. That he was working for the *Herald Tribune* now and freelanced as a correspondent for a few American magazines here and there. I had read a piece or two and then I stopped. It was nothing much: a mix of politics and lifestyle. One week he'd interview the prime minister about the possibility of the umpteenth fall of the Italian Government, the next it would be a list of the ten best extra-virgin olive oils one could find in Tuscany. Maybe I was being petty, but I wasn't impressed. I knew that he struggled, and he had been grumpy. And that Isabella refused to get a job because she said she had enough work coping with two babies.

"One wonders what she does in the house all day long," Alba continued. "It's such a mess, I can't even tell you. Sometimes she lets dishes pile in the sink for days. I don't understand why she's so disorganized. When I was her age I had two children, a pretty big place to run, a social life, and I never looked as untidy as she does. Did I?"

"Please, Mamma, can we change the subject now?"

What I couldn't help wondering was how everyone had so blithely moved on to the next chapter of Isabella's life. Nobody found it strange that now she had a husband—someone she once would have dismissed as an "imperialist pig"—who supported her and the kids by interviewing Italian politicians, state officials, and prosecutors who probably had all been on her list as "targets" at one time. I couldn't help wondering if these people knew who this charming American journalist was married to when he took them out to lunch on his *Herald Tribune* expense account.

One day, a cold, gray Sunday afternoon, while sitting in a traffic jam, I saw them come out of a building.

Isabella had gained weight, she looked almost heavy. Her hair had grown long and looked darker; it was tied in a loose ponytail. She had the smaller baby strapped to her stomach in a sling and was frantically rummaging through a large canvas bag till she found a bottle. Something had given way. All that tension that had been her backbone and had kept her sharp like the blade of a knife—it was gone. I could almost smell the diapers and the heated milk on her.

Daniel, in a thick down jacket, was struggling on the sidewalk with the other baby's stroller. I think the baby was crying. They both looked exhausted. Like two people who had headaches and wanted to get home fast. I watched them move along, zigzagging around the parked cars, coming toward me. She was trailing behind him, talking, while he stared straight ahead, in a daze, not paying attention.

They passed right by my car. I watched her stumble on the crowded sidewalk.

And I saw how, in a way, it had been the same all her life. First the Ballet Teacher, then the Revolutionary Boyfriend, then the Prison Guards, now the Husband: hadn't she always been looking for someone to bend her this way or that way? She'd deluded herself that she was a fighter, prepared to die for an ideal of justice and freedom—but hadn't she merely been searching for a way to bow her head down and be a prisoner?

Suddenly I felt like jumping out of the car and shouting after her:

What for? What was that all about, all that waste, all that violence? Why did you make us go through that horror for years, if this is what you wanted all along?

To be this wife, on a Sunday afternoon, droning on to your husband about what you have left in the fridge to cook for dinner.

I watched Daniel trudge along and disappear behind a parked car.

The romantic American, who wanted scars on his flawless skin. Who had come to a twisted, convoluted country he didn't understand, hoping it would have the power to turn his world upside down and make him more interesting and passionate than he had ever allowed himself to be.

CHAPTER TEN

———◆———

Alba's car pulls into the driveway of Casa Rossa just before lunch. She has stopped at the new Gulliver Supermarket on the way and has bought lots of food.

"All my favorite goodies in the world!" she squeaks as she takes the bags out of the trunk.

"Look, *ricotta salata, friselle al farro,* these great thick anchovies, fresh olive bread! Isn't this great? They have absolutely everything, I love that place!"

Rita and I look at each other and make a face.

"We hate it," I say.

"Oh, you two are such snobs."

Then she throws herself on Rita in an enormous embrace.

"*Ritina mia,* you're looking so good. And you've lost some weight, too!"

She walks into the house and takes a good look around, at the stack of boxes neatly piled up.

"Well, I guess this is it for Casa Rossa. Is this to be our last night?"

"Yes, the movers are coming tomorrow morning at seven."

"Good. I have a bottle of champagne, so we can celebrate." She turns to Rita. "It's so perfect that you're here. It was obviously meant to be. Oh, I can't believe I left my camera in Rome!"

We sit outside, around the old marble-top table in the patio. The same table where Oliviero had lunch with Lorenzo the first time he came to Casa Rossa. The same table visible in the background of the yellowing photos showing Renée sitting barefoot on the chipped stone step, staring into nowhere.

We eat with our fingers, straight out of the paper wraps, since all the plates and cutlery have been packed away. Eating like this puts us in a good mood, it makes the food even more delicious. Alba and Rita start talking in dialect. I can hardly understand what they're saying, but from the way they laugh I know they are joking and using dirty language. Suddenly I get a glimpse of the two of them as Beniamino and Alba, when they were just two awkward teenagers who knew nothing else but this place and had no idea they would ever leave it.

"Do you realize that you two could have easily been married to one another?" I say.

"It would have spared us a lot of nonsense," Rita says and laughs, licking her fingers.

We get the champagne out of the fridge and drink it, taking turns, straight from the bottle. I detect an imperceptible shift in our mood: it's as if Alba and I have suddenly become hesitant, as if we're not sure how to behave from this point on. Maybe the alcohol has made us more sentimental. I watch Alba as she leaves the table and paces around the garden, patrolling it, counting her steps. She's deeply absorbed, unaware of me and Rita watching her.

Rita looks at her watch.

"Well, girls, it was great to share this day with you, but I better get going now."

Alba looks disappointed.

"Why?" she asks. "I had this great plan. I was going to take you both out to dinner. I was thinking we could go to—"

"No, honey, I really need to get out of here. I'm not in the mood to hang around." She gestures toward me. "Alina will explain. Mine has been a rather frustrating mission."

So, reluctantly, we see her to her car. She sits at the steering wheel and puts on these enormous dark glasses *à la* Sophia Loren that look like giant TV screens. As she turns the ignition key, "I Will Survive" suddenly blares from her stereo. She pulls out of the driveway and Alba emits a deep sigh and shakes her head.

"Don't tell me she came here to see the Sisters of Santa Caterina."

"Yes, that's exactly what she did."

"Jesus, is she stubborn or what? I told her it was a totally absurd plan and that she shouldn't even—"

"I know, but she wanted so much to try. I bet she would have freaked if they'd accepted her. Can you imagine?"

Alba laughs. "I hate to think what she would be capable of organizing inside a convent."

I pull on her sleeve. "Mamma, there's something I really want to show you."

I've been waiting for us to be alone to do this.

"What is it?"

"A letter."

She looks at me surprised.

"A letter? From whom?"

"Come inside, I'll show you. It was at the bottom of the chest in Lorenzo's studio, inside a folder with some other papers."

She follows me inside the house. I take her upstairs, into my room. The letter is on my desk. I've been reading it over and over again for two entire days.

"It's only one page, the rest is missing," I say, handing it to her. "It has no signature, no date."

She takes it into her hand, holding it at a distance, like she does when she doesn't have her reading glasses. She arches a brow quizzically.

"It must be from your mother."

She looks at me, startled. It's always been Renée, and Renée only. She's never been "mother."

"I didn't know whether or not you'd ever seen it." I say softly as I move behind her and start reading the letter over her shoulder. "She must have sent this from Germany, after she left to go and live with Muriel."

She shakes her head slowly as she looks at the thin sheet of paper.

"No. I've never seen this before."

" I had a feeling you probably hadn't."

I look at the tiny, old-fashioned handwriting. The faded blue ink. I hold my breath.

"You must have been just a child when she wrote this . . .

. . . and what is unfair, and completely horrible, is the way you're us-ing politics to make everyone hate me. Muriel happens to be German, but this doesn't mean she's a Nazi in the way you like to think of her. I know that in your mind you have twisted all the facts already, so that they can feed your rancor, and you have turned me into this calculating monster, but I have to warn you: you will scar Alba for life if you instill in her mind all these despicable rumors. I beg you to be fair: don't lie to her about me like you have with everyone else. She'll grow up like a cripple. . . .

I think your resentment—your hatred, I should say at this point—comes from your need to blame me for all those things that didn't work out in your life: your career as a painter, the difficult situation you had to face with the Ovra in Paris, ultimately the failure of our marriage. It must have made things easier to shift all that weight onto me: I'm a woman. I don't have a family background. I'm an Arab woman who walked out on her husband and child. I don't think you have any idea what this means. But deep down, somewhere, you must know you've been taking advantage of my weakness and my regrets. . . .

Alba turns the sheet of paper, but the other side is blank. She looks at me. Her eyes are shiny, her cheeks flushed.

"That's it," I say, "only this one page."

Alba moves toward the window and stands there, her back to me, perfectly still. Then I hear the paper crackle in her hands, as she starts reading the letter once again. I silently slip out of the room and leave her alone.

It was '95. I was in my apartment in Rome at the height of summer and the light was still simmering behind the shutters. I was waiting for the afternoon to cool off. The phone rang.

"Alina Strada?" I heard a woman's voice I didn't recognize.

"Yes?"

"My name is Sonia, you don't know me." She cleared her throat. "I've made a couple of phone calls, trying to track you down, and then I actu-ally found you in the phone book."

"Yes. What is this about?"

"It's about your sister. Isabella."

"Oh. How do you know my sister?"

"We used to take the same yoga class a long time ago, before she had her second baby and moved to the country. Occasionally we spoke on the phone, things like that."

She hesitated, as if something was making her nervous.

" I hadn't seen her in a while, but I ran into her this morning in a café near where I live, in Campo dei Fiori."

"Yes?"

"Well, she didn't even recognize me."

I said nothing, waiting for her to continue. She lowered her voice.

"I think she needs some help."

"What exactly are you saying?"

"She looked extremely confused. . . . I don't know whether you're aware of the state she's in."

"No, I don't . . ." I broke into a sweat.

The woman sighed heavily.

"I just passed by the same café again. You know, I was a little bit worried, and she's still there. She's . . . talking to herself." She paused, embarrassed. "Totally crazy. You know . . . like a schizophrenic."

"What do you mean *schizophrenic*?" My voice turned into a whisper.

"Like, hearing voices, I guess." She cleared her throat. "She seems to-tally engrossed in some imaginary conversation. I tried to speak to her, but . . . nothing. She wouldn't even acknowledge me. But finally she gave me this deadpan look and said, 'You go call my sister Alina now.' She kept saying that over and over again. So I tried to find you, and—"

"Tell me again where she is."

"At the café on the left of the Cinema Farnese, in Campo de' Fiori. She was sitting at one of the outdoor tables. I told the owner I was go-ing to look for you, and to keep an eye on her. She said to hurry up or she was going to call the police. I'm at a phone booth right around the corner from where she is."

My eyes filled with tears. "Why the police? What is she doing, I mean?"

"You know what people are like. They get scared when they see someone out of control. She's just a bit . . ." She struggled to find the right word. "*Loud,* I guess. The café owner said she was scaring her clients away and she couldn't let her stay there."

"Oh my God."

"I'm *so* sorry."

"You have been so kind, taking all this trouble."

"She needs help, poor thing. She's such a nice girl, Isabella. I feel so bad for her."

"Yes, thank you, you have been really kind," I repeated, like a robot. I felt short of breath.

I flew out the door. I tried to hail a cab but couldn't find one—everyone seemed to be indoors in the shade, taking a siesta—so I started running.

I ran along Corso Vittorio, dense with traffic and orange buses, I turned into Via dei Baullari, then into the Piazza Campo de' Fiori. Early in the morning the piazza was always such a cheeerful sight, with all its vegetable stalls and brightly colored flower stands. The early morning air matched the crispness of the greens, the dew drops lingering on the peonies and the tulips. But by two o'clock the stalls had gone, leaving the pavement strewn with withered cabbage leaves and limp greens, overripe bananas and squashed plums. There was a loud sound coming from the sanitation trucks spraying the square with hoses. The square at this hour looked more like a battlefield, with all that decomposed matter dribbling warm juices on the ground.

I looked up, along the side of the movie theater. There was a small café with a few tables on the sidewalk. It was too hot for anybody to sit outside under the sun.

But there she was. Wrapped in a thick winter coat under the hot sun, legs crossed, foot shaking up and down. She held a cigarette between her fingers, waving it animatedly as she kept talking loudly, into space.

"Isa," I called her name softly as I touched her shoulder.

"Good," she said, looking me straight in the eye, "the man in the red car said it's time for you to go."

Her hair looked greasy, the front of her coat was stained, covered in crumbs. I could smell her. A sharp, animal scent. She blew the smoke in my face.

"I have to warn you, he'll try to do something very bad to you. It's none of my business, but just keep in mind I told you. He's a *complete fucker*!" Then she turned her head the other way and began to mumble away.

I sat down on the chair across from her and slipped my hand onto hers. Her fingernails were filthy.

"Isa." I felt my throat tighten. "Darling . . ."

She turned to me and our eyes met. It lasted only a moment, but I knew she was somewhere there, trapped behind those glassy irises.

"What's happening to you, what is it?" I whispered, my head now very close to hers.

She stared at me, surprised, as if I'd shaken her out of sleep.

"Tell me, please. What is it?" I caressed the back of her hand.

I brushed her hair, her cheekbone, with my fingertips.

I haven't touched her in so long.

She looked like she did when she was twelve. The day Angelica came to pick us up at school and took us out for pizza.

"My head is . . ."

Her face twitched a couple of times.

"Yes?"

". . . frying."

"Is it scary?"

She nodded, and for a split second I could actually *see* her fear. It was like a cloud moving fast across the sun, a ripple, then her eyes went flat and it was as if she had vanished again somewhere.

"He took all my notebooks," she said loudly, in that different voice. "He says he's going to keep them in a safe place, but I know exactly what he's going to do with them, the motherfucker."

"Darling, I think we should go now," I said quietly, still holding her hand in mine.

I paid for her cappuccino and asked a young girl sitting at the table next to ours if I could use her cell phone.

"I'm sorry to ask you, but it's an emergency."

"Sure, no problem." She gave me a sympathetic look, then ran her eyes across Isabella, who by then had taken up her mumbling again, completely unaware of my presence beside her.

I phoned Alba, hoping she would know what to do. I figured her husband could help. I told her where we were.

"Come right now with your car," I said. "And don't waste any time. You'll understand when you get here."

"I have no car. It was towed this morning.

"Shit! Then get in a cab and meet me at Giorgio's clinic. Isa is not well."

"I know, I know, Daniel phoned half an hour ago. He said she had disappeared early this morning. I was just going to—"

"Then hurry. *Please.*"

It wasn't easy to persuade Isabella to get up and follow me to Corso Vittorio so we could hail a cab. She raised her voice.

"No fucking way I'm giving them to you, you bitch! Guess what? I've already spoken to the press. It's going to be all over the place to-morrow. Right in your face, you cunt!"

I flagged down a cab and gently pushed her in. She seemed totally unaware of who I was or what I was saying to her. She had slipped off again, somewhere far away.

"Come, Isa, get in. We're going to see Giorgio. He'll make you feel better."

Once in the car, she got more and more agitated. Maybe having to sit so close to the driver made her nervous, but she was almost screaming and her face was twitching in spasms.

"I told you he was coming to pick us up. Why wouldn't you wait? Now we've lost him again, you idiot! You fucking moron!"

The driver kept checking back in the rearview mirror. I could feel his tension rising and filling the car. As soon as she started hitting the window with her fists, he pulled over.

"She'll have to get out, I'm sorry, *Signora.* She's going to smash my windows."

"Oh, please, it's all right, we're nearly there. She's not going to do anything to your car. Isa, darling, please calm down."

"You need a different kind of transport. I'm sorry."

He turned off the engine and gave me a sullen look. He was young-ish, unhealthy-looking.

"Like what?" I asked with hostility.

"Like an ambulance."

"Don't be ridiculous. This person needs help. Just take us to the clinic."

"No, you don't understand. I won't. You'll have to—"

"NO, IT'S YOU WHO DOESN'T UNDERSTAND!" I found myself screaming at the top of my lungs now. "SHE'S NOT DOING ANYTHING TO YOUR GODDAMN CAR, ALL RIGHT? You better drive us there or I'm going to raise such hell, you're gonna be fucking sorry you gave me any trouble!"

He drove on, in a frozen fury, while Isabella kept muttering to herself, quieter now. I caught her grinning at me and I squeezed her hand.

Giorgio Carlei worked in a private clinic surrounded by a vast park just outside the city. After lunch the patients wandered out on the lawn in their flappy pajamas and faded dressing gowns. They huddled together on a bench, all trying to squeeze into the same sunny spot, dangling their heads, some staring in space, others talking to themselves.

So this is what it's like.

Heavy medication, unwashed hair, a sense of annihilation. Feet shuffling in cheap slippers, thoughts lost somewhere, irretrievable. Scared of being abandoned there.

Lonely.

Alba and I watched them in silence, and I knew we were both thinking exactly the same thing. We were sitting on the steps, just outside the main entrance. Alba checked her watch nervously.

"Daniel should be here any minute. He said he had to find someone to leave the children with first." She shook her head and sighed.

I looked at the window on the first floor where Giorgio's office was. He had been with Isabella for over an hour by then. He had asked us to leave. He said he needed to see her alone.

"But what do you think it is? What sort of thing could this be?" I asked.

Alba shrugged.

"I have no idea."

"You know, manic depression is a chemical imbalance. It can be cured. One needs the right medication, that's all."

Alba didn't answer me. She stared at the patients sitting in the sun.

"I saw it coming. We all did. Yet nobody said anything," she said slowly.

"When did you see it coming? How?"

"She was getting so . . . sloppy about everything. Her personal hygiene, even. She seemed confused a lot, couldn't finish a sentence. I don't know, she had these . . . glitches. Like little short circuits."

Isn't that what breaking down means? I thought. The mesh in the net gets looser and looser, till it can no longer hold anything.

I wondered when this had all begun.

"She had it even as a child," Alba said, curled up on the step where we were sitting.

"She had *what*?"

"You know, this kind of obsessive quality. Everything she did, she always pushed to the absolute limit. Everything she believed in was like a law written in stone. How can anyone endure it?"

She wiped her eyes with the back of her hand.

"All that hatred she had. Why? The things she accused me of. You know, it's hard to live, knowing your daughter is convinced you have done something so horrible."

"Alba, please." I didn't particularly feel like discussing this again. "That's got nothing to do with it. And you know perfectly well she didn't even—"

"No! It does, it does." She searched in her huge handbag for a handkerchief and blew her nose. "How could I be the person I am today, had I done what she accused me of?"

"Mamma, this isn't the issue now."

It irritated me that she would want to talk about herself now.

"No, it is. This is *exactly* the issue. Do you think I could have married three times, be madly in love with my husband; do you think I could be the person I am today? A wife, a mother, a grandmother? A balanced person, capable of love?"

"What does this—"

"No, you see"—she shook her head vehemently—"I couldn't, because I'd be a wreck. *I'd be insane*."

I said nothing.

"Do you know what I mean?" she asked, her eyes narrowing.

I nodded.

"Yes, of course I do."

"Because nobody—I mean *nobody*—can live with that kind of guilt and go on hiding it for so long without going mad."

We sat in silence, looking at the lawn. We fiddled with our bags and looked for something to keep us occupied: mints, a fresh handkerchief.

"It's just not possible," Alba continued. "Even when nobody is expecting it any longer, the truth is going to push and push, till it pops up to the surface. And it'll disrupt everything you have built on top of it, in one big burst."

She turned to me.

"That's what happened. This is not a chemical imbalance. I know these things."

We saw Daniel appear from the parking lot. He walked toward the building, his head down. He looked smaller than I remembered him.

Alba got up and waved to him.

"I know these things," she repeated, keeping her eyes on Daniel, who had seen her and was now coming slowly our way. "My father, too—he ended up in a mental clinic for a year. Again, what do you think it was, that drove him so crazy?"

We started walking toward Daniel. I read his surprise as he saw me.

"It was all the lies he made everyone believe about Renée, all the stuff that *he* had been accountable for, that's what it was."

Alba stopped and grabbed my arm.

"By persuading the others, you're trying to persuade yourself that it never happened. But it did. I mean, it may be possible to forget our past, but the past is not going to forget us."

She was right, and I knew it. But still it bothered me, the way Alba always managed to put herself at the center whenever some particularly dramatic moment would occur. She never gave up playing the lead, even when the scene wasn't about her.

"Alina!"

Daniel's eyes were red, he looked disheveled, like a man who hadn't slept for days. He threw his arms around me and held me. I felt he wanted to be held tight. So I did, for a few seconds. I recognized his smell, the softness of his hair.

"How is she?" he murmured, breaking from me at last.

"We don't know." Alba kissed him on the cheek. "Giorgio is running some tests. She was very . . . confused."

We all exchanged a glance. We knew nothing, not nearly enough to even vaguely reassure each other.

"She disappeared this morning." Daniel struggled to find each word. "We had . . . a pretty bad fight last night. Lately she has been so . . . violent. Verbally . . . and physically, too. But I . . . I had no idea that—"

"I know," Alba broke in, "it's not your fault. Calm down, she'll be all right. It's probably just a crisis."

"Last night I came home from work and she was giving Claudia a bath. I heard her singing, but it was more like screaming. She went on and on, all nonsense words, it was so weird. Then I heard Claudia scream at the top of her lungs and cry"—suddenly his eyes filled with tears—"and I walked into the bathroom and saw she was playing with Claudia, pushing her under the water. It was almost as if . . . as if . . . she were trying to . . . drown her. I went totally berserk. She hit me . . . and then I was . . ."

He started sobbing, hiding his face in his hands. I held him again and felt his tears warming my neck.

Dissociative disorder.

That's all Giorgio said.

"I gave her something so she could rest. She's asleep now."

We were all sitting opposite his walnut desk, waiting for him to say more. He looked back at us, his hands crossed over his stomach. Professional.

"Is she . . . are you . . . keeping her for the night?" Alba asked.

He smiled professionally even when speaking to his wife.

"Of course, dear."

"But, when . . ."

"We'll have to see." He looked at Daniel. "I'm afraid this is not going to be a single episode."

Giorgio shook his head and quickly checked his fingernails. I caught him glancing at his wrist watch. He sighed, then raised his eyes again on all of us.

"Perhaps I should clarify: this isn't just a nervous breakdown."

He placed his elbows firmly on the desk, interlaced his fingers, and rested his chin on his hands. We didn't say a word, we just sat there. Dumb, helpless.

"But I need to keep her in the clinic for observation before I reach a conclusive diagnosis," he said and stood up. Our heads followed him simultaneously as he walked toward the door, as if we were following the ball at a tennis match.

"I have to run now. I'll see you at home. We'll talk about it later."

We understood finally that he had opened the door for *us*.

We kissed him in turn, Alba, Daniel, and I. Obedient and intimidated, like three children about to go somewhere far off.

"Come, I'll give you a ride," Daniel said to Alba and me in the parking lot as he opened the door of his rusty red car. I slid in the back, next to a padded baby seat. There were empty Coca-Cola cans rolling on the floor, comic books, tiny shoes. A stained pink T-shirt with a baby elephant on it.

Alba and Daniel kept talking about Isabella. Now that it was too late, they kept recalling signals, faint symptoms, things she said or did that sounded odd.

"I noticed she had started talking to herself, even when I was in the room. Like she would be constantly mumbling something."

I listened to them quietly. His Italian had become fluent, if still a bit loose around the *r*'s, somehow softened by his American inflection.

Their intimacy struck me—mother-in-law and son-in-law. So did my estrangement, the way I couldn't contribute to the conversation.

Daniel stopped the car in front of Alba's building.

"I'll call you later," she said to Daniel. "I'm sure Giorgio will want to speak to you when he comes home."

"Okay. Call me anytime, even late."

Then, once we were alone, there was a silence. He didn't start the car. He looked at me, deflated, his head hanging heavily.

"Don't go home yet, please," he said. "I want to talk."

I nodded.

"I need to or I'll go crazy."

"Okay."

He had taken up smoking. It was part of his Italianization, I suppose, this recklessness. He drove in silence through the traffic, puffing away. I didn't ask where he was taking me.

"I feel like walking. Do you?" he said.

"Yes. Fine."

He parked the car outside the gate of the Villa Doria Pamphili gardens. I didn't object, but I've always hated going for strolls in parks as a form of relief. There's something depressing for me about people trying to get a break like that, needing a breath of fresh air within the city. Such a feeling of constraint: couples walking hand in hand underneath the trees, gravel rustling under their feet, distant cries from children riding their bicycles while, in the background, the muffled roar of the city never stops.

We walked for a bit, and neither of us felt like saying anything. Yet somehow I felt it was all right to be like this, side by side, each one mentally reviewing the events of the day, comforted by the closeness of the other. We sat on a bench, surrounded by baby-sitters watching over small children, joggers, lonely men walking huge dogs. It was so unlike us, to be sitting in a place like this, after so long. Or maybe it was the easiest way to be with each other again. Amid a crowd, in such an open space.

"I think it's schizophrenia," he said, with a kind of finality.

"It's possible."

"I know the symptoms. I had a friend in college who—"

"How could you not see it?" I interrupted him. "I can't believe you never understood how sick she was."

"I thought she was unhappy. That much I could see. But I never thought it could develop into something like this."

"Jesus Christ, Daniel. All these years, and you never once imagined she might need help."

I realized I was feeling angry.

"You have no idea what it's like with two small children," he said. "You practically cease to exist. You're running around all day long trying to make ends meet. I don't know the last time Isa and I had a few quiet moments to have a proper conversation, just the two of us."

"Bullshit! Besides, I think she's been slipping away for a long time. Probably from even before she was in jail."

"I didn't ever see that. When I first met her I thought she was just in shock from spending almost seven years in jail—the solitary confinement and from everything else. . . ."

"Why don't we just say it was more convenient for all of us to see it that way?"

I turned my head away. As if to display indifference, as if this was stuff that I had already processed a long time ago.

"Also, she was probably much shrewder at disguising it then," I said.

I turned to look at him again and it all came back, in one big wave. How close we used to be, the private jokes we shared, how he made me laugh.

"If you want to talk more, then I need a drink," I said.

"Fine," he said and smiled.

We were back in the car, stuck in traffic for half an hour. Now and again we exchanged a quick glance, as if, after having opted for alcohol, we needed to reassure each other.

"Stop here, this is fine," I said impatiently, pointing at an ugly café on the other side of the street.

It was perfectly pointless to look for anyplace cozy for our conversation. So we sat at a table on the sidewalk, cars streaming by, fumigated by their exhaust, gulping down cheap raspberry vodka, overwhelmed by the noise of the street.

The café was crowded with young people in camouflage pants and army boots. The waitress had a pierced lip and a tattoo on the back of her neck.

Daniel stared into the bottom of his glass.

"Of course I'm aware that I've been responsible for part of her unhappiness," he said slowly, then went silent.

"*Which* part of her unhappiness?"

"Well, for instance, I never forgot what you said that day at the Hotel Locarno. I think you were right: I *did* project something onto her . . . and only later understood she wasn't the person I had wanted her to be."

I realized this was the moment—maybe never to come again—when I would be allowed to ask the question that I'd been wanting to shout

out loud in his face, at his answering machine, for years. Instead I asked it calmly, like it had just occurred to me.

"What was it, then? What kind of person did you want her to be?"

He looked away, uneasy. Then back into the ashtray.

"I don't know. I think she . . . When I first met her I immediately felt how lost she was. It was like . . . everything that she had once been, it had been erased, she no longer had a past. I felt she had a void, a blank space that I thought I could fill. I felt like a blank piece of paper too, in a way. Here I was in this country I knew nothing about. . . ."

He shook his head.

"I don't know, it's—"

"No, it's perfectly clear. You were trying to become someone else."

He nodded. "You said something like that, that day in my hotel room. Something like: 'You're trying to buy yourself a new biography.' "

"I remember that."

"But, you know, later, once Isa and I got to know each other more, things changed. She used to tell me that I made her feel like a squatter. Once she said to me, 'I live in the fear of being evicted from your life from one day to the next.' "

" And was she right?"

"Yes and no. I did feel that she had, you might say, taken a space that had been reserved for someone else. . . ."

He stopped to check my reaction, but I tried not to give anything away.

"But I had made a commitment and was going to honor it. I never actually considered breaking up our marriage."

"Why, if you were no longer in love with her?"

I don't even know how I had conjured the courage to actually ask such a direct question. But I felt like I was allowed, on a day like that. He didn't flinch.

"Because I do care about her and I don't want her to suffer."

"That's never a good enough medicine. It doesn't stop the suffering."

"It's different when you have children.

"Yes, maybe it *is* different. I don't know."

I slumped back in my chair, creating more distance between us.

The waitress came to take our empty glasses away. I looked at her tattoo as she bent over the table. It was a lizard crawling out of her scalp into the nape of her neck and sliding down her spine.

"We'll have another round of vodkas," Daniel said in his American-inflected Italian. She nodded, in that unfriendly manner young waitresses have when they want to look cool.

"That's smart," I said to her. "You can always grow your hair long if you get tired of it."

She gave me a blank look.

"The lizard," I said. "You might want to hide it one day."

"I can't see it, so I never get tired of it."

"Good point," I said dryly and suddenly felt a growing irritation.

"I wonder whether this would have happened—I mean, the way she has broken down—had things been better between us," Daniel went on, ignoring my exchange with the waitress, who was back in a moment with another round of frozen raspberry vodka shots.

He was asking to be acquitted, but I was the wrong person to ask.

"Daniel, tell me something."

"Yes?"

"Remember that night in New York when you wanted to know about all those letters I was receiving, and I told you about Isabella for the first time?"

"Yes."

"I didn't want to scare you off. I thought, you would . . . you'd just freak out. You know—my sister arrested as a terrorist."

He gulped down his drink and waited, the glass still close to his mouth.

"And?"

"And then, later that night, when we were in bed, you said, 'But you forgot to tell me the most important thing of all. Did she actually kill this man or not?' Remember that?"

"Yes, I do."

"And then I told you that in fact I had never asked her, that it was a very difficult question to ask."

He nodded slowly, cautiously.

"And that I hoped you would never have to ask that same question to someone you loved, because truth sometimes comes with a very high price attached to it?"

"Right." He patted his pockets, searching for another cigarette.

I didn't know until that very moment that we were heading in this direction. Round and round, in a big circle, back to that precise moment.

"I know what is it you want to ask me," he said and lit his cigarette. He turned his head to the side and waved his hand lightly, to fan the smoke away from his eyes. "And the answer is no."

I held his gaze and said nothing. I felt strangely close to him. We were together in all that was happening, in a way we had never been before. Like brother and sister.

"I never asked her," he said. "It was too hard. Especially after the children."

"Sure. I figured," I said.

We kept silent for a few seconds.

Because of the children. *What else,* I thought. Isn't that always the reason why we keep handing down our history in falsified, sanitized versions? So that our children will grow up intimidated by the questions they were not allowed to ask? So that the weight of the unanswered questions will make them crazy in turn?

A girl came over from the next table and asked Daniel for a light. She was very skinny and her flat tummy showed under the skimpy T-shirt. They fiddled with his lighter, which was running out of fluid. The girl gave a shrill laugh, with her head very close to his, as she kept trying to light her cigarette. He's still such an attractive man, I kept thinking while watching the scene. Women will always have a weakness for him.

"I'm exhausted," I said. "I need to go home."

"I'll drive you."

"No. I'll walk."

"Why? I want to take you, really."

I took his hand in mine and smiled.

"No," I said firmly. "I want to be alone. I need a bit of time on my own now."

He looked surprised. As if that couldn't possibly be my real wish.

"Oh. Okay." He put a couple of bills on the table and stood up.

"Well, then, I guess I'll see you tomorrow at the clinic," he said as we walked in the direction of the car. "You're going to come and see her, right?"

"I'm not sure, but I'll be in touch."

I didn't feel ready yet to slip into this new routine. Meeting at the clinic on visiting hours, playing family like nothing ever happened.

"You should go home and get some rest," I said. "It's been a long day for all of us."

I began to walk, my hands stuffed in my pockets, my eyes not focusing on anything in particular. It was a long walk to reach where I lived, but I needed to spend the energy.

On the way I didn't even think about the effect seeing Daniel Moore had on me. There wasn't much to think about, strangely enough: everything had slid into its natural place by itself. What had seemed so complicated, impossible to fix, had found its slot. As if it had been just a matter of time and nothing else.

Instead, as I walked with my head down, I was seized by vivid images of Isabella and me as children. They came in scattered fragments, like Polaroids from the past. Our tartan pleated skirts, a hairpin with a flower, our beloved Scrabble box, the old art books we pulled out of Oliviero's bookshelves and looked at on the Persian rug. As I walked up the stairs to my apartment, I could still conjure up the smell of the yellowing pages and the way they crackled.

A few months later I received a phone call from Marco Sestieri. He said he had been working on a book and he wanted me to see the galleys.

"It's a series of interviews with ex-terrorists and militants of the extreme left who have now returned to semi-normal life. Nothing new, so to speak," he said, in his usual understated way, "but it's very interesting, ten years later, how every one of them is able to talk about that time and their beliefs from an entirely different place."

There was a short pause. I felt I had to encourage him to go on with what he had to say.

"Yes, of course. Please send it to me, Marco."

"Well . . . as you can imagine, there's a pretty extensive interview with Isabella. We did it some time ago, before she . . ."

"Yes."

". . . and of course I was going to send it to her. You know, I wanted her to read it first and tell me how she felt about the way I had edited her statements. But at this point I'm wondering if she can . . . I mean, I don't know whether she is even capable of . . ."

"No, Marco, she isn't. Not right now, at least. She has a few moments of . . . when she's lucid, but I don't think she would be able to read it and discuss it with you. Maybe sometime later on. Let's hope."

"Yes, yes. I totally understand," he said, sadly. I could tell he still cared about her.

"Also, I don't think it would be a good idea for her to read that interview now."

"I agree. That's why I wanted to send it to you instead. Maybe you could go over it and tell me if you approve of it."

"Yes, if you'd like to. But I'm sure you've already done the best possible job with it."

And for a second I felt like saying, "Maybe you should have been the one to marry her, Marco. Maybe she wouldn't have had to run away from it all the way she did had she had you next to her." But of course I didn't; it would only have made him feel worse.

I got the galleys a few days later in the mail. Seeing her words on paper, I couldn't have been more grateful to Marco. He had found a way to put them somewhere before they got lost forever.

It's been hard—and it took a long time for me—to realize how a passionate belief can turn us into slaves. It was for passion's sake that we decided it was justifiable to kill, and once we crossed that threshold, everything became possible. I'm not going to try to look for excuses for what I and my comrades have done. I decided a long time ago that I was going to deal with the weight of my guilt all by myself, without trying to make it any lighter, yet I can't stop asking myself certain endless questions. One in particular keeps coming back: How was it possible that we decided it was right to kill? I still can't come up with an answer. I can only come up with abstractions—ideals of justice, beliefs, political fervor. But I still haven't found a concrete answer for that, something substantial. All I can say today is that I fought a war on behalf of a dream. And all that's left of that dream today is the pain of others, and of the lives we took.

EPILOGUE

Alba and I have decided to take a walk right after sunset. The light is perfect. We walk silently among the olive trees, climbing the low stone walls that divide the different properties. I watch her strong calves as she scissors her legs over a fence. Her body is still muscular and supple like a girl's, and I notice how easily she moves on this terrain. She has a way of grounding her feet, of rooting herself to the earth, just like every other woman from here. In spite of all the expensive suits she has taken to wearing lately, her body will always tie her to this place.

We walk past Stellario's *furneddhu*, which has been abandoned for years, and I see that her expression is suddenly alert. She doesn't stop, she doesn't peek inside, take refuge in its perennial shade, breathe its smell of stones and dry olive leaves. I think she wants to spare herself the spleen of remembering so much.

"Are you going to come back to Rome in the car with me tomorrow after the movers have finished loading up?" she asks after a while.

I nod.

"Good. I dreaded having to drive back all by myself."

"You know, I'm glad you came," I say, and I pat her shoulder lightly. She turns her face toward me.

"Yes. Me too."

We walk like that for a while, without talking. Just taking in the colors and smells of the evening.

"Mamma, there's one thing I need to ask you."

"What is it?"

"Do you remember the script Oliviero wrote for Esposito, the one about Lorenzo and Renée?"

"Yes, of course."

"I read it again a while ago. I realized how good a writer he was. He had a real gift for dialogue."

She nods, and, to my surprise, I see she's smiling.

"Yes. Oliviero could tell a story like nobody else. It was like . . . he saw a film in everything that happened around him and turned it into a great plot. He really had an amazing talent."

It's the first time in so long that she has talked about my father. So lightheartedly. And she has called him by name.

"Mamma, I've been meaning to tell you . . . I've been working on it, making just a few changes. You know, giving it a more 'contemporary' style."

She looks at me skeptically. I see those same golden specks in her light-brown eyes that Isabella and I have both inherited. I have to admit she still looks very attractive at sixty.

"How come you're working on it? Don't tell me Esposito wants to make that film again!"

"Yes. And he tells me he has some really great director and cast in mind. He wants it to be his next 'serious' film. He's tired of commercial crap."

She laughs.

"I can see why."

I swallow. This is not an easy thing to talk about, still.

"I know how you felt about the script back then. But I'm dying to work on a story like that for a change."

She interrupts me, waving her hand.

"At the time, you know, when I told your father I didn't want this story ever to be made into a film, Lorenzo was still alive. I didn't want to hurt his feelings. I felt very protective of him."

"Of course, I know. And you were right."

She has become animated.

"And part of it was that I was angry at Oliviero because of this way he had of turning everything into a plot—what I was talking about before."

"I know, I know, but . . ."

"As if it didn't matter to him what other people might—"

"Yes, of course, but—"

"But *what?*" She suddenly turns to face me.

"It's not about *us* anymore, Mamma. It's not about our family."

She stops and stands still in the middle of the path.

"What do you mean?"

"That film script he wrote? It's not about us. It's actually"—and I re-peat what Esposito said to me that day in the restaurant—"it's like . . . a metaphor . . . it's a story about truth itself."

She doesn't say anything, averting her eyes from mine, as if evaluat-ing my outburst from a different angle.

"I guess so," she concedes. "Well, in any case, it all seems so far away now that it doesn't really matter anymore."

There's a sudden gust of wind.

"Look," she says, pointing ahead of us. "It's going to rain again. We better head back."

And perhaps we have to become who we are, regardless of what really happened—or what we imagine has happened—I think. And as we start walking back toward Casa Rossa, the first drops of rain begin to fall.

The wind blows all night. I hear the whistling outside my window, the banging of shutters downstairs. I can't sleep. But I'm at peace, and I just lie in my bed and wait for the first light.

I feel Alba's presence in the next room, the same room where Rita had slept the previous night. I think I can hear her peaceful breathing.

I think of Isabella, sleeping in her bed in the clinic. Now I think of her every day, just like I did when she was in jail.

The little doll trapped in the dollhouse.

Giorgio says she won't be able to go home for now. Not until he sees some improvements.

I can't help thinking that her madness was something of a device of hers, one that would make the curtain fall earlier, so that she could fi-nally rest.

Daniel is slowly adjusting to the situation. Something has shifted between us, allowed us to position ourselves differently. He has his scars, and I suppose I have mine, too. We are finally learning to be close. We need to, now. Because we both love her.

Lately he and I talk on the phone often, we meet at the clinic. We go out with the children, take them for ice cream, or to the movies. They have learned my name. *Zia* Alina, they call me. They are such beautiful children, these two little sisters. One is three, the other one is four.

Such sweet girls, so well behaved.

"Alina! Alina! Get up, darling!"

I hear Alba at my door. I must have fallen asleep. I remember vaguely seeing the sky getting paler. Rain is pounding on the window.

"Yes. I'm up. What time is it? Are they here already?"

"Yes, they are." She holds a cup of fragrant coffee. She looks excited, in that childish way I know so well.

"They're loading the truck already. I'm surprised the noise didn't wake you up."

I spring out of bed and go over to the window.

"I was up most of the night. I must have dozed off just now."

I look out below and see the big truck parked outside. The movers, covered in raingear, are slowly loading the kitchen cupboard into it.

"I've got to show you something amazing," Alba says. "Hurry up, come down."

She hands me the coffee and I follow her downstairs, barefoot, in my white cotton nightgown. The men—there are at least five of them—are crowding the living room, shrouded in yellow raincoats. They look like a ship's crew in a storm. They are big, muscular, most of them probably Polish or Albanian.

"Good morning," I greet each one of them. They all greet me back politely in their foreign accents as they lift an armchair, push a table, slide a marble tabletop and wrap it in a curtain. I feel good knowing they are in charge now.

"Come outside." Alba motions me outside to the patio.

It's pouring. My bare feet feel cold on the wet tiles.

"Look." She gestures toward the wall of the patio.

"What?"

All I can see is how the wind and the rain have blown the leaves off the creeper and the patio wall now looks bare, except for the skeleton of the vine.

"Look more closely. Come."

She pushes me gently toward the wall. And I see it. Seeping through the red pigment that has been washed out. The faint trace of a foot, a leg, the roundness of a breast, an elbow. The naked figure, reclining like some kind of goddess, stretched all along the length of the patio.

Alba brushes the red pigment off with her fingertips.

It's a pentimento. The original idea.

"It's Renée coming back!" Alba laughs. "Isn't it extraordinary?"

"It's perfect," I say. "It took her so long, but she's made it just in time."

It's raining harder and harder. I feel the water running down my spine, streaking through my nightgown, sticking the cotton to my skin. The sound becomes deafening as the raindrops turn to hail. And suddenly I see beads of ice hitting and bouncing off the ground. Now they're pinching my skin like a thousand needles. Alba and I can't stop laughing, as our wet hair mats against our faces, the smell of drenched earth filling our lungs, and the movers staring at us as we hug each other and keep laughing, till we can't tell the tears from the rain.

RULES OF THE WILD

A mesmerizing novel set in the vast spaces of contemporary
East Africa, *Rules of the Wild* explores unforgettably our infi-
nite desire for a perfect elsewhere, for love and a place to call
home. Moving and wise, it gives us a sharp-eyed portrait of a
closely knit tribe of cultural outsiders: the expatriates living in
Kenya today. They all know each other. They meet at dinner
parties, they sleep with each other, they argue about the best
way to negotiate their existence in a place where they don't
really belong. At the center is Esmé, a beautiful young woman
of dazzling ironies and introspections, who struggles to make
sense of her own place in Africa and of her feelings for the two
men there whom she loves—Adam, a second-generation
Kenyan who is the first to show her the wonders of her adopted land, and Hunter, a British journalist sickened by its horrors.

"Remarkable . . . compellingly readable . . . makes you feel as
if you've come back from someplace very far away."
—*USA Today*

Fiction/Literature/0-375-70343-8